the INN *at* summer ISLAND

the INN *at* summer ISLAND

RACHEL MAGEE

Entangled Publishing, LLC
10940 S Parker Rd
Suite 327
Parker, CO 80134
rights@entangledpublishing.com

Amara is an imprint of Entangled Publishing, LLC.

Edited by Alethea Spiridon and Amy Acosta
Cover design by Bree Archer
Cover photography by runna10/Getty Images
aceshot1 and Lopolo/Shutterstock

Manufactured in the United States of America

First Edition August 2021

At Entangled, we want our readers to be well-informed. If you would like to know if this book contains any elements that might be of concern for you, please check the book's webpage for details.

https://entangledpublishing.com/books/the-inn-at-summer-island

For Kathryn.
I wouldn't be here without you.

Chapter One

Millie Leclair had arrived.

Not in the sense that she'd taken life by the horns and was living the dream. Not yet, anyway. But she had made it to her destination, her favorite place in the world, and things were about to change for the better.

"This is it, Bear. The first glance at our future," she told her caramel-colored labradoodle buddy, who was already enjoying the coastal breeze with his head sticking out the passenger side window.

The GPS voice piped up to let her know she still had another six hundred yards to go. Okay, technically she hadn't quite arrived at her destination yet, but after driving a thousand miles over the last fifteen hours, she was close enough. The fresh scent of tropical vegetation mixed with the briny tang of salt air floated into the car. The familiar smell caused some of her favorite childhood summer memories to flood her mind, and she let out a squee.

"Can you believe we live on Summer Island? The beach is practically our backyard. How incredible is that?"

Just to think, six short weeks ago, she'd been sitting in her tiny gray cubicle, wondering if winter was ever going to end in Chicago, when she got the call that she'd inherited her great-aunt's oceanfront property in the South Carolina Lowcountry. And now here she was, about to pull into her new life as owner and operator of her aunt's historic bed and breakfast.

"You're going to love Seascape, Bear. I suffered through the school year just so I could spend my summers in this magical place. The ocean is breathtaking and the house is…" She closed her eyes for the briefest of seconds and pulled up a mental picture of what she considered the happiest place on earth. Palmetto palms, vibrant teal shutters flanking every window, laughter floating alongside the sound of crashing waves. Millie let out a happy sigh as she blinked her eyes open.

In a word, this place was paradise.

The target on her GPS inched closer. "Our house is next!"

From where they were, she couldn't quite see it yet. A new modern concrete and glass monstrosity was blocking her view, but that was fine. It was like the extravagant wrapping paper around her perfect gift.

She slowed to a crawl, wanting to savor her first glimpse of her new home. Her dream. Her future.

Anticipation buzzed through her, making it impossible to sit still. She bounced in her seat, her smile so wide it strained her cheek muscles, as she inched past her new neighbor's house and—

The sight hit her like a sucker punch to the solar plexus. All of her air along with a good bit of her exhilaration gushed out, leaving her feeling as flat as a popped balloon.

"Oh."

It was the only word she could get out before she ran out of oxygen.

In her memory, the beachside beauty she'd called her happy place had been a whole lot more Cinderella's castle. What stood in front of her looked closer to The Haunted Mansion. She stared at the house in front of her, trying to reconcile what stood there with her dream-fueled expectations.

Admittedly, it had been longer than intended since she was last here, but it hadn't been that long, had it?

Millie winced at the stab of guilt in her chest. Of course, she had an idea of what happened, but she didn't want to think about that at the moment. If she did, she'd start placing blame. And since that blame would most likely fall square on her shoulders, it would be best to focus her attention on something more positive.

Hesitantly, she pulled down the long, crumbling drive. Tilting her head to the side, she examined the house again, hoping a different angle would make it look less in disrepair. Even in this sad state, the British West Indies–style house carried a certain elegance and southern flair that the newer homes in the neighborhood didn't have. Seascape used to be the only house down the road, a bright and welcoming sight.

Right now, though...

"I mean, it looks a bit dreary, but it has a solid, um, structure," she told Bear and prayed it was true.

She tried again.

"It's by the ocean so the sunrises are spectacular. And it has, you know—" Twisting her mouth to the side, she scanned the property for something else to add to the positive column. Although, it might've been easier to name the things it didn't have. Like the peeling paint that could now more accurately be described as the color of dirty sand or the many shutters that were broken and hanging by one corner.

"Character," Millie said. "It has tons of character."

The labradoodle pulled his head in the window and

whined.

"Come on, I'm trying to be positive." Millie scratched behind the dog's ear. "So, it needs a little work."

After parking, she got out of the car and walked over to examine the fountain that sat in the middle of the circular driveway. This used to be her favorite feature of the house. It was a cheerful welcome that set the mood for guests coming to stay at her aunt's inn. Now, the two cherubs sitting back-to-back were covered in a green mildew so thick that Millie wondered if the color was permanent, and all three of the scalloped bowls below them were cracked and chipped. The only indication it would still hold water were the lingering murky puddles probably left over from the last rainstorm.

To be fair, the estate lawyer who'd contacted her had said the house needed a little work. But this wasn't a little work. This was—

Nope. She wasn't going there. This was her moment. Her new life. She wasn't going to drag herself down dwelling on the negative.

Bear hopped out of the open car door and trotted over to her side.

Millie patted his furry head and stared up at the house. "What do you say we check out the inside?" Maybe it wasn't as rough as the exterior. After all, this place was operational only a few years ago. How bad could it be?

Digging the key out of her pocket, she marched across the driveway and up the wide stone steps to the porch. Bear followed and sat at her side.

Rust and decay had eaten away at the wrought-iron door handles, making it nearly impossible to get the key in the lock. Flecks of oxidized metal fell off as she tried to wiggle it into place. How long had it been since someone had entered this place?

Her great-aunt had been moved to a nursing home two

years ago—maybe three years now?—but Millie assumed someone had been checking the house since then. As Aunt Mildred's only living relative, maybe she should've been the one making sure of it.

Frustration, and perhaps a tinge of guilt, prompted Millie to give the key one final jab, thrusting it into place. She paused and wiped the sweat beading up on her forehead courtesy of the South Carolina humidity, then she tried to turn the key.

It didn't budge.

"It's probably a little stiff since it hasn't been used in a while. It just needs a tug."

Bear raised his furry eyebrows and tilted his head to the side. Sometimes she wished her dog had a less expressive face. It would make believing her own lies a bit easier.

She clutched the handle and gave the door a gentle shake, then tried again. No luck. Getting more aggressive, she pulled the door toward her with a firm tug, but the key still didn't budge.

"Ugh!" She planted her fists on her hips and took a step back, squinting through the sun's glare to stare up at the weathered exterior of her new house.

Well, no one said starting over was going to be easy. Although, she had hoped any setbacks would wait until day two. She deserved a break.

All her professional life, she'd worked as hard as she could, yet she was always the one left without a chair when the music stopped. Her love life wasn't any different. In fact, the residual ache from her most recent heartbreak still lingered in her chest. The one from when she dared to go all in on a workplace romance, thinking what they had was bigger than office politics. She'd thought wrong.

But all of that was in the past. This was her chance at a fresh start, her opportunity for a life full of adventure and unlimited access because she was the one who got to call the shots.

Except here she was, on day one, locked out of her own house.

"We'll just find another way in," she announced to Bear. She used both hands to pull the key out of its vise hold and headed down the steps toward the rear of the house. Maybe the key would work in one of the other locks, but she didn't have to go far before she spotted the break she was looking for.

The literal break.

One of the panes in the front window had a softball-sized hole. If she stuck her arm through it, she could unlock the latch and push the window up.

"Stay there, Bear. I'll be right back."

She grabbed a towel from her car and wrapped it around her arm as she hurried over to the window. It was higher off the ground than she'd originally thought. Luckily, among the items in her car was a small box she'd crammed full of her favorite books.

"They always say books can take you anywhere." She jumped over a bush to retrieve it from her trunk.

When the box was in position under the window, she stepped on it, raised as high up on her toes as she could, and reached in. The angle was awkward, but she nudged the lock with her first two fingers until it gave way, sending the window popping up slightly in response.

"Got it!" Millie pumped her fists in the air, and Bear, who was still sitting on the porch, wagged his tail in celebration.

"Stay, Bear. I'm coming for you."

Millie put both hands on the windowsill and pushed herself up like she was trying to climb out of a pool with a very tall side. Only, she'd never struggled this hard to push herself out of a pool.

Her first attempt didn't work out. So she tried again, this time starting out with a little hop. Her arms shook under the effort while her legs scrambled against the side of the house in an attempt to give her extra traction.

It wasn't pretty.

In fact, she was thankful no one was there to record it.

But she managed to push herself up far enough to get her stomach on the wooden ledge.

She paused for a second to catch her breath and stared at the Spanish tile floor inside the house. It was covered with leaves and other debris that must've blown in through the hole in the window. She shimmied herself forward and dove in hands first to walk herself inside the house, trying not to think about what else might have used the hole to get in. Hopefully, any critters that had let themselves in had already let themselves out.

Glancing around, she stood up and dusted herself off. She'd fallen into the dining room, and, unfortunately, the haunted mansion theme continued in the interior. The layer of dust covering the dining room table was so thick she'd have to carve through it, and the once stunning wrought-iron chandelier, which was short most of its bulbs, now hosted enough webs to be considered a spider condominium. All the place was missing was Casper gliding through the wall to greet her.

Okay. So the inn wasn't what she remembered, but it was still hers. For the first time ever, she owned something. Maybe it wasn't much at this exact moment, but it had potential, which was what really mattered. She just had to find it.

"Coming, big guy," she called as she walked through the grand foyer to the front door.

The lock on the front door was still tight on the inside, but she managed to get it to release. Out of breath and sweaty, she wiped her grimy hands on her shorts, then swung the heavy wooden door open.

"Who's ready to come inside and take a look at our new home?" she called out in a singsong voice while distracted by the peeling wallpaper. She'd always loved the faint metallic gold pineapples on the soft yellow background. What were the chances she could find the same print to replace it?

Finally turning her attention to the door, she jumped. Because standing right next to Bear on her front porch was a gorgeous stranger with an amused smirk.

"Tempting offer, but I'll take a rain check." There was a friendly glint in his eyes and the sunlight danced off his neatly cropped dark blond hair. If these were the kind of ghosts hanging out in this haunted mansion, she was totally in.

"Sorry," she said, looking around to where he might have come from. And how long had he been there? Surely he hadn't seen her not-so-graceful attempt at crawling through the window, right? "I didn't know anyone was here."

"I saw you pull in and wanted to stop by and say hello."

"Oh, hi. We just arrived into town." She motioned at the house behind her. "I inherited Seascape from my great-aunt, Mildred."

The stranger nodded. "I heard about her passing. I'm sorry for your loss." His gentle expression echoed the sympathy in his voice, which touched Millie.

"Thanks." She stuck out her hand. "I'm Millie by the way. Millie Leclair."

He stepped forward and grasped her hand with his firm grip. "It's nice to meet you, Millie Leclair." He let go and scratched the dog behind the ears. "And who is this guy?"

"This is my dog, Bear." Bear's tail happily thumped against the ground.

"I'm Braxton." His eyes sparkled in the sunlight. They were the exact same shade as the blue stripes on his pressed button-down shirt. Something about him looked vaguely familiar, and she racked her brain for some idea of how she might have known him. Before she could figure it out, he continued, "I live over there."

Millie leaned out the front door to take a look at the house in question. Of course this perfectly put-together, semi-familiar, gorgeous man would live in the modern concrete and glass beauty she'd admired on the way in.

"Now I'll know who's around next time I need to borrow a cup of sugar."

His brow furrowed in a sort of questioning look, but he recovered with a polite smile. "Right... Anyway, I wanted to say that we all want to see this property thrive in our neighborhood, so thank you for considering the—"

"Oh my gosh! You're that golfer." She'd recognized the camera-ready smile. "Braxton Channing."

Braxton shifted, losing the smile and looking slightly uncomfortable. "Used to be." He studied the ground for a second, then shook his head as if shaking away a thought. "I used to be a golfer. I'm still Braxton Channing."

"Used to be" was a good description. A few years ago, he was the most well-known PGA golfer in the US. Even people like Millie, who didn't know much about golf, had heard of him. He appeared on the scene at the age of twenty-four and took over, winning everything, and for the next five or so years the name Braxton Channing was synonymous with the PGA.

Being incredibly attractive probably aided in taking him from a golf superstar to a regular household celebrity. Everyone wanted to know more about the handsome athlete with the charming smile and the funny southern one-liners. Then about two years ago, he left the PGA, his face disappeared from the media, and the world stopped talking about Braxton Channing.

Except here he was, standing on her front porch, and she had to admit he was even more attractive in person than on the cover of *People*. A thrill jolted through her. She was living next door to a celebrity. Well, a used-to-be celebrity with some sort of mysterious disappearance from the public eye, but still.

"It's nice to meet you, neighbor." She started to ask him if he'd take a selfie with her but managed to stop herself before the words came out of her mouth. People who lived next door to celebrities probably didn't ask for pictures or autographs. At least not until they'd had a full conversation first.

"I'd invite you in but we've just arrived, and..." She glanced over her shoulder at the footprints she'd left in the layer of dirt on the floor. The stale mildew odor from the house drifted past her nose and she hoped it was from the house being closed up for so long and not because there was some sort of leak causing actual mildew somewhere.

"She's a bit of a mess right now, but the plan is to restore her to her former glory," she said, adding mildew check to the ever-growing fix-it list. "I guess we won't be taking guests yet, but before the summer is over, she'll be the thriving inn she once was."

"Inn?"

Millie turned to him. "Yeah. I'll probably run it more like a bed and breakfast than an inn. My aunt never really liked the B&B title because she—"

"You're not selling?" Braxton cut her off, his eyebrows knitted together.

"Selling?" The question caught her off guard. "Of course I'm not selling Seascape. Why would I want to sell something that's been in my family for generations?"

"You live in Chicago, so I guess we all assumed..." He let his voice trail off.

"I *used* to live in Chicago." She tried to sound patient, but why was she having to explain herself to this man? "Now I live here at 121 East Shore Drive where I'll be running Seascape Inn." She didn't want to be rude to her new neighbor on her first day in the neighborhood, but she couldn't help the hint of bite behind the words.

"Huh," Braxton said as he looked past her, his eyes sweeping across the front of the house. "You realize you can't turn this property into any sort of hotel, right? Using it for commercial business is against Oceanside Estates HOA regulations."

Her new neighbor might have once been known as America's most charming bachelor, but he was starting to get on her nerves. "I'm not turning it into a hotel. It *is* a hotel. Since it was built in the fifties, Seascape Inn has been a commercial business. This isn't something new."

"Perhaps in the past. But it's been vacant for a while." His gaze returned to her, no longer sparkling and friendly. "I can tell you with good authority that the current HOA rules are very clear. No businesses. Especially hotels."

"How can you make a rule prohibiting something that is already here?" She'd quit her whole life in Chicago and moved here to start over, to have the sort of life she dreamed about as a kid when she spent her summers here with her aunt. Reviving Seascape and running the inn wasn't just going to be her livelihood, it was a chance to keep her family's legacy alive.

Sensing her growing frustration, Bear abandoned his spot next to their new neighbor and sat next to Millie, his ears perked and on full alert.

Braxton offered another polite smile. She was growing to hate them. "I'm sorry to be the bearer of bad news, but the rules were designed to benefit everyone in the community."

Millie crossed her arms in front of her chest, defiance swelling inside her. "Well, I'm part of the community now, and I'm meeting with my lawyer later today. We'll see what he has to say about this."

It sounded a bit like "I'm telling my mom on you," but it was the best she could come up with after all the surprises she'd dealt with today.

"I always find a lawyer's opinion helpful." There was a bit of snark in his voice that only made the fire in her belly burn brighter. "And if you need any further clarification or want to file a complaint, you're always welcome to attend one of the HOA general meetings."

Braxton backed down the steps to where his slick new sports car sat on the crumbling and cracked driveway. He had gone from handsome celebrity to uptight know-it-all faster than that car went from zero to sixty.

"Great," Millie called out after him. "I'll be there."

He hesitated as he opened the door. "Then I'll see you there." He offered her one of his Braxton Channing famous grins, just as empty as his polite smiles. "And since you're moving in, I guess I should say welcome to the neighborhood." He slid into the driver's seat and the engine purred to life.

She stood there with her arms crossed in front of her chest and glared until his car drove through the rusted gate and turned onto the street.

"I'm glad we didn't ask him for a picture," she said to Bear. "It would've ruined our Instagram feed. And if I need a cup of sugar, I am *not* going to ask him for it."

Bear's tail wagged in what she assumed was agreement.

Millie drew in a deep breath and turned to stare at the dank and dusty inside of the house. "So it's not what we were expecting," she said again, scratching Bear behind the ears. But, honestly, when had anything in her life gone as expected? She was tired of sitting idly by and watching her dreams turn to dust because someone else told her she didn't deserve it. No. Not this time.

"This is our new life and nothing's going to stand in our way of making it great." Not a crumbling house in disrepair, not some stupid HOA rule, and certainly not some self-righteous former celebrity.

Chapter Two

Braxton pulled into the parking lot of Summer Island Memory Care Home for his daily chess game with his friend, still caught up on the conversation with the new owner of the property next door. That meet-and-greet hadn't gone at all like he'd planned. He hefted the giant flower arrangement out of the front seat and headed across the small parking lot, replaying the encounter in his mind. For starters, he hadn't expected the inheritor of the estate to be so young. Or so pretty.

But that surprise quickly gave way to the fact that she was moving into the property. He supposed he could appreciate wanting to renovate the place. The old beach house had a sort of vintage charm that could be beautiful once again with several coats of paint and lots of landscaping. But turning it into an inn?

The rules were clear. No commercial lots. Millie Leclair was in for a rude awakening if she came to debate the issue at the next HOA meeting. And he had no doubt she would be there, all feisty determination with passion burning in her beautiful caramel eyes.

Braxton shook his head at the image and pressed the buzzer with his elbow, moving the huge flower arrangement out of the way so the security camera could see his face.

"Hello, Mr. Channing. Come on in." The peppy voice came through the small speaker and the sound of an electric lock being disengaged hummed next to him. He shifted the flowers and pulled the door open enough to get his foot in so he could push it open the rest of the way. Veronica, the director of the facility, held the inner door open for him.

"Hello, Braxton. Mr. Henry is waiting for you. He's set up and reset that chessboard three times already." She took the flowers from him in her gentle brown hands.

"I'm running behind today."

"No worries. You're here now. And look, you used pink lilies this week. Aren't they lovely?" She took a big whiff. "They smell so good. Your flower arrangements always make our foyer so cheerful." Her dark sable eyes glittered and she gave him a wide smile before she shuffled off.

Braxton wiped the pollen off the front of his shirt and walked over to the table under the window where eighty-two-year-old Henry Donovan sat staring at a chessboard.

"Hey, Henry. How's it going today?" Braxton asked as he slid into the empty seat in front of the black pieces.

"You're late," the old man said grumpily.

Braxton moved his pawn to c5. "I know. I'm sorry. I had an errand to run before I came." The more Henry's Alzheimer's disease progressed, the more the man got agitated if things deviated from his normal schedule. Braxton knew this. But this morning, he hadn't wanted to miss his chance to personally thank the new owner for considering his client's offer to buy the abandoned property. He figured the effort would be worth the cost.

He'd figured wrong.

"I had to meet my new neighbor. Do you remember the estate next to me? Seascape?" He moved his rook in response to Henry's last move.

"Mildred Leclair owns Seascape." Henry studied the board before moving his knight.

Braxton nodded. "She did. But she died a couple months ago. I told you about that. One of her relatives inherited it. Her niece." He left off the fact that Mildred's relative was younger than he'd expected. And prettier.

Braxton moved his next piece.

Henry grunted. "Predictable move. You play chess like you play golf, only taking the safe shots."

Henry was the only person in Summer Island who dared to talk to him about golf anymore. Braxton wasn't sure if it was because his disease had caused him to forget it was an off-limits topic, or because he'd been Braxton's coach since he was a freshman in college and didn't think those rules applied to him.

Braxton preferred to think it was the latter.

"Sometimes safe moves win games."

"Only if the other guy makes a mistake, which I don't." Henry moved his rook and took Braxton's knight. His memory might be hindered, but he still had great game strategy.

"Mildred's sister. Is she going to take over running the inn?" Henry asked.

It took a second for Braxton to register the topic change.

At some point, probably when he first bought his house five years ago, someone had told him the rundown place next door had been some sort of famous inn back in the day, but it must've been *way* back in the day. Since he'd known it, there'd never been any paying guests that he'd been aware of, and the property was in desperate need of repairs. The situation only got worse when the elderly lady who lived there moved into a care facility some years back.

When Braxton first approached the estate's attorney about his real estate client's offer to buy the property from the new owner, the lawyer had reported the inheritor lived in another state and hadn't visited Seascape in at least a dozen years. Meaning there was a better than decent chance she'd be willing to sell, especially with the extremely generous offer being put forth. So when he saw her arrive this morning, he assumed she was here to settle the affairs and leave.

Imagine his surprise in learning that she wasn't only sticking around, but she wanted to reopen the inn.

Braxton held back a scoff. It just wasn't doable for a whole lot of reasons.

"Not her sister," he corrected. "It's her niece. Her great-niece, actually. But the neighborhood rules won't allow for it to be an inn anymore."

Henry stopped studying the game board and looked at Braxton, shock distorting his face. "Not be an inn? That's the most beautiful place to stay in town. In fact, if it wasn't for Mildred's inn, this town wouldn't even be a town."

It was often futile and upsetting to disagree with the old man, so he just nodded. "That nice, huh?"

"I could tell you some stories, but you'd have to be older. They aren't all PG-rated."

Braxton laughed. "Those I would like to hear."

"And that woman, oh, how she could bake. Sweetest treats I've ever put in my mouth." Henry closed his eyes and licked his lips as if he could taste the memories. After a second, he opened his eyes and made his next move. "Does she bake?"

"The new owner? I don't know. I didn't ask." Braxton wasn't interested in making new friends, whether or not his new neighbor caused a slight tingling somewhere deep inside his chest. After two years of being dead inside, the feeling was...unsettling. He pushed the thought of her out of his mind. "Are we here to chat about pastries or to play chess?"

Henry let out a heavy breath. "I thought we were here to play chess but you've gone and gotten yourself distracted by Mildred's beautiful sister."

"It's her beautiful *niece*." Braxton caught his slip almost as soon as he said it, but he didn't bother to correct it. It would only make him look like he was trying too hard to cover up something that wasn't there.

Henry raised a knowing eyebrow, the way he'd always done when he knew Braxton was lying to him, and moved his king in front of Braxton's queen. "Checkmate." He shrugged and settled back in his seat. "At least one of us still has our wits about us."

Braxton grinned. "Well played, old man."

In the past two years, Alzheimer's disease had ruthlessly overtaken what many would argue to be one of the most strategic sports minds of their time. These days, Henry often couldn't remember how to perform normal day-to-day tasks. He was starting to not recognize people and his short-term memory was almost nonexistent. It was heartbreaking to watch, but even in the midst of the struggle, his mentor still had a sense of humor about it.

"Best of three?" Braxton asked, starting to reset the board.

"Sure." Henry waved over one of the nurse's aides. "Since I won't remember who won this game, you gotta keep my friend honest. I'm up one to nothing."

The nurse's aide pulled up a chair next to their table. "I always love watching you play chess, Mr. Donovan, but since I've been here, I've never seen you lose a tournament to anyone."

Henry made his first move. "And it's not going to start today because Romeo here has gone and gotten himself distracted by the looker who moved in next door."

The nurse's aide eyed him.

Braxton shook his head and chuckled. "Just play your game, old man."

. . .

The bell on the door jingled as Millie walked into Daybreak Café the next morning. The charming coffee shop and bakery with its whitewashed shiplap walls and pink flowers in the middle of each table looked like something out of a picture book.

Delicious-looking treats sat upon vintage tiffany blue or white cake stands inside a glass display case, and shelves on the wall held neatly stacked, oversize white coffee cups and saucers. It was the kind of place that made everyone feel warm and welcome the second they walked through the door.

After yesterday's less than pleasant surprises, this little shop was an unexpected delight. Millie stood in the doorway and breathed in the sweet coffee and cinnamon scented air and let a glimmer of hope shimmy through her.

She chose a table in the back and dumped her laptop along with the stack of file folders she brought with her for the meeting with her lawyer on it. She had questions for him. A lot of questions. But first, she wanted a treat.

Millie strolled up to the counter and read the menu written in scripty white print on a black chalkboard. Normally, she'd order a black drip with a little room for cream. Someone had told her at some point that it was a sensible and efficient choice. But that was her old life, the one where she was always racing around and never getting anywhere.

This was her new life, and now she called the shots. Of course, she ate dry cereal for dinner and slept on a sleeping bag surrounded by candles because her new house didn't have electricity or a bed with clean sheets. But still, it was her house, her decisions, her chance to build something for herself.

No, she didn't drink boring drip coffee with a splash of fat-free milk anymore. This new adventure called for something decadent, something that needed to be sipped and savored and enjoyed.

A lady with a warm smile who appeared to be in her mid-sixties walked out from the back and wiped her hands on the front of her crisp white apron. "Good morning, dear. Welcome to Daybreak." She paused for a second and studied Millie before her entire body seemed to brighten. "Oh my! You're Mildred's niece. I've been wondering when you'd come to town." The older woman scurried around the counter and wrapped her arms around Millie.

The embrace caught Millie by surprise. People didn't hug like this in Chicago. And on the rare occasion they did, it was only among close friends or family. This lady, as far as Millie knew, was neither.

"Look at you, all grown up and just as beautiful as can be. You look like your aunt, you know." The hugger beamed at her.

Millie forced a smile. "Do I?"

"Oh, look at me going on and on and you probably have no idea who I am. I'm Bonnie Whitworth. My very first job was helping in the kitchen at Seascape Inn. In fact, I have your aunt to thank for my business today. She was the one who taught me how to bake."

"It's nice to meet you, Bonnie." So this warm, overly familiar community might take some time to get used to, but she liked it already.

"But enough about me. You came in here looking for some coffee, not to hear about my baking background." Bonnie went around the counter. "Now, dear, what can I make for you?"

Millie studied the menu again. "I'm still trying to decide."

"If you're in the mood for something sweet, you should try our mocha," Bonnie suggested. "Sophia, our resident chocolatier and owner of Sea Salt & Chocolate right down the road, makes our chocolate syrup. I don't know what she puts in it, but it's heavenly."

Millie nodded. "Sounds wonderful. And how about a croissant to go with it?"

"A perfect breakfast pair if you ask me." She packed the press with espresso and twisted it into place.

"It's nice to meet someone who remembers my aunt so fondly," Millie said.

"You'd be hard-pressed to swing a stick in this town without hitting someone who loved your aunt. She was a pillar of our community and will be greatly missed." Bonnie paused while the hiss of the steamer filled the air.

"And you're planning on sticking around, I hope? The rumor is she left you Seascape." Bonnie slid the coffee across the counter before she picked up a pair of tongs to grab a croissant.

At the same moment, the bell above the door jingled again, and the white-haired lawyer she'd only talked to via video chat walked into the café.

"That's actually what I'm here to talk about today. And it looks like my meeting just showed up."

"Well, I'll let y'all get to it." Bonnie slid the plate across the counter. "This one is on the house. Welcome to Summer Island, dear."

After the welcome she'd had so far, the sentiment warmed her heart. "Thanks. I appreciate that."

Bonnie patted her hand. "We'll catch up later." Then she turned to the man walking up to the counter. "Morning, George. You must thank your wife for those tamales she brought over last week. They were divine."

George nodded amicably. "I'll let Paula know you enjoyed them. She and her sister are talking about making another batch this weekend. I'm trying to persuade her to make some of her signature strawberry ones this time."

Millie carried her breakfast treats over to her table while the other two chatted for a second, then George Rodriguez joined her.

"It's nice to finally meet you in person." He shook her hand before he sat in the chair across from her. "Thanks for agreeing to move our appointment from the office to the café this morning. I thought you might like a chance to experience Beach Front Drive on your first day in town."

Millie took a sip of her sweet coffee and glanced out the window at the charming storefronts lining the town's main street. "It's so unique. I can't wait to check out some of the shops."

"Summer Island has a reputation for being a quaint beach town perfect for a relaxing getaway." He set his briefcase on the table in front of him and flipped the top open. "Your aunt's inn had a lot to do with starting that reputation. She offered beachside luxury with a small-town feel that helped put this town on the map."

"It seems the luxury part might have taken a hit in recent years."

George removed a neat stack of crisp folders from his briefcase before he closed it and set it on the floor next to him. "True. Mildred was a sweet lady, but she didn't always know when to ask for help. The inn was far too much responsibility for her in the later years. She stopped being able to care for guests and the estate long before she stopped being able to care for herself."

The familiar pang of regret seared her heart. Maybe Mildred should've called to ask for help, but Millie should've checked on her. If she had come for a visit, like she always promised she would, things could've been different.

"It is what it is," George said, as if reading her thoughts. "Our job now is to make sure all the paperwork is in order so you can move forward."

Millie nodded and took another sip of her mocha, hoping the smooth chocolate flavor would carry away some of her lingering regret.

George laid out two identical folders next to each other and opened both to the first page. "You signed most of the paperwork I had sent to you in Chicago. One final signature here will make the transaction complete."

She signed both pages.

George stacked one of the folders in front of himself and handed the other to Millie. "Congratulations. You're now the full owner of Seascape. Our next item of business is to talk about what you want to do with it."

He removed a single sheet of paper from the leather portfolio in front of him and slid it across the table. "Unfortunately, the house itself isn't worth anything. Anyone who bought it would most likely tear it down. However, the land is quite valuable. This is the value of the property according to tax appraisals."

Millie skimmed through the legal jargon and the lines of specs until she got to a big number at the bottom of the page. She read it and then reread it, making sure she'd counted the right number of digits.

She pointed to the number and looked up at George. "It's worth that?"

George nodded. "Being directly on the ocean with protected land on one side makes it quite rare and highly desired. This is only the tax appraisal. Like I mentioned before, you've already received offers on it. One in particular is especially interesting. I know you said you weren't interested in selling, but you'd be remiss if you didn't at least consider it." He slid another formal-looking document in front of her and pointed to the number in the middle of the page.

George must've thought interesting was a synonym for shocking, because that's what the number in front of her was. "The tax appraisal was over a million dollars less than that."

"That's not uncommon. Often there's a discrepancy in the numbers, especially for a unique property like this one."

Millie stared at the number again. She could've worked fifty years at the job she just quit and still wouldn't have made as much as this one sale would bring in. Of course, it wouldn't be enough to make her a trust-fund baby, but it would be enough to make her financially secure. Perhaps even comfortable, something she'd never known.

But just the thought of selling wrapped around her chest like a giant band, making it hard to breathe.

She shook her head and slid the paper back across the table, letting her eyes linger on the massive number. "I can't. It's been in our family since the 1950s. It was..."

Seascape and the two acres of oceanfront land it sat on was the only property any Leclair had ever owned. And now she was the only Leclair left. She wasn't just trading security for a dream; she was holding on to what was left of her family's legacy. If she sold their land, their legacy, to the highest bidder, then what was left? How long would it be before any trace of her family would vanish?

"Sell Seascape? Of course you can't sell it." Bonnie appeared and set a cup of black coffee on the table next to George. "That place is an iconic part of this town."

George gave her a warning look, and Bonnie held her hands up, backing away slowly. "I'm not meddling. I'm simply stating facts." She winked at Millie.

"She's right." Confidence surged through her. "I can't sell it."

George waited until Bonnie was out of earshot then heaved a sigh. "I had a feeling you would say that." He pulled another sheet of paper from his fancy leather-bound folder and slid it across the table. "I also took the liberty of mapping out the estate's current finances, so you'd know the fiscal state of the property."

The paper in front of her appeared to be some sort of spreadsheet with invisible lines dividing the big legal words on the left and the row of numbers on the right. She massaged her temples as she stared at the sheet, simultaneously trying to make sense of the numbers and push away the sinking feeling they caused as they dramatically shrank as they went down the page.

He pulled a pen from his pocket and pointed to the numbers starting at the top. "We use the tax-appraised value of the estate instead of the market value, because that's the number used for inheritance taxes, estimated here."

He pointed to the next number which made Millie swallow hard. It was big. Bigger than her annual salary.

"We discussed that at our initial teleconference. You have more than enough liquid funds in your estate account to pay this. That balance is here."

He pointed to a different number and Millie breathed a sigh of relief that it was bigger than her proposed tax bill. So far, she was still in the black.

"Of course, there's no lean against the property, but you will still be responsible for property tax and insurance." He paused and looked over his glasses at her. "With the risk of storms on the coast, it's a bit costly. However, it is something you will want to keep."

Hurricanes. Right. Millie was so excited to escape shoveling snow she hadn't even considered the kind of weather that caused problems here.

"You'll find that annual total here." George circled

another number. "And when both inheritance tax and annual property taxes along with insurances are subtracted, this is the remaining total."

He circled the smallest number at the bottom of the page.

"Oh."

It was still a positive number, which was good. She wouldn't have to dip into her personal bank account to pay the debts already owed, which was even better. But there was barely enough to live on for the two months she'd estimated it would take her to get the inn reopened.

She'd also been hoping to use the money from the estate to renovate the house. Her aunt hadn't done much with the place in the past few years, and being the responsible adult she was, Millie had made out a budget based on the money she *thought* there was left and the remodels she *assumed* she needed to make.

The problem was the work needed was far more extensive than she'd imagined, and after all the extra expenses she hadn't thought of, the amount left in the trust wasn't enough.

"Well...I guess I'll have to work with that." Millie smiled at George and took a sip of her coffee. So there wasn't enough in the bank to do everything she wanted. She'd been singing that particular song her entire life. It didn't make her dream of reopening Seascape impossible. It just made the process a little more complicated. But, like her dad had always said, all good stories had complications. Otherwise, they wouldn't be worth retelling.

Unfortunately, the dwindling bank account wasn't the only complication in this story so far.

"I had a talk with one of my neighbors yesterday," she said. "He seemed to think Seascape couldn't be reopened because of some HOA rule. That can't be right, can it? Seascape Inn has been there longer than any of the other houses in the neighborhood."

George pulled a file folder from the bottom and opened it, removing the top document. "I looked into that like you asked. I made a copy of the particular rule that will affect you."

He handed her the stapled group of pages. She had to flip three pages until she found the highlighted section. Millie read it, trying to weed through the hereinafters and whereases to find the meat of the rule.

"Basically," George interrupted. "Article 11b says all commercial deals are prohibited on these properties. Article 11c goes on to directly prohibit hotel accommodations, which it defines as accepting payment for lodging for a single night up to 364 days."

The knot in the pit of her stomach tightened, making her regret eating her croissant so quickly. "So what does that mean for the inn?"

"Unfortunately, the wording here is quite binding. The legal team that put this together was very thorough. But that doesn't mean we can't fight it. In fact, in my personal opinion, you should fight it."

Millie nibbled on her lip, commanding the welling tears to stay behind her lids. She wasn't sure what she was supposed to do in this situation, but she was positive crying wasn't it. "I don't have the first idea of how to do that."

George nodded, a warm glint shining in his sage eyes. "I contacted the HOA and their next general meeting is tomorrow night. Their bylaws also state that all grievances and formal complaints have to be presented in person by the resident." He closed the folder in front of him and passed it across the table to her. "However, I made a few notes of arguments I might make if I found myself in a similar situation."

Millie opened the folder and skimmed the top page. It had dates, times, and locations of all the meetings she would need to attend as well as arguments for each of the rules. Of course, this was just an outline and she would still have to do a lot of work to make the arguments her own, but at least she was pointed in the right direction. The iron knot in her shoulders started to release a bit.

She closed her folder and rested her hand on top. "Thank you," she said. "This means a lot."

George placed his remaining neat stack of folders into his briefcase and closed the lid.

"All you need is a solid case backed in evidence and a lot of passion." He wiped his mouth on his napkin before he stood. "Nothing is impossible. There are simply some tasks that require more effort than others."

The familiar words warmed Millie's heart and made her smile. "Aunt Mildred used to say that."

George nodded. "Her wisdom shaped a lot of lives around here. Once again, I am so sorry for your loss."

Guilt, sadness, and a whole lot of other feelings she couldn't quite identify pulsed through her, bringing a fresh round of tears to her eyes. She tried to utter the words "thank you" but they got clogged in her throat.

George seemed to interpret what she wanted to say and picked up his briefcase in preparation to leave. He stopped when he got next to her and laid a weathered hand on her shoulder. "I'll keep working on this problem." He crossed the shop and the bell above the door jingled as he exited.

Millie took another sip of her coffee and stared at the file folders in front of her, trying to decide where to start. It was like looking at a Jeopardy board full of topics she had absolutely no knowledge of. In her mind, moving down here and taking over her aunt's business wasn't going to have as many hoops to jump through.

"I'll take Financial Woes for a thousand, Alex," she said to herself as she lifted the center folder and flipped it open.

She'd just settled into her chair to try to get a better grasp on all the numbers in front of her when Bonnie reappeared to clear the abandoned dishes from the table.

"I couldn't help overhearing the conversation about the HOA rules. If you ask me, it's ridiculous. Mildred's inn has been renting rooms since before this town was even a town. To outlaw it now would be a travesty."

Millie couldn't help her smile. "Thanks. It means a lot to know I have people on my side."

Bonnie gave her hand a gentle squeeze then released it. "If you don't mind me asking, which neighbor was it that told you about this new rule?"

"Braxton Channing." Millie wanted to add "you know, the former golf star," but thought better of it.

There might've been a time when Millie had a small crush on America's favorite golfer. With that smile of his, who could blame her? She wouldn't admit it if asked, but she watched him more than once on a late-night show and read a few articles about him in a gossip magazine. That funny, charismatic guy who took the media by storm barely resembled the stiff and serious man she'd met the day before.

Bonnie pursed her lips. "Ahhh. Sweet Braxton. He's gotten progressively pricklier over the past few years." She picked up the dishes she had stacked. "But don't be fooled. Underneath all that pain, he has a good heart."

"Pain. What pain?"

Bonnie looked surprised. "I only assumed you knew. Most people know about Braxton's story. You know who he is, right?"

Millie nodded. "America's Favorite Golfer. Or at least he was until he left."

Bonnie nodded. "I'm not sure there was anyone who ever loved the game more than he did. And I'm not sure anyone played it more successfully, until that night." Sadness swept over her features and she lowered her head. "He hasn't been the same since."

It was on the tip of Millie's tongue to ask what happened when they were interrupted by the jingle of the door. Bonnie's attention turned to the delivery man struggling to get through the door with a stack of unwieldy boxes on a dolly.

"Oh my goodness, Seth. Let me help you with those." Bonnie rushed over, chattering in her cheerful voice the whole time.

Millie picked up her mug in both hands and settled back in her chair, mentally compiling her to-do list. At the top of it was find out exactly what happened to her overly serious, formerly famous neighbor, Braxton Channing. Right after she figured out how to get the electricity turned on in her house and memorized what George recommended she say at the HOA board meeting, of course.

Chapter Three

Millie arrived at the Oceanside Estates HOA meeting ten minutes before it started.

Her hair was still wet because, regardless of how much she pleaded with the electric company, they swore it was impossible to restore electricity to the property until the following day. Luckily the hot water heater was gas operated, so her shower was at least pleasant. But she had grossly underestimated the amount of time it took for her hair to air-dry in this southern humidity. The Lowcountry climate was going to take a little getting used to.

Millie followed the signs through the golf course's clubhouse until she found the room she was looking for. It was smaller than she'd imagined, with a long boardroom-style table taking up most of it. Of course, she didn't expect the board members to be wearing white wigs and dressed in black robes, because imagining this to be like English Parliament would have been foolish, right? But a group of people dressed in shorts and fancy flip-flops chatting over a charcuterie board was as far from anything she'd imagined as possible. If it wasn't for the sign on the door, she would've thought she was in the wrong place.

After a couple of questioning stares were thrown in her direction, she drew in a deep breath and stepped into the room. If she was going to be the shot-caller in her new life, she'd have to be willing to fight for things from time to time. She just wished she didn't have to be so alone while she did it.

She flipped open the leather-bound folder she was holding and glanced at her notes. According to the information George had given her, she had to register her official complaint on the docket before the meeting started. But where in this room of cozy friends and casual conversation did she find the docket?

A woman about her age in a brightly colored sundress and the most fabulous wedges Millie had ever seen came up to her. "You look like you could use some help. Can I point you in the right direction?"

"I could use a lot of help, actually. I just moved here and this is my first time at one of these things. I need to sign the docket but I'm not even sure what that is."

The stranger brightened. "Well, you're in luck. The secretary has the docket and I happen to be the secretary. I'm Sophia Gonzaga."

"Sophia? Are you the one who makes the chocolates?"

"One and the same." She beamed.

"I had one of your mochas at the coffee shop and it was fantastic." She shook Sophia's hand. "I'm Millie Leclair. I just moved into Seascape."

"Oh, Mildred's niece! We've all heard so much about you. I adored your aunt. Her business tips helped me get my shop up and running."

Millie had only been in Summer Island for three days, but it really seemed like her aunt had made a positive effect on everyone in this little town.

"She was an extraordinary lady."

"She was." Sophia motioned for her to follow her to an opened laptop computer at the head of the long boardroom table. "What would you like to add to the docket?"

Millie pulled out the top sheet of paper from her folder and handed it to Sophia. "I think it might be easier to let you read it instead of trying to explain it myself." George had done an excellent job of writing out the legal phrasing she'd need for each different step of this process. And while Millie had spent hours over the past two days going over all of this, she wasn't sure she could say it as eloquently as he had.

Sophia was quiet for a second while she read the paper. "So you want to resurrect Mildred's little bed and breakfast, huh? I hear it was pretty impressive back in its prime."

Millie thought she detected a hint of skepticism in Sophia's voice, which made her stand a little taller in defense. "It was listed in the top one hundred places to visit in *Travel Magazine* for fifteen years in a row. It was featured more times than any other privately owned hotel in the country." True, these were facts that George's team had given her to aid her arguments, but she should've known them. It was impressive. The town should be proud of Seascape Inn. "It's my intention to restore her to her former glory."

Sure, it seemed like an unrealistic goal when the house was falling apart, she couldn't even get the electric company to turn on the power, and apparently running the inn had become forbidden, but it could be done. Probably.

Sophia grinned. "I think Mildred would have loved that." She set the paper on the table and typed something into the computer. Millie surveyed the room again, her palms getting sweaty. Somehow, having to present her case in this cozy room full of people who all knew each other was more intimidating than what she'd imagined.

When Sophia finished typing, she handed the paper back to Millie. "You're all set. There are extra chairs set up along that wall over there. Here's an agenda. Your part will be at the end during new business."

"Thanks." She stared down at the agenda.

"If you have any questions about anything, just let me know. Welcome to the neighborhood."

Sophia's bright and cheerful voice sparked her confidence, and Millie wove through the tight space to the chairs along the back wall as an older gentleman announced it was time to get started. Maybe this meeting wasn't going to be so bad after all.

As soon as everyone had taken their seats, the older gentleman banged a gavel on the table and called the meeting to order. "We're still missing our president and a few others." He motioned to the empty chair at the head of the table. "But let's go ahead and get started with approving the minutes from our last meeting."

They were in the formal approval process when the door to the boardroom opened and an out of breath Braxton Channing stuck his head in. "Sorry I'm late."

Millie resisted the urge to roll her eyes. Typical. He was quick to critique everyone else's life but didn't bother to hold himself up to the same standards.

Instead of coming into the room, he held up a finger. "Hold on. Let me see if I can hurry her along." Before anyone could say anything, he disappeared again.

Seriously? He was already late and now he wanted the entire meeting to wait on him while he told someone else what to do? This guy had some nerve.

A minute later he returned, holding a giggling strawberry-blond toddler. "Once again, my sincerest apologies."

Millie took in the adorable two- or three-year-old on Braxton's hip who had his same eyes. Wait. He had a kid? This was new information. Maybe it was time she googled America's favorite golfer and found out what really happened after he left the sport.

Since the only empty chair along the back wall was next to her, she moved her bag to make more room. She wasn't overly concerned with Mr. Bossy-Pants's comfort, but the little girl deserved a place to sit.

But instead of making his way to the back of the room, he stopped at the head of the table. Pulling the tiny purple unicorn backpack off his shoulder, he sank into the vacant chair.

The president's chair.

"Where are we?" Braxton asked.

Millie's stomach plunged. Perfect. This was just perfect. Her uptight, know-it-all neighbor was also the HOA president. Could anything else go wrong in this new empowered life of hers?

"We were just about to get started with item one in old business." Sophia pushed her laptop in front of him then held her arms out to the little girl and lifted her onto her lap. "Alice, want to sit with me so your daddy can run the meeting?"

From somewhere, Sophia produced a bag of chocolate-covered pretzels and handed one to the cute little girl who sat contentedly on her lap and nibbled on it. "And be aware we have a couple of additions to new business at the end." She pointed to something at the bottom of the computer screen. Braxton appeared to study it for a long second and then looked up, searching the room until his gaze landed on Millie.

"Hello, Ms. Leclair." He offered a stiff and serious smile, but there was something about his stare, something in the way he looked at her, that seemed to go deeper than a polite greeting. It caused a slight flutter in her chest and she had to force herself to not squirm.

"I'm glad you could join us this evening."

Seriously, she'd never seen eyes that shade of blue before.

They were like the color of the sky on a beautiful, clear day. Perhaps she needed to focus on something other than his gorgeous eyes. Or his handsome face. Really, maybe she shouldn't look at him at all.

So she transferred her focus to Sophia. "I'm anxious to share my grievance."

Sophia flashed a friendly smile and handed the little girl another pretzel.

"Right." Braxton shifted in his chair. "Well, let's get started."

For the next forty minutes the board discussed everything from beautification projects to budgets to closing out a few violation inquiries.

"And that brings us to our final new item of the evening. The owner of 121 East Shore Drive has a grievance with one of the policies listed in the deed restrictions." Braxton looked up at the other board members seated around the table. "To remind you of the background of this property, the original owner, Mildred Leclair, recently passed away. The property has been inherited by Ms. Millie Leclair who is currently residing at the residence."

He shifted his gaze to Millie. "The floor is yours, Ms. Leclair."

Everyone turned to her and ice water flooded her veins, making the tips of her fingers and toes tingle. This was ridiculous. She was in a room among peers who owned houses in the same neighborhood she did. She had nothing to be nervous about, but reciting these facts to herself didn't change the fact that this felt like a giant game of which-one-of-these-is-not-like-the-others and she was the answer.

She stood, clutching the papers George had given her in her hand, and cleared her throat. "I'm coming before you today to make a formal complaint against article eleven section B as well as article eleven section C."

The complete silence at the end of her statement made her want to squirm. She shifted her weight from one foot to the other and continued reading off the sheet. "The aforementioned articles were put into place without regard for the current status of the property at 121 East Shore Drive. Since the property was established in 1953, it has been operated as a for-profit lodging facility. Furthermore, you will find in article four section A that all future regulations and changes which would negatively affect a property have to go through a separate approval process, which states..."

Millie could hear herself droning on and on with the mind-numbing legal mumbo-jumbo. From the glazed-over looks from almost everyone at the table, she wasn't the only one who felt that way about the words coming out her mouth.

She finished reading the paragraph she was on, then paused. She had a good case. George and his team had been very thorough. But she was missing the passion.

She didn't need any papers to guide her on this, so she folded them and addressed her audience once more. "Seascape Inn has been a pillar of the community long before the neighborhood was established. Its commercial business helped found the town. People who call this town home along with those who choose to come here year after year have good memories, priceless memories, of times spent at Seascape Inn. They're the kind of memories that give people hope and encouragement." Each word rang true, pushing away the chill of nervousness and the fear of the unknown. For the first time since she'd rolled into this town, she felt empowered.

"Our community needs those kinds of moments and those kinds of memories. Regardless of what's written in all of those articles and sections, we need Seascape to be what it has always been. It *deserves* to be a functioning boutique hotel." She took a slight step forward as she delivered the last statement, her posture tall and proud. Even her voice had risen a decibel to echo the passion burning in her chest.

Everyone in the room stared at her.

Crickets. Literally. The only thing that could be heard in the whole room was the annoying chirping of a cricket.

All of the wind got knocked out of her sails, and a flame of embarrassment brushed across her cheeks. She stood there as the silence became awkward, wondering what she should do next. Should she sit and let the board discuss, or should she keep talking? There were two more pages of legal mumbo-jumbo she could read to them.

"Thank you, Miss Leclair," Braxton finally said. "For clarification purposes for our minutes, you're requesting that the HOA reconsider article eleven section B that would prohibit the property at 121 East Shore Drive from operating as a business and article eleven section C that would prohibit said property from becoming a hotel."

"Not *becoming*, Mr. Channing. Remaining."

He nodded. "Very well. I motion to delay taking a vote on this topic until our next general meeting. That should give everyone on the board ample time to research the issue and will allow Miss Leclair time to display the renovations and a thorough plan for the property. Does anyone second?"

An older gentleman in a short-sleeved cotton guayabera shirt gave a second. Braxton turned to Sophia. "So for now let's leave this case open and put it at the top of the agenda for our next meeting." Sophia typed something into her computer and Braxton looked around the table.

"And unless I'm missing something, that concludes our meeting. Does anyone have any other announcements before we formally adjourn?"

• • •

Braxton banged the gavel against the table. Almost immediately people pushed back from the table and the room filled with conversation.

Not Millie, though. She dropped into her chair looking defeated.

Sophia swiveled her chair to face him, Alice happily sitting on her lap. "Is everything okay with Henry?"

From the moment he stepped through the door, Braxton had forced the drama from earlier today to the back of his mind so he could be 100 percent present here. But all it took was one simple question from his friend to bring it all flooding back.

Braxton rested his elbow on the table and massaged his temples. "He got confused and didn't want to take his medicine. Which led to him being belligerent, which led to all sorts of problems. But he had calmed down by the time I left. It helped that Lena could stay with him, but I didn't want her to have to watch Alice, too."

Lena, their sixty-year-old nanny and housekeeper, had also helped take care of Henry before he moved into the memory care home and was the only other person Henry still trusted.

Sophia ruffled the little girl's hair. "That's not a problem because we don't mind Alice hanging out with us, do we?" She turned back to Braxton and put a sympathetic hand on his arm. "But I'm so sorry you have to go through this. I know it's hard to watch."

Henry had always been one of the gentlest, most patient people Braxton knew. Never would he have ever expected to be called out for Henry causing problems, but this condition was changing everything. The more confused he got, the more frustrated he became. And the more frustrated he became the more his fight or flight reflex kicked in. Unfortunately, lately he was prone to the fighting side.

"I made a doctor's appointment for him next week. Maybe she'll have some suggestions on how to manage it better."

Sophia smiled. "You're a good friend to him. He's lucky to have you."

Braxton shrugged. "It's the least I can do."

"Well, I'm going to take Alice to see the fish tank in the lobby. Take your time finishing up whatever you need to do in here." She turned her attention to the little girl in her lap. "Chiquita, want to go see if we can find Dory?"

Alice clapped her hands together and they got up to leave. "Bye-bye, Daddy," she called as she bounced to the door holding Sophia's hand.

"Bye, Little Foot. I'll see you in a minute."

His daughter grinned at him with an expression that was an exact replica of her mother. He watched her walk with Sophia until they disappeared into the hallway. He turned back to the computer to finish up the notes he needed to make, but the stress headache that had started earlier still pounded in his head, making it hard to concentrate. Maybe he needed water.

He pushed away from the table and headed toward the snack table. But halfway there, his new neighbor, Millie Leclair, appeared in front of him with her hands on her hips and her lips pressed together in a grim line.

"Why do you hate my aunt's legacy?"

Braxton frowned. "I have nothing against Mildred's legacy. I thought she was a lovely woman."

Her eyes narrowed. "Then why are you trying to buy up her land and block her hotel?"

It'd been a hard day and all Braxton wanted was to drink some water, finish his work, and get home to put Alice to bed. He let out a sigh and reached around her until he could snag one of the bottles on the edge of the table. Still, he admired her tenacity.

"I'm not trying to block you." He twisted off the top and raised an eyebrow. "Plus, I thought you said you wanted it to be more of a bed and breakfast." He took a long pull from his drink, keeping his gaze on her.

She blinked in rapid succession. While he'd managed to catch every word she'd said on their first meeting, he'd somehow missed how pretty her eyes were. They were the color of rich caramel and they simultaneously calmed and ignited something within him.

"It's...well...yeah. So you were listening."

Braxton nodded. "Of course I was listening. My job, however, is to make sure everything that happens in the neighborhood is in everyone's best interests."

She propped her hand on her hip again, regaining her footing, and passion ignited in her beautiful eyes. "And you don't think my great-aunt's legacy, my livelihood, is what's best for the community?"

He took another swig of his water, trying to turn his attention to anything other than the way her eyes sparked when she spoke. Or how they were causing a flurry somewhere deep in his chest.

"I didn't say that, but there are a lot of things at play here. The bylaws were written to protect our residents, our neighborhoods, and our beaches." It might be an unpopular opinion, but he happened to like rules. They protected things that needed to be protected. They kept people safe.

"What exactly do you think I'll be doing at the B&B? Holding midnight raves and dumping my trash on the beach?"

"I wouldn't think so, but one should never assume." He leaned in as if sharing a secret. "By the way, if you're planning on the rave, you should make it an early evening thing. There's also a noise ordinance that goes into effect at eleven." He gave her his best *what-can-you-do?* look and shrugged.

She rolled her eyes and the flurry in his chest upgraded to a fluster, which he immediately stomped down. He didn't have time for that, no matter how much he admired her gusto.

"My intention, Mr. Channing, is to restore a legacy. A legacy that, as I said before, helped build this community. A legacy that should've never been blocked."

"And as the HOA president, if one of our rules or regulations is unfair, I'm dedicated to making it right. Which is why I asked for more time to fully review your case." He nodded once, confident he'd made the right call. "If reopening your B&B is what's best for our community, convince us."

"Oh, I will. Seascape's renovations are going to have her looking even better than she did before. And I won't just have a plan to show you. I'll host an open house before the next board meeting so you can see it in person."

He hoped she had deep pockets because it would take a small fortune to pull that off.

He held up his drink in a salute to her. "No one is looking forward to seeing that more than I am."

"In that case, you better hold on to your socks, because I'm about to knock them off."

Chapter Four

Millie stood on her front porch with Bear by her side and watched the last of the contractors drive off down her crumbling circular driveway. From the estimates she'd received today, fixing said driveway would cost anywhere from three to six thousand dollars. More if she wanted stamped concrete, which was what they all recommended.

She glanced down at the price sheet in her hand.

Bathroom remodels, roof repairs, rotted siding that needed to be replaced...

The list was five pages long. Five pages of things that needed to be repaired, updated, or simply redone. Hardwired smoke detectors installed, broken windowpanes replaced, lighting fixtures. And, at best, her bank account could only handle about half of the costs.

Sure, there were bank loans, but the fact that her small business technically wasn't allowed to be a business at the moment made her an "undesirable candidate." And she would consider asking a friend for a personal loan as an investment, but that would require her having friends with money. Which she didn't.

"Where are we going to find the money?" she asked Bear.

She sank down onto the step and scratched her dog behind his ears, looking out over the front lawn. It was a gorgeous summer afternoon. Fluffy white clouds hung in a blue sky and the vibrant scent of flowers mixed with the fresh salt air. It was the kind of afternoon that made you want to relax by the pool with a glass of iced tea. Only her ice maker was broken and her pool needed a new pump and to be resurfaced before it could be filled again.

"Homeownership is a lot harder than I was expecting." Bear lay down next to her, resting his head on her leg.

She opened the file folder she'd been holding and spread it across her lap, adding the new estimate page to the top. There were four of them in total. Four different contractors offering four different ideas of what she needed to do, each with four very different price tags.

"I don't know, Bear. Which one of them did you like?" She started to flip through the reports when she was distracted by a shiny chocolate-brown convertible bumping down her driveway. It pulled to a stop in front of her steps and Sophia stepped out, wearing a blue and white striped sundress with her long, dark hair pulled up in a high, swingy ponytail.

"Hello, neighbor," she said in her cheerful voice. She reached into her passenger seat and pulled out a turquoise box tied with a brown satin ribbon. "I've come to bring you a housewarming present."

Bear's ears perked and he trotted down the steps to greet their guest. Millie gathered up all the papers on her lap and shoved them back into the folder before she stood.

"That's so thoughtful." Millie accepted the box. "I'd invite you to come in, but it's a bit of a mess in there."

Sophia waved off the suggestion. "I can't stay anyway. I'm on my way back to my shop. I just wanted to drop this off first."

"I'm glad you did." Millie tucked the file folder under her arm and pulled the ribbon to open the box. Inside were rows of picture-perfect chocolates in varying shapes and colors. "These are almost too beautiful to eat." She took one out and examined the way the white drizzle fell over the round milk chocolate surface. "However, I've never met a chocolate I can say no to." She popped it in her mouth and moaned as the velvety cocoa cascaded over her taste buds.

"This is amazing," she said through her mouthful. "And the kind of pick-me-up I needed."

Sophia flashed an amused smile. "I'm glad you like them. That one is my abuela's famous secret recipe." She motioned to Millie's file folder. "What are you working on?"

Millie forced herself to put the lid back on the box instead of eating another sweet and retrieved the folder from under her arm.

"These are the estimates for the renovations."

"Ahhh. The dreaded reno. I've been in my current shop for almost three years, but I still remember the drama of the buildout like it was yesterday."

"It went that well, huh?"

"It turned out gorgeous, so all the blood, sweat, and oh-so-many tears were worth it."

Millie giggled. "So the tears are a normal reno occurrence?"

"If you haven't cried at least once, you're doing it wrong." She grinned. "Actually, Mildred gave me the best advice when I was building out my first shop. She said 'even marathons are run one single step at a time.'"

Millie looked up at the dilapidated house and loneliness ached in her chest. "I wish she was here to help me now."

Sophia pointed to the folder. "I'm far from having Mildred's wisdom, but I've been down the reno road a few times. I'd be happy to take a look at what you've got if you'd like."

"That would be really helpful, actually." She handed Sophia the folder. "I've been trying to ask Bear for his opinion, but he's more of the strong, silent type."

Sophia nodded as she flipped through the different estimates in the folder. "I have a couple of fish and they're the same way."

The sound of a sports car engine revving filled the air, and Millie looked up in time to see her infuriating neighbor pull out of his driveway onto the main road.

"What about Mr. Everything By The Rules? Should I be worried he'll file official HOA complaints about every little thing I do?"

Sophia looked up from the files. "Braxton? No way. He's a great guy. Ever since the accident he comes across a little grumpy, but he has a heart of gold."

She'd once again forgotten to google the man, but it was twice now that something in his past had been brought up as the reason for his less than neighborly attitude. "Accident?"

"Jade, his wife, was killed in a car accident about two years ago. Alice was only about a month old at the time." Sadness filled her eyes. "She was one of my best friends and an amazing mother. Her death was a tragedy."

Millie held back a gasp.

It was still no excuse, but she could understand. She was no stranger to loss, so she knew firsthand what it felt like to grieve. But losing a wife? She couldn't even imagine how painful that would be.

"I had no idea."

Sophia stared off in the direction his car had gone, as if looking at a memory. "Braxton was devastated. We all tried to pitch in with the baby, but Henry, his golf coach, played the biggest role in helping him through it. He even moved into

Braxton's house for a while to help out when Alice was really small." Sophia laughed. "Henry never had kids and Braxton was a first-time dad. I can only imagine what kind of skit their two men and a baby situation looked like until Braxton hired Lena."

"Henry sounds like a good friend."

Sophia nodded. "Braxton is the closest thing to family Henry has. They're really close. Which is why it's so sad to watch his condition get worse so quickly. Braxton now visits him in the assisted living facility every day."

A twinge of guilt pricked at her. Even though he hadn't given her the best impression or the warmest welcome to Summer Island, maybe she had judged him too quickly on that one interaction. He had been infuriating at the HOA meeting as well, but that had felt more like teasing, which left her flustered for a whole other reason she would not think about right now. Well, at the very least, she would try to give him another chance and be civil during their next interaction.

Not that she was anticipating one or wanting to see him again.

She was still wrangling her wayward thoughts when Sophia handed her one of the estimate packets.

"I like Gus. He's honest, hardworking, and sticks to his timelines. Plus, he's very considerate of your budget. I used him when I moved into the shop I'm in now." She stacked the rest of the papers neatly in the folder before handing it over. "I ended up having to do some of the work myself because of budget restrictions. It's how I learned how to tile a backsplash."

"Wait. You tiled it yourself? How did you learn how to do it?"

"One of my brothers and YouTube."

Of course. Why hadn't she thought of that before? Millie stared at the line items on the sheet and the numbers attached.

If she did some of the work herself—okay, *a lot* of the work herself—she could save quite a bit of money.

She grinned. "I might be calling you to give me some of your expert tile-laying tips."

Sophia clapped her hands together. "I love a good DIY project! You tell me when you're ready to start tiling and I'll come over and help." She glanced at her watch. "Except right now I gotta run."

"Thanks for the chocolates and the help. I needed both this morning."

Sophia waved goodbye and climbed into her car. Millie watched her drive down the cracked driveway. It needed to be fixed since it was the first thing visitors saw, but pouring concrete sounded much too technical to be in her YouTube-aided wheelhouse. Like it or not, she'd be spending six grand on a part of the estate no one would notice as soon as it wasn't falling apart.

She turned to examine the front of the house with a different eye. While pouring concrete was out of the question, there were still plenty of things she could do herself. Like use a power washer. She'd never tried before, but she'd seen people using them. It didn't look that hard. Painting the exterior of the house sounded like a giant task, but she was more than capable of using a paintbrush.

She balanced the folder on top of the box of chocolates and pulled the pencil from behind her ear to circle those two expenses on her list. Combined, they cost about the same as the driveway. It wasn't enough to save the entire project, but it was a start.

She sat down on the steps and opened the box of sweets, selecting a white chocolate rectangle striped with dark chocolate. "If we're going to do this, Bear, we're going to need all the sustenance we can get. Don't judge."

Bear wagged his furry caramel tail. She scratched his

head as she scanned other items on her list. All she had to do was whittle the reno price tag down by half. Which meant, since she still had to rent equipment and buy materials, she was going to have to do more than half the work herself.

"It's a lot, Bear, but we can do it." She circled another item on the front page. "How do you feel about polishing and resealing the tile floors?"

· · ·

The next day Millie stood inside Summer Island's hardware store with her trusty notebook, a pen, and a crick in her neck. This fact-finding mission should've been an easy—and possibly fun—task to cross off her to-do list. She'd thought wrong.

In order to set her final budget she needed to know what the materials would cost on jobs she intended to tackle on her own. Admittedly, it was a long list full of things that fell into the category of "I'd never heard of that" or "I'd never even thought about those." But since she wasn't making final decisions today or spending money she didn't have, she figured it would be pretty low stress.

What she didn't factor in was the vast number of options she would have to choose from for each item on her list. Take the doorknobs, for example. They seemed pretty straightforward, right?

Wrong.

An entire aisle from floor to ceiling full of different doorknob choices awaited her, to be exact. And the longer she stood staring at them, her neck getting sore from constantly looking up, the more overwhelmed she became. Should she go with brushed nickel or antique bronze? Or maybe just straight black? Of course there were also glass knobs if she wanted something more original. Then she had to consider the shape. Did she want a lever or round? And how could there be so many different ways to interpret the word "round?"

The knobs were starting to blur in her vision when a voice interrupted her internal debate. "Would you like a stranger's opinion?"

A woman about her age dressed in a long-sleeved rash guard with a local dive shop logo, shorts, and a sun visor stood in the middle of the aisle holding a set of wrenches. "Sometimes I find that a stranger weighing in can help you figure out which one you really wanted to begin with. Either you agree with their opinion, or you're ready to argue with someone you don't even know about why it should be the other one. Regardless, you walk away feeling good about your decision."

"You had me at decision," Millie joked. "I'd actually love a second opinion. Or any opinion, really. What are your thoughts on doorknobs?"

"I find them pretty handy when trying to open a door. Other than that, I have to admit I've never given them much thought." She pushed a few stray strands of sun-bleached blond hair out of her eyes as she turned to examine the options.

"That makes two of us." Millie sighed and refocused her attention on the wall of knobs. "The only thing I know is that I need a lot of them." She glanced down at the numbers on her page. "Seventy-two to be exact."

"What are you doing with so many doorknobs?"

"Renovating my great-aunt's house." Millie shifted, trying to push away the chilly disappointment that started to creep up every time she talked about the house. "At least, I'm trying to. It turns out the process is a little more difficult than I'd thought."

"Oh, wait." Recognition flickered in her green eyes. "You

must be Mildred's niece. My friend Sophia told me you were in town."

Millie extended her hand. "That would be me. Millie Leclair. Great-niece of Mildred and new owner of Seascape Inn."

"I'm Tessa Foster. Welcome to Summer Island."

"Thanks. I'm glad to be here." It was the truth. Being in Summer Island felt right. Even if her struggles were piling up by the day and her bank account was shrinking by the minute, she felt more at home at Seascape than anywhere else she'd ever lived. Now all she had to do was convince Braxton Channing and his HOA cronies to think the same way. She took a deep breath before the thought overwhelmed her. "Although, I'm not sure everyone is as happy that I'm here."

Tessa nodded. "I heard you had a little run-in with the Oceanside Estates HOA."

"Do you live in Oceanside too?"

"No. I live on the other side of the island. But they're known for having a very, shall we say, involved HOA."

"I'm starting to see that."

Tessa gave her an encouraging grin. "Don't worry. Aside from their occasional warning letter, they're all good people."

"Good to know." Millie would have to take her word for it, because as far as she was concerned, the verdict was still out.

"But back to your knob situation, I like those." Tessa pointed to one in the middle of the wall. "It seems like a normal shape and comes in a box of eight. If nothing else, it'll make it easy for you to carry them out of the store."

"Great recommendation. I'm going with it." Millie wrote the part number and the price in her notebook. "Thanks."

"My pleasure." Tessa jerked her thumb toward the front of the store. "I was about to meet Sophia for lunch at The Bait Shop. You should join us."

Millie glanced at her binder. There were a lot of empty lines on her price estimate sheet and she'd only gotten about a quarter of the way through the store. But on the other hand, it would be nice to make some friends in her new hometown.

"I'd love to, but there's one problem," Millie said.

"What's that?"

"The stranger's opinion thing really worked, and I still have a long list of items to pick out."

Tessa laughed. "The good news is a friend's opinion is even better. And we have a few minutes before we have to be at lunch. What's next on your list?"

"What do you know about bathroom faucets?"

"Not a thing. But let's go pick one out and then I'll introduce you to the best fried oysters on the island."

"Sounds great." Millie felt lighter as she followed Tessa to the faucet aisle. Today's successes were only small steps in her reno-marathon, but at least she wasn't at the starting line anymore. And every bit of road that was behind her put her that much closer to the finish line.

Plus, she'd run just about any race that included eating fried oysters.

Chapter Five

Friday afternoon, Braxton shoved a quarter of his club sandwich into his mouth while listening to Jenna, the beautification chairwoman, give her update at their board meeting. He'd come up with the idea of switching the monthly meeting of the HOA's nine board members to lunchtime and having Oceanside Estates clubhouse restaurant cater it as a way to maximize time.

Braxton was nothing if not efficient, and he was determined to check off all the items on the agenda and eat his lunch by the time he had to roll out of here at one thirty, even if it meant he had to inhale his sandwich while the various chairpersons were reporting.

"Lastly, as usual we'll have a board displaying the fall color scheme and plant selection for the six shared space gardens at the next general meeting for the residents to see. And that's all from the beautification committee."

"Thanks, Jenna." Braxton took a quick drink of water and wiped his mouth with his napkin. "That closes out our committee updates, moving us to new business. First on the list is the property at 121 East Shore Drive."

"Do you really think that place could ever be a functioning inn again?" Lori, one of the members-at-large, asked.

"No." Stan, the board's parliamentarian, didn't have any hesitation in his voice. "I don't know why we delayed the vote. There's only one way this thing can go."

"Because it's our job to make sure we're 'protecting the rights of our residents while providing a beautiful, safe, and secure place to call home,'" Braxton quoted the board member oath they all took when they were sworn into their positions. "Since she's a resident, we owe it to her to listen to her complaint and make an educated decision about the situation based on the facts."

"The fact is the place is a dump," Stan said, eliciting a couple of muffled snickers from his end of the table. "I still don't know why she doesn't sell. It would be so much easier to start over."

Jose, the chair of the standards committee, nodded. "It does seem like a full renovation to get it up to code will be a challenge."

Braxton had to agree, which was why the real estate agent in him originally pounced on the idea of finding a buyer for the premium lot. But his spirited new neighbor was set on staying.

Would it be easier for her to take the generous offer his clients had put forward and start over? Or any one of the other two offers that he knew were on the table? Absolutely. There were several turnkey waterfront properties available that she could move into tomorrow, all well below the amount they were willing to pay her.

But Millie Leclair didn't want a vacation home. She wanted to hold on to a legacy.

He just wasn't sure it was a legacy she *could* hold on to.

"George Rodriguez said Ms. Leclair isn't interested in

selling. She's not entertaining offers of any sort," Braxton said. "Since she has decided to remain in the property, we will have to make a decision regarding her formal grievance. To do that, what information do we need?"

"Isn't looking at the place enough?" Stan said under his breath, drawing chuckles from the end of the table once more.

Braxton shot him a warning look. Normally, Stan was a good guy. Loud at times and certainly opinionated, but good. What was his problem today?

"If her claim is that it's always been operational, I guess we need proof that Mildred never closed the business aspect," Jenna offered.

Braxton wrote that down on his pad. "That's good. What else?"

"How long will the renovations take? And what are her plans for the inn once it reopens?" Lori added.

Braxton nodded as he jotted down the next two items.

"Does she have and can she obtain all the permits required to do the work she's wanting to do?" Jose threw out.

"We could play a part in that." Stan's lip curled up.

"She's hiring Gus Richardson as her contractor," Sophia announced, glaring at Stan. "He's done a lot of work in this neighborhood and is very thorough about getting the building permits he needs."

Braxton looked across the table at her. "How do you know that?"

"I stopped by to drop off some welcome-to-the-neighborhood chocolates just as she'd finished meeting with him."

"You took her chocolates?" There was a hint of disdain in Stan's voice which Braxton didn't care for. Apparently Sophia noticed it, too.

"And I had lunch with her yesterday." Sophia focused on Stan, not trying to hide the irritation in her voice. "Welcoming someone to the neighborhood is polite. I did the same thing when you moved to town. It's how I met your wife, who I now consider a close friend." She shifted her gaze to the rest of the table. "Also, Mildred would've wanted us to welcome her family member with the same open arms she extended to each one of us."

Braxton couldn't have said it better himself. He gave Sophia a slight nod of appreciation.

"Exactly, which brings us back to the task at hand." He tapped the list he'd made. "These documents seem like a good place to start. The actual vote has to be done at a general HOA meeting that is open to all the residents, but it might be worth it to have Ms. Leclair and her contractor show us their plans."

"Seems like a lot of work for one vote." Stan sat back in his chair, crossing his arms in front of his chest.

Braxton had to agree with him on this point. It was a lot of work, and he had his doubts that the vote was going to be favorable for Millie. But that didn't mean it wasn't the right thing to do.

"I'll take care of gathering the documents, and we'll go from there." Braxton made sure to add a tone of finality to his voice as he closed out the subject. As long as he was president, they were going to do things right, which meant Millie Leclair's case was going to get a fair review.

However, she would need all her i's dotted and t's crossed, because he had a feeling that the HOA board wouldn't have much grace.

· · ·

"What's wrong with you? You seem grumpy," Henry said as he made his next move in his daily chess game with Braxton.

"I'm not grumpy. I just have a lot on my mind today." He

moved his bishop to f5 which Henry promptly captured.

"Whatcha thinking about that's making you grumpy?"

Braxton shook his head. Lately, Henry said whatever thought popped into his mind, whether or not it would offend someone. More often than not, at least where Braxton was involved, it made him discuss things he'd rather not talk about. "If you must know, I'm thinking about Seascape."

Henry's eyes had the same blankness that had become increasingly more standard these days. "What's Seascape?"

"It's the name of the property next door to me. It used to be an inn run by Mildred Leclair."

"I know Mildred. She's…" His voice trailed off and a flicker of recognition lit up his eyes.

"She's what?" Braxton abandoned the game and focused on his friend.

Henry stared off for another second, still lost in the memory that brought life to his eyes. A hint of a smile tugged at his mouth and he returned his attention to the game board. "Wouldn't you like to know."

Braxton chuckled and made his next move. "Mildred's niece now lives in her house and she wants to reopen the inn."

It would've been easy to avoid telling Henry that he was struggling with the decision about Millie's request to overturn the no hotels rule. But the truth was the topic made him uneasy and he valued Henry's advice.

"Mildred's inn is one of the nicest in town. I could tell you some stories."

"I know, I know, but I'm not old enough," Braxton finished. "The thing is, there are rules now about having a business on the beach, especially hotels. They aren't allowed."

The blank stare returned and Braxton picked up on the signs of Henry's building frustration. "Everyone is always changing the rules. Why don't people just leave them the way they were? How is anyone supposed to focus on anything when the rules are always changing?"

"Sometimes new rules make things better."

"And sometimes they complicate things."

Braxton considered that. Did the new deed restrictions make things better for the neighborhood or more complicated? Having rules to keep property values high benefited all the residents, didn't they? Opening the door to add hotels and vacation rentals on the beach would only bring more traffic and pollution, right? It would be a lot harder to protect their beaches when the people using them were always coming and going.

"In this case, I didn't make the rule. It's just my job to uphold it." And to protect the best interests of everyone in the community.

Henry made his next move. "Then you better make sure the rule is worth upholding."

Chapter Six

Demo day.

After a week of picking a contractor, deciding on materials, then working and reworking her budget to get everything in, it was finally time to get started on the actual work. Task number one was to rip everything out, which also happened to be the first project on her list to tackle on her own.

Millie had been excited to get started this morning. Those TV home reno shows always made demo day look like fun. Walls, cabinets, and disgusting old flooring popped right out, and the homeowners blissfully carried it all to the dumpster waiting right outside their door, looking as fresh and as made up as they did at the beginning of the segment. By the next commercial break, entire houses were cleared out and swept clean and no one had even broken a sweat. Easy breezy.

She could now confirm they were a bunch of liars.

For starters, her dumpster wasn't anywhere near her front door. To toss her debris, she had to walk all the way down her 207-foot driveway without tripping to the perimeter of her property because apparently if she was intending to redo the driveway, the dumpster couldn't be anywhere in the way of it.

Also, per the safety instructions on the do-it-yourself video she watched, she had to turn off all the power to the house in case she accidentally hit an electrical line. Meaning she hadn't even swung a sledgehammer yet, but sweat was dripping down her face, her torso, and other places that made it really uncomfortable to move with her clothes sticking. She'd spent forty-five minutes trying to open every window in the house, hoping the coastal breeze would help with the rising interior temp.

Now, covered in the dust from windows that hadn't been touched in years and already sticky from the humidity, Millie stood in the first bathroom and stared at the step-by-step directions on the phone in her hand.

"They say start with the vanity. 'Swing the sledgehammer upward at the underside of the vanity where it meets the wall.'" She stared at the spot it suggested and shrugged. "Sounds straightforward enough." Plus, she really felt like hitting something. "Here goes nothing."

She slid her phone in her pocket and pulled her safety goggles over her eyes. "Stay out there, Bear."

The dog remained in the doorway, his gaze intently on her. Millie widened her stance, grabbed the heavy sledgehammer in both hands, and swung with all her strength.

The vanity didn't move. In fact, other than chipping one of the tiles, it didn't appear as if she'd done anything. She let go of the tool with one hand, letting it fall heavily to her side, and tried to wiggle the countertop. Nothing. Not even a shimmy.

With a deep breath, she tried again, this time swinging it upward at a different angle. Still nothing. "Seriously? All the things falling apart in this house, and this hideous gold tile is the one thing that's indestructible?"

She wiped the sweat beading on her forehead with her sleeve, frustration building inside her, and got ready to swing again. Maybe third time was the charm. Or maybe the frustration was enough to give her super strength.

"Knock, knock! Anyone home?" The familiar voice made her pause.

Confused, Millie stepped out of the bathroom and peered around the corner into the grand foyer. There, standing right in the middle, was Sophia dressed in worn overalls with a blue bandana holding her dark hair back. Tessa was next to her, wearing work gloves. Both were holding buckets full of cleaning supplies.

Bear trotted over to greet them.

"Sorry, we tried ringing the doorbell, but it didn't seem to be working so we let ourselves in," Sophia said.

Millie stepped all the way into the open foyer area. "What are you girls doing here?" She tried to counterbalance her confusion with a friendly smile.

"We heard you were doing some demo work today and thought we'd stop by and lend a hand," Tessa said as casually as if someone had just asked why she was at the mall.

"You came to help me with demo day?"

"Of course. That's what we do in this town. We help each other." Sophia nodded at the platter in her hand. "And we bring snacks. I brought my famous chocolate chip cookies."

Millie took the treats. The sweet scent drifted up, triggering memories from her childhood summers at Seascape Inn. Also, they reminded her she hadn't eaten breakfast yet.

"That's so kind." Millie broke one of the cookies in half and popped it in her mouth. "Thank you."

"Where do you want us?" Tessa asked.

Millie motioned at the bathroom as she swallowed the bite in her mouth. "I'm starting in there, but ripping out the vanity is harder than I thought it'd be."

Tessa pointed at Millie's sledgehammer. "May I have a whack at it?"

"Be my guest." Millie handed her the tool, but before she could follow the two women into the bathroom, the front door swung open again.

"Yoo-hoo!"

Millie spun around just in time to see Bonnie sweeping through the door with two men Millie hadn't met yet following right behind her. Of course, all of them were dressed to work and carrying an assortment of tools.

"We haven't missed it, have we?" Bonnie stopped in front of Millie and leaned her broom against the wall.

"Miss the demo? I just started on the first bathroom and there are six more to rip out."

"Oh good. We can start on the next one. Which way?" Bonnie asked.

"All the guest rooms are upstairs. I guess we should start with the first room on the right?"

"Perfect." Bonnie held up the tray of brownies in her hand. "And where should I put these?"

"I'll take them for you. They look delicious."

"It's Mildred's recipe. They're still a bestseller at the café."

"How thoughtful!" Millie resisted the urge to eat one right now. No one needed a brownie *and* a cookie for breakfast.

She'd just returned from putting the trays of treats in the kitchen when the front door opened again. Her lawyer and two young men he introduced as his sons walked in followed by her contractor and his wife.

It continued like that until her house was full of people from the community. All seven bathrooms were being ripped out at the same time while other people hauled out old furniture and carpets. Millie raced from room to room answering questions, pointing people in the right direction, and trying not to slow down long enough to let her emotions catch up with her. Because if she even stopped for one minute to fully process the magnitude of kindness surrounding her, she'd be reduced to a mess of grateful and overwhelmed tears.

She was coming down the stairs when Sophia walked in with an empty wheelbarrow.

"One bathroom vanity successfully removed." She beamed at Millie. "The toilet is up next. You want to help us bag it?"

Millie clapped her hands together. "How did you know that's the part I've been looking forward to?" She hurried down and followed Sophia into the half empty bathroom.

Tessa was on the floor unscrewing the water line. "It's all unbolted and ready to go." She draped the rusted hose over the toilet bowl and stood up.

Sophia moved to the front of the toilet where she could lift it up. "Is everything in here original to the house?"

"As far as I can tell." Millie grabbed a plastic trash bag and squatted next to the toilet to slide it under the bottom as soon as the girls lifted it up. "Since the house was built in the early fifties I'm calling them antiques. It sounds more optimistic than old."

"I like it. Are we ready to move this antique commode?" Sophia asked.

"My grandmother's neighbor had an old potty in her front yard with flowers planted in it. So you have options. We could skip the dumpster and plop this guy right in the flower bed," Tessa said.

Sophia stared at her with a slightly horrified expression. "A toilet? In her front yard?"

Millie giggled. "The HOA would love that."

"So that's a no to the potty planter?" Tessa grinned as she twisted the toilet so she could get a grip on the tank side.

"I think this antique is dumpster bound."

Together, the three awkwardly carried it out and tossed it in with the other debris.

"Can I ask you a question?" Millie asked as they were walking back to the house, the muffled sounds of banging drifting through the air.

"Sure." Sophia rubbed her work-gloved hands together to get rid of some of the dirt on them.

"Don't get me wrong, I'm very grateful for the help. I just don't understand why people would give up their Saturday to rip out my old toilets."

Tessa wagged her finger. "Antique toilets."

Sophia smiled. "Two reasons. One, it's the kind of town we are. I know you got off to a rocky start with the whole HOA zoning thing, but I think you'll find that, in general, the residents of Summer Island are one big family."

Millie swallowed around the sudden knot in her throat. "I'm getting that picture. What's the second reason?"

"There's not one person in town who Mildred didn't help or who doesn't have at least one happy memory of this place. I think we're all eager to give back to it."

"That's the truth. My first kiss was here. Out by the pool at one of the Valentine's Dinner Dances Mildred used to do." Tessa got a wistful look on her face. "Jeffery Stevens in eighth grade. I wonder what happened to him."

"I sat at that dining room table and cried because the bank wouldn't give me a loan to open my first shop. Mildred made me tea and helped me figure out a way to make it work without it."

Another wave of regret swept over her. Aunt Mildred spent so much of her life helping and encouraging those around her. Even now she was indirectly helping Millie by providing a house full of people to support her. And Millie had never found the time to come out and visit her in her later years.

She sucked in a deep breath to try to ease the guilt that gnawed at her chest. The past couldn't be changed, but she could make it her goal to carry on Aunt Mildred's legacy. "She was an amazing lady."

Tessa nodded. "She was. And now it's your turn to be the amazing woman."

Millie squared her shoulders, more determined than ever to make her dream of reopening the inn work. No way was she going to stand by and let some dumb HOA rule prevent the world from experiencing the kindness and encouragement that had become synonymous with Seascape Inn. "One more question. How did everyone know about this?"

Sophia and Tessa both chuckled as they jogged up the steps to the front porch.

"Oh, honey. This is small-town living at its finest. Everyone here knows about everything," Sophia said.

"Welcome to Summer Island." Tessa grinned.

· · ·

The rest of the morning went quickly. The residents of Summer Island made a great demolition crew, and they had gotten further by eleven o'clock than Millie had expected to get by the end of the weekend.

Words couldn't express how thankful she was to these strangers, so she decided to use food instead. Although, ordering lunch for so many people with an hour's notice was no easy task. Luckily, Via Marco, the local Italian restaurant, could put together a baked ziti and salad lunch for twenty-five in less than an hour and they didn't even mind delivering it so Millie could keep working.

"I put myself through culinary school by cleaning rooms at Seascape Inn," the owner told her. "Delivering this food will be my pleasure."

By the time the food arrived at one, all of the guest rooms, bathrooms, and living areas were nothing but empty shells while the dumpster at the end of the driveway was full to the brim.

Her houseful of friends and neighbors gathered in the freshly swept and mopped dining room to make plates and claim a spot around the newly scrubbed long wooden table. Laughter once again filled the room, the same way she remembered as a kid, and the view warmed her heart.

This was what she wanted. This was what she was fighting for. The HOA might be worried about preserving their precious community, but this was worth preserving, too.

Millie floated around the table, carrying a pitcher of water in one hand and a pitcher of sweet tea in the other, refilling plastic cups and listening to different stories about the inn. One by one people left until only Tessa and Sophia remained.

Tessa tossed a handful of plastic cups she'd gathered into the trash bag Millie was holding. "I wish I could stay and help you clean up in here, but I have to dash. I have a scuba-diving tour going out at three."

"Sadly, me too." Sophia flashed an apologetic smile. "I have to get back to the shop."

"Please, you both have done enough today." Millie left the rest of the trash where it was and walked her new friends to the front door. "Really, thanks for everything. I can't imagine where I'd be without your help."

"My pleasure. Ripping out antique toilets is always a great way to spend the morning." Tessa gave Millie a quick hug. "And now you have to come to our book club on Friday. Talk her into coming, Sophia," she said as she jogged down the steps to her car.

"You'll love the group. This month it's at Joyce's house, who lives just down the street." Sophia motioned in the direction of all the beautiful new houses that lined East Shore Drive.

On the one hand, Millie loved the idea of getting to meet more of her neighbors and having a night off from the never-ending reno projects sounded like a welcome break. But there was one detail holding her back. "I'd love to but I haven't read the book."

Sophia waved away the concern. "At least one person shows up every month without reading it."

Millie laughed. "In that case, I'm there."

"Great! I'll send you the info."

They hugged before Sophia headed down the stairs and climbed into her car. She pulled around the fountain, then down and out the gate.

Millie was about to go back into the house when another car pulled through the gate. A very recognizable silver sports car.

Braxton Channing.

He was pretty much the last person she wanted to see bumping down her driveway, but after the amazing day she'd had she was in such a good mood that even Mr. Neighborhood Hall Monitor couldn't bring her down.

She stood on the top step and watched him get out of his car. "Well, look who it is. What brings you to this side of the fence?"

"Besides the fact that you had a party and didn't invite me?"

"Your invitation must have gotten lost in the mail." She shrugged and pulled a face to show her mock sympathy.

Braxton chuckled. It was a legit laugh that caused little wrinkles to appear around his eyes, as if laughing was something that used to happen often with him. The sight of it made her feel... Well, it made her feel a lot of things, but the one she was going with was friendly. Besides, didn't her aunt always say the best way to make the world a better place was to be friendly to anyone and everyone?

"What's with the flowers?" She pointed at the giant flower arrangement secured in his passenger seat with the seat belt, looking for any distraction from the friendly debate bouncing around in her head.

Braxton glanced over his shoulder. "I, er, am on my way to deliver those."

The arrangement of cream and pink roses mixed among white lilies in a vivid green vase was breathtaking. And huge. In fact, the only other time she'd seen one this large in person was when her ex-boyfriend took her to brunch to celebrate her birthday at the Waldorf-Astoria in Chicago.

"Lucky girl."

"Lucky girls," he corrected, adding extra emphasis to the plural. "They're for the Summer Island Memory Care Home."

Millie remembered what Sophia had told her about his friend Henry, and a hint of warmth that had nothing to do with the sunny South Carolina day spread through her. "How thoughtful. I'm sure they'll love them." Maybe there was more to Mr. By The Book than she'd originally given him credit for.

Braxton paused, as if trying to decide if he should say more.

"I deliver them weekly in honor of my wife." He threw a glance at the flowers in question. "Umm, late wife. Her name was Jade, hence the jade vase. And lilies were her favorite flower."

The incredibly sweet sentiment combined with the fact that Braxton would share such a personal detail with her momentarily knocked her off balance. For the first time she could see the pain lurking deep in his eyes and something ached in her chest.

"They're beautiful." She tried to pour all her sympathy into the two simple words.

"Thanks." He stared at his shoes for a moment, taking a deep breath. Then the sadness flickered away and the cool, collected HOA president returned. "I'm actually here on official HOA business. I'm gathering the documentation we need for the official inquiry. One item missing is the operating license for Seascape Inn."

"The operating license?" And just like that, all the confidence she'd gained from the day crumbled away as she was reminded of how wildly inadequate she was for this new life she was determined to make for herself. An operating license sounded like something official and important she should have, or should be applying for, but it was yet another thing she would have to google when she got inside.

"You know, the documentation your aunt needed to operate this place. I need to make a copy of it for the file."

"Oh right, the operating license." Millie had no idea what he was talking about, but she wasn't about to admit it, especially if whatever this document was would make a difference in the ruling of the board. "It's in my aunt's office with all her other important documents."

According to her aunt's official will, all her important documents were in the file folders in her desk. And after one peek into her aunt's office at Seascape, Millie was willing to take her word for it. It seemed every paper since 1953, important or otherwise, was stuffed in that room.

"Unfortunately, I don't have a copy machine yet. But I can run down to the shipping store to make a copy tomorrow then drop it by your house." Of course she'd have to wade through lakes of papers first, but she left that part off.

"I have a scanning app on my phone and I only need a PDF file. It won't take but a second to snap a picture of it."

Shoot, she hadn't thought of that. Dumb modern

conveniences were making her life anything but convenient at the moment.

Millie kept her cheerful smile plastered on, although her cheerfulness was starting to wane. "Oh sure, right. Yeah, come on in," she said, but found it hard to move from the door.

Braxton narrowed his eyes. "You do have an operating license, don't you?"

"What kind of question is that?" She forced out a laugh that came out a tad too loud. Not suspicious. At all. "It's just a little messy in there, that's all. With all the demolition today, everything is out of place. It might take me a few minutes to find it."

Braxton looked unsure, but he trotted up the front steps anyway.

Millie pushed open the door to the house and led him in. "It looks worse now but it's about to look a whole lot better." Her voice echoed in the now empty house.

"I lived through a reno before," he said. "You have to go through a whole lot of it looking worse before it starts to look better."

"Thanks. I feel better now knowing I'm in the 'worse' phase of it," Millie said as she led him past the giant empty living room.

Braxton chuckled. "Glad to help."

Millie shook her head and continued toward the downstairs hallway that held her personal living quarters, made up of the master bedroom, bathroom, and office. They also happened to be the only three rooms that were not getting any renovations. The creaky bed and rusted clawfoot tub might not be glamorous, but they were functional. And at the moment, functional was good enough for Millie.

"But don't worry," Braxton said. "The final product is worth it. At least ours was."

The unexpected dose of encouragement in his voice combined with the *friendly* feeling that was still lingering from before left her unsteady. What was happening here?

"You don't mind if I let my dog out, do you? He's been shut in my room all day so he wouldn't get in the way of the swinging sledgehammers." Plus, she could use a little moral support from her furry best friend right about now.

Bear came bounding out when she opened the bedroom door and ran right up to Braxton who petted his head rather enthusiastically. Traitor.

Millie shook her head, fought back a smile, and led them to the office. The dusty smell of old papers tickled her nose. "Come on in. The document you're looking for should be in my aunt's desk, so make yourself comfortable while I find it." Millie motioned to the only worn leather wingback chair not covered with stacks of file folders.

Braxton glanced at the chair and walked around it to study the pictures on the wall. Not that Millie blamed him. She wasn't sure she would sit in dusty furniture, either.

Instead, she dropped into the creaky wooden desk chair and pulled open the first drawer that looked like it could contain important files. Bear followed their new friend around the room, his tail happily wagging.

"These old pictures are amazing. I had no idea what this place looked like when it was new. And is that Joe Frazier, the famous boxer? In front of this house?" He pointed to one of the yellowed black-and-white photographs, a look of astonishment on his face.

"Oh, yeah. I guess he liked to come to dinner out here when he needed to get out of Charleston and relax." At least, she remembered stories from her aunt to that account.

Millie shuffled through the contents in the drawer, which didn't appear to be much more than an old metal lock box and a jar with pens. She closed it and pulled open the drawer below it.

"When did this place open?"

"They bought the land in 1940, but then America got into the war and it took a while for the house to be built. I think it was 1953 when they officially opened the doors. And even then, it was easier to get here by boat than by car."

"Interesting."

There wasn't much inside the second drawer, either. An old evening handbag, a box of old lipsticks. She shuffled through the things, hoping the license papers would magically appear. Way in the back, buried under a small notebook and a couple monogrammed handkerchiefs, there was a stack of envelopes tied together with a red satin ribbon. Since they looked important, she pulled them out.

The top one was addressed to her aunt in neat, cursive handwriting. She assumed they were business correspondence, but they didn't look official enough to contain the document she was looking for. She set them on top of the desk to go through later. Where could the license be? And if she couldn't find it, how fast would Braxton and the HOA cancel her plans?

Starting to panic, she opened the larger drawer on the other side of the desk, but it was empty.

"Harry Truman stayed here? For real? President Truman stayed at your aunt's house?"

"Inn," Millie corrected, slightly annoyed now, not just at the interruptions, but at him destroying her lovely afternoon with requests for elusive papers. "It's a small boutique inn in a charming seaside town, ideal for people trying to get away from the spotlight, like Truman or Frank Sinatra." She pointed to the picture of her aunt posing with Ol' Blue Eyes on the wall next to her.

Of course, no one of that caliber had stayed at Seascape since the sixties. And no one else would unless she could get the HOA to change their dumb new rule. To do that, she needed to find that license.

She pulled the last drawer in the desk, but it didn't budge. She pulled harder. Still nothing. Fueled by the building frustration, she tugged with both hands and glared at the lock just above the handle. "It's locked."

She opened the long center drawer. Frantically tossing aside stubby pencils and pens that had long stopped working, she searched for the key.

"What's locked?" Braxton came over from where he'd been examining the photos on the wall.

She motioned to the file cabinet–sized drawer in question.

"And you're sure it's in that drawer?" He raised an eyebrow, which only annoyed her.

She wasn't sure about anything when it came to this house. Nothing had turned out the way she'd thought it would, but she wasn't about to throw in the towel. She closed the drawer and gave Braxton the most determined look she could muster.

"It's here." One thing she did have faith in was her aunt. If she needed some license to officially run her inn, Millie was confident she had it.

All Millie had to do was find it.

"I'm just not sure where she kept the key." She opened another one of the drawers she'd already searched and dug through the random contents.

Braxton joined her. "May I?" He gestured at the collection of small trinkets on the desk, some of which had lids.

"Be my guest."

"Not without an operating license." Braxton shot her a teasing look then gently opened the lid of one of the knickknacks he'd pointed to.

"Ha ha." Millie made a grand gesture of rolling her eyes

at his lame joke. Although, she had to admit it caused the corners of her mouth to twitch upward and that *friendly* feeling to return. She shook off the feeling, opening one of the trinkets at the other end of the desk. Hers contained a couple bobby pins and a few rubber bands. The second one held a roll of stamps that were so old they had to be licked, and the third one had nothing but dust inside.

Two more trinkets were all that stood between her and the last of the obvious places to store a key. After that she'd have to...

One stolen glance at the overstuffed file cabinets and teetering towers of boxes caused that thought to ricochet in a hundred different directions. She'd have to what? Start digging through the endless piles of papers in here? Search Aunt Mildred's bedroom? Consider the possibility that it had been carried out with the other renovation debris and was now buried somewhere in that giant dumpster?

She stopped herself right there. Panicking wasn't going to help anything. What was it that Aunt Mildred always said? Put first things first, and the rest will fall into place.

"What are these?" Braxton asked, breaking the silence and her mental storm. He pointed to the ribbon-wrapped letters.

"Found them in the desk. I thought I'd go through them later so I could properly file them. Why? Do they look familiar?"

He stared at them for one more second then shook his head. "I thought I recognized the handwriting, but it's probably just the era. Everyone wrote in cursive back then."

"It's the equivalent of what our grandkids will think of emojis."

"True." A slight look of amusement flashed in his eyes but disappeared before it could travel to the rest of his face. He glanced at his watch, which made Millie's already heightened sense of urgency kick up a notch.

She reached for the last jar and pulled the lid off. There, among a single clip-on earring and a tarnished nickel, was a small, old key. Triumph soared through her as she pulled it out and held it up for him to see. "Ta da!"

Swiveling in her chair, she pressed the key into the lock, only it wouldn't go in. Her soaring spirits took a nosedive as she flipped the key over, hoping she was trying to insert it the wrong way. No luck. The key was about twice the size of the lock on the drawer.

She slumped back in her chair and let out a frustrated sigh. "Never mind. False alarm." Her gaze swept the room. The key could be anywhere, and even if she found it she wasn't 100 percent sure the document she was looking for would be in that drawer. This search had the potential of being long, and she had no desire to add to her stress by letting Mr. Stone Cold And Serious stare over her shoulder.

She tossed the bad key on her desk and stood. "I hate to make you wait while those beautiful flowers are wilting in your car. Why don't you let me keep looking for the key and I promise the minute I find the document, I'll let you know."

Braxton glanced around the office with a look that fell somewhere between overwhelmed and uncertain. "Great. But I'd like to have it by the end of the week."

Millie was aware she was nodding far more animatedly than necessary, but she couldn't help it. "No problem. I'm on it."

And she would have to be, because not finding the document and having the HOA shut down her plans was not an option.

Chapter Seven

"No nap!" Alice stomped her tiny foot on the ground on Monday afternoon. She scrunched her face in the most determined look a two-year-old could muster, then yawned.

Braxton chuckled and scooped his little girl up, kissing her on the forehead. "Yes, nap. Naps are a requirement if you want enough energy to play at the park later."

"Daddy come to park?" She rubbed her eyes. Despite her best attempt to avoid the nap, he was sure she'd be asleep before her head even hit the mattress in her crib.

"I can't come to the park. I have to work this afternoon."

Ever since the car accident, Braxton had made a commitment to stay home to raise Alice. It was unfair enough that she'd lost one parent; she deserved to have the other one around as much as possible. However, being with her every minute of every day was almost impossible.

Of course, he'd given up golf, which had occupied so much of his time for the majority of his life. He hadn't even touched a golf club since the night he got the life-changing phone call. But there were still other commitments he was responsible for, like his part-time career as a real estate broker. And Henry.

Yes, what he had to do was valid and important, but it didn't take away the guilt of leaving his little girl when she looked at him with those baby blue eyes. "But your friends will be at the park. And I'll be home in time for dinner." He handed the wiggly child over to his amazing nanny, Lena.

"Right now, though, you have to take a nap. And I have to take Henry to the doctor."

Henry had been his number one fan for decades. He was the one who had recruited him with a full college scholarship. When Braxton ventured into being a professional golfer, Henry left his job at the university to go on the PGA tour with him. Then when Jade died and Braxton felt like his life was falling apart, Henry had made it his full-time job to pick up the pieces and help Braxton put them back together.

Now that Henry needed help, it was Braxton's turn to stand in the gap.

Fighting back the urge to stay just one more hour with Alice, he ruffled her hair one last time and watched her sleepy eyes droop as Lena carried her up the stairs. As soon as they were out of sight, he headed out the front door.

It was a beautiful day on the island. The sun was warm, but the breeze blowing off the Atlantic kept the temperature comfortable. Maybe, if Henry was having a good day, he'd bring him back here after the doctor's appointment. A walk on the beach would be good for him. The soothing sounds of the ocean always relaxed him. Although, the faint banging noise might be a problem. Anything out of the ordinary seemed to set him on edge lately.

Braxton paused on the front porch to search for the source of the racket. It didn't take him long to trace the sounds to the house next door. Millie's house.

They both had large lots, so her house was a ways away,

but he could still make out her figure on top of her roof. There was a box next to her and she appeared to be hammering something. Was she putting new tiles on the roof? By herself?

As a professional athlete, he'd seen determination before. He knew what it was like to get up before everyone else and push past all the pain to achieve his goal. But there was something about her determination and fiery stubbornness that impressed him.

He had a few minutes to spare. Maybe he should stop by her house and see what she was up to. Besides, he needed to see if she'd found the operating license he'd asked for the other day.

Braxton headed next door in his car. The broken concrete crunched under the tires as he drove around the circle and came to a stop next to the old fountain before climbing out.

Banging drifted down from the roof, but there was no sign of how she'd gotten up there. He made his way over the patchy grass around the side of the house, looking for the ladder she'd used. He had to go all the way to the back of the house before he found it.

There, on the uneven, rocky ground was a very tall and very wobbly-looking ladder leaning against the side of the house with her curly-haired dog lying in the shade nearby.

"Hey, Bear." The dog hopped up when he saw Braxton and trotted over with his tail wagging. "You let her climb up that?"

It was possible the ladder would have been tall enough to reach all the way to the roof if it had been positioned in the courtyard, or even at the front of the house, but the ground at the back of the house was lower than any other point, making the wall of the house even longer. It left the ladder short, stopping about six inches below the roofline.

Had Millie been standing on it to hang Christmas lights or paint the trim, this setup could have worked. It would've been unsafe and he wouldn't have approved, but it could've worked. As it was, he had no idea how she'd managed to get herself from the top of the ladder to the top of the roof without falling.

"How does she plan to get down?" he asked Bear, who whined in response. He cupped his hands around his mouth and called out to her. "Hello? Millie?"

Could she even hear him over all the hammering?

Braxton checked his watch again. Now that he'd seen her hazardous setup, he couldn't leave without making sure she was safe.

"I guess I have to go up," he told Bear, although he had no desire to climb that haphazard contraption. He gave it a jiggle, making sure it was firmly planted on the ground, then climbed the bottom two rungs to check the stability. Was he satisfied with the results? Absolutely not. But since he had no choice, he hesitantly moved up the death trap toward the edge of the roof.

"Millie?" he called again. "You up here?"

He made it almost to where his hands could touch the roof, about four rungs from the top, when her head appeared over the pitch.

"Hey. What are you doing here?" She had the same peppy tone and optimistic grin she always had and their effect swept over him like a refreshing ocean breeze, calming some of his apprehension.

"I came to ask you the same question."

Millie held up a hammer and wiped the sweat from her forehead on the back of her arm. "Fixing the roof."

"Do you know how to do that?" Braxton was impressed. He didn't know how to fix a roof. He wasn't sure he'd even be motivated to learn how to do it. But here she was, hammering away and looking content about it.

"Not as well as I probably should. But the video didn't

seem overly complicated."

He strained to see past her, looking for someone who might be helping her. "Are you by yourself up there?"

"Well, yeah. I mean, I tried to convince Bear to come up here with me, but he's got this thing about heights. And ladders." A joking glint flashed in her eyes.

The sight of it caused his heart to do a little shimmy.

"I don't blame him." Braxton glanced down at the dog sitting at the foot of the ladder, reminding him just how high they were. A fresh wave of fear rolled through him. "Although, in all seriousness, you shouldn't be up here by yourself."

"Is roof repair like swimming? Do I need to wait twenty minutes after eating, too?"

"I heard the twenty-minute rule was an old wives' tale, but it never hurts to be on the safe side."

"Interesting tip. I'll keep it in mind." She waved her hammer at the roof behind her. "If that's all, I gotta get back. These tiles aren't going to hammer themselves."

"Actually," he called, stopping her in mid-crawl. "I hate to do this, but now that I've seen your setup, I can't in good conscience let you stay on the roof by yourself." He pulled his mouth into the most sympathetic face he could muster and threw in a slight shoulder shrug for good measure.

Her eyes narrowed. "For real? You're making me get off my own roof?" There was an edge of annoyance in her voice that might have concerned him if he wasn't worried about one of them plummeting to their death.

"Just until you have someone else here. I don't want anything to happen to you." The truth that so freely rolled off his tongue surprised him. It was natural to be that concerned about his new neighbor, wasn't it? He added on a bit of sarcastic humor, just to prove the point to himself. "We finally got someone to take care of this lot. We'd hate to lose that too soon."

She studied him for a second and he wondered what was going through that mind of hers. "Fine. It's probably time I hydrate anyway." She slid her hammer into her belt loop with a little more force than he thought necessary.

Braxton climbed down a couple of rungs to give her space. She rolled onto her stomach and inched down until her legs dangled off the side, her feet reaching for the top rung.

"You're still about a foot away. Keep coming."

She edged down a bit more, her feet still well above the ladder she was blindly scrabbling for. His pulse started to race.

"Keep coming."

She pointed her toes, clearly reaching for the ladder she couldn't seem to find. Finally, her feet stopped moving and she hung there for a second. "I could, uh, use a little help."

"I got ya." He reached up and cupped his hand around the heel of her tennis shoe, guiding her foot to the first rung. She inched farther down, her stomach still pressed against the roof, and secured her second foot on the same rung. With one hand holding on to the side of the ladder, he reached up and gently pressed the other against Millie's back to give her support until she was able to grab the sides of the ladder herself.

The connection of their touch buzzed through him, which caught him off guard. He would've pulled his hand away, but since he was more concerned about her safety, he left it in place until she was securely on the ladder.

Once they got to the ground, she dusted her hands on her shorts and looked anywhere but at him. "Well, thanks for that."

"My pleasure. But, in all seriousness, that was incredibly dangerous. Promise me you won't climb onto the roof from a ladder that's too short again."

"Sure thing." She gave him a salute. "Next time, I'll prop the ladder up on rocks before I start." A sly smile pulled at the corners of her mouth and she waggled her eyebrows before she turned and started around the side of her house with Bear following along by her side.

He fought back a smile and jogged to catch up with her. "Just make sure you teach Bear how to call 911."

She nodded thoughtfully. "Not a bad idea. I think that's the first good tip you've had since we moved in." They reached the front of her house and she jerked her thumb at the front door. "We're headed inside to rehydrate, so thanks for dropping by." She turned and trotted up the first few steps.

"Actually, I swung by to ask about the operating license. Were you able to find it?"

She paused mid-step, looking like a student who forgot their homework.

"Right. About that, I'm still looking for the key. If I don't find it tonight, I'll call a locksmith to open the drawer tomorrow."

"So I can drop by to get it tomorrow? Say around five o'clock?"

"You know what, why don't I drop it off at your place as soon as I rescue it from Fort Knox."

"Great. Thank you." He nodded once and walked around to open his driver's side door. As he did, he caught sight of her trash cans. "Oh, by the way, trash cans have to be brought in by sundown of trash day. It's kind of a thing here."

He always felt the need to warn new residents about that since it was the first and only violation letter he'd received. There were a lot of things he loved about living in Oceanside Estates, but the one thing he still didn't understand was their obsession with trash cans.

With her back still to him, she held her hand over her head in a thumbs-up.

"I'll add it to the list."

• • •

Later that night, Millie let out a tired sigh as she carried the box of roof tiles inside and spied the trash cans still sitting next to the curb under the lit streetlight. With all the other problems she had to hurdle to reopen Seascape, Braxton and his HOA posse had the audacity to split hairs over her trash cans? Did they not think her impossible dream was impossible enough?

To be fair, Millie didn't realize she was signing up for an impossible dream when she quit her job, loaded her car, and moved to Summer Island to start a new life. Yes, she thought it'd be hard. Yes, she was aware it would require some work. But she never anticipated *this*, which probably was just as well. If she'd known what she was signing up for, there's a good chance she would've chickened out.

Instead, she went all in, and since living her impossible dream was the only choice she had, that's what she was doing, one how-to video at a time. At least she could now add roof repair to her list of unique skills and qualifications.

It had taken all day, but she'd finished. Of course, someday she would need to invest in a whole new roof, but her repair job on the damaged parts should fix the leaking problem for now.

She carried the box of the leftover roofing tiles to the storage closet in the laundry room and stood on her toes to place it on the top shelf with the optimistic assumption she wouldn't need it again for a while. She still had to get on the roof with a water hose to make sure the leaks were all fixed, but that was a two-man job and at the moment she was here all by herself.

As much as she hated to admit it, Braxton was right. She

shouldn't be on the roof without anyone else around. Luckily, during the day, Gus and his crew were constantly coming and going as they worked on their part of the construction project. They made the perfect safety buddies. Once they had gotten back from their lunch break, she made it her new habit to tell them what she was working on, and someone came out and checked on her regularly. Plus, it turned out that Gus had a ladder that was a much better fit for her tall roof than the antique she'd found in the garage.

But the sun had set a while ago, and all of the crew had gone home to their own families, leaving Millie alone in the big old house with the one task that had given her more anxiety than playing on the roof—finding the key to Aunt Mildred's desk.

What if she couldn't find it? What if she found the key but the document wasn't in the locked drawer? Or, worse yet, what if the document backed the argument of the HOA?

Her blood pressure skyrocketed, making her temples beat to the rhythm of her racing heart as she stood in the office doorway, clutching her hot tea between her hands.

"It has to be here somewhere," she said to Bear and stepped over the threshold. "We just have to think like Aunt Mildred."

Aunt Mildred was the closest thing to a maternal figure Millie had ever had. Every year, all through elementary and middle school, she and her father would fly down to Summer Island the first week of summer to stay at Seascape. They'd spend the week together playing on the beach and exploring nature. Then her dad would go back to work, while Millie stayed and helped her aunt around the inn until he came back to get her just before school started. Summer was always her favorite time of the year.

Of course as she got older, her personal life got busier and around the time she started high school, summer jobs and friends replaced the seasonal escape. The excuse had been that she'd come next time. Only, next time never came.

Sure, she could blame it on circumstances. Her dad got sick. Balancing taking care of him and her full college workload took every bit of her time. After he died, she was dealing with grief and drowning in medical bills and student loans. As soon as she got her head above water, she was stuck in the corporate world chasing promotions she couldn't catch and falling in love with the wrong men.

But the bottom line was she hadn't made time to come check on Aunt Mildred. She'd sent Christmas cards and Mother's Day cards claiming she'd plan a trip soon until time had run out.

Millie dropped into the creaky wooden chair in front of the desk and studied her favorite picture on the wall—the one of her, her great-aunt, and her father. Bear followed and lay down on the floor at her feet, picking up the bone he'd left in here.

"What I wouldn't give to spend one more summer here with both of them." Loneliness ached inside her. But at least she was here now. Being in this place where she'd made some of her favorite memories with two of the most important people in her life made her feel closer to them.

"That's our goal." She motioned to the picture on the wall, focusing on her twelve-year-old self's genuine, carefree smile. "We want to be part of the legacy that helps people create happy memories with the ones they love. That's going to make all this work worth it."

The tower of old papers teetering below the picture caught her eye. At close to three feet tall, Millie was a little amazed it could stand without falling over. Were the cobwebs holding it in place? She made the mistake of checking out the stacks of papers next to it, which led to following the mess all around the room. A decent amount of the floor space along with every single surface was covered with stacks of yellowing papers and worn file folders.

"Let's hope we find the key before we have to start digging through all of that." Cleaning the grout on the tile floors that stretched across all four thousand square feet of the downstairs area seemed less overwhelming.

Bear lifted his head and cocked a shaggy eyebrow before he settled his head back on his paws. Millie chuckled and bent down to rub the dog's head. "My thoughts exactly, boy."

She decided to comb through each one of the drawers again, checking every nook and cranny. When that came up short, she moved to the first six-foot metal filing cabinet. The key wasn't in any of the baskets on top, and the first two drawers that she opened were so full of papers that she couldn't imagine putting the key in there.

Frustrated, she slammed the drawer shut and turned to the picture of her aunt with her and her dad. "Any sort of hint would be nice. The inn is kind of on the line, here."

And then a thought came to her.

If it was her favorite picture, what if it was...

Her heart pounded as she took two slow steps toward it. Drawing in a deep breath, she carefully removed it from the wall.

There, on the nail that held the frame, hung a key.

Millie almost laughed at the sight. Of course her aunt would hide the key behind the people she trusted the most in the world, which simultaneously filled her with joy and regret. She grabbed the key and rehung the picture on the wall, pausing to touch the image of her aunt.

"I should've come sooner," she whispered.

She could almost hear her aunt's voice whisper the one piece of advice she often gave to Millie. "The past is behind you, dear girl. Focus on what's to come."

Hopefully whatever was in the locked drawer would help

firm up the shaky future of Seascape.

"The moment of truth," she said to Bear. He sat up next to her, his ears perked.

She slid the key into the lock and rotated it. There was a clicking sound as the lock disengaged. She did a little victory shimmy and then pulled the drawer out. The very first file was titled "Seascape Business Documents" in her great-aunt's neat cursive writing.

"Bingo." She lifted the folder out and opened it on the desk. Excitement glimmered through her. The document on the top was the hotel operating license. But that wasn't all. Behind it was the certificate of occupancy and the fire safety permit along with a host of other official-looking documents for Seascape Inn.

"Woo-hoo! We found it, Bear!" She broke into a seated version of a happy dance. This didn't solve all her problems, but it proved that Seascape Inn was perfectly legal and operational—even if it wasn't operating—up until her aunt was admitted to the nursing home.

She neatly stacked the documents and closed the folder. "Tomorrow, you are coming with me. We are making some copies!"

As she slid the folder to the center of the desk, she caught sight of something else. There, next to the mug she'd abandoned earlier, was the stack of envelopes tied together with a red ribbon she'd found the other day when Braxton was here.

Still floating from her success, she pushed the mug aside and picked up the stack, wondering what kind of important documents it contained. She slid the first letter from the stack without untying the bow and carefully pulled the folded piece of cream-colored paper from the matching envelope. A single gold *C* was stamped into the top of the stationery.

February 4, 1955

My darling Mildred,

Millie paused as a different kind of excitement sparkled through her. These weren't official property documents but handwritten love letters to her aunt. The only handwritten note Millie had ever gotten that was even slightly romantic had always come on the inside of a store-bought Valentine's Day card.

She refolded the bottom third of the letter, covering the bulk of the words, and contemplated if she should read it. Aunt Mildred had never married or had a lover, at least not one she'd presented to the family. Which meant these were very personal, private letters meant only for her great-aunt to read.

The other part of her, the part that loved happy endings and wanted to believe in fairy tales, couldn't pass up the chance to read the sweet words of someone falling in love.

"You don't think she'd mind, do you, Bear? At this point, it's considered history not snooping, right?"

Bear continued chewing on his bone which she took as affirmation. Millie settled into her chair and unfolded the letter.

My life during the last four days has become more colorful. The trees that line my walk are a brilliant green. The yellow feathers on the finch that nests outside my window seem more vibrant. And, as of late, the rich azure ocean sparkles as if it's full of jewels.

All of this is because of you.

Your radiance brightens the world around you. Your joy overflows and enhances everything in your path. I

*myself have never felt as alive as I do when I am with
you. How blessed I am, my darling, that you have
come into my existence. Though it hasn't been long,
my heart already beats for you.*

Always,

Millie dropped the letter to her lap and stared at Bear.
"People don't write letters like this anymore. Just imagine..."
She picked it up again, reading the sweet words out loud. A
warmth fluttered in her chest as she imagined what it must
have been like for a young Mildred to read this on a balmy,
starlit February night.

She picked up the ribbon-wrapped stack and thumbed
through it. There had to be at least twenty letters there. She
slid out the next one. The date was February 14.

Dearest Mildred,

*I've just left you, and I can't help but count the
minutes until I am in your presence again. When I'm
with you, I feel like a man who can fly. You give me
wings, and your exuberance is the wind that carries
me off the ground.*

*Tomorrow evening seems a long time to wait until I
can see you again, until I once again can fly in your
presence. But until then, I will relive every one of our
moments together. Until then I send you all of my
love.*

Always,

Millie read three more letters after that, each more
beautiful than the one before it. The love radiating from the
old yellowed paper caused the swell in her chest to rise.

"But none of them are signed," she said to Bear, reexamining the envelope for any hint of the author. Other than the gold *C* at the top of the stationery, there was no identifying information on any of them.

"Who's Aunt Mildred's mystery Romeo?" She leaned back in her chair, looking for clues in the photos hanging all around the room.

Aunt Mildred had never married. On one of Millie's last visits, she'd asked her aunt about her decision to remain single.

"Life, my dear, is full of all kinds of adventures," she had said. "Choosing some adventures means leaving other ones behind. But don't ever get so caught up on what was left in the past that you don't get to appreciate the excitement waiting for you."

At the time, Millie thought she was advocating an independent life, but what if it was something else? What if it wasn't a missed opportunity she left behind but a heartbreak?

One thing Millie knew for sure was that Aunt Mildred had been involved in a love story. Of course, the story thus far was one-sided and lacking a lot of information, but Millie was dying to know how it ended.

Chapter Eight

Friday evening, Millie quit her projects earlier than normal to make it to her first neighborhood book club on time. The last thing on her list for the day was to check the mail. So she walked out to the rusted old mailbox next to where her long drive met the street and pulled out the handful of envelopes that were inside. She flipped through them as she strolled back to her house.

Electric bill. She skipped right over that one since she didn't need whatever astronomical number was inside to ruin her perfectly good mood. A letter from a local insurance company claiming they could save her hundreds on her car insurance. She highly doubted their claims would hold true if she actually called for a quote, but depending on the electric bill, it might be worth a shot. Then she got to the envelope on the bottom.

Millie rolled her eyes. She'd already received a letter from the Oceanside Estates HOA earlier this week. It had been a formal warning of a deed restriction violation—leaving trash cans out—signed by her trusty neighbor, Braxton Bossy-

Pants Channing.

Why send her a formal warning after telling her about it in person? It was a waste of a stamp, but she was glad it made him feel better. She'd filed the letter in her kitchen trash can, to be dumped in the very same receptacle that got her in trouble in the first place. It only seemed fitting.

Millie let out a huff as she tucked the other letters under her arm. She wanted to file this one in the same place as the last one, but since the board held the fate of her B&B in their hands, she ripped open the envelope and pulled out the paper inside.

To the valued property owner of 121 East Shore Drive,

It has been brought to our attention that one or more aspects of your property is out of compliance with the Oceanside Estates Deed Restrictions. Please address the item(s) listed below.

Requested legal documentation not submitted

Please note that the HOA executive board will not be able to consider your formal grievance if these document(s) are not submitted.

This is your first warning regarding the above violation(s). You will be given ten (10) days to rectify this matter.

Thank you for your cooperation and dedication to keeping Oceanside Estates a wonderful place to call home.

Kind Regards,
Braxton Channing

Oceanside Estates HOA President

A cold anxiety swirled in her gut as she remembered the documents still sitting on her desk. She'd gotten so distracted by the love letters that she'd forgotten to make the copies or take them to Braxton.

"But, really? He had to send me a formal warning? That's so unnecessary," she said to Bear who was waiting for her on the front porch. She headed straight to her office to grab the file folder with the documents in it, letting her anxiety and embarrassment morph into anger. If he was so desperate to get it, she'd drop it by his house right now. She might even tell him exactly what she thought about all of his formal letters while she was at it.

She headed to the kitchen to grab her keys, letting the anger fuel her, only to find Bear sitting next to the back door with his leash in his mouth. The sight added another pang of guilt to her already complex assortment of emotions.

"Oh, right. I promised you a walk, didn't I?" She checked her watch. "How about we walk down the beach to get to Braxton's. That way you get a walk and I get to drop off these papers along with a piece of my mind."

Bear wagged his tail in response, which she took as the go-ahead to tell Mr. HOA President what she thought of his formal letters. She could always trust Bear to be on her side. She clipped on his leash and they headed out the back door.

It took her walking halfway across her wide backyard for her thumping pulse to drop to a normal-ish level. To her, the world didn't offer a more stunning view than this one right here, and it always caused a sense of calm to wash over her. She loved the way the sea oats sat atop the sand dunes and swayed in the breeze as if beckoning her to the beach. The greenish-blue of the waves that gently rolled into the shore reminded her of the color of her favorite crayon as a child. The private deck that led over the dunes to the beach always felt like a sort of magical bridge leading from reality to paradise.

Of course, the bridge didn't look magical at the moment. It more closely resembled a rotted pile of jagged splinters that almost guaranteed a trip to the doctor for a tetanus shot. And it currently was the thorn in her side. Somehow, this item had been missed when they were making up the original budget. But since it was hard to offer beachfront accommodations without beachfront access, it had to be done.

"You're on the list. We'll get to you soon enough," Millie said to the structure as she navigated over it, careful to step on the parts that looked the least rotted. Once she got to the other side, she stepped onto the beach and slipped out of her flip-flops, letting her toes sink into the sand.

She took a deep breath of the salty air and let it go, along with the rest of her annoyance. "We have an HOA who hates us, a boardwalk we have no idea how to repair, and the only functioning toilet has to be manually flushed from inside the tank," she said, unhooking Bear's leash. "But we live here, Bear. In a house that gave me all the best summer memories. And I'm not ready to give that up."

Bear wagged his tail at her words, then bounded past her into the water, jumping over the small waves rolling into the shore. She strolled down the beach, mentally going over what she was going to say when she saw Braxton. She wanted her words to be well thought out and pack the most powerful punch. It wouldn't hurt if she had the perfect last line she could deliver right before she turned on her heel and marched away like one of those stick-it-to-'em scenes she loved in movies.

She was so involved in her own thoughts that she missed the figure walking down the beach until she was less than twenty yards away from the very person she was coming to see.

Only, it didn't look like the Braxton Channing she knew. He was wearing his signature button-down shirt and shorts, but his shirttails were untucked. He was squatting down at the water's edge with his adorable daughter pointing at a crab scuttling across the sand in front of them.

As soon as the crab scurried into the water, Braxton picked up the little girl and tossed her in the air. She was only a few inches higher than his hands, but it still elicited a round of giggles. The smile on his face was best described as fatherly adoration.

Millie stood there for a second taking in the sweet father/daughter scene and trying to reconcile the serious man sending her HOA violation letters to the doting father in front of her. While he still had his faults—lots of them—it was becoming more and more evident that there was also a soft, caring side. At least when he was around his family.

The spirited speech she'd planned out in her mind started to fade away.

Bear, who'd been preoccupied with the waves up to this point, froze as soon as he noticed the other people on the beach, his head cocking to one side.

"Oooohh! Doggie!" The little girl screeched and held both hands out, as if in an attempt to grab the dog, while looking up to her dad for permission.

Bear, who loved kids more than any other humans, wagged his tail and bounced in anticipation.

It was time to announce herself, whether she was ready or not. After telling Bear to sit and stay, she awkwardly held up the file in her hand, suddenly feeling guilty for encroaching on their family time. "Hi. I'm coming over to deliver the documents you asked for."

It took a second for recognition to register on Braxton's face. When it did, he nodded once. "Great."

Meanwhile, the little girl seemed unfazed by Millie or her

documents and made a beeline for Bear. "Hi, doggie! Hi!"

Braxton scooped up the kid before they reached Millie and her dog.

"Is it okay if she pets him?" Braxton asked.

"Absolutely. He loves kids." Millie stepped closer to her dog.

Braxton lowered Alice to the ground next to Bear, and immediately she grabbed fistfuls of the curly fur on his head with both hands.

"Be gentle, sweetheart." He scratched behind the dog's ear while keeping a protective eye on Alice. Bear panted happily. "He's a nice doggo, huh?" Braxton said to his daughter.

As if agreeing with him, Bear stood, licked Alice on the cheek, and trotted off.

"Doggie!" Alice squealed in delight and went with him, leaving Millie and Braxton to follow along behind them.

"I guess you haven't officially met my daughter Alice yet." Braxton kept his eyes on the little girl.

"She's adorable. How old?" she asked.

"Two," Braxton said. "Well, two and a half and one hundred percent sugar and spice and fearless." He glowed with pride as he watched his daughter, which Millie found endearing. Doting father looked good on him.

"Fearless is a good thing. You need a bit of fearlessness to do great things."

Braxton diverted his attention long enough to look at Millie. "Like moving someplace new and taking on the HOA on your first day in town?"

She smiled and a streak of warmth shot through her. He thought she was fearless? "It was my second day in town. And that was necessity. I didn't have an option."

Braxton nodded. "I've had some experience with necessity myself." A hint of sadness passed over Braxton's face as his gaze returned to Alice. The little girl was examining a piece of driftwood that had washed onto shore, Bear at her side.

"What did you find, Little Foot?" Braxton stepped up to look at the log with her.

Millie watched them, captivated by the sweet gentleness he had around his daughter. There wasn't a contest about which of them had to be more fearless. Suddenly, becoming a single father to a newborn baby didn't even compare to renovating a house, and he seemed to have conquered his role with excellence. All she had to do was watch YouTube videos to figure out how to replace the flushing mechanism in a toilet, and it still wasn't working.

After a few seconds, Alice and Bear took off again, and Braxton dropped back to where she was.

"What's on your agenda for the rest of the evening?" he asked. "More solo roof repair? Standing on the top rung of the ladder with a chainsaw to trim the palmetto palms, perhaps?"

"I haven't tried the ladder against a palmetto…yet." She couldn't help the grin that spread across her face, and she tapped her chin as if she were considering the hazardous idea. "But that will have to wait because tonight I'm going to a book club that Sophia and Tessa invited me to."

"Ah yes, the neighborhood book club. From what I hear, there's a lot of talking but it rarely revolves around the book."

"Since I only read the first chapter, that's not a bad thing. Plus, it'll be nice to spend the evening in a house where I don't have to step over power tools and stacks of two-by-fours." She bent down and picked up a large pink and white shell that was just above the water line. "How about you two. Any big plans on this Friday night?"

"Absolutely. After our pre-bedtime walk, we have our own nightly book club. Right now, Alice and I are reading a riveting family saga about a baby bird trying to figure out who is her mother." He gave a nonchalant shrug. "I hate to give anything away, but it has a pretty good plot twist at the end with a big, scary crane."

Millie chuckled, thinking about the famous children's book she'd read when she was younger. "Sounds like a good way to kick off the weekend."

"The best." He stared at his daughter with an adoring look in his eyes. "Then one of us is going to hit the hay while the other gets caught up on work."

"Tell Alice not to work too late. It is the weekend, after all," she teased.

He shot her a playful look that sizzled through her. "I'll pass the wisdom along."

This conversation had taken a very different turn than what she had planned when she first stepped on the beach. And what surprised her even more was that she was enjoying this twilight stroll with her dog and his daughter. What was happening here?

They caught up to where Alice and Bear had stopped to stare at a crab scampering across the sand in front of them. Braxton scooped up the little girl. "Are you almost done exploring?" He tossed her up in the air and caught her, eliciting another round of joyful squealing.

The little girl pointed a chubby finger to where Bear was sitting next to Millie. "Doggie."

"I know. He's a good-looking doggie. Maybe Miss Millie will let us play with him again."

Millie smiled, unable to deny Alice anything at this point. "Any time."

"Bye-bye, Doggie." Alice waved at the dog then rested her tired head on her dad's shoulder.

"So we might be here for the dog, but we'll tolerate it if you come along."

Millie chuckled, completely caught up in the moment

and this new—dare she say attractive?—side of Braxton. "I get that a lot."

He flashed a charming grin. It was the same type of grin he was famous for back in the day with one major difference. This one wasn't just polite, it was personal, and something inside her soared. "Have fun at your book club."

The combination of the grin and the soaring nonsense made her feel off-kilter. "Thanks." She forced one of her own smiles as she tried to regain her footing.

Braxton turned and headed for his own private boardwalk over the dunes toward his house, rubbing small gentle circles on his daughter's back. He was almost halfway across his property before Millie realized she was still holding the file folder in her hand.

"Oh, wait!" She held the folder over her head. "You can't leave without this."

See, this was what happened when one took walks on the beach with handsome neighbors and their adorable daughters. Important things got forgotten. And according to the formal warnings he kept sending her, she couldn't forget anything else.

She jogged to catch up with him and handed over the folder. "I'd hate for you to have to send me another letter."

He looked a little confused as she paused to catch her breath from the short jog.

"It's the operating license, along with a few other documents you might find helpful." She tapped on the folder just to clarify.

"Great. Thanks for bringing them over."

"Any time. Have a good night." She gave him an awkward wave and turned to head home before she did anything else to embarrass herself.

She didn't want her spirits to soar when she looked at Braxton Channing. Just because it turned out that he had a softer side didn't mean that she needed to fall in love with him. Besides, he was still the same guy that was trying to stand in the way of her dreams.

In fact, at the moment she wasn't planning on falling in love with anyone. Love, at least in her experience, was always lopsided. One person made all the sacrifices while the other person walked away as soon as there was a better offer. It had happened in every single relationship she'd been in. Even her mother had left when having a family got in the way of her career.

Millie was done with it all.

From the moment she decided to move to South Carolina, Millie vowed this new chapter of her life would be entirely about her. This was her time to focus on *her* goals, to take *her* future in her own hands, and make *her* dreams come true. Nothing would stand in her way. And she wasn't going to give up on anything because some charming smile made her heart go pitter-patter.

• • •

Millie hadn't factored a walk on the beach into her evening timeline.

By the time she got home and gave Bear a bath to get all the sand and saltwater off him, she was behind schedule. She pulled up to the address Sophia had texted her almost ten minutes late. Nervousness rattled through her, making her belly flutter and not in a good way, as she rolled down the window and leaned out to press the buzzer on the call box.

She strained to see past the large wrought-iron fence that surrounded the house, looking for signs of someone she knew. But, like hers, the house was down a long driveway and the only car she might recognize was Sophia's anyways. Millie tugged on her seat belt, shifting in her seat. There was something intimidating about trying to get into a private party at a million-dollar home whose owner she'd never met.

Sure, at the moment, Millie also owned a home in this same million-dollar neighborhood, but she didn't have a big fancy fence or know enough people to host a party, private or otherwise, so it was a different playing field entirely. Still, neighbors were neighbors. And meeting them was the neighborly thing to do, right?

"Hello?" came the voice from the call box.

"H-hi." Millie leaned out of her car window to get closer to the speaker. "I'm Millie Leclair. Sophia invited me to the book club meeting tonight."

Book club meeting? What was wrong with her? No one called these things meetings. She dropped her head back against the seat and rolled her eyes, realizing only too late that there was probably a security camera pointed on her. She snapped her head up and focused on the box, plastering a smile on her face. "Well, I mean, not a meeting. Just the, you know, book club."

This was getting worse as it went on. With her tense smile—more like a grimace—still aimed at the call box, she moved only her eyes to search for where the camera might be.

"Millie! We've been expecting you. Come on in."

An electric buzz sounded and then the gate slowly swung inward.

Millie pulled through, following the long driveway to the house and parking behind the last car. Tucking her ereader into her bag, she closed her eyes and took one last deep breath before she opened the door. "Here goes nothing."

Joyce Huffington, a woman with carefully styled short dark hair and a hint of laugh lines around her warm smile, stood on the front porch of her beautiful oceanfront mansion, dressed in casual slacks, a flowy top and bare feet.

"We're so glad you could make it tonight! As a lady of

Oceanside Estates, joining us for our monthly book club is a requirement," she declared with a teasing lilt, waiting for Millie to join her. Once at the top, Joyce took both of Millie's hands. "You know Mildred was a regular at our book clubs when we first started them."

Yet another detail Millie hadn't known. Her aunt had loved to read and had often sent her book recommendations when she was in high school and college, but they'd never discussed them. Being here in the same place surrounded by the same women Aunt Mildred had shared her thoughts with about the stories she read somehow made her feel closer to her aunt. Millie smiled and squeezed Joyce's hands. "No, I had no idea. It seems I keep discovering things about her every day."

"Well, she was always our favorite because she had such interesting things to say. Even when it was a dull book, she managed to make the discussion exciting." Joyce's eyes glimmered and she gave Millie's hands a gentle squeeze back before she let go.

"I hope you're not expecting me to take her place. I only started the book last night and I'm afraid I don't have the same insight into life that Aunt Mildred did." For probably the hundredth time since she'd gotten here, she wished she'd made visiting her aunt a bigger priority.

Joyce waved away the thought, ushering Millie through the wide front door. "You'll be fine simply being you."

They walked through the house to the covered patio. It was as beautifully decorated as any of the interior rooms, with heavy wooden outdoor furniture and plush cushions placed in a semicircular conversation area. The long gauzy drapes that hung down at each corner of the patio were blowing in the sea breeze.

Six other women were already gathered.

"Millie, do you know everyone?" Joyce pointed to Bonnie

first. "Bonnie owns the Daybreak Café and loves any story set during World War II whether or not it's a good book."

Bonnie shrugged. "Guilty. And a little warning, I brought two World War II books to pitch for next month. It's great to see you, Millie."

Joyce pointed to the next lady who had long, flowing silver hair and appeared to be about the same age as Bonnie. "This is Camilla. She runs Summer Island's Charity League and is a lover of memoirs."

"People's stories are just so interesting, don't you think?" Millie nodded. "Agreed."

Joyce moved on to the next lady, who had to be close to eighty years old. "Betty lives next door to me. She reads everything and likes to tell anyone who will listen that she's lived in this town longer than anyone else."

"The only person who had me beat was your aunt. She was a dear friend," the lady said. "And I'm sure you don't remember this, but I once met you when you were a little girl. It's a pleasure to see you again."

Finally, Joyce motioned to the last two people in the room. "And of course you know Tessa and Sophia. Sophia likes the thrillers while Tessa's responsible for all the romance books we read."

Tessa grinned. "What can I say? I like happy endings."

Sophia patted the empty cushion on the loveseat next to her. "We're excited you could make it."

Millie took the seat and put her bag on the floor. "Thanks for inviting me. It was nice to have a reason to take a break from the renovations and socialize with other people. Plus, I love to read, so this is right up my alley."

"Since Joyce told you all of ours, what's your favorite type of book, dear?" Bonnie asked.

Millie twisted her mouth to the side in thought. Deciding on a favorite genre was like trying to choose a favorite chocolate. How do you pick just one when they're all so good? "I think I would consider myself more of a dabbler. But what I've been reading lately, besides *Home Remodeling for Dummies*, is a collection of love letters."

"Ohhh, a real-life romance. Who are they to?" Tessa asked.

"My aunt." Millie paused to let this news sink in. "I found them when I was going through some of the things in her office."

"Love letters to Mildred?" Joyce looked as surprised as Millie had been when she found them. "Who are they from?"

Millie shrugged. "I'm not sure. They aren't signed."

"A secret admirer? This keeps getting better." Tessa leaned in, looking intrigued.

"I don't think it was a secret admirer. They're very personal. So personal that I think the writer didn't need to use his name. Any idea of who might've been in love with my aunt?" Millie surveyed the faces around the patio, hoping one of them could shed some light on the mystery.

Unfortunately, they all looked just as baffled as she'd been.

"Mildred never had a romantic interest as far as I knew, but I've only been here for about twenty years. Betty, you knew Mildred for ages. Any ideas?" Joyce turned her attention to the oldest woman in the group.

"So Mildred had a lover after all." Betty tapped her chin. "This is news to me. As long as I knew her, she was always single. We'd sometimes give her a hard time about it, because no matter who tried to pursue her, no one ever piqued old Mildred Leclair's interest."

Camilla leaned forward and poised her pen above her journal, ready to take notes. "Is there any identifying information in the letters at all? An address or personal details? Maybe we can try to figure it out."

Millie pictured the letters in her mind, thinking about what other clues she could've missed. "There's not much to go on. There are twenty-three letters written between 1955 and 1956. None of them are signed and there's no return address. But they were all written on the same stationery monogrammed with a single *C*."

All eyes in the room turned to look at Betty, who just shook her head. "I moved here in 1959 and Mildred was a little older than I was. We didn't really get to know each other until after I graduated. I could probably come up with some people whose name started with *C*, but it would be a stab in the dark."

Tessa clasped her hands over her heart. "Can you imagine someone writing you a love letter on monogrammed stationery? I barely got a sappy text from my ex."

Bonnie nodded. "Love letters are a lost art form. My husband wrote me a few love letters back when we were dating almost thirty years ago, but nothing since."

"Mine too," Joyce chimed in. "And I can't remember the last time I purchased any stationery, monogrammed or otherwise. Perhaps the world wouldn't be such an angry place if we all took more time to send each other letters."

Camilla nodded. "Agreed."

"So what happened? Why did the mystery relationship end?" Sophia asked.

Millie thought about the last few letters in the stack, the ones she hadn't read yet. In fact, she hadn't even pulled them out of their envelopes. "I'm not sure. The love story has been so beautiful so far that I'm not ready for it to end."

"A tragic ending." Joyce's eyes lit up. "What do you think it could be? He was already engaged to someone else? Someone he felt he had to marry because of financial reasons?"

"Mildred wasn't hurting for money back then. If it was a

financial reason, she could've covered it," Betty said.

"What if he got shipped off to war or had to move away?" Tessa threw in.

"Don't you think if he went away, he would've still written letters? I feel like distance wouldn't have stopped them. It had to have been something else," Bonnie said.

Millie made mental notes of these details about her aunt. Each new fact helped her form a more complete picture of young Mildred in love.

Joyce leaned forward in her chair, almost knocking the book on her lap to the floor. "Oh honey, you have to finish reading those letters before our next book club. We have to know how the story ends."

While the first person Millie would've wanted to discuss these letters with was her aunt, getting to share the story and hear the thoughts of these women who all knew Mildred in a different way was a good consolation prize. "Absolutely. I'll be ready to give you a full report of everything I learn in the final letters."

"I have to wait a whole month to find out what happens? You do realize I'm the girl who reads the last chapter first, right?" Tessa said.

"Life doesn't give you the final chapter first. You have to live it to find out how it will go," Betty said, then turned to Millie. "Your Aunt Mildred used to say that."

"Fine." Tessa slumped in her chair with a sigh. "I won't make Millie take us all to her house right this second to read the last love letters. But if y'all are going to make me wait, I'm expecting some really rich discussion about what-could've-beens and what-should've-beens. You have lots of time to think about it."

"Just think about it? I'm doing some research. Someone in this town has to know something about Mildred's affair," Camilla said. "Millie, do you mind if we ask around about it?"

"Not at all. I'm dying to know who this mysterious Romeo was and what happened."

"Any chance you'll let us read some of them?" Sophia asked.

Millie considered the request. The letters did seem personal, but they were history now, right? And the beautiful history of the house deserved to be shared. "I can bring some of them."

"And in honor of Mildred, I'll bring her famous brownies," Bonnie added.

Joyce clapped her hands together. "It's a date, then. Four weeks from tonight, we find out how Mildred's secret affair ended."

Chapter Nine

Braxton walked up to the memory care home on Saturday at noon with Alice on one hip, a bag with their takeout lunch dangling from his other arm, and a tray of drinks in his hand, feeling like he was long overdue for a nap.

Spending the morning with his daughter was one of his favorite activities, but that didn't make it any less exhausting. So far today, after they stopped for a treat at Bonnie's café, they hit up story time at the library, ran two errands, and had just enough time to stop by Henry's favorite beachfront restaurant to pick up a couple of blackened grouper sandwiches for lunch. Hopefully, they both had enough energy left to eat with their friend.

Since he was all out of free hands, Braxton had to squat down a bit to ring the buzzer with his elbow.

"Hello, Mr. Channing," the bright voice on the speaker called. "Come on in." There was an electronic buzzing of the door being unlocked and Braxton did his best to pry open the heavy wooden door with a combination of using the hand holding Alice and his foot.

"Here we go. Time to eat lunch," he said to the toddler.

"Well, hello, cutie-patootie! It's been a long time since I've seen you!" Veronica held the interior door open for them.

"Hi-ee." Alice waved her plump little hand at their favorite administrator.

"Let me help you with that," she said to Braxton, taking the tray of drinks from him. "Mr. Donovan is sitting in the dining room waiting for you."

"How's he doing today?" Braxton didn't bother hiding the concern in his voice. Over the past several weeks, Henry's good days had become fewer and further in between. His mind was getting fuzzier and he was experiencing more bouts of extreme confusion and angry fits. Not that Braxton blamed him. Just watching his friend's mind deteriorate without any way of helping him made Braxton want to launch into an angry fit of his own.

"He's okay." Veronica shot him a sympathetic smile. "I think he's real excited about the fish sandwiches. Been telling everyone who will listen about them."

They wound through the grand living room to the dining room. Henry was sitting in one of the heavy wooden chairs at a square four-person table, wearing one of the golf shirts with Braxton's old logo on it.

Veronica raised her voice when they approached him. "Mr. Henry, look who I found at the door. This good-looking duo brought you lunch."

"Being good-looking is a curse in this sport," Henry grumbled with humor. "Too many pretty ladies around to swing a club. If you ask me, he'd be a better golfer if he had an ugly mug."

Veronica shook her head, her smile never fading. She set the cardboard cupholder of drinks on the table. "From what I heard, he did pretty well."

Braxton placed the bag on the table. "Enough with the

golf talk. How about we eat lunch?"

Henry reached for one of the drinks. "So touchy." He picked up a straw and stared at the cup, his look of confusion rapidly turning into frustration.

The sight made Braxton's heart ache.

Veronica reacted first and gently took it out of Henry's hand, removed the wrapper, and stuck it in the drink for him as if forgetting how to put a straw in a cup was no big deal. "You know what, I forgot to pull out the highchair. Let me get it for you." She patted Henry on the shoulder before she scurried off.

Braxton let Alice stand in one of the chairs while he unpacked the takeout boxes, trying not to let the little incident bother him. Struggling with normal everyday tasks was nothing new. They were the first thing to go when the Alzheimer's disease started to progress. In fact, not being able to dress himself without help was one of the main reasons they'd made the decision for him to move into this home-like assisted living center designed specifically for people with dementia. But lately it seemed like he needed help with almost everything.

Braxton didn't want to dwell too closely on that. Today, he wanted to enjoy lunch with his two favorite people and maybe even pretend like everything was back to normal and his life, once again, made sense. He pulled out the first box, opened the lid a little to check what was inside, and placed it in front of his spot before he grabbed the next box.

Henry took a sip from his straw and smiled at Alice. "Who is this?" he asked in a pleasant voice.

Braxton froze, his hand holding the box hovering in the air as he looked back and forth between his daughter and her godfather who were making eyes at each other. His stomach plunged, and for a moment he thought he might be sick. It took all the willpower he could muster to keep the expression on his face neutral. This was the first time Henry hadn't recognized someone so close to him.

Braxton took a breath to steady his voice before he answered. "This is my daughter, Alice." Tears stung his eyes, but he commanded them to go away. He couldn't react to this. Not in front of Henry. It would only make things worse.

"Hi-ee, Hen-wee. Hi-ee." Alice waved both of her hands and danced in the chair, completely oblivious to what was happening. "We have wunch with Hen-wee!" There was joy in her voice and excitement to see the man who had helped raise her for the first two years of her life.

"Your what?" Henry's innocent smile was replaced by a shocked look of confusion.

"My daughter, Alice," Braxton repeated, setting the box in front of Henry. "She came to have lunch with us today."

"Your daughter." Henry's face screwed up, making him look angry, which caused a lump to form in Braxton's throat.

"Here you go." Veronica made her way through the wooden tables with the highchair in front of her. Henry took his eyes off Alice and watched their friend place the seat in the spot between Henry and Braxton. As if someone had pulled a plug, all the tension drained from his face, leaving him with nothing but a blank expression and a vacant smile.

Veronica did a slight double take when she saw Henry's expression then she shot Braxton a quick questioning glance.

She laid a hand on Henry's arm. "You are one lucky man getting to eat this fancy lunch with these fine people. Last time I ate at Coral Reef, it took us an hour just to get a table. And here you are not having to wait at all."

Henry nodded, still staring blankly at the spot in front of him. Braxton busied himself with buckling Alice into the highchair while he tried to swallow the lump in his throat. Now wasn't the time to mourn his own loss. The best thing to do was to make Henry comfortable and offer support. For years, Henry had been his rock, and now it was his turn to be that for his mentor.

Veronica laid a comforting hand on his shoulder as she walked by, her eyes filled with sympathy. "Let me know if you need anything."

Braxton nodded, forcing a smile. "Thanks, Veronica." He took one more breath, then turned his focus to opening everyone's meal. "How about we eat before this all gets cold." He opened the box in front of Henry first, turning it to offer the easiest access to the food inside. He didn't want to give Henry any more reasons to get frustrated. "You don't mind if Alice takes one of your fries, do you? Of course not." He took a couple of the large home-cut French fries and put them on Alice's tray.

As he pulled Henry's plasticware from the wrapper and handed it to him, he watched Henry's gaze follow the fries as Alice picked one up and tried to shove the whole thing in her mouth.

"I like those kinds of fries." His voice still had a vacant quality to it.

"I know you do. I've watched you take down a double order by yourself on more than one occasion." Braxton opened a smaller box containing the grilled fish nuggets and fruit for Alice. "In fact, you're the reason she likes them so much. You gave them to her when she was a baby. It was the first solid food she ate."

Henry put one of the fries in his mouth and chewed slowly, visibly relaxing a bit. "Seems like a reasonable thing to do. Life's too short to not eat good food."

Braxton chuckled. "That's what you said then, too." He cleared the giant bag from the table, then took a seat, opening the meal in front of him. "Which is why I didn't think you'd mind sharing with her."

Henry stuck another fry in his mouth, looking at Alice.

"You should tell him to get you your own order."

"Sage advice if ever I heard any."

"Well, I've been giving you advice for a long time and you won't take it. Maybe I should start on the next generation." He looked at Alice. "The secret to a great golf swing is to keep your head down."

Braxton took a bite of his sandwich and let relief flutter through him. Maybe there was hope of recovering this lunch after all. "Maybe you should try giving her advice that would be useful like always eat your vegetables, don't stay out past midnight. That sort of stuff," Braxton joked.

Henry stared at Alice for a second, then shifted his focus to the food in front of him, getting quiet. "My mind is getting worse," he whispered, all his attention focused on poking at the fries in front of him.

Braxton's heart broke. "I know."

Silence settled over the table as they both contemplated the heavy truth hanging between them. Even Alice sat completely still.

Finally, Henry looked up, pain and confusion glaring in his eyes. "It's…" There was a long pause as he searched for the right word. "Trouble," he said eventually.

Braxton nodded. It was troubling. It was also terrifying, heartbreaking, frustrating, and unfair. And that was just from his perspective. He couldn't begin to imagine what it was like to deal with it from Henry's side.

Henry continued, "Trouble in the same way that you can't keep your head down when you swing your nine iron." He looked up at Braxton with a sly smile.

Braxton let out a loud laugh. Some of the heaviness lifted off his chest. "But you still have your sense of humor."

Henry shrugged and picked up his sandwich, some of the life returning to his eyes. "Mmmm. This is good."

"Only the best for our Henry. Right, Alice?"

Alice grinned and popped another fish nugget in her mouth.

Henry nodded his head at the little girl. "She swing a golf club yet? Maybe I should give her some lessons after lunch. We wouldn't want her to pick up any of your bad habits."

This journey they were on was hard and promised to only get more difficult, but it wasn't over yet, which made Braxton thankful. He needed to hold on to Henry for as long as possible. "Just eat your sandwich, old man."

Braxton knew from the moment Henry didn't recognize Alice that he'd be spending the rest of the day at the Summer Island Memory Care Home.

Braxton was like Henry's security blanket. He anchored him when he was feeling his most confused and staying with him was the right call. It was the call Henry would've made if the situation was reversed. But that didn't make it less difficult.

Entertaining a two-year-old while trying not to disrupt Henry's normal schedule was a challenge. Luckily, Alice was a good sleeper and took a nap in her stroller while they played chess. She thought the daily exercise class was great fun and ran around the courtyard while they sat outside to have his afternoon lemonade. But by the time they finished dinner, Braxton was emotionally and mentally drained. He stayed around until the staff change was complete and Henry was ready to head off to his room for his nightly TV-watching ritual.

That gave Braxton just enough time to get an overtired and overstimulated Alice home before she had an epic two-year-old meltdown. After a quick bath and reading her current favorite board book three times, his little girl was finally asleep in her crib and Braxton had a moment to himself.

He grabbed the handheld baby video monitor and stepped outside to unwind in the quiet summer evening. From his patio, he had an unobstructed view of the Atlantic stretching all the way to the horizon. It was—when he took the time to admire it—breathtaking. In fact, this picture-perfect view of the ocean was what had inspired him and his wife to buy this house. Of course, that was back in a carefree time when he lived a picture-perfect life and the world made sense.

He drew in a lungful of warm, salty air and let the sound of the waves wash over him. How had his life gotten so off course? He'd had the world on a string, and he was so consumed with his own selfish ambitions he didn't even realize it. And look where it got him.

He headed down the concrete steps to the boardwalk, the weight of his situation like a physical heaviness on his body.

What if... It was a game he liked to play when everything seemed like it was crumbling around him. He replayed his past from every angle, like when he used to watch videos of his golf swing, looking for specific moments where it all went wrong.

What if he hadn't been on tour the night of the car wreck?

What if he hadn't been so consumed with his own need to be number one that he missed the early warning signs of his coach's chronic condition?

What if he had never swung a golf club to begin with?

He stepped off the end of the boardwalk and let his feet sink into the sand, guilt pecking away at him. He stared at the orange horizon, wondering what he could've done to make it all turn out different.

"Hi there, neighbor." The optimistic, airy voice sliced right through his heavy thoughts, bringing with it a sort of lightness that caught him off guard. Slowly, he pivoted in the direction of the sound.

Millie sat on a driftwood log with her dog at her feet. Her dark hair fluttered behind her in the gentle ocean breeze and the setting sun highlighted her in a soft glow. She looked content and serene and lovely and the sight of her made something stir inside him.

"Hi, yourself." He lifted his hand in a wave.

Millie leaned over and looked down the beach around him. "Where's the little one?"

"Dreamland." Braxton held up the monitor in his hand to show the image of a sleeping Alice.

"Awww." She nodded and pressed her lips together in a sort of polite smile of someone who had cycled through all of their conversation topics.

The silence between them grew.

He could've offered a simple "see ya later" and headed back to the privacy of his own patio. But he didn't. The truth was, seeing her made him feel a little lighter, as if someone had just thrown him a lifejacket when he was struggling to stay afloat.

Perhaps he should've asked himself why the mere act of her presence felt like a lifejacket. It seemed like the kind of realization that should've set off warning signals. But instead of diving down the "why" rabbit hole, he pushed the thought away and took a step toward her.

"What do you have there?" He motioned to the stack of papers in her hand.

"These?" Millie held up the papers in question, giving him a better look. "They're love letters written to my Aunt Mildred."

"Love letters, huh? From her husband?" He strolled toward her to get a closer look.

Millie wiped a few grains of sand off the top page then straightened the pile and settled it on her lap. "Nope. She never married. Never had any sort of serious commitment we knew about, so there's a bit of mystery."

"A secret affair?"

Millie giggled. "That would be scandalous. But no. I don't think it was secret, it just didn't last." She let out a sad sigh. "I have two left to read, but they seem so in love right now. I'm not sure I want it to end. Listen to this." She flipped to one of the pages in the middle of the stack.

"'Each night I lie awake thinking about your beauty and the way it has changed me. Your zeal for life and love for humanity breathes life into my spirit. You, my love, are my reason for being.'" She flipped to the last page. "And this one. 'I am a rich man, indeed. Rich in love. Rich in you. Forever with you simply isn't long enough.'"

She dropped her hands back to her lap and stared out at the ocean, a blissful look softening her delicate features. "Isn't that beautiful. How could something like that end?"

The guilt and pain he'd been carrying around squeezed his chest like a vise. He could imagine how something like that could end. It started with a golf swing and ended with a car crash. "Bad choices and bad luck."

Millie froze, as if the words had shocked her, and she studied him for a second. Shock turned to sympathy and the gentle look in her soft brown eyes caused the vise on his chest to loosen just a bit.

"Are you okay?" And there it was again. The vibe that radiated from her wrapped around him like a compassionate hug, soothing him. Only this time, instead of explaining it away or ignoring it, he closed his eyes and allowed his aching soul to rest in it.

"It's been a hard day." He breathed the words out, letting the freedom of voicing them lift some of the burden.

She scooted over a bit and motioned to the space on the log next to her. "Want to sit? It's a beautiful evening and Bear is a pretty good listener." At the mention of his name, the dog lifted his furry head.

Braxton stared at the log. Did he want to sit? Standing here and shooting the breeze with a woman who inexplicably made him want to smile was one thing. But sitting? That felt like something else entirely.

He didn't need one more thing to complicate his life, and his new neighbor with a money pit house and a livelihood that was currently blocked by the rules of a group he was president of sounded like a major complication.

Still, it was just a log and only a conversation.

He took the vacant spot and petted the dog, hoping focusing on this task would make the words come out easier. "We had a little setback with my friend, Henry, today." He paused, backtracking a bit. "Have I told you about Henry?"

"Your old coach?" Millie asked, seeming somewhat familiar with the name.

He nodded. Coach was one word to describe him. Or mentor, confidant, friend...

Loss tugged at him as he scrolled through the list of titles that described one of the most important people in his life. "He has Alzheimer's disease and it's progressing more rapidly than we'd hoped. And today, for the first time, he didn't remember who Alice was."

"I'm so sorry."

It wasn't just the words that resonated with Braxton but her tone. Heartbroken, sympathetic, and supportive all rolled up into three little words that comforted his deepest wound.

Perhaps it was because the setting sun cast a golden glow that made the world look too good to be real, or the way the gentle waves rolled onto the shore in an almost perfect rhythm. Or perhaps it was the way Millie's kindness hit him square in the chest. Whatever the reason, Braxton didn't stop at his surface-level woes. Nope. Tonight he went straight for the deep stuff that he'd never voiced to anyone.

"Sometimes I wonder if it's my fault."

"Oh?" She didn't seem shocked by this statement or intent on trying to correct him. Instead, she sat, her caring eyes focused on him, ready to listen.

Encouraged, he continued, "My whole focus for so long was being the best. Youngest golfer to win back-to-back Masters. Youngest golfer to win all the majors. Most wins in a single season. It wasn't enough to be good. I had to be the best."

He ran his hands through his hair and stared out at the obscure spot where the ocean met the sky. "Because of that game, I lost everything."

"Or maybe because of the game, you gained everything you had that was worth losing."

Her words made him pause.

Golf *had* brought him some great things. His golf coach, the physical therapist he met when he was recovering from a back injury who later became his wife, the daughter they had together. His whole life had come together because of the one thing that ultimately sent his life into a spiral.

He nodded toward the letters in her hand. "Maybe my life is one of those stories with a tragic ending."

Millie held up the letters. "I'm not sure what happened with this part, but my aunt would not have said her life had a tragic ending. A sad chapter? Maybe. But her overall story was remarkable." Millie reached over and gently squeezed his hand. "Your story isn't over yet."

Her words—or maybe it was her touch—caused a flutter inside of him. Something warm and golden and shimmery. Hope. It flowed through him, past the barriers he put up, past the part of his heart that he had closed off, touching the darkest, loneliest places that had been off-limits for quite some time.

This was exactly why he shouldn't sit on logs.

"Thanks. I appreciate that." He let his hand linger under her touch for another millisecond before pulling it away and standing. "I should probably head back." He held up the baby monitor for good measure.

"Me, too. The first guest room was finished today and I was going to try to get a coat of paint on tonight." She grabbed the ball at her feet and gave it a quick toss down the beach in the direction of her house. Bear scrambled to his feet and bounded after it. "I wanted to give Bear a little exercise first."

"Thanks for letting me hijack your peaceful sunset."

"Anytime." She flashed a sort of sympathetic half grin that made her nose wrinkle in the cutest way then turned and headed in the direction of her house.

Friends. That's all they were. Nothing complicated. Nothing noteworthy. Just a friend. Besides, one could never have too many friends in their life, right?

At least that was the story he was sticking with as he watched her walk away.

Chapter Ten

Millie shouldn't have stopped to get the mail when she was backing out of her driveway on the way to the hardware store the next morning. Lately, nothing good came out of her mailbox. There were no party invitations or greeting cards, and she didn't even have any fun magazine subscriptions.

All that landed in the rusty old mailbox was junk mail, bills, and—on especially frustrating days—official warning letters from Braxton and the Oceanside Estates HOA.

Today was a frustrating day.

She idled in her driveway to open the dreaded letter. Was this number four or five? She was starting to lose track.

"At what point do you think we'll hold the record for most violation letters received in the shortest amount of time?" she asked Bear who was in the backseat. "And do you think we get a plaque for that?"

She could joke all she wanted, but the familiar apprehension swirled within as she unfolded the letter. She needed Braxton and the HOA to be on her side if she had any hope of reopening Seascape. And judging by the amount of problems they found with her property, there was very little chance of getting their approval for reopening.

Before she read anything else, she glanced at the bottom. Just like the rest of the letters, it was signed by Braxton, which caused a different stab of disappointment.

She didn't get him.

Sometimes, like last night on the beach or when he was playing with his daughter, she saw glimpses of a great man with a big heart. It was the kind of man she might fall for—if she was in a place where she'd let herself fall for a man. Which she wasn't.

But it didn't matter, because as soon as she started to think she'd misjudged him, the uptight lover of rules and neighborhood hall monitor showed back up.

Last night, she'd thought they'd connected, that their relationship had taken a turn toward friendly. She even considered calling him a friend next time it came up. But clearly she had misread the whole situation because a *friend* would've mentioned a problem before sending a formal violation letter. Or, at the very least, he could've given her a heads-up that it was coming. Braxton, however, had said nothing, as if her work on Seascape and all the time and energy she'd poured into it was nothing more than a business matter for him to check off his list.

"Whatever," she said out loud. "We don't need him to like us. Seascape is going to speak for herself."

Bear wagged his tail in agreement.

She glanced at the rest of the letter to find out what his beef was this time.

It has been brought to our attention that one or more aspects of your property is out of compliance with the Oceanside Estates Deed Restrictions. Please address the item(s) listed below.

Exterior stain used on doors is not on the approved list of colors appropriate for the exterior of a dwelling.

This is your first warning regarding the above violation(s). You will be given thirty (30) days to rectify this matter.

Her fingers clenched around the paper, crinkling it a bit. For real?

She looked at the two large wooden front doors that she'd spent the entire previous day refinishing. It hadn't been easy. In fact, one of them she had to re-sand and start over after a disastrous dripping incident, and there was still sawdust in her hair. But all the work had been worth it. They turned out amazing. The finish was exactly like the inspiration picture she'd used from the front of *Coastal Life* magazine.

Yes, she'd known that the stain she chose wasn't on the HOA's approved list, but that list hadn't been updated since the early 2000s. The stain Landon, the paint expert at the local hardware store, had recommended was a new formula that held up better under the extreme oceanfront elements. According to him it was very popular and being used all over the island. She thought it was close enough to the approved color that it was impossible to tell the difference.

Apparently, a certain next-door neighbor thought differently.

She tossed the letter onto the seat next to her and shifted her car into drive. The newly painted doors were barely even dry. Was he constantly watching her house to make sure she followed every single rule to the letter?

"I hope he at least noticed how fantastic they look while he was comparing the shade to his color chart," she said to Bear.

She let out a sigh. Under different circumstances she might have left them and seen what happened after the thirty-day deadline, but she didn't have that luxury. She couldn't afford to give the HOA any additional reason to not allow Seascape to reopen as an inn. If she had to sand and re-stain those doors for that to happen, she'd do it.

But not for twenty-nine more days.

• • •

Two days.

It had been two days since the infamous spilling of his soul on the beach to his new neighbor, and Braxton still couldn't get it off his mind. What had he been thinking?

Yes, it had been a stressful day. In theory, he knew at some point Henry would forget them, but he never expected it would be this soon. He'd also known that day would be hard, but the extent of it was a crushing blow. It was still no excuse for him to pour out his woes to Millie, no matter how optimistic her smile made him feel.

But he had, and now he had to fix it.

He'd seen her power washing the front of her house when he was walking out to his car, and there was no time like the present to mend the proverbial fence between them. So he pulled up to her house, parked well out of the way of the work she was doing, and walked over to her.

"Hey there," he said, trying to keep his voice as casual as possible as he yelled to be heard over the noise of the machine.

She paused mid-stroke and looked over at him. Her expression morphed from surprise to annoyance. "Oh, it's you."

The bite to her words left him momentarily frozen. After their last conversation, he assumed things would be awkward, but he hadn't expected her to be angry.

She leaned down and turned off the machine, killing

the noise of the motor and powerful spray. "Did you come to lecture me about the safety protocols of power washing?" She grabbed the water bottle that was next to her and took a quick drink. "Is a buddy required for this job, too?"

He shrugged. "The buddy rule is appropriate in a lot of situations."

"Bear has my back. If I find myself incapacitated by a life-threatening power washing accident, he'll go for help." She recapped the water bottle and returned it to its place. "What would a power washing accident look like? Hand cramp? Water in the eye?"

Braxton tried to keep his tone light to counterbalance the rising tension between them. "You know, tripping is the second most common cause of serious accidents that happen in the home. There's a high trip risk when you're moving while staring at a big wall."

Millie huffed and rolled her eyes. "You're like a walking doomsday Google search."

"Knowledge is power." He shoved his hands in his pockets, trying to figure out how to get this conversation back on track. He'd come to apologize for oversharing, but now he wanted to figure out what had her ready to power wash *him* off her porch.

"And on that front," she continued, "I'll have you know I checked to make sure the paint color I'm about to use on the shutters is on the HOA approved list. I even made Landon double check the mixture to make sure it was right."

Okay, so it was about the rules again. Had she bought the wrong paint at first and then discovered the list? How was that his fault? "I applaud the effort." Then, hoping to clear the air, he said, "So, listen, about the other night—"

"You could've just said something," she snapped, fire blazing in her eyes.

"Said something?" He did say something. In fact, his

problem was that he'd said too much, thus the reason he was here.

She took a step closer, wagging her sprayer at him like a giant finger. "I'm a big girl, Braxton. I can take a bit of constructive criticism without falling to pieces."

Criticism?

"I mean, seriously, after that whole conversation the other night, you couldn't slide in a simple, 'oh, and by the way, your doors can't be that color?' I would've listened. I probably wouldn't have been happy about it because, seriously, the color is amazing and you need to update your dumb approved list, but I would've listened. It would've saved you a stamp."

Braxton frowned, completely at a loss. "What are you talking about?"

"The letters you keep sending me." She propped her hands on her hips, sending drips of water from the sprayer running down her shirt. "I get it. There are rules. But would it hurt you to mention them to me before you send me the big formal letter with the threat of a fine?"

He held his hands up defensively. "Can we back up a bit? I came over to apologize for oversharing the other night. It had been a hard day and I wasn't quite myself. But I didn't need to dump my problems on you."

She paused and tilted her head to the side, examining him. "Why would you apologize for that? You're human. You're allowed to struggle when life gets overwhelming."

There was a kindness in her voice once more, like there had been that night.

He swallowed. "But they're not your problems. I didn't need to burden you with that."

"Problems aren't meant to be carried alone."

The truth of her words once again chipped away at the walls around his heart, deep enough to reach his soul. But he didn't need anything or anyone touching his soul. That's how oversharing happened.

"Thank you, but I don't—" He stopped and rewound her argument. "Did you say I was sending you threatening letters?"

She let out a huff, the kindness vanishing from her eyes. "The formal HOA warnings you keep leaving in my mailbox." She held up her fingers and started ticking off examples. "Not submitting my document on time, leaving my trash cans out past sundown, too many work vehicles being parked on the street, and now the stain on the front door not being on the approved color list."

"And they're official letters from the HOA?" While he wasn't a huge fan of the violation letters the HOA sent out, he understood the reason for them. The rules were in place to protect everyone who was part of the community and occasionally, when a friendly mention didn't rectify the situation, a reminder in the form of a letter was needed. But he had no idea they had sent any to Millie.

"Sure, I guess we can consider them from the HOA since they have the HOA letterhead. But since you signed them, I'm gonna say they're from you."

Shock reverberated through him. "My signature is on the letters? You're sure?"

She let out a huff of air, clearly exasperated with him. "They say Braxton Channing. Is there another Braxton Channing around here?"

Violation letters usually went out from the standards committee, not from him. Not only did he not have any idea these letters were going out, he had no idea that they were using his name. Something was not right here. "May I see them?"

Millie frowned at him, but then sighed. "Sure. A couple of them are in my kitchen. Let me grab them." She handed him the spray wand and disappeared into her house. A minute later she returned holding some papers.

"Here you go." She handed the stack to him. "Four violation letters signed by our fearless HOA president."

He flipped through the pages, blood draining from his face and leaving him cold at the signature at the bottom of every page. *His* signature. It was the official electronic signature that was on file for legal reasons which was only supposed to be used with his permission. And he most definitely didn't give his permission for a violation letter.

"I had no idea."

She tilted her head, studying him with an intense gaze. "So you didn't send them?"

He shook his head out a combination of disbelief and anger. "No. And there's no excuse for these. All of these are ridiculous. Of course you have work vehicles at your house. It's under construction. But they haven't blocked the road, which is the actual violation."

Whoever was sending these out had to be looking for any complaint they could find, probably to add to the case against her. It wasn't just awful, it was unethical. But what made it even worse was that they were using his name to do it.

"On behalf of the HOA, I'm going to figure out who's been sending them. The deed restrictions are set up to protect residents, not torment them. This shouldn't be happening."

"Thanks." She offered a weak smile. "I appreciate that."

"On a personal note, I'm sorry. This is a lot of added stress you don't deserve."

She held his gaze for a second as if she was trying to read something in his eyes. "Thank you."

He wanted to say something else, but his mind was too jumbled from finding out about the letters.

Millie shook her head slightly as if snapping out of it and turned to look at the wall beside them. "Well, I better get back to de-griming this monster. I was hoping to get it done before it gets dark, and, as my Aunt Mildred used to say, we're burning daylight."

Braxton stared at the house, too. She'd worked hard on this place, harder than he'd seen anyone work in a long time. Her dedication was admirable. Inspiring even. And the fact that someone was using his name to discourage her was deplorable.

Yet, even thinking he was the one who'd sent the letters, she'd still listened patiently to him the other night and encouraged him. He only wished he could somehow ease her mind in the same way. In fact, an idea teased his mind and he opened his mouth before thinking too much.

"Actually, let me make it up to you."

She paused and stared at him, confusion written all over her face. "Make it up to me?"

He shrugged, trying to cover up a sudden bout of nerves. "Not so much make it up to you as prove that Summer Island is a pretty great place to call home. Despite what some might have led you to believe."

"Okay." Her voice had a hint of caution in it. "What do you have in mind?"

He took a breath.

"Let me take you to the Beach Front Festival this weekend."

"Oh yeah, I heard some of the ladies talking about that," she said, her eyes lighting up. "What exactly is it?"

"It's our version of a main street festival. You know, local vendors, artists, live music." Memories of the annual festival where their community came together floated through his mind. It was one of his favorite events in Summer Island and the thought of sharing it with her made him buzz with excitement.

He'd be sharing it as an ambassador, of course, to try to

repair any damage the letters might have caused her. He just had to keep repeating this until he believed it.

"Alice and I are already planning on going," he said. "As your neighbors, we'd love to show you the best our town has to offer."

Millie raised an eyebrow. "As my neighbor?"

He nodded. "Consider it a peace offering. Plus, parking is always a problem, so they encourage ride sharing when possible."

Millie twisted her mouth to the side, considering it. "Well, in that case, how can I say no?"

His heart did a funny thing that had him inhaling sharply. "Perfect. I'll pick you up Saturday at ten?"

She smiled one of her optimistic, hopeful, Millie smiles. "Sounds like a plan."

Another shot of excitement buzzed through him. "Great. See you then."

Chapter Eleven

The following Saturday morning, Millie pulled out the sundress she'd bought in Chicago the day she decided to move to South Carolina.

It was a splurge, especially for a casual dress, but the cheerful pinks and turquoises that made up the tropical pattern had looked like a preview of what her new life would be. In her mind, living on the coast would be full of breezy and laid-back days where she became the kind of person who wore casual resort wear on a daily basis. Even work would be more leisure than chore.

But reality had hit a little different when she arrived.

These days, she was the kind of person who wore old T-shirts and shorts she didn't mind ruining while keeping her hair pulled back with a baseball cap. And her list of chores to complete the renovation grew every day.

But today she was taking a break from the never-ending reno projects to go to her first Summer Island festival. It was the perfect event to debut her new dress. And her decision to wear it had absolutely nothing to do with the neighbor with whom she was going. Nothing at all.

She slipped the sundress over her head. "It's official, Bear. Welcome to our resort-wear life." Using the scissors on her dresser, she cut off the tags. "Now to find some shoes to go with it."

She was digging through the box marked *shoes* in her closet trying to find the dressy flip-flops that went with her outfit when the doorbell rang.

"Coming," she called, fully aware there was no way anyone at the front door could hear her. There was a good chance anyone standing in her room would have a tough time hearing her voice muffled by all the things in this closet. She really needed to clean it out, go through Aunt Mildred's old clothes and shoes, and finish unpacking her things. But that was low on her priority list at the moment.

What was high on her priority list was finding a match to the sandal in her hand.

In desperation, she dumped the box on the floor. She'd probably regret this decision later when she was cleaning it up, but it did help. The lost flip-flop turned up on the top of the pile. She grabbed it and hopped down the hall as she slid them on her feet.

She paused at the front door to take a calming breath. Jittery excitement pulsed through her, mostly because she was looking forward to the festival, and it had nothing to do with the man standing on her porch. While she was now willing to admit her initial snap judgments of him might have been slightly off base, today's outing was simply her neighbor showing her around to ease his guilty conscience. Plus, they were helping with the parking congestion problem, which only made sense.

Still, she didn't want to look a mess. She ran her hand through her hair before she swung the heavy front door open.

"Who's ready for a festival?" she asked in a singsong

voice.

"I feel fairly confident Alice has no idea what a festival is, but she's been claiming she's ready all morning."

The little girl, dressed in a pink and white seersucker sundress, beamed. "We go fess-ee-val!"

"I'm with Alice on this one. I have no idea what to expect, but I'm hoping it includes some really sinful food and live music." She turned all her focus to Alice. "And maybe even some dancing." She wiggled her hips in a sort of exaggerated attempt at a dance move. Alice giggled and squatted slightly, doing the toddler version of the twist.

Braxton shook his head. "I can guarantee both food and music. As for me dancing?" He gave her an apologetic shrug. "I wouldn't get my hopes up."

Millie shook her head in mock disbelief and addressed the adorable little girl still wiggling on the porch. "If there's music, there's dancing. Right, Alice? Don't let the wallflowers tell you any different."

"And on that note, shall we?" Braxton held his arm out toward the car. "Your chariot awaits."

The car parked on the drive was not the expensive, flashy sports car Braxton usually drove. Instead, there was a nondescript silver minivan.

Not bothering to hide the shock on her face, Millie turned to Braxton. "You drive a minivan? Like a legit family-style dadmobile. What happened to the fast car?"

Braxton chuckled, grabbing Alice's hand to help her down the concrete steps. "Not a dadmobile. This is a luxury family transportation unit playing only the finest selection of cartoon theme songs in a never-ending loop. Which, by the way, I happen to know every single lyric to."

There was something adorable about the proud way he shared this detail. "Impressive."

"I know." He waggled his eyebrows at her as Alice

stepped off the last step. "And watch this action." He hit the button on his key fob and the automatic back doors to the car slid open.

Millie couldn't help the grin that spread across her face. "Be still my beating heart."

"What can I say? I've got it going on." He bent down to pick up Alice and hoisted her into her car seat.

Millie locked her front door, trying to calm the stray butterfly that had unexpectedly taken flight in her stomach. When she finished, she tossed her keys in her purse and turned to the waiting minivan. Braxton, who'd finished buckling Alice in, stood next to the vehicle with his eyes fixed on her, and instead of leaving, that darn butterfly invited a few friends to the party.

"You look nice, by the way."

"Thanks." Feeling off balance, Millie glanced down at her bright sundress, hoping the heat in her cheeks wasn't causing a visible flush. "I appreciate the excuse to wear something other than clothes covered in paint stains and sawdust."

She jogged down the steps, and as soon as she reached the driveway, he opened the passenger side door for her. The gesture caught her off guard. Had a man ever opened the door for her, even on a real date? Not that this was any sort of a date at all. In fact, it was the opposite of a date. It was a non-date, which maybe made the door-opening thing more normal. Chauffeurs opened doors all the time, didn't they?

She slid into the seat, pushing the internal debate aside. "Thanks."

"Here at Channing Transportation, we aim to please." He shut the door for her and walked around to the driver's side.

Millie quickly closed her eyes to regroup. The excitement pulsing through her was because of the festival. She'd already determined that. It had nothing to do with Braxton, or his lovely daughter, or the way it all felt like a family outing.

But all her denials didn't change the fact that he continued to surprise her.

Braxton climbed into the seat next to her and pressed the ignition button. "All right, ladies. Next stop, Summer Island's Beach Front Festival."

They drove the short distance past the state park to the main street area. Once parked, Braxton took a stroller out of the trunk and threw a small sequined unicorn backpack and a blanket in the basket on the bottom. He buckled Alice into the seat and they started off.

Beach Front was a wide street that ran from the river side of the island all the way to where it dead-ended in a public beach access parking lot on the ocean side. Both sides of the streets were lined with boutiques, shops, and restaurants that charmed visitors and defined Summer Island.

But today it looked different.

The street had been closed to traffic. Tents occupied by local vendors selling everything from delicious-smelling food to art ran all the way down the middle of the street and outdoor displays were set up on the sidewalk outside every shop. A main stage was in the beach parking lot at the end where a group of little girls in sparkly costumes were doing their dance routine while proud parents recorded it with their phones. A couple of bouncy houses and other large inflatables had been set up in the surrounding areas, with lines of kids waiting to get in.

Millie glanced to her left and right, trying to get her bearings. "It's a little overwhelming. I don't even know where to start."

Braxton nodded his head at the west end of the street. "I like to start at one end and work my way down. That way we won't miss out on the best food."

Millie scanned the many food booths set up along the

street. "Which one has the best food?"

Braxton shrugged as he turned to walk to where the barricades marked the beginning of the festival area. "I'm not sure. But if we don't try them all, there's a chance we'll miss it."

"I like the way you festival."

Braxton steered the stroller to the first food stand. "It's taken years of practice, but I think I've finally perfected it." He gestured to the busy street in front of them. "Every restaurant in a thirty-mile radius is offering a tasting menu today. Some of the best food you'll ever eat is here."

Millie's stomach growled, reminding her she'd skipped breakfast. Perhaps her mismanagement of time was going to work out in her favor. "And you plan on hitting up every one of them?"

"Absolutely. But this challenge is not for the faint of heart. It takes a lot of strategy and pacing to make it to the end. Not everyone can do it."

Millie chuckled, getting in line behind him. "Good thing I came with a pro."

"Right? You're welcome." Laughter danced in his eyes as they got to the front of the line. The server handed each of them a plate with three small cups containing a bite-sized sample of what they claimed were their most popular dishes. There was a seafood paella with a succulent pink Lowcountry shrimp on top, a tiny pane de tomato, and a small ham croquette.

They strolled over to the shade of a giant oak tree to eat. Mouthwatering scents drifted up from the offerings in Millie's hand. She picked up the paella first, admiring how artful even their samples looked.

"This looks delicious, but I don't think I've ever had paella at ten thirty in the morning."

Braxton picked up his own cup. "Rule number one,

festival days forgo traditional meal-time conventions." He dropped the sample size spoon back in his paper tray. "Bottoms up." He clinked his sample cup with Millie's then tossed it back in one big mouthful.

"Apparently, it forgoes traditional utensil use as well," Millie joked.

"The only utensil required around here is a stick." He winked, sending a round of tingles dancing through her which she promptly dismissed.

After they finished their first plate, they grabbed a sample of gelato from the next booth, then strolled past a tent selling photographs of local nature and wildlife. Millie stopped to admire one of the pictures with a bright white seagull flying against a bright blue sky and then the one next to it of a grand oak tree with Spanish moss hanging down from it. Fog swirled around it, creating interesting shadows.

Braxton stopped next to her. "Did you hear about the photographer who had to quit her job?"

Millie turned to him, concerned. "No. Why?"

"She kept losing focus." He spooned a bite of ice cream into his mouth.

Millie chuckled. "Did you just make a joke?"

Braxton shrugged. "I think I did."

His nonchalant attitude made her laugh harder. "I mean, it was a total dad joke, but still. Look who's turning into a funny man."

He flashed her a charming smile. "Stick around. I might have a few more up my sleeve." He took another bite of his ice cream, his eyes meeting hers in a way that made the flock of butterflies return.

Before he could bust out any more cringeworthy one-liners, he waved to an older gentleman Millie remembered from the HOA meeting. "Will you excuse me a minute?"

Braxton steered the stroller over to talk to the man, and

Millie continued wandering around the tent, admiring the art.

"Millie!" She looked up, searching for the source of her name, to find Bonnie waving to her from the sidewalk. She'd been so consumed by the crowds and the booths in the middle of the street she hadn't realized they were standing almost right in front of Daybreak Café.

Millie wove through the crowd on the street to the sidewalk.

"Hello, dear!" Bonnie said, pulling Millie in for her typical greeting hug. "How are you enjoying yourself?"

"This is amazing." Millie's gaze swept the area, taking in the smiling faces, laughter, and comradery that surrounded her. It was the kind of crowd where people called one another by name and asked "how are you" with a genuine interest in knowing the authentic answer. While this sort of open-book life took a little getting used to, there was no doubt in her mind that this was where she was meant to be and continuing her aunt's legacy of offering a home away from home as friendly and caring as the town itself was what she was meant to do.

Bonnie nodded, surveying the crowd. "It's a good turnout this year. Did you come by yourself?"

Millie tossed a glance over her shoulder to where Braxton was still talking with the other man. "No. I came with Braxton Channing."

A look of surprise flashed across Bonnie's face before the corner of her mouth pulled into a knowing smirk.

Millie waved her hands in the air as if erasing Bonnie's thought before it could even be voiced. "No, it's nothing like that. Since I'm new in town, he wanted to make sure I saw the best of what Summer Island had to offer."

Technically speaking, Millie could see how someone would think there was a possibility for something to be there.

Braxton had more than a few good qualities. He was a good father, a loyal friend, and he even cracked the occasional joke that was so bad she couldn't help but laugh. Someone *might* be interested in a guy like that. But she wasn't up for romance of any kind.

And even if she was, Braxton Channing had far too many complications in his life. He would not be interested in adding one more to his pile, especially not one trying to DIY an inn by herself while fighting the very HOA he led.

"He's just... He's being a good neighbor," she finished, not sounding as sure as she'd like.

"Of course he is." Bonnie's smile was more teasing than anything as she handed Millie three colorful paper cupcake wrappers, each holding a small square of her famous iced brownie. "Any new discoveries about the love letters?"

Millie balanced them in her palms, careful to not let the icing touch the sides of the paper cups. "Nothing yet, but I still have a couple more to read. Were you able to find out anything about who the author might be?"

Bonnie shook her head. "Unfortunately, no. I chatted with Camilla yesterday, and she is just as stumped. She can't find any link to Mildred and anyone with a *C* in their name."

Millie let out a sigh. She'd been hoping the ladies might uncover the mystery. "I keep thinking there has to be a clue somewhere that will reveal his identity."

Bonnie patted her hand. "Something will surface." Her gaze flickered for a second to something behind her before she looked at Millie. "Love is one of those things that shows up in the most unexpected places."

They were still talking about Aunt Mildred's letters, weren't they?

"Right." She held up the treats in her hands. "Well, I better deliver these before I'm tempted to eat them all myself."

"Enjoy your day, dear," Bonnie called as Millie crossed the street to where Braxton was waiting for her. As a neighbor. And perhaps a friend.

But absolutely nothing more.

• • •

Braxton couldn't remember the last time he'd had such a good day. It had been the kind of day where everyone was happy and enjoying themselves and the worries of life seemed to be miles away. It was a nice break from the stress he'd been dealing with lately.

"One more, Daddy. Pweese." Alice's face was still red from her last stint in the sea-castle bounce house, which was her sixth inflatable in a row, not to mention the pony rides and petting zoo.

"Not now, sweetheart," he said, not bothering to hide a groan. "It's time for a rest."

"Slide, Daddy, pweese." She pushed her lips out into a pucker and stared at him with those baby blues that made it almost impossible to say no.

He looked up at the line to the inflatable slide in front of them. It was the shortest he'd seen it all day. Plus, Alice did love the slides.

He sighed in defeat, which made Millie smile beside him. "Okay. Last one. Then we rest."

Alice giggled and darted over to get in line. Only, she didn't go to the small five-foot-high slide with giant cartoon zoo animals on it. She ran for the tall slide next to it and got in line behind a kid who had to be three times her age.

"She's very adventurous. That's a tall slide for such a little girl," Millie said as they followed her. "I like that about her."

Fear twisted in Braxton's gut as he studied the slide. It was much too big. He couldn't even reach all the way up the steep ladder side to make sure she didn't fall off.

"Me, too, but I think she overshot this time." He squatted down to get eye to eye with his fearless daughter. "Not this one, Little Foot. That one." He pointed to the smaller toddler-sized slide.

Alice shook her little head. "No, Daddy. Big swide. I go fast."

She squinted her eyes, scrunched her face up, and pulled in her arms in what he could only assume was Alice's interpretation of what she thought she looked like when she went fast. But the sight of it, with her forehead furrowed and her feet widely planted but knees pulled in together, was adorable.

Yes, he wanted her to have adventures and be bold, but within reason. It was his job to keep her safe and giant slides that were out of his reach seemed like a big risk. He couldn't let her put herself into situations where she could get hurt.

"It's too tall, Little Foot. I can't help you get to the top and be there to catch you."

"I can catch her," Millie said, catching him off guard. "That dad followed his kid up the ladder side and someone else is going to catch him."

Anxiety pulsed through him at the mere thought of his daughter at the top of that thing. And leaving her landing in another person's hands? "The risk is too high."

"She's a great climber." Millie gave Braxton a sly look. "And I happen to know from experience that you're pretty good at helping people on ladders."

There was no way he was letting his daughter do something that could go wrong in so many different ways. "She could fall." Among other things, but he didn't feel like rattling through the entire list.

"She won't." There was confidence in her voice, but unless she had some talent involving a crystal ball he didn't know about, there was no way she could know that.

Millie turned her attention to the slide in question. "I've been watching it for a while now, and it seems totally safe. I haven't seen one close call yet." A little boy not much bigger than Alice slid down to the waiting arms of the woman below. "I think Little Speed Racer's got this."

Of course she'd think this. She was one of the most fearless people Braxton had ever encountered. It allowed her to do amazing things like move to a town where she didn't know anyone and learn how to renovate a house. But it also made her reckless at times, like the whole roofing incident.

Braxton stared at the steep ramp ladder again. The main problem was *he* wasn't sure he had this. For Alice to do it, he'd have to let go of her at some point. He physically couldn't protect her the entire way.

As if she could hear the debate in his head, Millie laid a gentle hand on his arm. "You'll be with her all the way up and I'll be waiting for her at the bottom. Trust me. It'll be okay."

There was something about the optimism in her voice combined with her confidence that blew through his soul like a gentle breeze, easing some of the constant fear he carried around.

"You've got this."

Braxton stared at the tall ladder, unsure. Letting go after all that had gone wrong in his life was infinitely harder than he ever imagined it could be. He stared at the inflatable in front of him. But it was only a slide, and Millie would be there to catch them—

Her. Catch her. She was there to catch his daughter at the end of the slide. And he did trust Millie with his daughter, a revelation he didn't have time to look at closely right now.

"Okay," he said before he could talk himself out of it. "Let's do it."

"Big swide!" Alice cheered and scrambled up the ladder.

He followed her all the way to the top, letting his protective hand hover just behind her back, but she never even wobbled. In fact, she made it to the top with less of a struggle than he did. Before he could climb back down, she plopped herself at the top of the slide and pushed herself down.

"Weeee!" Alice held her hands up over her head, a wide smile spread across her whole face as she flew down the brightly colored nylon slope. Millie stood at the end, her arms out ready to grab the child if needed. But Alice stopped well before the end of the inflatable part and crawled the rest of the way to get off. Millie lifted her up and set her on the ground at the same time as Braxton joined them.

"Woo-hoo." Millie pumped her fists in the air, her full attention on the little girl. "You were the fastest!" She turned to Braxton. "And you were pretty great, too."

Braxton picked the little girl up and hugged her into his chest, feeling a bit euphoric. Yes, it was a small fear, but it felt like a big step.

"Again! Again!" Alice chanted.

"That was the last time, remember. It's time for a rest."

"No nap!" Alice swiftly shook her head, rubbing her droopy eyes as she did.

Braxton shot Millie a look to see if she'd caught the difference between Alice's words and actions. She met his gaze and gave him a knowing half grin, then she yawned and stretched her arms over her head. "I'm pretty tired. I could use a rest, too. Maybe we should all take a rest."

Alice stared at Millie as if trying to decide if this was some sort of trick or actually a good idea. "Millie's nap time?"

Millie nodded. "Yep, Millie's nap time, too."

Alice studied her for another second and then she did something that both shocked Braxton and warmed his heart. She held her arms out for Millie to hold her.

"Oh." Millie looked surprised by the little girl's request

and looked from Alice's outstretched arms to Braxton. Braxton gave her a slight nod.

"Okay." Millie looked the most out of her element that he'd ever seen her, but she held her arms out to accept his daughter anyway.

As soon as they made the transfer, Alice patted Millie's face with her little hand. "Millie." There was a hint of adoration in her little voice and her eyes sparkled as she looked at their new neighbor.

His heart surged into a gallop as Alice laid her head on Millie's shoulder, and Millie, already looking more confident, hugged the little girl into herself, rubbing her back.

Braxton grabbed the stroller with one hand and pointed to a shady spot off to the side of the grandstand. "How about we head over there?" He whispered the words, not wanting to break the trance sleepy Alice was under.

Millie nodded, and instinctually Braxton settled his other hand in the small of Millie's back to support her as she walked with the child. At the touch, a warm glow rolled through him as if someone had just turned on the lights in his soul.

He glanced sideways to try to gauge Millie's reaction, and he wasn't quite prepared for what he saw. There was a soft smile on her face, and she looked comfortable holding his daughter and walking with him. Even more shocking was that he felt the same way.

A flurry of emotions swirled through him—tenderness, affection, worry, hope—but he stomped them down to deal with later. His life was complicated. But right now, on this June afternoon with the sounds of a local band lazily drifting through the late afternoon air, he wanted to unwind and enjoy. It had been a long time since he'd felt like this, and he didn't want to mess it up with a bunch of complicated emotions about life and love and loss.

When they got to the patch of grass under the big oak tree, Braxton pulled the picnic blanket from the stroller's basket and spread it out.

"Is she asleep?" Millie twisted around so Braxton could see Alice's face.

The toddler's eyes were closed, her mouth slightly open, and her breathing had become slow and even. Yep. She was out.

Braxton nodded. "Apparently, you're magic. Care to come over every afternoon around two o'clock?"

Millie chuckled quietly, which brightened the glowing feeling already pulsing through him.

He grinned and motioned to the blanket. "You can lay her down there. She should stay asleep."

Millie's eyes darted to the blanket, a look of concern crossing her face, and then glanced back at him. "What if I wake her up?"

The vast majority of the time, Braxton felt like he had no idea what he was doing when it came to being a dad. Alice had only been six weeks old and so tiny and helpless when they'd lost Jade, who had been a fantastic mother. Those weeks that followed were a hazy crash course of him and Henry trying to figure out how to take care of an infant. But they did it. Somehow he got from those long, scary nights—where he had to google everything from how to mix a bottle to what stores sold diapers at two in the morning—to here. And the look of fear combined with the newness on Millie's face reminded him of just how far he'd come.

He gave her what he hoped was an encouraging smile. "She's a hard sleeper. If you move slowly, she won't wake up."

Millie bit her lip in concentration and stared at the blanket for a second before she slowly sank to her knees. She leaned over and gently laid his sleeping daughter on the blanket. But she didn't stop there. She hovered over the little girl, gently brushing Alice's hair out of her face, as she made sure she was going to stay asleep. The gesture was so gentle and sweet, it took Braxton's breath away. Who was this fearless and compassionate stranger who had rolled into their lives?

"I think it worked," Millie whispered, keeping her gaze on Alice.

Braxton nodded, trying desperately to think of something other than how his feelings for her were getting dangerously close to moving past the friend zone. "You're a natural."

Millie rocked back onto her feet and scooted over so she was sitting on the farthest corner of the blanket from the sleeping toddler. "I wasn't so sure that was going to work out."

Braxton chuckled. "Welcome to parenting. It's one giant experiment. And you know what they say about experiments."

Millie shook her head. "No. What?"

"You have to think like a proton and stay positive." He chuckled at his own joke. "I'll show myself out."

Millie rolled her eyes, but at the same time, her lips curled up in an amused grin which made his own smile brighten. "You're killing it with the dad jokes today."

"Baby, you ain't seen nothing yet." He waggled his eyebrows at her, ignoring the swoop in his stomach at how easily the endearment had come out. "How about I get us some drinks? Ruthie's makes the best frozen pineapple-mango smoothies."

"Sounds great. I'll hang here and hope she doesn't wake up."

He left them in the shade and headed for the food truck that made his favorite frozen tropical concoctions, feeling lighter than he had in a long time. He was so consumed by this new emotion that he almost missed Sophia, who was leaning against a tree with her arms crossed in front of her chest, watching him.

"Look who finally remembered how to smile." She gave

him a knowing look.

Braxton pressed his lips together, trying to contain the goofy grin that had spread across his face. "We're at a festival. Isn't that what one does at a festival?"

Sophia shrugged, looking unconvinced. "Some people, maybe. But not you. You're usually too busy calculating the risk assessment."

He shook his head at his longtime friend and continued walking toward the food truck.

She followed him. "And I even spotted a confirmed Braxton Channing laugh." She widened her eyes in a look of fake shock.

Braxton stepped into line, scanning the festival menu to make sure they were offering his favorite drink. "Maybe your eyes were playing tricks on you. Too much sun can do that, you know. It's important to stay hydrated at these kinds of events."

She nodded. "Right? At first, I thought I was imagining it, but then there it was again, plain as day right in front of me."

Sophia's tone switched to something more serious. "It's been a while, a very long while, since I've seen you laugh. It was nice to see you've found someone who can make you do it again."

Braxton looked over at where they'd set up the blanket for nap time. Millie was bobbing her head to the beat of the music as she glanced down periodically at Alice sleeping next to her. The same complicated swirl of emotions twisted through him again.

The truth was, it had been a great day, one full of carefree fun and laughter. Braxton couldn't remember the last time he'd had a day like this, but it had been a while. Sure, he'd had happy moments here and there, but entire happy, carefree days? Life just hadn't dealt him one of those recently. Was the last time he felt like this before Henry went to live at Summer Island Memory Care Home? Or before the accident? Or had it been even longer than that?

But the fact that his first joyful day in years was with Millie had to be simply a coincidence. It was the same way when he shot a near-perfect round on his favorite course on a still, sunny day. It had nothing to do with the color of his shirt or who he was paired with. When the conditions are perfect, great things happen, regardless of who you're with.

With a slight shake of his head, Braxton dismissed Sophia's suggestion. "It's nothing. I only offered to show her around the festival as a goodwill gesture after the whole HOA letter thing. Speaking of which, did you find out anything?"

He'd called Sophia and told her everything, enlisting her help in discovering who'd been sending out the warnings without approval from the board or him.

"Nothing that would be very useful." Sophia switched to her serious businesswoman attitude that made her an excellent HOA secretary and his most trusted ally on the board. "I keep a record any time someone uses your signature, but anyone on the board could access it. They'd have to do some digging or know where it is, but it wasn't password protected."

"We should probably fix that."

Sophia nodded. "Already done."

"So you think it's someone on the board?"

"It appears to be. But I can't imagine who on the board would do something like this."

Braxton couldn't either. To be honest, the thought that a board member would do this was disturbing. Not only did they all take the same oath to protect their neighborhood and their neighbors, he considered each of the other eight members a friend.

He shook away the thought as he stepped up to the

window to order. Today was much too pleasant of a day to get bogged down with that. "Well, thanks for checking." He motioned at the window. "You want anything? I'm buying."

"Anytime. And I'd love a pineapple-mango fusion."

Braxton held three fingers up to the server. "We'll have three of those. Thanks."

The teasing glint returned to his friend's eyes. "She makes you laugh and you're buying her drinks? Doesn't sound like nothing to me."

The server passed him the first two frozen concoctions topped with little umbrellas and brightly colored paper straws.

"You've been known to crack a joke, and I'm buying you a drink. I'm quite certain there isn't anything between us." He handed her both cups for emphasis. "Besides, I thought we were finished with this conversation."

Sophia took the drinks. "Simply calling it how I see it." She flashed him a knowing smile and made a dramatic show of taking a long pull from one of the striped paper straws.

"Then maybe it's time you get your eyes checked," Braxton joked. He grabbed the last drink and turned toward the blanket where Millie and his daughter waited.

Sophia walked with him. "All I'm saying is that it's nice to see you happy again. You deserve it."

She flashed him a sympathetic smile just before they reached the blanket, then switched all of her attention to Millie.

"Hey!" She dropped her voice to an excited whisper as she squatted down next to Millie on the blanket. She handed Millie one of the cups and gave her shoulders a squeeze with her free hand.

"Thanks for this," Millie whispered before she took a sip.

"It's from Braxton. I just got the privilege of carrying it over." She motioned to where he was standing behind them.

"But I've been looking for you. I am totally free Thursday and Friday to help you with tiling the bathrooms. Tessa said she'll be in and out with her tours, but she's excited to help. With the three of us working on it, I bet we can knock out at least three or four of them."

"The three on the south end are all ready to go, so that'll be perfect. And Gus said we could use his tile saw." Millie gave a small fist pump.

"Great." She rocked back on her heels and stood. "I gotta run. The Sea Salt & Chocolate booth has been busy all day. But y'all enjoy. The band that's coming up next is fantastic."

Braxton took her place on the blanket. "A tiling party? You ladies know how to have a good time."

Millie took another sip of her drink. "They're just being kind to the new girl in town who never goes out because of the never-ending renos. Plus, I think they're worried if I don't get enough human interaction, I'll turn into one of those lonely old ladies who doesn't just talk to dogs but thinks they talk back."

"I've met Bear. The way he looks at you, there's a very high probability he might talk back."

Millie nodded. "I keep telling people that, but they don't listen."

"But I resent the statement that Bear is the only one you talk to. I've rescued you from your roof and interrupted your peaceful twilight walks on the beach. How much more human interaction do you need?" He pulled a face to show his mock offense.

She grinned, her eyes sparkling in the sunlight. "And don't forget driving me to the festival while singing carpool karaoke to princess songs."

He shrugged. "You're lucky to have such a great neighbor."

"Great's the adjective we're settling on?"

"I'm not opposed to spectacular if you think it's a better fit. Or maybe awesome?" He was fighting a losing battle with the smile tugging on his lips.

She raised an eyebrow.

"Or we could drop the adjective all together."

"Yes, let's go with that."

He chuckled. "Fair enough."

She held up her frozen drink. "To neighbors."

He clinked his clear plastic cup with hers, meeting her gaze in a way that sent electricity racing through him. "To neighbors," he echoed.

He took a drink, not even bothering to try to make the electricity stop. His already complicated life was about to get more complicated if he wasn't careful.

Chapter Twelve

On Friday night Millie and Sophia stood in the shower of one of her guest bathrooms, pressing the custom cut tiles that Tessa handed them into the thin-set mortar on the wall.

"I'm not going to lie. Tiling is kind of therapeutic." Millie stepped back and examined the wall she was working on, breathing in the satisfaction of seeing all the shiny white rectangles lined up in perfectly spaced rows. "I think I've found myself a new hobby."

Tessa pushed the safety goggles to the top of her head and looked at the wall, too. "If you like this, you should try helping Soph hand-pack her chocolates during her busy seasons. There's nothing quite like making those perfect little rows surrounded by the scent of chocolate."

"That sounds like a project I can wholeheartedly get behind." Millie turned to Sophia. "Count me in."

"I'm glad you find it therapeutic. Those seasons stress me out. Without fail, the tighter the deadline, the higher the likelihood of something breaking. Last Valentine's Day, it was my wrist. Do you know how hard it is to whisk with a broken wrist?" Sophia let out a loud, exaggerated sigh.

Tessa nodded. "Why does it always work like that? Next week is one of my busiest weeks so far this summer. Almost every tour is fully booked, and now we have this dumb hurricane lurking in the Atlantic."

At the word "hurricane" the hairs on Millie's neck stood up. "Did you just say a hurricane is coming here?" There was no denying the hint of panic in her voice. She looked from Tessa to Sophia.

Sophia waved an airy hand as she reached for the next tile, as if the threat of a violent storm was inconsequential. "It's nothing to worry about yet. Right now it's way south and it's only a tropical depression that's predicted to become a hurricane. It'll be almost a week before it makes it this far north."

"But it's coming here?" Maybe it was time she started watching the local news for the weather report. In the time that she'd lived here, the weather had been so consistent, she hadn't been concerned about it. But now a big storm was headed their direction in less than a week?

Tessa shrugged. "Forecasts have it heading this way, which means I have to start thinking about contingency plans. Even if it doesn't hit us, it'll make the seas around here rough. And I can't take a dive trip out with a high-sea warning."

Sophia shot her a sympathetic look. "Maybe it'll blow itself out before it gets here. It's still pretty far away."

Clearly, Millie needed to do a little more research on this hurricane thing if she was going to live next to the ocean. "Can it do that? Blow itself out? Like it just disappears?"

"Sometimes. That's the thing about storms. They're not super predictable. They tend to have a mind of their own." Tessa pulled the pencil from behind her ear and marked the cutline on the tile in front of her. "But Sophia's right. It's still too far out to get concerned about yet. We'll have to wait and see what it does."

"But there's a different, much more pressing topic we need to spend some time on." Sophia paused and shot Millie a scandalous look. "One that involves a certain neighbor."

"What's going on with Braxton?" Tessa asked, because apparently there was no need to clarify which neighbor.

Millie didn't feel any more at ease with the new topic, so she picked up the next tile, trying to distract herself. "He lives next door. Nothing to talk about."

"They were hanging out at the Beach Front Festival," Sophia said.

From the corner of her eye, she could see Tessa's eyebrows shoot up. "Really? How did I miss this?"

"Because you were busy running the bodyboarding and standup paddling workshops. You never made it off the beach," Sophia said.

"*Because* there was nothing to miss," Millie added. "We weren't hanging out. He gave me a ride since parking is such an issue." She tried to ignore the fluttery excitement that seemed to show up every time she thought of Braxton.

"If your definition of not hanging out means sampling food together, playing with Alice and setting her down for a nap, and then sitting on a blanket sharing drinks while listening to the music show then, yeah"—Sophia grinned—"you totally didn't hang out."

The heat firing up Millie's cheeks no doubt gave her away, and she groaned.

"Methinks thou doth protest too much." Tessa flashed a knowing grin.

Millie rolled her eyes. "If there were scandalous details, I'd give them to you. But the reality isn't that exciting. He drove me to the festival in his minivan and pointed me in the direction of the best food booths. At the end of the day, he dropped me off in front of my house. That's it."

"He laughed," Sophia told Tessa.

Memories of Braxton's laughter floated to the front of her mind. That part she couldn't deny. Yes, he'd gone a little overboard with the dad jokes, but it was more than that. He was witty. And smart and interesting and...

She let the thought fade away because, like she said before, it was nothing.

"Braxton laughed, huh?" Tessa exchanged a glance with Sophia.

"I'm pretty sure it was the festival that made him smile. I just happened to be the one who rode in the car with him." It was true, after all, wasn't it? Just because it was a great day didn't mean there was anything there. She wasn't interested in anything more, and he had more than enough going on in his life. They were neighbors. The end.

She went back to tiling. "It's nothing. In fact, I haven't even seen him since."

She left off the part that she had, however, noticed his house had been unusually still the past couple of days and she wondered if he'd gone out of town. Which, by the way, didn't say anything about how she was feeling. After all, watching his house was a very neighborly thing to do, wasn't it?

• • •

Saturday morning was quiet around Braxton's house and it made him anxious. Over the past couple days, he'd taken Alice to Atlanta to spend the week with her maternal grandparents. It was something he did twice a year, since it gave Alice a chance to bond with her mother's side of the family. It also gave Braxton a little break from the constant demands of being a single father while giving Lena a much-needed week off.

Braxton knew it was a good thing, but the quiet house

was always a bit unnerving.

So far today he'd gone to the gym, spent the morning getting caught up on work, and paid his daily visit to Henry. It was only two o'clock and Braxton had already finished everything on his to-do list, leaving him alone and restless in his quiet, empty house.

He walked out to the back porch as he sorted through ideas of how to fill the rest of his empty hours. He could read. There were a couple new books he'd been wanting to get to. Or he could take his kayak out and go fishing. It'd been a while since he'd paddled through the marsh. Those were exactly the kinds of activities his former in-laws suggested he do with his "free time."

Braxton pulled his phone from his pocket, ready to look up the tide schedule, when something else caught his attention. A single someone was at the edge of the long exterior wall of the neighboring house. There was a good amount of space between where he was on his deck and where her house started, but he could tell it was Millie by the dark wavy hair pulled back with a pink baseball cap. She was painting the wood siding armed with nothing but a single paintbrush and a ladder.

He watched for a second as she dipped and painted, dipped and painted, over and over until she had adequately covered the small area she was working on. She stepped back to study it and wiped her forehead with her arm. The amount of area the fresh paint covered looked painfully small next to the amount of wall that remained. She would have to repeat that process hundreds of times to finish the entire side of the house.

Seemingly undeterred by the amount of siding left, Millie dipped her brush in the paint tray and went back to work. There was something about watching her tackle the enormous job stroke by tiny stroke that impressed him, and

Braxton suddenly had a great idea for how he could spend the rest of his day.

After a quick wardrobe change and grabbing two cold bottles of water from the fridge, he headed down his front porch and walked out to the end of his driveway.

This was the first time he'd ever walked to his neighbor's house. After five years of living in this house, he'd only ever visited his neighbors by car, which now felt very impersonal.

He walked past the crew of workers going in and out of Millie's house and around to the side.

"Hey there, neighbor," he said as she came into view.

She paused mid-stroke and a grin pulled at the corners of her mouth.

"Is this my daily safety protocol lecture?" There was a joking tone to her words and she rested her paintbrush on the paint tray while all her attention was focused on him.

"I racked my brain but can't think of one safety tip for painting." He shrugged and handed her one of the bottles in his hand. "Seriously, though, if you'd like some help, I'd love to lend a hand."

She took a long drink of her water and then stared at him.

"You want to spend your afternoon helping me paint this behemoth?" Her eyes narrowed as if she doubted what she'd heard.

Braxton couldn't decide if he should be offended at her disbelief, but he filed that thought in the back of his mind to be revisited later. "Painting behemoths happens to be my specialty."

"Really?"

"Believe it or not, I've painted a wall before."

"The mighty Braxton Channing has painted a wall?" she teased.

He waggled his eyebrows, easing into their now familiar banter. "I'm a man of many talents."

"Clearly. And you want to put those talents to use today on the exterior of my house?"

"Yours seems to be the only house around getting a new paint job today, so..." He looked around as if searching for other houses to paint. "I guess I'm here by default."

That made her smile, which sent sunlight dancing through him.

She handed him the paintbrush she was holding. "Well, I don't let just anyone paint my house. You'll have to prove you're worthy of the task."

He took the brush from her. After dipping it in the tray on the ground, he pressed it against the wall. Since he was almost a foot taller than she was, he could reach farther up, and he started covering the part just above where she had been.

She stood next to him, staring up at the wall with her hands on her hips until he had fully covered a two-foot square and he needed more paint.

"Not bad."

"What? You think all I do is stand around and look good? I'm more than just a pretty face."

"Awww, that's sweet." She playfully patted his cheek. "You think you have a pretty face."

Braxton shook his head, but this banter confirmed the reason he came. Being around her was fun. A lot more fun than casting a fishing line by himself. He didn't need more alone time. He needed—

"I guess you're hired. You want to paint, and I don't want to hinder such a natural talent. Have at it." She motioned to the wall in front of them.

He reapplied paint and returned the brush to the wall.

Millie watched over him for a minute before walking over to the tub of supplies near the corner of the house. "Where's the little miss today?"

"Biannual visit with her grandparents." He painted a few strokes as he considered how to explain the situation that was complicated at best. "Her, um, mother's parents. They live in Atlanta."

Millie pulled out a second paintbrush and stepped up next to him. She dipped it into the paint and began to cover the patch of wall in front of her. "What a great way to keep her mother's memory alive."

Braxton had to agree. Sylvia and Thomas were the kind of warm and devoted parents everyone dreamed of having, and it seemed they were made to be grandparents. They'd doted on Alice from the moment they found out she would be coming into this world. Every child deserved to have someone like that in their life.

"But it must be very hard on you. You're brave to let her go."

Braxton considered her words. Was he brave? He didn't feel brave. Everything he'd done for the past two years had been done out of necessity. Raising Alice alone, moving Henry into the assisted living home, simply trying to survive.

Taking Alice to Atlanta to visit her maternal grandparents was the right thing to do. Braxton knew that in his soul. Alice deserved to be around her biological family and learn from them how amazing her mother had been, and Braxton trusted Jade's parents. But it always came with mixed feelings.

On the one hand, it was a nice break to not have to be in charge all the time. He enjoyed having a moment of freedom. There was nothing brave about wanting to sleep past 5:30 a.m. or eating a leisurely meal whenever he felt like it. But on the other hand, leaving Alice in another state in the full care of someone other than himself was hard. When she was out of his direct care there was no way he could keep her from getting hurt, and that terrified him.

Plus, with Alice gone, the house was too quiet, especially

at 5:30 a.m. and during mealtimes.

"She's playing with cousins and getting completely spoiled by her grandparents. It's a good thing." At least that's what he kept telling himself. "And it's a short visit. I'll fly there on Sunday to get her."

Millie squatted down to focus on covering the bottom edge of the house. "So you're living the bachelor life for the next six days, huh? What wild and carefree adventures await you?"

Braxton dipped his brush in the tray, then wiped it on the side to prevent any drips. "There's this monster house that needs painting and I am armed with a paintbrush and a five-gallon barrel of paint. So this party is about to get lit."

She chuckled. "Lit, huh? I guess it's a good thing you showed up. Before you got here, I was starting to think this was the most monotonous task I'd attempted so far."

Playfulness danced through him. It had been a while since he felt like this. Sure, he'd had moments of fun, and there had been plenty of excitement over the past several years, but he hadn't felt playful. There was just something about being around Millie that made him want to smile again. Hope again. Laugh again.

And even though every logical thought in his brain told him to run the other direction, this time his heart won and he stood firmly where he was, wide goofy grin and all.

Chapter Thirteen

Millie hadn't expected painting the exterior of Seascape to be fun. In fact, she'd been dreading the task since the moment she circled it on the reno task list.

There was even a little note next to it declaring it the first item moved to the contract's list if she came up with extra money, which now seemed laughable. Just this morning, she'd maxed out her last credit card as Gus's crew started construction on the new boardwalk over the dunes so her future guests wouldn't have to hop from one large rock to the next as she'd been doing. It wasn't the boardwalk she envisioned, or even the one she wanted—it was more of a low wooden walkway without handrails—but it was all she could afford.

To be honest, it was more than she could afford, but at least it'd be finished on time. She hoped.

When it came to renovations, there was never any extra money or extra time. However, there was no lack of surprises.

Like Braxton showing up for the second day in a row to help her paint the house. Together, they'd finished the long side wall and most of the back, which was far more than she'd thought she'd be able to accomplish on her own. She was even ahead of schedule. A few more days like this and she might actually have a chance at having everything done before the open house which was rapidly approaching.

He propped his paintbrush against the paint bucket and stepped back with his hands on his hips to examine the wall they were working on. "Not bad. What do you think?"

Instead of admiring their work, Millie admired Braxton. Somehow, when he was busy lecturing her about HOA rules and safety protocols, she'd missed how attractive he was. And now that she'd noticed, it was hard to look away.

"Not bad at all." She was at least partially referring to the wall. Probably. "But I think you missed a spot."

He squinted up at the wall. "Really? Where?"

"Right here." She dabbed her paintbrush against his cheek, leaving a seashell-white smear along his strong jawline.

The expression on his face was priceless. It went from serious and stony to wide-eyed with shock then softened into a playful grin. It was a micro glimpse of how his attitude had changed since she met him, and the transformation made her giddy. "No worries. I got it for you."

"Oh, so that's how it's going to be." He wiped the spot on his face and surveyed the amount of paint that had come off on his fingers. "I should probably wash this off."

He grabbed the hose and leaned over, as if he was going to spray the water on his face, but just as he squeezed the handle, he flipped his wrist, pointing the nozzle right at Millie.

The cold water hit the side of her body, causing her to gasp. She jumped out of the way, water dripping off her arm.

"Oops. Didn't see you there." He shot her the kind of roguish grin that made her heart do a stutter step.

"It happens." She shook off the water droplets from her left arm and fanned the side of her shirt to air it out a bit.

"However, this also has a tendency to happen." With a swift move, she picked up her brush and spun it, swiveled, and then ran it down his arm.

Braxton stared down at his shirt, his mouth hanging open. "Hey! This is my favorite shirt."

The outburst caused Millie to pause. Maybe she'd taken it too far, but to be fair, she hadn't meant to paint his shirt. She was aiming for his arm but the fancy move threw her off.

She laid her brush down and grabbed the rag she had hanging from a loop on her toolbelt. "Sorry. Let me just…" She stepped closer to him, ready to dab the paint off his sleeve, when icy water hit her right in the chest. The shock combined with the coldness momentarily took her breath away.

"Just kidding. Who wears their favorite shirt to paint?" Mischief sparkled in his cobalt eyes and a wide smile stretched across his face.

Millie stared down at her drenched shirt. "So that's how we're going to play this, huh?" She backpedaled, grabbing for the brush to defend herself. She tried to dodge the water spray as she swiped at him with the paintbrush, but it was no use. In this situation, the water hose was the more successful weapon. She squinted through the spray and reached for one final attempt of smearing him with ivory paint. But she missed, running the roller across Bear instead, who'd come off the porch to check out the situation.

"Oh no!" She let the paintbrush fall to her side as she rubbed the dog's head. "Sorry, buddy. I didn't mean for you to get caught in the crossfire."

Braxton let go of the sprayer, stopping the heavy stream of water coming from the hose. "Guess everyone's getting a shower tonight." He walked closer to Millie to examine the ivory strip running down Bear's caramel fur. "Although, I gotta say, the color looks good on you, boy."

Millie giggled. "Will you spray him off so we can get the

paint out before it sets? I'll grab some shampoo." She made a grand gesture of setting her brush down and holding up her hands in surrender as she backed toward the porch. "And how about we call a truce before anything else gets painted?"

"Deal." Braxton wiped his face on the sleeve of his shirt which did nothing more than smear the paint all the way across his cheek. "I don't know about you, but all this manual labor has worked up quite an appetite." He switched the sprayer to the gentle shower setting and held it close to Bear's back.

Millie returned with the shampoo and squirted a line along the paint stripe. "Same. Since I've started full-time home improvements, I'm starving by the end of every day. Now I know why Gus always has a jar of peanuts with him."

"Would you like to come over for dinner? I have a freezer full of gourmet meals Lena left me before she went on vacation." He rubbed his head, looking a little unsure of himself for the first time since she'd met him. "You know, nothing fancy. I can throw one in the oven and you could come over after you get cleaned up or dried off or whatever."

Wait? Had Braxton just asked her out? Suddenly, her wet clothes weren't the only thing making her cold. Icy apprehension pricked her chest. "Oh, umm…" She pretended to focus on lathering the shampoo in her dog's thick fur as a thousand thoughts raced through her mind. Dinner? With Braxton?

Sure, today had been a lot of fun, but it just sort of happened. It didn't mean anything. Dinner was different.

"Nothing formal," Braxton said, stepping forward with the hose to rinse off Bear. "Food that's already prepared. Maybe even served on paper plates."

"Right, no. It's just that…" She let her words trail off again, because what was it? Dinner—at his house, no less— felt personal. It felt like the kind of thing that could lead to something more. Something she promised herself she wasn't getting involved in, especially with someone like Braxton Channing.

"I have a lot I need to work on tonight."

The excuse was sort of true. Seascape was a lot to work on all the time. The list of projects that still needed to be done before the open house in just over two weeks seemed never-ending. And once she finally checked every single one of them off, it would be time to start phase two. *If* Braxton and his board decided to approve her appeal.

But the overwhelming list of projects and the looming deadline weren't the only reasons she was passing on Braxton's dinner invitation. The truth was, she found herself looking over at his house more often than she should, and the way her heart fluttered when he flashed one of those charming grins made her nervous.

She didn't have a great track record when it came to relationships. In the past, she'd let one relationship after the other derail her dreams, realizing too late that the only person doing any sort of sacrificing was her. She wasn't about to do it again. Not this time.

A hint of disappointment flickered across Braxton's face but he quickly replaced it with his easy grin and a nonchalant shrug. "Sure. No big deal."

They gave Bear one final rinse, then she released the dog so he could shake off the excess water. Braxton turned away, busying himself with winding up the hose. Millie replaced the lid on the paint bucket, still considering his invitation. Turning him down was the right thing to do, she was sure of it. Yes, she enjoyed his company and appreciated his help, but anything more would complicate things too much.

She was being smart. So, why did a tinge of regret nudge at her?

Annoyed, she pushed the feelings away and focused on

the task, which was moving the almost full five-gallon paint bucket to the part of the covered porch where she was storing the painting supplies overnight. She squatted slightly and, using both hands, hefted up the bucket. It wasn't that it was too heavy for her to carry, but combined with the awkward size, she had to sort of waddle to move across the yard.

"Here, let me help you." Braxton jogged over and grabbed one side of the handle, instantly making the load lighter. She dropped one hand and they walked side by side the rest of the way to the porch.

They set the bucket down on the drop cloth she'd spread out earlier to protect the patio, and Millie propped her hands on her hips to catch her breath.

Braxton was tying the top of the trash bag he'd been filling before he stopped to help her. Beyond him, the sight of the freshly painted walls caught her eye.

"Thanks for all your help the past two days." She hoped the sincerity in her voice portrayed the magnitude behind those simple words. "I really appreciate it."

"My pleasure." He lifted the trash bag. "Would you like for me to throw this in the dumpster on my way out?"

"Since you spent your afternoon helping me, the least I can do is walk you out." She reached down and scooped up the pile of oversize garbage items waiting to be taken to the dumpster. "But I'm not going to pass up the opportunity of having someone make a trash run. If you carry the bag, I can carry all of this."

They walked around the long side of the house toward the front yard, both carrying armfuls of trash. "The biggest surprise about this whole renovation process is the amount of garbage it has produced. I'm doing my best to recycle what I can, but there never seems to be an end to the stuff going in the dumpster."

Braxton nodded. "I remember that feeling. But it gets

better."

"That's what you keep saying." They reached the dumpster and she tossed her things over the top, then turned to examine the front of her house. "I think I'll have to see it before I believe it."

"From what I see, it's already looking a lot better." He grinned. "In fact, you'll have to give me the name of your painter."

Millie shrugged, knocking back the unwelcome but ever-present fluttery feeling. "I'm not sure you can afford him."

Braxton chuckled. "I really enjoyed today." His eyes met hers with an expression that sizzled through her.

"Me, too," she said, which was the truth. "Thanks for everything."

She watched him pause in front of his gate to pull his phone from his pocket. He hit a few buttons, then waited while the giant wrought-iron structure swung open. He threw one last glance back in her direction, held his hand up in a wave, then disappeared onto his property.

Millie turned back to her own house. As she paused on her front porch to dry off Bear with one of the towels she left by the door, she tried her best not to let thoughts of Braxton distract her. She had dozens of other things she needed to be thinking about. There were reno decisions she had to make. Those new cabinet pulls weren't going to pick themselves out. Plus, she needed to start considering an advertising and marketing campaign for once she was able to officially open.

And of course there was the more pressing issue of what she was going to eat since she declined Braxton's dinner invitation. Satisfied that Bear was as dry as she could get him with a towel, she strolled through her house into her outdated kitchen. She washed her hands then pulled open the freezer to examine her dinner options, confident she'd made the right decision.

The only problem was that he seemed to occupy the valuable real estate at the front of her mind. And her mood must be transmitting somehow, because suddenly Bear was at her side, nudging her knee. Or maybe it was the prospect of food.

"It's nothing, Bear. I'm just processing the events of the day, which is totally normal." She popped an unappetizing frozen dinner into the microwave and studied the nutrition information on the package to distract herself from thinking about what sort of gourmet meal Braxton was heating up. Or the conversation they might have had if she'd taken him up on his offer.

But when a comprehensive examination of the entire box only took thirty seconds into her four-minute wait time, she decided she needed another activity to occupy her mind.

"How about we get out of these wet clothes." She tugged on the damp shirt, actively trying to avoid thinking about how she got wet. "We've got more work to do tonight."

Sure, she'd had fun hanging out with Braxton and painting all afternoon. And she probably would've had fun if she'd joined him for dinner. But fun wasn't the point. The point was that she had other things she had to do. Important things. And she wasn't going to sacrifice them for some other person's important things.

She made her way through the empty rooms to her private suite on the other side of the house

"After dinner, what do you say we get a jump start on cleaning the tile floors in the guest rooms? If we knock that out today, we can reseal them tomorrow." She scratched Bear behind his ears before she peeled off her damp clothes and hung them over the bathtub. "See how productive we can be when we stay focused?"

The stack of clean T-shirts in her closet was dwindling down to almost gone and there was only one pair of shorts left. It looked like a load of laundry needed to be added to her to-do list.

With her dry clothes on, she grabbed a laundry basket and started filling it. On her way to the laundry room, she paused in her room to collect any stray clothes that hadn't made it into the hamper in her closet when the stack of love letters sitting on her bedside table caught her eye.

There were still two left. Two neatly folded sheets of stationery were all that stood between her and the end of the love story. She paused and ran her finger over the satin ribbon that held them together. What could've happened that made it end? Mr. C was clearly smitten with Mildred and from the way he talked in the letters, that love was reciprocated.

Millie was dying to know what happened to end the romance that, according to the dates on the top, had spanned from at least February to April the following year, and at the same time, she wasn't ready for their love story to be over.

"What if we just read one of them," she said to Bear. The dog wagged his tail, which she took as a sign he supported her plan.

She slid the second-to-last envelope from the pile and a familiar warmth surged through her. She loved these letters. Just the thought of reading them made her feel less lonely. It made the house seem less empty. Imagining her great-aunt here, with the man she loved and a house full of guests and, well, furniture, even made her footsteps seem less echoey.

She dropped the letter on the kitchen counter while she started the load of laundry. When she returned to the kitchen, she pulled her flavorless-yet-convenient frozen dinner from the microwave and, sinking down onto the barstool, took the letter out of the envelope.

"And now, Bear, for your dining entertainment, the latest edition of Aunt Mildred's romance."

She took her first bite of rubbery chicken and started

reading.

My darling Mildred,

I imagine sunsets along this particular stretch of beach have always been inspiring. But they are never quite as lovely as when I am enjoying them with you.

Tonight's sunset was perhaps one of the most stunning I have ever seen. The brilliant pinks and lavenders in the sky reflected in the oceans, turning even the deepest blue at the horizon a rosy shade of pink. After living here most of my life, I've never seen anything quite like it. But what made it most special, my love, was that I got to experience it with you.

It is true that the sun would have set whether or not you were with me on the beach tonight. The rhythm of life continues from one setting of the sun to the next as the world slowly spins in its predictable pattern. Daily tasks, however mundane, are required and completed and checked on a list. However, I am considered one of the lucky ones for even my most mundane task sparkles when I have you to share it with.

But every once in a while, something astonishing happens. We get a break from the mundane and the opportunity to gaze upon sheer perfection. From here on out one thing that can never be taken away from me is that I once experienced the most amazing sunset imaginable, and it was even more special because I got to share it with you.

Always,

Millie laid the letter on the counter and closed her eyes, letting the words echo in her mind.

"That was the most romantic one yet." She opened her eyes and combed over the words again, letting the love resonate off the page. "'Even my most mundane task sparkles when I have you to share it with.' Isn't that beautiful?" She forked a few limp green beans into her mouth and chewed.

Maybe the relationship didn't work out, but at this moment, she envied her Aunt Mildred. Sure, Millie had had boyfriends before. She might even go so far as to say she'd been in love before. But not one of her past love interests had adored her the way this man adored Aunt Mildred.

She looked down at Bear. "What would it feel like to have someone like that in our lives?"

Her dog cocked his furry eyebrows.

"What? Don't give me that questioning look. We've never had that. Especially not with…" She let her voice trail off, not even wanting to speak the name of her most recent failed relationship. Her gaze drifted out the small window over the kitchen sink as she considered all the ways that particular relationship had been doomed from day one.

And that's when her eyes caught sight of Braxton's house.

The sight of his house and the thought of his deep laugh filled her with a bright, bubbly feeling.

Wait—a light, bubbly feeling while eating a more than mundane freezer dinner, echoes of laughter while completing her most dreaded project… Could it be that she…?

She let that thought trail off, too, because it was ridiculous. They were barely at the point of being friends.

Bear continued to stare at her with those cocked eyebrows and a judging look.

Millie looked away to try to avoid him and kept eating her dinner. "It's nothing. Just two friends who had a little fun while painting a house. I don't even know why I'm letting a dog make me rethink it." She glanced back at Bear's sweet face. "No offense."

Bear let out a loud sigh and flopped down on the floor next to her feet, as if to acknowledge that neither one of them was buying the nonsense she was spewing. Whether or not she was willing to admit it out loud, Braxton had made her mundane tasks sparkle. And what made it even worse was that even her dog seemed to know it.

She let out her own long sigh and picked up her phone, well aware that she was arguing with a dog. "Fine. I'll ask him if he wants to come help paint tomorrow. But don't be surprised if he says no. It's not like he's writing us love letters."

She typed the message and hit send before she could rethink her decision, then plonked her phone facedown on the tile counter with a loud *thud*.

"There. Done. Happy now?" She wasn't sure if she was asking Bear or herself, but she rolled her eyes for good measure and stuffed another oversalted-yet-bland bite of her dinner into her mouth. She hadn't even finished chewing when her phone dinged to alert a new message.

She paused mid-chew and stared at the turquoise phone case in front of her. Surely, that wasn't from him, was it?

Slowly, she lifted it up and turned it over to look at the screen.

I'd love to. See you at 3?

He'd *love* to?

She quickly liked his reply and flipped the phone back over, promising herself that she wouldn't read more into it than there was. Still, she couldn't stop one corner of her mouth pulling up into a grin.

"He's just being nice and he's trying to keep his mind off his daughter being away. There's nothing to get excited about," she told Bear. But it didn't matter what she said.

Braxton Channing said he'd love to come help her with the mundane task of painting her house, and at the moment, everything around her seemed to sparkle.

• • •

On day four of living the single life, Braxton was starting to feel in rhythm.

In the morning, he took care of all his realtor duties. After a quick lunch, he'd go to Summer Island Memory Care Home for his daily game of chess with Henry. And by three o'clock, he'd be at Millie's house, ready to help her with whatever project was on deck. And, although it'd taken some convincing, they now topped off the evening with a late dinner on his patio, compliments of whatever Lena had left in his freezer.

Braxton wondered what kind of project he'd be helping Millie with later today as he pressed the buzzer at Summer Island Memory Care Home just after noon. While he fiercely missed hearing Alice's sweet giggles and footsteps around his house, this week was turning out to be not so bad.

"Hello, Mr. Channing. Come on in." The voice rang through as the electronic buzz signaled the door opening.

As usual, Veronica was waiting for him on the other side of the second set of doors. "You're early today."

"I had some extra time, so I thought I'd spend it here. Is he finished with lunch?"

"He finished a while ago, and I'm not sure where he's gone off to now. He normally wanders around the gardens until the alarm on his phone tells him to meet you in the parlor."

"Not a problem. I'll wait over there until he's ready."

"Are you kidding? Seeing you is the highlight of his day. He'll be thrilled you showed up early. Let me go see if I can find him." Veronica patted his hand and then scurried off in the direction of the door that led to the courtyard garden.

Braxton headed over to their usual table, thinking through the rest of his day. Since he and Millie finished painting the exterior of her house last night, she'd mentioned maybe they could get started on the landscaping today. It'd been a while since he'd spent much time digging in the dirt. Maybe when Alice came home he should plant something with her. Tomatoes or herbs or something else that could grow in pots, maybe. It would be good for her to watch something grow.

While he thought through the prospects, he squared up and gripped a pretend golf club as if he was getting ready to hit a pretend golf ball in front of him. His thoughts drifted back to Millie. Maybe she'd like to come over and help him and Alice plant their new garden. Alice seemed to like her, and it would be good for her to have positive female role models in her life.

He swung his pretend golf club in a practice swing. His lower back was stiff, but what bothered him the most was the way his right shoulder dipped. That particular faulty form had plagued him his whole life. He'd spent hours at the driving range working on breaking the bad habit. As if on autopilot, he quickly reset and swung again, paying close attention to his shoulder.

"Wow. Mr. Channing."

Braxton, still holding his back-swing position, looked over his shoulder at where Veronica was standing with Henry. Shock covered Veronica's face while something that looked more like smug satisfaction covered Henry's.

And then it clicked why his back was stiff.

He hadn't done that motion in more than two years.

Dropping his pretend golf club, he shoved his hands into his pockets and turned to them. He worked hard to keep his conflicting emotions from showing on his face. Did he really just take a practice swing without even thinking about it? What had possessed him to do such a thing?

Veronica's shock melted into a sort of starstruck look. "I've never seen you swing before. At least not in person." She knew all about his story and the reason he'd walked away from the sport, but they'd never once talked about it.

In fact, he didn't talk about it with anyone. The last time any words about golf were spoken was when he wrote a letter about it to put in Henry's journal of "things I should know about my life."

"You looked good, Mr. Channing." Veronica smiled up at him as she pulled out the chair for Henry.

Henry still had his smug grin. "You were meant to swing a club. It's in your blood."

Braxton sank into the chair across from him, his mind whirling. "It's nothing. Just a habit."

Henry shrugged. "If you say so." He moved his pawn to e4, a classic opening move. One that was more indicative of when they used to play on the road for golf tournaments.

Of course, it wasn't nothing. It'd been more than two years since Braxton had done anything related to golf. The moment he arrived home that dreary morning to try to piece together the life that had been destroyed, he locked his golf clubs away and banned the sport from his life. For a long time, he couldn't pass a golf course without feeling the sickening grip of regret and defeat. What had once been his passion became a painful reminder of all that he'd lost. He'd lost his wife, Alice had lost her mother, and the world was losing one of the greatest coaching minds it had ever seen all because Braxton had been too busy trying to master a game that couldn't be mastered.

And yet here he was, swinging again.

Braxton clunked his own pawn down in an equally predictable move. "How about we forget about it and just play chess?"

He didn't want to talk about why he was swinging again or think about what it meant that he would do it so naturally at a time when he was feeling—dare he say—happy. And he sure didn't want to consider how a certain new neighbor and the time they'd been spending together played into all of this.

It was a slip of focus and an old habit. Nothing more. End of discussion.

Henry nodded and studied the board. "I suppose we could do that."

Six long ticks of the clock passed as Henry stared at his pieces. Finally, he picked up his pawn again and set it down in c4. Another classic move from any *How to Play Chess for Beginners* book. Braxton let out an annoyed huff and rolled his eyes.

Henry didn't play chess robotically. Even after the Alzheimer's disease had claimed so much of his brain that he couldn't remember how to button his own shirt, he still made daring, almost genius, moves on the chessboard. The only exception was when he was trying to make a point.

Henry looked up from the game and met Braxton's eyes with a challenging gaze. "Or we could talk about the, umm." He glanced away, frustration scrunching his face as he searched for the word he wanted to use.

Another wave of sadness crashed over Braxton as he watched his mentor, the man he admired more than anyone else, fall victim to a ruthless disease. This was why he left the sport. He'd sacrificed too much already. He couldn't give it any more. "The elephant in the room?"

"Yes, that." He crossed his arms in front of his chest. "You know golf didn't kill Jade. A drunk driver did that."

The sudden moment of clarity caught Braxton off guard, making Henry's words even more powerful. They hit him right in the solar plexus, taking his breath away.

From time to time, patients in advanced stages of the disease would have brief moments of clarity. There was no explanation as to why it happened and such episodes were reported to last for as little as a minute or two, or, in one rare instance, up to an hour. But at the moment, Braxton didn't care about the specifics he'd read about. He was accepting this rare gift any way he got it.

For so long, Braxton had to be the strong one in order to manage the disaster that had become his life. He'd pushed his own pain about the event deep into a dark place to be dealt with later. Except later never came. But seeing his friend, his mentor, the man whose opinion mattered more to him than anyone else in the world, with clear eyes and understanding written all over his face was enough to let all of that pain come pouring out.

Braxton closed his eyes, trying to keep the tears from sliding down his face. "But I could've been there. I might have stopped it."

Henry bobbed his head from side to side as if considering the options. "Maybe yes, maybe no. There's no way you could ever prove that. She could have died anyway. You could've died with her." He let the words hang between them for a moment before he continued. "'What if' is a dangerous game. One you'll never win."

Tears stung Braxton's eyes and he blinked to keep them away. "I miss her," he whispered.

It was the truth that hung on him like a weight. One he tried to hide in order to be strong for everyone else. One that, if he was being totally honest, was holding him back from moving forward with his life, moving forward with Millie.

Henry nodded with a look of sympathetic understanding. "Of course you do. But don't forget, it's like sweatpants."

The random conversation switch caused Braxton to pause, momentarily distracting him from the emotion welling up in his throat. His brow furrowed and his eyes darted from side to side as if something in the room would explain why they were suddenly talking about loungewear. "I'm sorry?"

"The heart. It's like sweatpants." Henry waved his hand in the general direction of Braxton's chest. "It expands to allow as much room as you need. Moving forward doesn't mean you have to replace her. You're adding to the list of love in your life. And there's always plenty of space in your heart to go around."

Braxton let the words marinate in his soul. As they did, some of the weight he'd been carrying around got a little lighter, making it feel like he could finally take a deep breath.

So maybe he couldn't have saved Jade, but he could've saved Henry. He looked up and met his mentor's eyes, finally voicing the guilt that had been eating at him for a long time. "If we hadn't been so busy chasing titles, we could've gotten you the help you needed earlier."

Henry settled back in his chair and looked out the window. His mouth twisted to the side, and a sadness Braxton hadn't seen in a long time filled his eyes. "That decision was all on me. I could've walked away at any time. You would've been fine with Mike or Jake or Beau coaching you. It might have even served you better in those final days." He turned back and looked Braxton in the eye. "I stayed for me. Because I wanted to live a life where my biggest regret would be not being able to remember it. Not a safe life, where I didn't have anything to forget anyway."

"Leave it all on the course." Braxton whispered Henry's famous advice that had become his catchphrase. He'd said it to Braxton often, but most famously, he'd said it right before the first time Braxton won the Masters tournament.

Braxton had hurt his rotator cuff teeing off on hole seventeen. Somehow, he managed to finish the hole, but the pain radiating from his arm was so intense he wasn't sure he could walk to the locker room on his own, let alone finish the round. He only had one more hole, and he was in the lead by two with almost no likelihood of the four golfers behind him catching him. All he had to do was finish eighteen and he'd get the coveted green jacket.

Henry had looked him right in the eye and said, "I know you're hurtin', but you're almost there. Four swings are all that stand between you and your dream. There's time for ice and rest and all that other bullshit tomorrow. Let them carry you in on a stretcher if you have to, but right now, you can't be done until you've left everything you got on that course."

Braxton went out after that and played a near-perfect hole, sinking his birdie putt to the cheer of thousands. *Leave it all on the course.*

But Braxton hadn't been the only one there that day celebrating, and it wasn't just his dream, was it?

Henry gave a slight shrug. "We did some great things out there, kid."

Braxton had to clear his throat. "Yeah, we did."

"I don't regret my decision at all." A smile lit up Henry's face. "In fact, if I had to play it over again, I'd do it all the same way."

"Even knowing what you know now?"

"Especially knowing what I know now." He leaned forward in his chair, focusing his clear eyes on Braxton. "Injury and heartache are going to come your way, but you can't let them stand in the way of your dreams. Life, after all, is for the living."

Braxton closed his eyes for a moment to let the wise words sink in. He'd been playing it safe thinking nothing could hurt him that way. But it was all a lie. No one could control what life gave, the surprises it sprung, unannounced, in the form of beautiful next-door neighbors.

"So there's this amazing woman." Braxton blinked his

eyes open and searched Henry's face for any sort of reaction.

Henry scoffed. "It always has to do with a lady."

Braxton chuckled and made his next chess move. "So you say."

Henry eyed the move then flashed Braxton a disapproving look while he made his own play, capturing one of Braxton's pawns. "What is it about her that makes you want to swing a club again?"

"I didn't say she made me want to pick up the game again. I just said she existed." Braxton's argument was as much for himself as it was for Henry.

Henry raised an eyebrow, clearly not buying it.

Braxton huffed. "Fine. She might've had a little to do with that. We've been spending some time together recently and she just makes life feel so…" Visions of Millie filled his mind as he tried to come up with words to adequately describe her. "Hopeful," he said at last. "She makes life fun and bright and hopeful."

Henry nodded, as if he had experienced the same kind of thing himself. "Those are the best kinds. She sounds like a keeper."

Braxton shrugged as he picked up his piece and rolled it around in his hand. "I don't know. It's not quite that simple." He had Alice and Henry and deep-seated pains and regrets that had closed off his heart. What if he got hurt again? Worse yet, what if one of them got hurt?

"Newsflash. Life isn't simple. If you're waiting for things to get less complicated, you're going to be sitting on your derrière for a while, cause it ain't happening." He clasped his hands together and leaned forward, looking into Braxton's eyes. "The trick is to find someone who'll hold your hand and walk through those complications with you. Someone who reminds you that hope is just on the other side."

For so long Braxton convinced himself that it was better

if he did things on his own. There was less risk of everyone getting hurt that way. But he was starting to realize maybe that wasn't true.

"And it never hurts if she's good lookin' either." Henry winked.

Braxton gave Henry a warning look. "You have to watch what you say. Women are more than their looks. This one in particular. She's talented and hardworking and has a great laugh." He couldn't help the grin that crept up on his face. "She's unlike anyone I've ever met before."

"Then why are you sitting here with me? You need to go get her before she figures out you're a bonehead."

Braxton chuckled. "You aren't holding any punches today, are you?"

Henry glared. "In all our years together, have I ever held back?"

"Touché."

They sat in silence for a moment as Braxton considered everything Henry had said and cherished the conversation.

"Seriously, why are you sitting here?"

Braxton didn't think he'd ever get to the point where his mentor's disease wouldn't leave him heartbroken and angry, but today he didn't dwell on that. Today, he was grateful for the moment and the advice.

"How about we just play best out of three?"

Henry moved a piece, capturing another of Braxton's pawns. "So, we're only playing two, then?"

Chapter Fourteen

Millie came out her front door Friday evening on her way to Braxton's for dinner because she wanted to take one more look at her new landscaping. The scent of fresh mulch wasn't exactly appetizing, but it did smell like gratification. The bright flowers and manicured beds made the house look warm and inviting. Just one step closer to having Seascape Inn ready for visitors—and for the HOA board.

She walked all the way to the road then turned back and paused for a moment to take in the view. That house with the gorgeous new paint job and the crack-free drive lined with flowers was *hers*.

She drew in a deep breath of warm, salty air. The glow of peace and joy filled her from the top of her head down to the tips of her toes. She probably wouldn't admit it to anyone, but there were times when she thought getting through the renos on the tight timeframe with her impossible budget would never happen. But here she was, on schedule and almost on budget.

Of course, she hadn't done it all on her own. Gus and his

team had been amazing. Then there were her new friends. Sophia and Tessa had been an invaluable help with all of the bathrooms. And Braxton… Well, he was just another friend, wasn't he? Which made this meal at his house simply dinner and not a date.

For starters, her casual shorts and flip-flops were only a slight upgrade from the work clothes she'd worn earlier to plant countless flats of flowers. Her hair was still wet from her recent shower and the only makeup she'd bothered to put on was lip gloss. She would've gone to a lot more trouble if it was a date, right? This was just two friends eating a casual dinner on his patio after a long day's work.

To prove to herself this dinner wasn't any more exciting than any other household activity going on, she decided to check the mail on her way over. That was definitely something not done on a date. She opened the latch and pulled out the handful of envelopes that were inside. On top was another letter from the HOA. Millie ripped open the envelope and pulled out the letter as she strolled over to Braxton's front gate.

To the valued property owner of 121 East Shore Drive,

It has been brought to our attention that one or more aspects of your property is out of compliance with the Oceanside Estates Deed Restrictions. Please address the item(s) listed below.

Curbside mailbox made of plastic.

*Curbside mailboxes should be constructed in a style reflecting that of the property, painted an HOA approved color found on the exterior of the main home, and made of metal, wood, concrete or other

HOA approved building materials for the exterior of a home.*

This is your first warning regarding the above violation(s). You will be given thirty (30) days to rectify this matter. Subsequent violations of any item after receiving a formal warning will result in a fine in accordance with the Fines and Penalties section in the HOA deed restrictions.

Thank you for your cooperation and dedication to keeping Oceanside Estates a wonderful place to call home.

Kind Regards,
Braxton Channing
HOA President

She was still shaking her head over the violation letter when she punched the call button on Braxton's front gate.

"Come around the back. I'm on the patio." His voice floated through the air as the wrought-iron gates in front of her swung open.

She walked around the side of his house and up the exterior staircase.

"Hey, you," he called as his pool deck came into view.

She held up the letter as she continued up the last few steps. "The mysterious Braxton Channing violation letter strikes again."

Braxton came over and took the letter from her. His expression turned serious as he studied it. "Plastic mailbox? That's a reach."

Millie chuckled and dropped the rest of the letters on a nearby table. "First of all, my new mailbox is a high-density polyethylene and there are two others just like it on this street alone."

Braxton shook his head. "It's not a valid complaint. While plastic itself is not listed on the approved materials list, several specific plastics are, like polyethylene." He flipped the letter over to check the back, then reread it.

"While I still hold firm to my belief that you have some really dumb rules, I have been very careful to abide by them. Even the ones cited in these mystery warnings." Millie sighed. "I'm just trying to prove that Seascape Inn will be an asset to the neighborhood, not a liability."

Braxton returned the letter to her. "Did I tell you that not all of the letters are in your file? Only the ones with valid violations like the trash can and the paint color made it into your official file. The rest of them never existed, according to our records."

Millie mentally flipped through the violations mentioned on the different letters she'd received and what Braxton had told her about each one. There had to be at least four or five letters missing from her file. "What does that mean?"

Braxton shrugged. "Maybe someone's trying to scare you into leaving. Or trying to make me look unethical. Or maybe both."

"And your signature's still locked?"

"Yup. Sophia and I are the only ones who know the password. I chatted with her earlier this week and she said no one has even asked for it since we added the restriction."

"Which means it's probably the same person sending all the letters. Once he or she saved the first letter to their computer, it wouldn't be hard to change the date and rewrite the violation." Millie couldn't decide if that new clue made her feel better or worse. It was starting to look more and more like only one person had a problem with her, not the entire HOA, which gave her a glimmer of hope. But if that person had enough of a problem to go to this much trouble, they'd likely not give up, meaning she could almost guarantee there would be more of those letters popping up in her mailbox before this whole thing was over.

"I agree, which means we won't be able to catch the culprit based on HOA server usage."

Millie slipped the letter into the envelope and added it to the pile of mail, letting go of her concerns before she fell too far down that rabbit hole. "Well, I'm in much too good of a mood to stress about that tonight."

She paused, taking in the scene in front of her. Braxton was wearing a heavy khaki apron and held long-handled metal tongs. The smell of wood fire and pepper floated around them. "Wait, are you grilling?"

"I am." A proud grin tugged at the corners of his mouth, and he held up the tongs, clicking them together. "I thought it was time to eat something that didn't come out of the freezer for a change. And contrary to popular opinion, I do know how to cook."

"Painting, planting, and grilling? You're a man of many talents," she teased, and walked over to join him by the grill. She closed her eyes, breathed in deeply, and let the stress from the HOA letter drift away. "It smells amazing. What are we having?"

"Steak, roasted corn on the cob, and grilled peaches from a local orchard. I like to call this menu Summer on the Patio."

"Aptly named."

He tossed his tongs on the counter next to his built-in grill and reached for a pitcher on the table.

"And since neither of us is driving and I'm kid-free, I mixed up some margaritas. Would you like one?"

"After having to read another one of those annoying letters from my uptight neighbor, I'd love one," she joked.

He grabbed one of the glasses that already had ice in it from the table and filled it. After handing it to her, he grabbed the second glass and poured one for himself. Then he held it up in a toast. "To uptight neighbors."

"And plastic mailboxes." She clinked her glass with his and took a sip of the sweet and tangy concoction, keeping her eyes on him. Everything got quiet for a second except for the sound of the steaks sizzling on the grill. Or was it the air between them that was sizzling?

Millie looked away, trying hard not to roll her eyes at herself. She was being ridiculous. Sure, they had fun together and these daily dinners after long workdays together had become the highlight of her week, but there was nothing more.

In fact, even if she wanted there to be something more, it simply didn't make sense. She'd been over this a million times. She wasn't in the market for a relationship.

She swirled her drink, letting the ice clink against the side of the glass, desperately looking for something else to think about. "I should be the one making you dinner to thank you for all your help this week. There's no way I would've been able to complete all those projects without you."

"Happy to help." He exchanged his glass for the metal tongs and turned back to the grill. "Your hard work is paying off. The house looks great. The board is going to love it."

Would they? It seemed like every time she turned around there was another violation notice. The familiar apprehension twirled through her like a brewing storm. She'd sunk every last penny into the renovations and dedicated six long, tiring weeks and countless scrapes, cuts, and bruises to transform Seascape into the bed and breakfast it deserved to be. And now all of it hinged on a group of people approving that what she had done was good enough for their aesthetics and neighborhood vibe.

"Fingers crossed."

"Trust me. They'll be blown away." He turned back to

her. "You exceeded all my expectations."

Perhaps it was his tone, or the way he peered into her eyes like he could see into her soul, but it felt like a wave crashed over her, sending tingles swirling through her body. Suddenly a little disoriented, she grabbed the back of the chair to steady herself.

Luckily, he didn't notice as he'd turned back to check on the grill.

"I think it's done." He grabbed the two plates sitting on the counter next to the grill and held them out to her. "Hold these while I serve it up?"

The sweet and savory scents mingled together as he plated the food, making her stomach rumble. But this was good. Focusing on the food and not on the intensity between them was good.

"I don't think I've been this excited to eat dinner since I moved here." She turned away to place the full plates on the table.

"Wait a second," Braxton said. "I'm not finished. You're missing the best part."

She stared at the plates in her hands, both looking pretty perfect. She narrowed her eyes at him. "Please tell me you're not one of those people who ruins a perfectly acceptable meal by adding something weird like fermented beet salad."

Braxton chuckled. "Is that what you think of me?"

Millie shrugged. "Maybe. I don't know what kind of bizarre health trends you South Carolina folks follow."

Braxton held up a bottle. "We like honey here. Just good ole honey, fresh from the hive. For the peaches." He flipped the lid open and held the bottle over Millie's plate. The golden liquid drizzled down over the hot peaches, sending a waft of summer sweetness into the air.

Her stomach rumbled in approval. "I knew I liked it here. You're not going to have a problem if I eat my dessert first, are you?"

He snapped the lid shut, returned it to the counter, and grabbed one of the plates from Millie. "Isn't that the best part about being a grown-up?" He shot her a devious smile, sending her pulse galloping through her veins.

Millie took a seat at the table and focused on putting her napkin in her lap as she tried to rein in her surging emotions. She grabbed her knife and fork and sliced through the peach before taking her first bite. "This is delicious."

Braxton flashed her another one of his charming smiles, which didn't help with the whole surging emotions thing. "I'm glad you like it." He took a bite of his own and hummed. "Did you finish reading the love letters?"

Welcoming any topic that would get her mind off whatever was happening with her *neighbor*, her thoughts switched to her young and in love Aunt Mildred.

"I read the last one last night." She took another bite of her peach. "Writing love letters really is a lost art form. Every one of them was so beautiful."

"Did you figure out what happened?"

Millie shook her head. "The last one seemed as optimistic as the rest of them. It ended with, 'Until tomorrow.'" She replayed the words from the final letter in her mind and shrugged. "I guess we'll never know how it ended."

Braxton took another sip of his drink. "Or who he was."

"Yeah..." She sighed. "Even with everyone in the book club looking into it, nothing has turned up. I guess we might never know the true identity of Mr. C."

Millie looked out over the ocean. It was the same water her aunt had stared at with her mystery man, the same beach she'd walked on as she was falling in love. How did something as perfect as what was in the love letters just dissipate without so much as a trace?

"You know, my aunt used to say love was a force more

powerful than any other in nature. Used wisely, it could change the world."

"I hear Mildred-isms all over town. But I think that one has to be my favorite." Braxton's gaze was fixed on her and something powerful surged through her.

There were a lot of reasons Millie had come to admire Braxton. He was funny, kind, compassionate, responsible, and a great father. But the number one thing that made her heart soar was the way that he looked at her. For some reason, when his kind eyes focused on her, she felt seen. Known. Validated.

She could feel heat flushing her cheeks and working its way down her neck, and she hoped the dim light would prevent him from noticing. She couldn't be falling for Braxton. Yes, he was a great guy. But love had to be used wisely, and falling in love with Braxton was the opposite of wise. There were a million warning flags flapping all over that idea. For starters, they shared a fence. If things went south, she'd still have to spend the rest of her life connected to him.

Not to mention she had no intention of getting involved with anyone. This was her turn to do her own thing on her own terms without anyone else telling her what to do.

How on earth did she let herself get into this situation?

Braxton motioned to her plate. "How is everything?"

"Great." Millie painted the politest, non-enamored smile she could muster on her face and did her very best to look at anything except his eyes.

After all, it was just dinner, wasn't it?

• • •

Dinner had been amazing, and it wasn't just because the butcher happened to hook Braxton up with the perfect cut of steak or that the fresh South Carolina peaches he'd picked up at a local stand were at the peak of the season. No, what elevated tonight was the woman sitting across from him.

Millie Leclair was simply beautiful. For the past two hours, he'd sat mesmerized by her. Her eyes sparkled with passion as she spoke and her warm, endearing smile pulled him in. Their banter was effortless and fun.

For the first time in more than two years he felt alive. More than alive. He felt vibrant.

True, the new emotions were enough to set off warning lights in the back of his mind, but tonight he chose to ignore them. He didn't want to let anything stand in the way of their nearly perfect evening.

"Oh, wow. It's dark," Millie said as their conversation finally came to a lull. "Where has the time gone?"

Braxton had the same thought. Time had flown by and stood still at the same time. It was as if his patio was under a beautiful spell and he didn't want to do anything to break it. But all good things had to come to an end.

With a soft smile, she pushed away from the table. "It's probably time for me to go home."

Braxton pushed back, too. "Can I walk you?"

Millie met his gaze and the connection that they'd had all night crackled through him. "I'd like that."

They strolled down the steps to the bottom level and he unlocked his gate, pushed it open, and held it for her to pass through first.

"Thanks." She slid past him, leaving her intoxicating scent of coconut and tropical flowers trailing behind her, causing all his logical thoughts to scatter.

For years, Braxton told himself he was off-limits. There were many reasons he had to back up his decree, and every one of them was valid to some extent. Losing his wife had scarred him, dealing with the guilt of not being able to save her crushed him, and raising a daughter on his own took every bit of his energy.

Being emotionally unavailable to love was understandable. He had more than enough emotional obligations vying for the fractured pieces of his heart as it was.

And then came Millie.

If he was being totally honest with himself, he'd been enthralled by Millie from the moment he saw her animated smile when she opened the door the very first day they met. He hadn't even known her name or anything about her, but the way joy danced in her eyes and life flowed of out her had captivated him.

But being emotionally off-limits, he'd disregarded the feelings.

Until the festival. Until this long week working side by side on her dream home. Until tonight.

Millie looked out over the ocean as they strolled down the sand. "I thought I'd seen beautiful night skies in the city, but I wasn't prepared for this."

Braxton nodded. "There's nothing like a clear night sky over the ocean."

She paused and breathed in deeply as if trying to absorb the moment. "I have to admit I love a full moon over the ocean, but without it, the stars are brilliant. It's like being surrounded by thousands of sparkling diamonds."

Braxton looked out over the ocean too. While the stars did seem extra bright tonight, their brilliance wasn't what enamored him. For better or worse, the only thing he could see was Millie, and the thought both energized and terrified him. He was swiftly moving into uncharted waters he wasn't sure how to navigate.

"It's hard to imagine that there's a storm raging out there." He pointed to the southeast. "Right now, it should be somewhere in that vicinity."

Millie's gaze followed to where he was pointing. "I'd

almost forgotten about the hurricane." She shivered. "I still can't believe it's so close to us but is going to pass right by. How does that happen?"

"There's no use trying to explain the weather. It does what it does. Something about high pressures and low pressures, so maybe if we all stand on the coast and blow at the same time…"

Millie giggled. It was a beautiful sound. One that resonated with hope and joy. "You might be joking, but there's no limit to the absurd things I'd do if it meant I didn't have to drag out all those ancient storm shutters and try to figure out which window they belong to."

"What? Now that you're reaching the finish line, you've lost your sense of adventure? Where's the woman who climbs tiny ladders to the top of tall buildings?"

"That woman had a leaky roof and no time to overthink things. Plus she's addicted to the way those particular roof tiles turned out." Millie gestured in the general direction of her house.

"Fair enough."

Millie's cheerful smile faded away and worry lines crinkled her forehead. "In all seriousness, I read everyone on the coast should have a hurricane preparedness plan. I don't even know what that means let alone how to come up with one."

She let out a defeated sigh as her arms hung limply by her side. "Sometimes I wonder if I'm in way over my head here."

Insecurity echoed in her whispered words and Braxton realized that for the first time since they'd met, Millie was being vulnerable with him. Most of the time she walked around with the kind of fearlessness mixed with confidence that made her seem larger than life. She was strong, brave, and caring, a combination that put her on the winning side of almost any challenge. More than once his own vulnerabilities and insecurities had been strengthened by her words and actions. But she'd never shown her weak side before. At least not to him. And not on purpose.

An urge so powerful he couldn't stop it came over him, and he did something else they'd never done before. He wrapped his arms around her and pulled her into his chest.

"Batteries, flashlights, and water. Those are the basics," he said gently, hoping to ease her worries. "Oh, and maybe some hurricane snacks."

"I like snacks. Snacks seem pretty important," she mumbled into his chest.

He softly chuckled. "See. You're already prioritizing things."

Her arms wrapped around his waist and she relaxed into him. He stood there, holding her on their beach, marveling at how good she felt nestled against him. They fit perfectly, as if they belonged together.

And as soon as the thought entered his mind, he pushed it away. He was barely past the point of adamantly denying she was anything more than a neighbor. He needed to take this one baby step at a time.

"In all honesty, you're killing it," he said. "You took on a job that would've had most people running the other direction and you've knocked it out of the park."

"I think it probably helped that I've never done this before. If I knew what I was doing, I probably would've run the other direction, too."

"Well, I for one am glad you didn't. What you've done to Seascape is remarkable. You've earned my vote, and I have a feeling the rest of the board will be equally impressed."

"I hope so." Millie's voice still lacked her normal unstoppable optimism, but there was a hint of confidence that wasn't there before.

"I know so," he said. "And as soon as the renos settle

down a bit, we'll pull out all those shutters and figure it out."

Millie pulled away and looked up into his eyes, a bit of hesitancy in her voice. "We?"

Braxton forced himself to release her and shoved his hands into his pockets. We? Now he was thinking in terms of we? Was his heart not listening to a single thing his brain was saying?

"Y-yeah. I mean, I know you can do it on your own. I just thought you might want some help," he said cautiously. "Or, you know, maybe you'd like the company?"

Because the truth was, regardless of what he wanted to feel, *he* liked the company. He wanted to spend more time with her.

She turned all her attention to the sand, chewing on her lower lip. Either she was really interested in her toes or she was giving his offer serious consideration.

"Help is good." She glanced up at him from under her lashes. "Though I gotta warn you, it's kinda creepy inside that shed. Lots of spiders." The joking glint in her eyes had returned.

"Spiders don't scare me."

"Really? Because I'm pretty sure I heard you squeal the other day when that big spider dropped down from the windowsill and landed on you."

"That…that was different. It just caught me off guard, was all."

She laughed, which echoed out over the waves. "Just wanted to give you a heads-up in case you need to find a hazmat suit before you come over."

He loved making her laugh. He loved how she took on the world with a sense of humor and a spirit that wouldn't back down. He loved…

He stopped that train of thought right there.

He was willing to admit that he might have more

emotional capacity than he once believed, and that Millie ignited something inside him. He'd even admit she was quickly becoming one of his favorite people. But no one said anything about the L-word.

"I should probably have my bug guy come by a couple days before we start, just to be on the safe side. I'd hate for anything to bite you."

She rolled her eyes. "How chivalrous of you."

"I'm a giver like that." He tucked the stray strand of hair that blew across her face behind her ear. "Good night, Millie."

"Good night."

He watched her walk across the sand to the brand-new, refinished boardwalk that led over the dunes to her backyard. She climbed the three steps and then paused at the top.

She turned and met his gaze through the starlit darkness. "For the record, I like the company, too."

And despite his best efforts to avoid it, his heart reopened the conversation about the L-word.

Chapter Fifteen

Braxton did something the next morning he hadn't done in almost two and a half years—he stepped onto a golf course.

He stood at the first tee box with his golf bag slung over his shoulder and stared out at the course in front of him. Fog rolled out from the trees and across the green grass as golden rays of dawn painted the sky. There'd been a time when this place felt more like home than any place he actually slept. A place where he belonged. A place he'd come to feel renewed, invigorated.

Then life had gone south and everything changed.

He'd been caught in a wave of grief, unable to tell up from down and fighting just to get his next breath. And when the wave finally washed him up to the shore, darkness had settled over everything.

Perhaps he could've fought his way back then, but he was too bruised and battered to find the will. So, he let fear and regret dictate where he could and couldn't go and what he could or couldn't do. Easier that way. And safer.

But lately a tiny glimmer of hope had pierced his dark

world. And hope, even when it was tiny, was a powerful force.

The sun had risen and set many, many times since he had stood in this spot, but everything about it felt familiar. The way the gentle morning breeze skimmed his skin, the earthy smell of freshly cut grass, the way the excited buzz hummed through him. Everything about it felt right, as if nothing had changed.

"I'm sorry, sir, but the course isn't open yet," an unfamiliar voice called out from behind him. "You'll have to make a tee time."

Braxton turned toward the person. The guy was young, early twenties at best, and wore one of the golf club's logoed staff shirts and was accompanied by the course's golf pro.

"Wait, you're..." The kid's voice trailed off, a look of astonishment on his face.

The golf pro chuckled next to him. "Good morning, Mr. Channing. It's nice to see you out here."

Braxton nodded, taking a second to look around the course. It felt nice to be here, which was a welcome surprise. "Thanks, Grant. I was just going to try to get in a couple of holes. Is that still okay?"

Grant nodded. "Absolutely. We just finished mowing the front nine and our first group doesn't tee off for another hour and a half."

"Thanks. I'll be off before they start."

Grant nodded once more to show he understood. "Let us know if you need anything." He slipped his hands in his pockets and continued walking past Braxton.

The new guy followed right on his heels. "That's really Braxton Channing? I thought he didn't play golf anymore."

"Apparently he does today," his old friend said. "And Mr. Channing prefers to practice when the course is empty before it opens. It's part of the arrangement he has with the club."

The golf pro's voice trailed off as they walked away.

Braxton waited until they were out of sight to put his bag down. Anticipation was building inside of him, but he didn't want an audience for his first swing.

He teed up his ball, grabbed his favorite club, and set up for his first drive. The breeze skimmed his skin, bringing with it a sense of calm. And then he did it.

Without so much as a practice swing, he pulled back and swung through, sending a satisfying *thwack* of the club hitting the ball in the exact spot echoing through the morning calm. He stood there with his golf club still over his shoulder as he watched his white ball sail through the air in a perfect arc. Farther and farther it flew, pushing away the darkness that had been hanging over him. It landed in the middle of the fairway, bounced once, and rolled to a stop some three hundred yards from where he stood.

Braxton dropped his club to his side and, closing his eyes, lifted his face to the sky. It didn't matter that it was a perfect shot or that the ball landed in an ideal position. What mattered was that exhilaration pulsed through his body, and for the first time in two and a half years, he could breathe.

He slid the club back into his bag, hoisted it over his shoulder, and started down the hill to where his ball lay waiting for him.

"Hello there, gorgeous," he said as he approached the ball. He set his bag on the ground next to him and grabbed a nine iron. Gripping the club between his hands, he stepped up to the ball. When he was satisfied with how he was standing, he lifted only his head to look at the exact place he wanted the ball to land on the green.

A grin tugged at the corners of his mouth. He was comfortable with where he was and knew where he wanted to go. How long had it been since he'd said that? Hope did some bizarre things.

With each stroke, Braxton felt lighter. His world seemed

brighter, and it wasn't just because the morning sun was rising over the trees. Something had changed over the past couple of months, and it wasn't a coincidence that the timeline coincided with the arrival of his new neighbor.

"Nice shot." Jerry, one of the groundskeepers, drove up after Braxton had sunk his putt on the second hole.

"Thanks. This was a tricky pin placement." He gestured to the hole as he bent down to pick up his ball. "I don't think I've seen it here before."

Jerry hopped out of the cart and picked up the long flag to put back in the hole for Braxton.

"We've changed up the rotation of some of the holes. And I guess you've heard about the new twelve? New tee box, new green. You're hitting across the creek now for a par five instead of a par four. It's nice."

Braxton stared out in the direction of the area of the course where holes ten through eighteen were located. Had he heard something about them changing a hole? A familiar zing of excitement pulsed through him.

"I don't think I'm going to make it to the back nine this morning, but maybe I'll start over there tomorrow."

Jerry placed the flag back in the hole. "You tell me what days you want to start on the back nine and we'll make sure they're ready for you."

Braxton picked up his bag and they both headed toward the cart path. "I appreciate it. I haven't figured out my new practice schedule yet. But as soon as I do, I'll let you know."

Jerry nodded as he climbed into his golf cart and released the brake. "It's nice to have you back, Mr. Channing."

The smile that crept across his face was genuine. "Thanks. It's good to be out here again." In fact, it had energized him in a way he hadn't expected and by the time he finished the third hole, everything looked different.

After he placed the pin back in the hole at the third

green, he paused and looked out over the course. Everything even appeared more vivid than it had in as long as he could remember. The deep green of the oak leaves was a vast contrast to the soft gray of the Spanish moss that hung from them. The sky was a brilliant azure striped with wisps of pink-tinged clouds.

It was like someone had lifted the foggy veil that had been hanging over his world so he could see color again. And he knew exactly who that someone was.

Millie.

Just the thought of her sent a jolt of excitement buzzing through him and he savored the feeling. For the first time in years he felt like himself.

Somewhere along the way he'd given up the idea of ever feeling like this again. It wasn't a conscious decision, but something that sort of evolved out of self-preservation. His main focus for so long had been to survive. Every ounce of his energy went to putting one foot in front of the other. He hadn't had any time to try to figure out how to deal with the pain or figure out how to dig himself out of the emotional void he was falling into.

As time wore on and his daily steps fell into more of a routine, he'd embraced it. So what if the world around him was colorless and he felt dead inside? He was making it, wasn't he? That was all he could ask for in his situation.

But then, when he was least looking for it, Millie showed up with her bright, sparkling eyes, big smile, and unrelenting optimism and shined a light on the darkest depths of his soul. She managed to breathe life into the parts of his heart he thought had died long ago. The result was nothing less than intoxicating.

Now that he realized what he'd been missing for the past few years, he wasn't willing to let it go. From this point forward, everything was going to be different.

Sure, there was an underlying fear that everything could go south again. The one thing he knew for certain was that life had no guarantees. Everything could change in a split second, but now he had hope. And hope changed everything.

He marched with a new determination to the fourth tee box.

He'd just set his bag down and pulled out his club to tee off when his phone buzzed in his pocket. After bending down to tee up his ball, he quickly pulled out his phone to make sure it wasn't anything important. While he wasn't a slave to fear, he did have a responsibility to two very important people. Hopefully, if he played his cards right, that number would increase to three soon. His mind swirled with the possibilities of what a future with Millie could look like as he read the message on the screen.

It was a local news alert about the hurricane, and he was about to slip the phone back into his pocket when something stopped him.

With a hurricane in their vicinity it wasn't unheard of that he would be getting updates about its path. It was so close to the coast that they were expecting rain from the outer bands as it passed by them later this afternoon. The media loved to hype up anything that seemed exciting in their sleepy little town. He almost ignored it, but he paused. There was something else about the message, something his subconscious had seen that prompted him to take another look.

He clicked on the alert and read the full headline: *Hurricane Makes a Sudden Path Change, Heading Straight for Summer Island.*

It felt like someone pulled out a plug and every last ounce of warmth in Braxton's body drained out through his feet. Shivering, he scanned the article, searching for some sort of good news to counteract the bomb dropped in the headline.

Then he reread it again just to make sure he'd read it right.

When he got to the bottom of the article for the second time he looked up, stunned. This couldn't be happening. Hurricane Axel wasn't supposed to hit Summer Island. It should've glided right past them. Every strand of the spaghetti model had it making landfall farther north, almost a state above them.

Well, every model but one. That single strand had it taking a sharp left turn right around where they were. But they'd called that chance an anomaly. No one paid any attention to the outlier, least of all him. He played the odds, and the odds said the storm was headed north.

Only this time, the odds weren't winning.

Acid roiled in his stomach as he pulled up the official announcement from the National Hurricane Center. As soon as his eyes flickered across the last line, his head popped up.

Rogue outlying model or not, the storm had turned.

Still holding his golf club in one hand, he flung his golf bag over his shoulder and broke into a sprint for the parking lot. Hurricane Axel was now predicted to make a direct hit to Summer Island and the only thing that Braxton could think was that someone needed to tell Millie.

Chapter Sixteen

Millie stood in her front yard and read the final step for installing the new pump that would return the splash to the three-tiered fountain that sat in the middle of her grand circular drive as the first welcome to guests of Seascape Inn.

Twenty-three steps were printed in the manual that came with the new pump. Twenty-three steps that turned out to be way more technical than the glossy directions made them sound.

But now that she was on the final step, her hands tingled with anticipation. "Here we go, Bear. You ready for this?" The satisfaction of finishing a project never got old.

Triumphantly, she held up the plug then squatted down to complete the final step. Bear's tail wagged. Anticipation crackled as she made the final connection and then...

Nothing.

Millie's soaring spirits fell flat, and she rocked back to sit on the driveway, staring at the motionless fountain.

"I was sure we did everything right." She grabbed the

manual next to her and flipped through the steps, searching for something she could've missed. It only took a second before the lightbulb went off, and she rolled her eyes at herself.

"Power, Bear. We forgot to turn the power back on." She sprang up and jogged around to the side of the house to where the breaker box was located and flipped the switch in question. "All right. That should do it."

She heard the old fountain sputter to life before she saw it, and as soon as she and Bear rounded the corner, it was flowing once again.

Pride caused her lips to twitch at the corners, and she stood a little taller as she propped her hands on her hips and watched the water flow. Nope, the satisfaction never got old.

"Look at that, Bear. We did that." She rubbed the dog's head, her lips giving way to a full-fledged smile. Bear's tail thumped happily against the ground.

A familiar sound distracted her from the cascading water, and her grin widened as Braxton's sports car rolled down her faux-cobblestone driveway.

There was no denying it anymore. Whether she wanted to or not, she was starting to fall for the boy next door. Last night had solidified that. The second he wrapped his arms around her, she knew there wasn't anywhere else she'd rather be.

His car rolled to a stop and his door opened at almost the exact same moment. Millie opened her mouth to greet him but was cut off by his non-greeting.

"Where's your phone?" There was a mild look of panic on his face.

For real? She understood his hypersensitive concern about safety, but seriously, there was little risk of getting hurt when installing a new water pump.

Millie shrugged. "I don't know. The front porch, maybe."

She looked over her shoulder, scanning the yard for where she might have last used her phone.

"I've been texting you. You haven't answered." There was a hint of bossiness in his voice, and her mild offense was on the verge of blossoming into annoyance. His concern for her safety was endearing, but this might be bordering on the mildly possessive side.

"I turned the notifications off because they kept popping up over my YouTube videos." There might have been an edge to her voice that she didn't bother removing.

"You can't do that."

"Sure I can. Do you have any idea how annoying it is to—"

"Millie."

She was about to launch into the story of how all the news alerts and texts kept popping up and would pause the how-to video she was watching. It was dragging the twenty-minute video out to a time limit she didn't have patience for. But the way he said her name gave her pause. Before she could question him, he put his hands on her shoulders. Worry swirled in his eyes, sending a flutter of panic streaking through her gut.

"What's wrong?" Possible scenarios of emergencies involving Alice and Henry raced through her mind as she considered all the things that could ignite panic in Braxton.

"The hurricane has turned."

Since she'd been expecting the news to have something to do with one of the two people in his care, the words didn't register with her at first. She tilted her head to the side as she untangled what he'd said. "The what?"

Braxton closed his eyes and drew in a breath, as if he was trying to figure out the best way to deliver the news.

For a second, everything around them got perfectly still. The wind stopped blowing. The birds stopped chirping. Even the fountain got quiet.

Braxton opened his eyes and his gaze flickered to the house behind her before they focused on her face. "The hurricane turned. The National Hurricane Center is now predicting that the eye will make landfall somewhere between the Broad River and Pelican Sound."

Millie pulled up a map in her mind, mentally plotting the coordinates Braxton had said like the computer models they were always showing on TV. And that's when it sank in. "Wait. *We* are between the river and Pelican Sound."

Braxton nodded once, and the worry on his face was starting to make sense.

"But that can't be. All the computer models pointed north. The weatherman. That Allan something or other who's been tracking hurricanes for like thirty years said it was going north. It's supposed to hit North Carolina tomorrow."

Bear whined at her side, probably from the high pitch her words had taken.

Braxton shrugged. "That's why they call it a prediction. Sometimes it's wrong. This time, the high pressure from the north didn't come as far down as they were expecting I guess and it's pushing the storm west."

"But..." Millie's mind went blank. She looked over her shoulder at the sliver of water she could see between hers and Braxton's house. That was the ocean right there. Landfall would be in her backyard. Everything surrounding them would be in the catastrophe zone. The new paint job, the roof repairs, the landscaping, even the fountain. Everything she'd spent the past month and a half working on would be in the storm's direct path.

This couldn't be happening.

She turned back to Braxton. "I...I don't even have a hurricane preparedness plan." It was a dumb thing to say. Of course a storm didn't care if she had a plan or not. But at the moment, it was the only thing she could think of.

Braxton gently rubbed her arms, sending the slightest hint of comfort cascading over her. It wasn't enough to calm the nerves playing ping-pong inside her mind, but it was enough to slow them down so she could form a coherent thought.

"You do now. Step one is move everything you can inside and secure the rest. Step two, I'll start pulling out your shutters so we can board the windows."

Move everything inside. Right. She could do that. She nodded her head once, focusing on the tools she had dragged out to repair the fountain. She could start there. "How long do we have?"

"Eight hours."

"Eight hours?" Her words came out louder and slightly more screechy than she'd intended, and there was probably a horrified look on her face. How could they possibly get everything ready in eight hours?

Her eyes darted around her yard as she created a mental list of everything that needed to be accomplished in that time. Were the ancient hurricane shutters even functional? The ones on the front of the house had taken almost a day of work to fix, and that was just a drop in the bucket compared to the number of glass doors and windows along the back and sides of the house.

Millie sucked in a deep breath, trying to calm herself down. Panic never helped anything. If that was all the time they had, she was going to need every second of it to get things ready. "So eight hours, huh? I guess we'll be ready in eight hours."

"Not exactly. The eye is forecasted to make landfall in eight hours. The actual storm will hit before that. Maybe five or six hours." His hands slid down her arms until he took her hands in his. "But it's enough time. We can get it done."

She highly doubted that but arguing with him seemed

like a moot point. It was all they had. "Okay, so six hours. And then we evacuate?"

He paused before answering as if weighing his words. "Well, no." He looked in the direction of his house. "To evacuate we'd have to leave now."

A fresh wave of fear swept over her. "But don't we have to? What about the storm? What about Alice and Henry?" Admittedly, she didn't know much about hurricanes except they were massive storms that caused major destruction and people fled from them in droves. Staying was risky, especially when living right on the coast with the beach as your backyard, wasn't it?

"I spoke with Alice's grandparents in Atlanta. They're totally safe and happy to watch her as long as needed. And Memory Care is at a high spot on the island, which means there's little risk for flooding. And they're taking all the necessary steps to fortify it from the wind."

That news calmed some of the fears racing through her, which were causing her mind to spin at a rate that made it hard to focus. But there was still one concern that made her blood feel like it had turned to ice water. "What about us?"

Braxton's words came out calm and confident. "My house is made of solid concrete and my hurricane impact windows are tested to withstand winds far stronger than anything this storm will throw at us. After we board up your house, we'll ride the storm out at my place."

"But…"

He squeezed her hands and gazed deep into her eyes with a look of confidence that felt as strong as the concrete that made up his house. "We're going to be fine. We've got this."

And there was that word again. *We.*

When she moved here six weeks ago, she was determined the only "we" in her very long-term future would be referring to her and Bear. She, the Lowcountry version of herself, was a solo act. Even when her heart did the tango the first time she met her once-famous neighbor with the hypnotic blue eyes, she was determined this chapter in her story would be only about her.

But things had changed. Over the weeks of getting to know him, of working side by side with him, her *me* started shifting to *we.*

It was a scary realization, because her past failed relationships had left the deepest scars in her life. She didn't want that to happen again. Doing life on her own was the safer option. But what if it wasn't the better option?

Yes, falling for Braxton was a risk. And if life had taught her anything, it was that there were no guarantees. But right now, when the storm was threatening to destroy everything, *we* was giving her the strength to move forward.

"Okay." She nodded with a new determination. Pushing the noise out of her mind, she focused on what needed to be done. "Let's do this."

Chapter Seventeen

Millie remembered the days when six hours was a long chunk of time. In fact, back when she spent the majority of her waking hours as a cubicle jockey, there were several days it seemed two o'clock would never come. However, today, when she needed every second she could get, the minutes ticked by in double time.

At first it was hard to imagine a massive storm was coming in their direction. The sky was a bright blue with big, fluffy clouds. By the time noon rolled around, she was a hot, sweaty mess and silently questioning if all the prep work was for nothing.

Braxton had left at around one o'clock with Bear to get his house ready which, considering that was going to be their safe haven for the duration of the storm, she was more than willing to let him do.

Around that same time, gray clouds had started to move in. These storm clouds were different than anything she had seen before. They weren't the large and heavy kind that slowly rolled in and settled in place until they dumped their inches of snow or rain. These clouds were lighter, nimbler, and swept across the sky from the south to the north, bringing with them sudden gusts of wind and random spatterings of rain. Then they'd disappear out to sea, like a scout going back to report the enemy's position.

Then, at two o'clock, almost exactly six hours from when Braxton had pulled into her driveway that morning, the storm rolled in.

Millie wasn't sure "rolled in" was the right term when one was referring to a hurricane. "Blew in" would be a better description, because instead of falling straight down from the sky, the rain blew sideways, sneaking in through any corner not shut tight. She only had two sets of French doors left to shutter when the raindrops started pelting her, stinging her skin. She turned and glared at the sky. "Back off. If you were in such a hurry to get here, you should've let us know sooner."

As if in response, a sudden gust blasted her. In frustration, she banged with all her might against the metal track the ancient hurricane shutter was supposed to slide into. Millie wasn't sure of the last time someone had boarded up this house for a hurricane, but the combination of time and the salt air had done a number to the hardware that held the shutters in place. With two out of thirty-two sets of shutters left, she hadn't come across one yet that hadn't needed some sort of repair. With all the other repairs she'd done to the house, this shouldn't be surprising, but it was about time she caught a break, wasn't it? And if her house wasn't going to give it to her, she was going to need the weather to do her a solid.

"Like I said." She banged the hammer against the metal with all her might, trying to force the opening wide enough to allow the shutter to slide in. "Not. Yet." With the last swing of her hammer, the metal gave way and widened enough for the shutter.

"Finally." She tucked the hammer into her toolbelt

and hoisted up the giant door-sized shutter, sliding it into the track. She locked it into place, then turned to survey the ocean. Angry white-capped waves careened through a murky sea before crashing onto the shore, each one washing farther up the sand than the one before it.

Millie stood on the second-story exterior walkway and watched it, both mystified and terrified at the same time. Sweat dripped off her forehead and soaked through her shirt while she stood in awe of the power of nature.

"I'm almost done," she whispered to the winds. "Please, just a few more minutes."

Without waiting for a response, she moved down the walkway to the next door, and in less than ten minutes she was locking the last shutter into place. She hurried down the exterior stairs. Grabbing the overnight bag she'd left under the covered porch, she headed through her courtyard on her way to Braxton's house. It wasn't until she got to the gate that she paused to take one last look at her house.

She stood there, trying to burn this picture of the fresh paint job and newly refinished pool deck into her mind as a single tear ran down her cheek. She had no idea what tomorrow had in store for her, but she wanted to remember that she'd done it. When faced with an impossible challenge, she, Millie Leclair, had laughed in the face of adversity and conquered the impossible.

"Godspeed," she whispered to the house and blew it one last kiss. Then she crossed the boardwalk on the way to whatever the future had in store for her.

As she trudged through the sand, a sudden blast of wind slammed against her. She slowed to a stop and widened her stance to keep from being knocked down. A loud crash caught her attention, and she turned in time to see a massive palm frond drop to the ground somewhere to the right. Fear raced through her as she scanned the sky. The raw power of nature was relentless. The rain beat against her face and the angry waves crashed onto the shore. She had to get out of the danger zone. She had to get to Braxton's house.

With a new determination, she pulled the hood of her raincoat over her head, leaned into the wind, and headed toward his boardwalk. Fixing her gaze on the ground, she moved forward one step at a time. More crashing sounds rang out around her as the waves drove closer to her feet, but she focused on one thing. Braxton. She just needed to get to Braxton.

"Millie!"

At first she thought she'd imagined it or that perhaps the storm was taunting her, but after hearing it a third time, Millie looked up. Braxton was jogging down the beach in her direction.

In the middle of the storm, with the wind bearing down on her and an angry ocean raging at her side, an overwhelming warmth surged inside Millie. There wasn't anything that she wanted more than to be in Braxton's arms. She could face whatever this storm—or life—threw at her if she had him by her side.

And even more amazing was that thought didn't even scare her. In fact, it actually calmed her.

She picked up her pace, jogging, then running toward him. For the first time since she found out about the storm, she was oblivious to what was going on around her. The only thing she was focused on at the moment was the man in front of her.

"I finished," she panted. "It's all—"

But before she could even finish her sentence, he slid his hands behind her head. With his thumbs caressing her cheeks, he leaned down and kissed her.

It was deep and full of desire, with an energy that reverberated through her body, causing everything around her to fade away. The storm, her fears, all the questions about being with Braxton that had raced through her mind over the past few weeks just melted away. She wrapped her arms around his neck and kissed him back.

Rain fell all around them, but in his arms she didn't care.

When she finally took a breath, she looked up at him. He flashed one of his charming grins that made her feel all woozy inside.

Or maybe it was the kiss that made her feel woozy.

"I have something to tell you." He brushed a strand of dripping wet hair out of her eyes and tucked it inside her rain jacket hood. "I…"

It was her turn to cut him off. "I like you," she blurted out over the howling wind and the rain dripping down her cheeks. It probably wasn't the most eloquent way to tell him how she felt, but the truth just sort of burst out of her.

There was something warm and friendly in his eyes. "I was going to say my house is secured and that Bear and I are waiting for you." He shrugged. "But I kind of like what you said better."

His arm snaked around her back and pulled her close. He rested his forehead against hers, stroking her cheek with his other thumb. "Also, for the record, me too."

The words swirled through her, making her feel warm and giddy, even as the cold rain dripped onto her. "This could get complicated."

The warning was as much for her as for him.

"You're always telling me I need to take more risks in my life."

"True." She stood on her tiptoes and pressed her lips against his again. This time, the kiss was slower and gentler, but almost more powerful. It flowed through her, setting every sense on fire. Kissing him was rapidly becoming her new favorite hobby. She didn't know exactly where this thing between them was going, but at the moment she didn't care.

Right here was good enough for now.

Another crash from somewhere behind Braxton had them jumping apart. Braxton wrapped a protective arm around her shoulders and pulled her into his side. She searched through the wind and the sideways rain clouding the air in front of them for the source of the latest destruction, a shudder of fear edging in on her euphoric glow.

Okay, so maybe right here didn't mean this exact location.

"It's getting bad out here," Braxton said, his eyes darting around as if taking in the dangers for the first time. "What do you say we finish this conversation inside?"

"Conversation?"

Braxton's eyes sparkled. "We can finish other things, too."

With his arm around her shoulders, they ducked into the wind and jogged across his boardwalk to his gate.

His house looked different. With all of the patio furniture gone and the normally overflowing infinity pool drained to three quarters of its capacity, his house looked cold and vacant. But at the moment, it had never been more inviting to her.

They raced for the door, stepping inside as another large gust of wind blasted them. Braxton pushed the door closed and locked both dead bolts, drowning out the storm and securing them inside.

Braxton slid out of his jacket and hung it on a rack next to the door, positioning a towel on the floor under it to catch the runoff. He held his hand out to Millie, and she shrugged hers off, trying not to splatter water everywhere. The whole time she kept her gaze locked with Braxton's, the heat between them building.

Once both jackets were hung up, Braxton placed both hands on her hips and pulled her toward him. "So, where were we?"

"You were saying something about how you feel."

"Oh right. That. Let's see, I think it went something like this."

A thrill rushed through her as he bent down to kiss her again. But this time they were interrupted by the muffled sound of his phone ringing in his pocket.

Part of her wanted to ignore it. Even if it was an emergency, what could either one of them possibly do about it until the storm passed? For the next couple of hours, they'd be locked inside the safety of Braxton's house. Of course, she had in mind a few things they could do to kill the time. But a tiny voice kept nagging her.

"You going to get that?" she asked between kisses.

"Look who has become the cautious one now." Braxton's look smoldered through her. "But if it's nothing, I'm leaving my phone in here and taking you someplace more comfortable."

The idea of that sent sparks sizzling through her. "Deal."

He slid his phone far enough out of his pocket to be able to read the message on the screen. Then Braxton tensed up. He took another step away from her and pulled his phone all the way out of his pocket. Hitting a button on the screen, he held the phone up to his ear.

"Hey, Veronica. What's wrong?"

He stared straight ahead as if concentrating on the words being spoken on the other side of the phone. His brow furrowed with concern.

"Already?" With each question, the playful passion that had just been dancing on his face was replaced with rigid concern.

Finally, he grabbed his car keys and, with an apologetic glance at Millie, said the words that sent a shudder of fear through her.

"I'm on my way."

Chapter Eighteen

"A tree just fell on the mechanical building at Summer Island Memory Care Home and took out their backup generator." Braxton reported this to Millie as he grabbed his dripping raincoat off the rack where he'd hung it. He tossed it over his arm, not paying any attention to the water he was flinging around.

"Oh, no. That's awful." Millie trailed behind him as he crossed the house. "Can they fix it before they lose power?"

"Not in this storm. And since several of their residents require medical equipment that needs electricity, they can't be without a backup plan."

He opened the door to the interior staircase that led to the ground-floor garage. His mind spun with the possibilities of what might happen if the power went out before he could get there. Flipping on the light, he trotted down the steps.

"So what are they going to do?" Millie followed him down, a hint of fear in her voice.

"They're gathering as many portable generators as they can find. They have one but it'll take two just to run everything that's medically necessary."

He strolled over to where the first of his two generators was set up, ready to be turned on when the power went out. When this system was designed right after they moved in, he was sure the two generators, each located in his two different garages, was overkill, especially since part of his house ran on the power from solar panels anyway. Would there ever be a time when he lost both solar power and city power and still needed to run every single thing in his entire house?

But right now, he'd never been so grateful for an overcompensation.

"If the solar panels get damaged, you can run almost everything you need from the other generator. It can handle the main floor air-conditioning unit, lights, and the refrigerator. Just try to steer clear of drying any clothes and running the dishwasher at the same time." He unplugged the large metal box-like structure from the wall and wrapped the cord around it, getting it ready to load into the back of his minivan. "The whole house should be secure, but if you start getting nervous, the interior laundry is the safest room."

He wheeled the giant machine toward his minivan. "Keep your phone by you. I'll call to check in."

"Wait. You think you're leaving me here?"

Braxton stopped by the trunk of the vehicle and straightened up to look at her. "Of course. The house was built to withstand this kind of storm. You'll be safe here." He kissed her on her forehead. "But can you help me lift this into the minivan before you head upstairs?" He folded down the backseat to make space for the generator.

Millie shook her head. "No."

He shot her a questioning glance. True, the three-foot motor was heavy, but Millie was stronger than she looked. He'd seen her lift some pretty big things all on her own while doing the renovations.

"I could make a ramp out of plywood, but I'm kind of in a hurry. Can you try to lift it first, and if it's too heavy I'll work on a plan B?"

"Of course we can lift it. I meant no, you're not leaving me here." Before he could argue with her, she squatted down on the other side of the generator and counted down. "Three, two, one." Together they lifted it high enough to get the two wheels in the back of the minivan.

"I'm going with you. Plus, if we fold down the middle seats, we can take both generators, and it sounds like they could use them."

Braxton stopped what he was doing and stared at Millie. The thought of her driving with him through the storm, one that was already blowing down trees and knocking out power, flooded him with fear. Here she was safe; out there on the road with only the thin metal of the minivan to protect her was a risk he wasn't willing to take.

"No way. It's too dangerous." He rolled the generator farther into his car, making sure there was enough room to clear the tailgate. As far as he was concerned, this conversation was over.

"Apparently, it's not too dangerous for you to go." There was a hint of defiance in her tone. She wasn't one to back down even when things got tough.

Normally, he liked that quality in her, but now… "That's different."

Millie propped her hands on her hips and glared at him. "How? Because I'm a woman?"

She had his full attention now, especially with that fiery look in her eyes that ignited something in him, the fierce determination he adored. But fear gripped him, squeezing so hard it was getting difficult to breathe.

"Because out there I can't keep you safe."

Her hands dropped to her sides and for a second a

different emotion flashed across her face. Something that more closely resembled the look she gave him right after he kissed her.

She nodded and stared at her toes for a second before she reached out and took his hand in hers. "You're never going to be able to keep everyone you care for safe. Not me, not Alice, and not Henry. Things are going to happen that are beyond your control." Her words were soft and caring, wrapping around his wounded heart like a warm embrace. "And right now you need me. You could use an extra set of eyes to look for hazards as you drive and an extra set of hands to help you lift this. And the other generator will do a lot more good there than here with only me and Bear."

A knot formed in his throat, because she was right, and not just about him needing her help. It was impossible for him to keep all of his loved ones safe. For so long he'd been doing everything in his control to physically protect the people he loved, but control was just an illusion. What he'd really done was shield his heart so it wouldn't hurt so bad when things went sideways. But that was no way to live.

Millie had broken through his barriers and shown him that.

She gently squeezed his hand. "It'll be okay. Let me come."

The thought of something happening to her terrified him, but he drew in a deep breath, letting her confidence give him strength. "You sure you want to sacrifice the second generator? You might be singing a different tune when you're sleeping in sweltering heat without air-conditioning."

She flashed one of her dazzling grins. "I haven't had a good reminder of summer camp in a while."

Braxton's heart tripped. While he might not be able to completely protect her all the time, he sure wanted to do his best to keep her around for a long, long time. "Why don't you grab Bear and I'll meet you at the other garage to load the other generator?"

Millie cocked an eyebrow, looking around. "You have a second garage? Fancy."

Braxton chuckled. Leave it to Millie to help him keep his stress level in check. "You have six bedrooms, but I haven't said anything."

She shrugged with a sort of mock humility. "Seven, but who's counting?"

Ten minutes later, the second generator was loaded into the minivan and he, Millie, and Bear pulled out into the rain. He'd driven in heavier rain before. The Lowcountry had a history of letting the skies open on a moment's notice, dumping blinding sheets of rain on any poor soul who was unfortunate enough to still be on the road. They still hadn't invented a windshield wiper setting fast enough to keep up with it.

Hurricane rain was different, though. It wasn't as solid. Instead, it came in random blasts, blowing in from every direction at once. Sometimes, it even seemed to be coming up from the ground.

He knew this drive well. He'd done it almost every day for the past year. But today the familiar road looked eerie. There wasn't another car anywhere to be seen. The big oak trees that lined the road shook angrily as he passed and the palmettos blew so far to the side that they threatened to touch the ground. Gusts of wind blew the minivan around as if it were an empty tin can, and he struggled to keep the car centered on the vacant road.

Finally, after what felt like the longest drive of his life, he pulled into Summer Island Memory Care Home's vacant parking lot. Storm shutters covered every window and door, and if he didn't know for sure that there were people inside, he would've thought it was abandoned. He drove around to the back entrance that the manager had told him to use.

Millie pulled out her phone and dialed the number they'd been using to communicate with Memory Care's staff during their drive. "Hey. We're here." She paused. "Yeah, we're at the back entrance."

She paused again, listening, then laid her gentle hand on his wrist. Warmth billowed through him. It wasn't lost on him how easily she fit into his life.

She lowered the phone from her mouth and looked at him. "He said you should back all the way up to the door."

Braxton nodded and shifted the minivan into reverse. "Backing in."

He swung around so the tailgate was pointed at the doors and slowly moved the van backward. Millie twisted around in her seat to watch his progress.

"I think if you get close enough to the building, I can climb through the car and help them unload it."

Braxton kept his eyes on the backup camera. "Deal. Then I'm going to try to park under that covering over there." He pointed to the overhang of the maintenance building. "It's not total protection, but it's better than nothing. And it's an easy sprint to the door."

"Bear and I will wait to let you in."

"Good plan. I feel like we should be putting our hands in the middle to do some sort of team cheer," he joked.

Millie stuck her hand in between them. "Go team on three?"

He shifted the car into park. But instead of putting his hand on top of hers for the cheer, he leaned across the seat so his face was inches from hers.

"Go team." He gently kissed her lips. "Be careful."

She blushed and a spontaneous grin pulled at the corners of her mouth. "Always."

She climbed out of her seat and crawled through the car

as he opened the liftgate.

"You must be Millie," a familiar voice said. Braxton leaned around in his seat to see Ronnie, the head of maintenance. "Hey, Braxton. Thank you so much for this. You have no idea how much these two generators will help out."

"Anything for y'all," Braxton said, holding his hand up in a wave.

Millie climbed over the generators and helped Ronnie and one of the medical assistants lift them out.

Once both were removed, Braxton pulled forward, parked under the overhang of the maintenance building, and turned the ignition off. The main building was less than a hundred yards away. It was an easy walk across a paved parking lot, but with the winds picking up, the thought of running across it made his heart race.

"On the count of three." He said the words out loud, as if some unseen person in the car was going to force him to go on the appropriate number.

Pulling his rain jacket hood over his head, he twisted around to look at his target. Through the rain, he could barely make out Millie's face behind the glass door.

It didn't matter what kind of storm was raging outside, she'd always be worth running to.

"Three," he said, not bothering to count down the rest of the way. He flung the door open and dashed out into the rain. The wind blew at his side, but as he got near, Millie opened the door for him.

"See. Nothing to it." She handed him a towel. He used it to dry his face as she locked the glass door. Turning the key that was stuck into the hole on the wall, the automatic storm shutter slowly lowered down, covering the glass doors.

"Where are the generators?" Braxton asked.

"Already in the process of being installed." She grinned

at him. "They said everyone is gathered in the formal room. That means nothing to me, but I'm guessing you'll know how to get us there."

"Formal room, huh? We're going to have to socialize with some people."

Millie shrugged. "I hear there's a pretty exciting game of bingo going on at the moment. And a TV set to live coverage of the storm. You can choose your poison."

Braxton flung the towel over his shoulder.

"It's a tough decision, but I do love a good game of bingo." He made sure the storm shutter had lowered securely into place before he opened the interior door for Millie.

"Come on. Fun is waiting."

He took her hand and they walked down the empty back hallway in the direction of the noise with Bear trotting along by their side.

"This place seems nice." Millie's head swiveled around, taking in the sights of the empty hallway. "I haven't been in a lot of nursing homes, but they all had a sterile, hospital feel. This place feels homier."

The dark wood floors, crown molding, and private rooms did make it feel more like a home, which was what Braxton wanted. When it became clear that Henry was requiring more help, Braxton didn't want his dearest friend to move into some cold institution. If Henry couldn't stay at home with him, he wanted the closest thing to home they could get, and this was it.

They walked to the end of the hall where it opened up to the common space. Veronica stepped out of the kitchen holding a tray with two pitchers of iced tea.

"Braxton! You're our hero as usual. Ronnie tells me your two generators, along with the one another family member lent us, will be enough to power all the medical devices, keep our kitchen functional, and maybe even allow the lights and air conditioner in the main part of the public spaces to stay on." She beamed at him. "He's hooking them all up right now so we'll be ready when the power goes out."

"Anything for Summer Island Memory Care Home." Braxton swiftly shifted the attention to Millie. "I don't think you've met my friend Millie yet. Millie, this is Veronica Nicholas, the heart and soul of this place."

"It's a pleasure to meet you, Millie. And who is this handsome fella?" Veronica looked down at Bear.

"This is Bear. I hope it's okay we brought him. I didn't want to leave him alone in the storm."

"Okay? Darlin', he's going to be a bigger hit than the generators." She balanced the tray on one hand and reached down to scratch the top of Bear's furry head with the other. "The residents are going to love you."

"Can we give you a hand with something?" Millie motioned to the tray Veronica was holding.

"Actually, I'd love a bit of help, as long as you're offering. We're a little short-staffed at the moment and the storm has made some of our friends pretty anxious."

"Just tell me what to do, and I'm here for you."

Veronica shifted her gaze to Braxton. "I like her," she said, nodding her head at Millie.

Braxton's heart did that flip-flop thing again. He couldn't agree more.

Before he got lost in the moment, Veronica had shoved the tray of pitchers in his direction. "Braxton, you take this into the main room. Millie can help me carry in the other two snack trays. And Sir Bear." She turned to the dog whose tail wagged happily at the mention of his name. "You just be your doggone handsome self." She scratched him behind the ears again.

As the ladies and Bear disappeared into the kitchen, Braxton made his way out into the main part of the facility.

It was more active than usual. Kimmie, the activity's coordinator, was calling a game of bingo in the dining room which occupied most of the residents while several medical aides sat in the formal room trying to comfort a few of the more upset individuals.

Braxton set his tray down on one of the empty tables and went to join Henry who was sitting at a table by himself with three bingo cards in front of him.

"That's a lot of cards to keep up with for an old man," Braxton joked as he slid into the chair next to his friend.

"There's a big storm outside. Big storm. I didn't know it was coming."

Braxton's heart lurched as he caught sight of the panic on Henry's face. "Naw. Nothing you haven't seen before. Plus, it gives you a chance to win back some of your money at this all-day bingo tournament. I know your bingo dollar bag was getting a little light."

"What are you talking about? I always win at bingo," Henry grumped. He paused for a second as Kimmie called the next number and marked it off on two of his cards.

"Why are you here? You're too late for chess."

"I had to bring over a generator. But since I missed our chess game today, I thought we might be able to play later. You know, as soon as you finish losing your money at bingo."

Henry grunted. "I'll see if I can fit you into my schedule."

Braxton chuckled and settled back into his chair to survey the room. With hurricane shutters covering all the windows, it had a cave-like feeling. There was a general air of nervousness hanging over the room, but the staff was doing their best to overcome it with their bright smiles and reassuring voices. Braxton twisted around in his seat to take it all in when he caught the brightest smile of all.

Millie, carrying a tray of cookies, emerged from the hallway that led to the kitchen. Bear stood by her side, his tongue hanging out of what appeared to be his own happy grin and his leash wrapped around her wrist. When she met his gaze across the room, he jumped up to help her.

He grabbed Henry's shoulder. "Also, I brought a friend with me today. Someone I'd like you to meet."

"You what?"

Braxton headed away from the table and reached Millie just in time to grab Bear's leash, so she didn't have to balance the tray as the dog tugged.

"Mildred?"

Braxton jerked and turned to stare at Henry, who'd gotten up from his seat. It wasn't so much the word as the tone that caught him by surprise. It had a ghostly hint, as if he was far away.

"No, it's..." Braxton started, but it was as if Henry didn't even see him. Henry hobbled, more unsteady than usual, through the tables in their direction, his eyes fixed on Millie.

"Mildred, it's you."

Braxton's gaze darted back and forth between Millie and Henry.

Millie's welcoming smile never faltered as she stood there holding her tray of goodies.

"Yes, it's me. But most people call me Millie. And I'm guessing you're Henry."

Henry had a look on his face that Braxton had never seen before, and something about it troubled him.

"My sweet Millie." Henry kept walking toward Millie, the far-off look in his eyes almost enchanted. And that's when Braxton's confusion turned to concern. While there was something about this particular expression Braxton hadn't seen before, he knew this look. The hollowness in his eyes, the lack of expression on his face. Henry's mind thought he was somewhere else.

This happened from time to time. His mind would

think he was somewhere from his past. He would mistake people and situations from those in his fractured memory. As the episode went on and more things didn't connect, the confusion ramped up and frustration would set in.

"I was hoping you'd come. I was hoping I'd get a chance to apologize. And look, here you are."

Veronica had noticed the situation and stepped closer. "Mr. Donovan, I think you've gotten confused. This is Braxton's new friend Millie. She recently moved here from Chicago." She spoke in a loud, even tone. "You're at Summer Island Memory Care Home, where you live. And there's a hurricane today so we have a few new people here to help us out. This is Braxton's friend Millie. You've just met her," Veronica repeated.

Henry ignored her. "I wrote you a letter explaining everything. It was all a misunderstanding. A big, horrible misunderstanding."

"A letter?" Millie kept her wide smile, though it was starting to look a little more forced. She threw a questioning look at Braxton.

"Henry, this is my friend Millie. Millie Leclair. She was the one I was telling you I wanted you to meet." Braxton used a voice a little louder than normal, patting his friend on his shoulder, but his words seemed lost on Henry.

Henry shook off Braxton's hand. "I know Millie Leclair," he said, then turned, beaming at Millie with that same far-off look in his eyes. "You came back, my love. I was afraid you wouldn't read my letter. But here you are."

Veronica had set her own tray down on the table and now laid a gentle hand on Henry's other shoulder. "Mr. Donovan, why don't you come sit down and rest a while? It has been such an exciting day. You are safe. You're at Summer Island Memory Care Home where you live and we're taking good care of you. Let's sit and relax."

Braxton recognized Veronica's calm, soothing words. They were the basic facts given to help anchor Henry when he was having a moment of confusion. She would continue repeating them until he recognized something or calmed down enough to relax. Usually, Braxton helped with this process, but right now he stood spellbound by the scene.

Mildred. My love. Letters.

It must have clicked for Millie at the same time, because she whispered, "He thinks I'm Aunt Mildred? Did Henry used to date her?"

This was new information for Braxton, too, and his gaze bounced between Henry and Millie as the pieces of the past started to come together like a long-lost jigsaw puzzle. Perhaps he should've made this connection before, but honestly it'd never occurred to him. Part of that reason was due to the fact that when Henry mentioned he knew Mildred Leclair, Braxton assumed it was because everyone knew everyone in this small town, and he never bothered to stop and think about when he would've known her.

But perhaps the biggest thing that had thrown him off was the little-known fact that he hadn't remembered until right now. Henry's first name, a name he claimed was only ever used by his mother and the only trace of it left was on his birth certificate, was Christopher.

Meanwhile, Millie had refocused on Henry, her forced smile turning more genuine. "I'm Millie, Mildred's great-niece." She kept her voice bright and some of the concern lines that had crept up around her eyes started to fade away. "She was an amazing woman, so I'm flattered to be mistaken for her. I'd love to hear more about how you knew her." She held her hand out to Henry in a friendly attempt to restart their introduction.

"Henry's Mr. C," Braxton blurted out without thinking, then winced as soon as the words had left his mouth. He didn't want to create more confusion, but the discovery was blowing his mind.

Millie paused, her hand still hovering in front of her. "Henry Donovan is Mr. C?"

Henry's face screwed up in frustration. "What are you talking about? Why does everyone keep changing names?"

"Mr. Donovan, you're at Summer Island Memory Care Home where you live. Braxton came by with his friend Millie to help us out today." Veronica rubbed his arm and tossed a warning look at Braxton.

But Braxton kept his focus on Henry. "That letter, Henry. What did you explain to Mildred in that last letter?"

Henry turned to him, his eyes narrowed and his expression turning angry. "Letter? What letter?" Confusion clouded his voice and Braxton knew whatever memory had captivated him was now fading. Times like this often led to his biggest episodes, but Braxton couldn't let it go. This could be the only shot he had to find out the truth.

Millie took a step back, looking uncertain.

Veronica's gaze narrowed on Braxton, clearly telling him to back off before he upset Henry. "Braxton, why don't we table this conversation until another time. You and Mr. Donovan can play a game of chess. This dark and rainy day is perfect for chess, don't you think?"

Braxton probably should've listened to her advice, but he couldn't leave it alone yet. Henry's answers were important, not just for Millie, but for himself. Treading carefully, he pushed forward. "Your stories of Seascape, the ones I'm not old enough to hear, they're about Mildred, aren't they?"

A hint of recognition flickered in Henry's eyes. "Mildred," he whispered. He looked from Braxton to Millie to Veronica. His face screwed up with a combination of frustration and fear, as if trying to recall the memory was like trying to grab onto a fading tendril of smoke.

"Were you in love with Mildred?" This discovery felt big. It was a part of Henry's life story that Braxton didn't know and could explain a lot of questions about why he took the route he did, about the advice he'd always given Braxton. About the path Braxton himself should take because of it. "The Big Regret you always talk about? Did that have to do with Mildred?"

Henry pursed his lips together, his breathing becoming more rapid as he glared at Braxton. "I don't... I can't..."

"What happened with Mildred? Why was she The Big Regret?" Braxton could feel his own pulse racing, but he didn't stop. They were so close to the truth.

Henry glanced again at Millie, then at Veronica, and finally at the room around him. He squeezed his eyes shut in angry frustration, color rising from underneath the collar of his shirt.

"Braxton!" Veronica wedged herself between Braxton and Henry, putting an arm around the old man's shoulders. "Mr. Donovan, you're at Summer Island Memory Care Home where you live and you're safe. Why don't you come over here with me and we set up this chessboard? Let's get those pieces in the right place." She steered him off in the direction of a small table that held the antique chessboard Braxton had donated to the facility just after Henry came to stay here.

Braxton watched his friend relax into one of the chairs, the dedicated and amazing Veronica calming him down before the situation got out of control. There should've been relief flowing through him that she was able to deescalate the situation as quickly as she did. And perhaps, somewhere deep down, it was there, but mostly he was consumed with all the other thoughts scurrying through his mind.

Millie stepped up next to him. "You okay?" She slipped her hand into the crook of his arm.

Braxton sorted through the cacophony of emotions. On

the one hand, he just learned an important piece of Henry's past. It was the piece that explained why Henry chose the path he did. It also brought a fresh clarity to advice and life coaching Henry had given him over the years.

But on the other hand, his heart broke once again at the thought of not being able to have a conversation with Henry about it. The deep feeling of loss formed a lump in his throat.

"Yeah, I'm okay," he said eventually.

Millie leaned her head on his shoulder, and her quiet support poured into him, giving him strength. "When you're ready, want to talk about my aunt and your coach? You seem to know a bit more than I do."

A grin tugged at the corner of his mouth. Who would've thought? "You want the short version or the long version?"

"Whichever version includes why he used stationery monogrammed with a *C*, and why my aunt was known as The Big Regret."

· · ·

Millie watched Henry as Braxton finished explaining all the bits of the story he'd gotten from his mentor without knowing he was the mysterious Mr. C.

She was mildly aware her mouth was hanging open. "Wow." She'd spent quite a bit of time thinking about who'd captured her aunt's heart with his eloquent words, but she had to admit she'd never even considered Henry. "I mean, he's been right here the whole time."

"Actually, he hasn't." Braxton stole a quick glance at his mentor. "He grew up here, but he left Summer Island shortly after high school to pursue his golfing career, sometime in the mid-fifties."

"Probably around the time of the last letter," Millie added.

"Exactly. And once he left, he never came back. He always told me that other than the best golf course in the world, this town had nothing for him. Even after I fell in love with Summer Island and bought a house here, he only ever came for short stays to play golf with me. The only reason he officially moved back was because Jade died and I needed him."

Millie sorted through all the details in her mind, trying to put together the story that had captivated her all summer. "So what happened? Why was she The Big Regret?"

Braxton shrugged. "That's the part I don't know. Henry would talk about The Big Regret from time to time. It was always a cautionary tale about not letting opportunities pass you by and seizing the moment. I always thought it had something to do with his golf career." A hint of sadness flickered in his eyes. "I do know that it was the one thing he'd do over if he had the chance. I think he never stopped loving her."

"Based on some of the things my aunt used to say, I think the same was true for her." Millie leaned back in her chair and watched the author of her aunt's love letters. "I wonder what happened that drove them apart."

"I think there's a chance we might never know all the details, but at least we have this piece of the puzzle."

"For sure." Being able to put a face to the voice behind the letters was oddly satisfying, even if she didn't know the whole story. "So now what?"

"Now we play chess. Do you know how to play?"

A hint of nervousness fluttered through her. "Are you sure that's a good idea?" The last time she stood in front of Henry, it'd caused quite a scene. She didn't want to upset him a second time. This day was already upsetting enough as it was.

"These kinds of episodes can be hard to watch, but it's

the disease not the person. And it has nothing to do with you." There was a kindness in Braxton's eyes that made sense after she'd experienced this part of his world.

"Henry's a big part of my life. I wish you could've gotten to meet the real Henry, when his mind was still his. You would've liked him. But this is hard. And if you don't feel comfortable, you don't have to interact with him."

Once again, Millie was overwhelmed by the magnitude of Braxton's responsibility. Day in and day out he selflessly gave of himself to care for those he loved. He was one amazing man. It reinforced her desire to be part of his life. Not just the easy fun parts, but also the hard parts.

She looked up at him from under her lashes. "Did I ever tell you I was on the all-district chess team in junior high?"

"You keep getting better." He waggled his eyebrows, which sent familiar tingles racing through her. "Let's give him some time to settle down, then I'll introduce you again. Formally this time." He picked up the two pitchers of tea from the nearby table and held them out to her. "In the meantime, how do you feel about refilling some drinks?"

Millie took the two pitchers of tea from him, reading the labels. "Regular and unsweet? Isn't that the same thing?"

Some of the stress that was weighing on Braxton seemed to lift and a corner of his mouth pulled up in an amused grin. "Regular means regular sweet tea. Apparently, it's a southern thing."

"I have to admit, the stuff can be addictive."

She and Braxton spent the next thirty minutes circulating the dining room full of heavy square wooden tables, refilling drinks and offering cookies to the bingo playing residents. Braxton greeted every one of them by name, offering kind remarks and encouraging smiles. Some acted like they recognized him, but most stared up at him with empty looks in their eyes. Sympathy pulled at Millie's heart.

At the same time, watching Braxton interact with them made whatever magnetic draw that was pulling her to him even stronger.

When they'd worked the whole room, they returned the tray and pitchers to the serving table. "You sure you're ready for this?" Braxton asked.

Millie nodded. "Let's do it."

Braxton took her hand, lacing his fingers through hers as they headed for the table where Henry was playing chess with Veronica.

"Hello, old man." He clapped his friend on the shoulder.

"You're late." Despite the grumpy tone, Henry's expression lit up with the sort of excitement that said he was happy to see his friend, late or not.

Braxton pulled a chair from the neighboring table and placed it next to him. "I am, but I guess Veronica here has been telling you there's a hurricane outside. Hurricane Axel. It's appropriate someone finally named a storm after that golfing imposter."

Henry let out an annoyed sigh. "I don't know why they let him on the tour. But if the storm's anything like the golfer, it won't do much."

Braxton chuckled. "Henry, I want to introduce you to my new friend Millie and her dog Bear."

A spark of nervousness zinged through her as she stepped in front of Henry. Not only was she still a tad concerned that her presence would cause another episode—it had only been half an hour after all—but this was Braxton's person. His opinion mattered. And nothing said meet the family like rolling in during a natural disaster after a day full of manual labor.

"It's nice to meet you."

Henry studied her, but this time there was no recognition in his eyes as he took her hand.

"Pleasure."

"Millie also happens to be a champion chess player, so I hope you brought your A-game today."

Henry shot Braxton a look. "I always bring my A-game."

Braxton settled back in his chair and crossed his arms over his chest. "That's not what you told me when I beat you last week."

As they bantered back and forth, Henry seemed to relax. They had a special relationship, and getting to witness it was a treat. The last of the guards she'd put up around her heart faded away.

She handed Bear's leash to Braxton and slid into the seat across from Henry that Veronica vacated. "It's been a while since I've played. I hope I live up to the hype."

Henry made his first move. "I'd take it easy on you, but they say my memory's going and I'll probably forget my word before the game's over."

His ability to make the best of his situation made Millie grin. "Fair enough." She made her first countermove.

So maybe he wasn't exactly the same man as before the disease captured him, but there were hints of the great man who inspired Braxton and wrote beautiful letters to her aunt.

Henry looked over at Braxton and, not bothering to be discreet about it, nodded his head at Millie. "So, you sweet on her?"

Braxton chuckled. He met Millie's gaze and the familiar jolt of excitement surged through her.

"Yeah, something like that."

Chapter Nineteen

Millie lay on her back in the darkness in the women's on-call room and stared at the bunk above her. The storm had stopped hours ago, but since it was dark and the electricity in the whole city was out, she and Braxton had decided to wait to leave until the sun came up, which, according to her phone, would be any minute.

Millie had been a fan of the idea partly because of the safety aspect, but also because being here kept her mind off everything else. As long as she was pouring drinks or doing dishes, she didn't have to think about how one day had derailed her life.

On top of the list of things she was still trying to come to terms with was the whole kiss situation. From here on out, everything with Braxton was going to be different, which was a good thing, right? This wasn't one of those situations that when the stormed cleared and they stood in the light of day looked a lot more like a mistake than a good idea, was it?

Of course, thinking about storms clearing was her second most inevitable topic. She didn't want to imagine what the howling wind was doing to her renovations or what it would take to do more repairs. She didn't want to wonder how high the storm surge came or whether the trees were still standing or had gone through her house. She'd rather think about scrubbing deep pots until they gleamed.

But now the storm had passed and a new day had dawned, and it was time to face the music.

She crawled out of the creaky bunk bed and dressed in the darkness, careful to not wake any of the sleeping staff members. Quietly gathering her things, she made her way out of the dark room into the lit hallway with Bear lazily trotting along behind her.

Veronica was already up and dressed, looking as cheerful as always while she rearranged the chairs in the dining room. Bear sidled up to her and looked up with expectant eyes, waiting for her to pet him.

"You're one good boy." Veronica scratched behind his ears before she looked up at Millie. "He was the single most successful tool to calm down our upset residents yesterday. Thanks for letting us use him as a comfort dog."

Millie set her small bag and raincoat on a nearby chair, wishing she'd had the forethought to bring a toothbrush with her. "I think he enjoyed it more than the residents. There's nothing this guy likes more than attention and getting petted."

"You know, if you and Bear can find time in your schedule to come by once or twice a week, we'd love it. We've been looking for a companion dog ever since we lost our last one a couple months back."

Bear was surveying the empty room with his tongue hanging out the side of what appeared to be a wide, openmouthed grin.

"I think he'd like that. He loves putting a smile on people's faces."

"He wasn't the only one who caused some smiles. I caught

someone else who couldn't stop smiling when he looked at you." She shot Millie a knowing look that caused another round of nerves to skitter through her.

She shifted and tried to play dumb. "Who? Braxton?" It was a complicated subject she wasn't quite ready to dive into yet. Not until she had coffee, anyway.

Veronica raised a questioning eyebrow. "Honey, all I can say is I wish I had a man who looked at me like that."

There was that fluttery thing in Millie's chest again, but she tried to play it cool. "I mean…it's…" Millie quickly looked down at Bear in hopes to shield any of the lingering expressions that would give her thoughts away and make her more vulnerable than she already felt.

There was kindness and understanding in Veronica's dark eyes. "Everyone here adores Braxton and it's been a while since we've seen him smile like that. It's nice to see he found someone who makes him happy."

This time, apparently Millie couldn't keep the mixture of emotions surging through her from being reflected on her face, because before she could respond, Veronica gently patted her arm.

"He's one of the good ones. A real keeper."

Heat flared in her cheeks, but before she could say anything, Veronica looked over her head. "And speak of the devil. Good morning, Braxton."

Millie took another second, hoping the color in her face would fade, before she looked up to see Braxton strolling toward them with his confident gait.

"Morning, ladies. I hear the sky is clear and Summer Island hasn't been washed away. How 'bout we raise up these shutters and take a look?"

He was extra adorable with the rumpled T-shirt and hair of someone who'd just woken up. He stopped next to her so his shoulder grazed hers.

"We were about to get to that. But you two have done quite enough for us already. It's time for you to go home and check on your own places." Veronica made a shooing motion.

"You sure? You have enough staff to help you out today?"

"Our building is still standing and the power company assured me an hour ago that we'll have full electricity restored before lunchtime. We're fine here. Go. Take care of your own stuff."

"If you say so." He turned to Millie. "You ready?"

A whole different set of nerves danced through her. "Yes," she said while shaking her head no.

Braxton chuckled. "Time to see what kind of punch ole Axel packed." He gave her hand a reassuring squeeze before he turned back to Veronica. "I'll try to come back up to check on Henry today, but depending on what the houses look like, it will probably be later this afternoon."

"No rush. We've got everything under control here. Be careful out there." She turned to Millie. "It was lovely to meet you, Millie. We'll talk soon."

"Absolutely." She hugged her new friend, a gesture that had become more natural in the six weeks since she'd moved to Summer Island, and then followed Braxton down the long, dark hall toward the door they had entered barely more than twelve hours before.

She wiggled her fingers then balled and opened her fists, trying to expel some of her nervous energy. This was the first hurricane she'd been involved in, and she had no idea what to expect of the aftermath. They'd be able to get their car out, right? Would the roads be passable? Was there anything left of her house?

When they got to the end of the hall, she held her breath as she waited for Braxton to raise the storm shutter and push open the door. Half blinded from the bright light of morning, she stepped outside. And what she saw stunned her.

Tons of leaves and branches littered the grounds. A broken plastic lawn chair was upside down in the middle of the garden and what looked like a section of metal fencing was curled up like a tumbleweed in the vacant parking lot. But other than that, everything looked okay. All the buildings around them were standing and the roofs appeared to be attached. Even Braxton's minivan seemed to be unharmed.

"Only two trees down. The one that took out the generator at the beginning of the storm and that one over there." Braxton pointed to the giant uprooted oak tree on the edge of the property. "I'd say they were pretty lucky."

"I can't believe it." Millie walked out to the middle of the grassy lawn, careful to step over the fallen sticks and branches, and a sense of calm washed over her as she slowly turned in a circle to take it all in. "All the howling and banging during the storm, and only two trees came down."

It was going to take quite a bit of cleanup, and the trees that had been stripped of a good chunk of their leaves and more than their fair share of limbs were going to look bare for a long while, but what she saw was encouraging. Much more encouraging than what she'd been expecting. "Let's hope our houses did as well."

Braxton slid his arm around her shoulders and gave her a squeeze. "Regardless of what we find when we pull onto East Shore Drive, we can fix it."

There was that word again. We. It hung there in the air between them, begging to be addressed.

"You're only saying that because you're still sad you missed the chance to put on a new roof the last time I offered it," she joked, trying to calm her jittering nerves as they walked toward his car.

He hit the unlock button and the back door slid open for Bear to hop in as they both walked to their own sides. "Exactly."

Braxton tried to engage her in mindless chitchat on the ride home, which Millie appreciated, but she was having a hard time focusing. Every turn, every time they had to drive around a fallen tree or some sort of hurricane-caused damage, Millie's body got more tense. By the time they turned onto their street, all her muscles were in one solid knot. Her heart started to race and her palms got sweaty.

She squeezed her eyes shut. "I can't look. You're just going to have to tell me if it's still standing."

Braxton wrapped his hand around hers. Leaves and twigs crackled and popped as they drove over them. Occasionally, she could feel the car swerve to the right or left as she assumed they dodged larger debris on the road, and finally they slowed to a stop.

"Okay, we're here. Do you want to look for yourself?"

Millie's heart thundered in her chest. She clamped her hands over her already closed eyes. There was no way she could look. At this point, she was struggling just to breathe. Every worst-case scenario played through her mind along with some that didn't have anything to do with damage from a hurricane. She was fairly certain there wasn't a smoking meteorite crater where her house used to be, but that image flashed through her mind nevertheless.

"Just tell me. I think I can deal with whatever it is if I know before I see it." At least she hoped that was true.

The car inched forward and then made a sharp turn.

"Wow." Braxton's voice had a hint of amazement that made her rapid heartbeat kick up a notch.

"Is that a good wow or an it's-worse-than-I-imagined wow?"

Braxton chuckled, a warm sound that calmed her overactive nerves just a bit. "It's a good wow. Lots of leaves and branches. I mean, *lots* of leaves. I'm not even sure where they all came from. Are those pine branches? Is there even a pine tree around here?"

Millie was tempted to crack her fingers and take a peek at the mystery pine branches, but the fear of what else she might see made her squeeze her fingers tighter together.

"The house. How's the house?"

"There used to be a house here?"

She could hear the joking tone in his voice. "Braxton!"

He chuckled. It wasn't the forced, nervous chuckle of someone trying to figure out how to share bad news. It was a legit, joyful sound of someone who was happy. It wasn't enough to calm her fears, but it did make her pounding heartbeat relax just a smidge.

"The house looks fine. All those flowers I planted the other day took quite a beating, which I'm taking as a personal offense, but from this angle, the house looks good."

Slowly, she spread her fingers and peeked through the cracks. He had pulled the car all the way around so her door opened at the base of the front steps and from what she could see, it didn't look like there was one bit of damage to the house.

Dropping her hands, she took in the full site, fear turning to shock. "It's still here." She opened the door and stepped out, careful to step over a large palm frond sticking out from under the car. "And it has a roof."

Her eyes were probably the size of dinner plates, but she couldn't help it. She'd imagined a lot of scenarios over the past twenty-four hours, but this scene was never one of them.

Braxton walked around the front of the car to join her. "It does still have a roof. In fact, I don't see any major damage to the house."

"It's still here," she said a second time. Relief cascaded over her, leaving behind a warm, euphoric feeling in its wake. "Let's look at the back."

Without waiting for him, she headed around the side of

the house, taking in the paint job. There were places that looked scratched and scuffed from where debris must have hit it, and it was missing that fresh glow it had before, but it still looked decent. Bear trotted along beside her sniffing one fallen limb or leaf pile after the next.

She rounded the final corner and without looking out over the yard, she immediately gazed at the back of the house. And she gasped.

Braxton followed and stopped next to her. "I'd say the wind is no match for Seascape. Look at that, it doesn't look like even one of those shutters moved an inch. You're quite the installation beast."

Millie shook her head, walking along the patio and gently touching the old wooden shutters covering the many French doors she'd struggled to lock into rusting tracks. "It worked." She paused in front of one that had given her particular trouble and gave it a shake. "I wasn't so sure it would when I was putting them up."

Shock gave way to excitement and she turned to Braxton and flung her arms around him. "The shutters worked! Thank you so much for helping me. I couldn't have done it without you!"

His arms wrapped around her waist and she marveled at how nice it felt to be held by him. "I battled the spiders, but you pretty much did the rest."

She let go of him and gazed up at the house again. "You feel like battling those spiders again? I guess now that they've done their job, it's time to take them down and store them for next time."

"I don't think the spiders made it." He pointed to something behind her. She turned around and took in the rest of her yard. This time she could feel her eyes getting wide for a whole different reason.

"Oh my." She'd been so focused on any damage done to

the house, she hadn't looked at the damage done to the rest of the property. One of the tall palmetto trees that lined the property had fallen right on top of the wooden shed where the spiders lived and the shutters were stored, crumbling the entire back half of it. "Honestly, that thing was already falling down. I'm surprised the wind didn't knock it over."

There were several other trees down, and the fence between her property and the nature preserve next to her was going to need some repairs. Then her gaze landed on her newly finished boardwalk. Or perhaps it would've been more accurate to say it landed where her newly finished boardwalk *used* to be.

She pointed in the direction of the dunes. "It looks like my bridge to the beach was washed away." There was a spike of disappointment as she considered the cost that had been carried out to sea. That boardwalk had been her biggest nemesis during this whole renovation. It was the one thing that no matter how hard she tried, still refused to be conquered. She was determined to beat it, but right now, she had to admit it had her against the ropes.

"It's possible you'll find the wood in there. Along with half the trees from the neighborhood." Braxton pointed to her pool which was completely full of leaves, branches and random other things that had been blown into it, sending murky water sloshing out the top.

"What is all this stuff?" Millie let out a chuckle as she walked over to examine the ludicrous sight. "Eight feet. That's eight feet of leaves and branches at the deep end. It's like Axel dropped all his junk right here in my pool."

Braxton stood on the edge and peered into the mounds of branches heaping over the side. "You could hold a botany class on all the vegetation on Summer Island right here. There might even be some things that blew over from other places it visited." He pulled a branch out from the pile near his feet.

"Like this thing. Do you recognize these leaves?"

Millie scanned her property for a tree boasting similar leaves but came up short. "Not from my yard."

Braxton tossed it to the side and shrugged. "On the positive side, the spiders have a new place to call home."

Millie giggled again. After all the stress of the past twenty-four hours, it felt good to laugh. Some of the insecurities that had been weighing her down lifted just a little.

"If finding the money to build a new boardwalk and deforest my pool is the biggest job I have, I'd say I'm pretty lucky."

Braxton nodded. "Yes, we were. It looks like even the storm surge didn't come up as high as they were predicting. You can see the waterline way out there."

He strolled out past the pool to where a jagged line of seaweed, dirt, and bits of fishing nets ran across her yard about four feet from the end of her patio. He stood on the line and looked across to his house which sat closer to the beach than hers did.

"It looks like it stopped right along the back of the garage. With any luck, there's not any flooding."

Millie studied where the waterline hit the concrete wall that separated their properties. "You should check on it. Do you want me to come with you?"

His gaze lingered on his house for another second before he looked toward the road, his face filled with concern. "I'll check on it in a minute. But first there's something else I need to show you."

"But we've seen the whole house." Her newfound confidence gave way to nerves that had plagued her all night. "What else is there to show me?"

She wanted her argument to prompt his confident grin to return along with a joke about the mess she'd have to clean up. Instead, his look of concern shifted into sadness.

"You didn't see everything. There's one thing you missed."

. . .

Braxton led Millie back to the front of her house, wishing she didn't have to see what he was about to show her.

"But it's fine. The front of the house is fine." Panic flickered in her voice, causing a pang in his gut. He didn't want to walk her back to the front of her house and point out that her beloved fountain, the one she had worked to restore for three solid days, had been crumpled by the storm.

"No, yeah, the house is fine. It's not the house."

Maybe he should've pointed it out as soon as they pulled up, but he just couldn't stand that being the first thing she saw. After how hard she'd worked on this place for the past six weeks, she deserved better. That was why he chose to park as close to the house as he could, using the van to block her view. Then he tried his best to keep her focus on the house in front of her when she opened her eyes. In fact, if he could've used misdirection to keep her focus on cleaning up the mounds of yard debris in the back while he restored the one feature of the house she loved best and spared her from the pain, he would have. But the fountain was beyond repair.

"Tell me it's not the driveway. I am not paying to have that driveway redone again. Seriously. The driveway cost the same as three bathrooms. Three. If the driveway washed away, my guests are now parking on the dirt."

"It's not the driveway." It was much, much worse.

"Then what could it be?" They rounded the minivan and the fountain, or lack of a fountain, came into view. Millie stopped in her tracks and her whole body sagged as if all her air had just been let out. "Oh."

She let go of his hand and walked across the wide driveway

to where the remains of the fountain lay. Her bottom lip quivered, and she squatted down among the rubble. She ran her finger along what was left of one of the bowls. His heart broke.

"Did you know this was the first thing that was built on this property? My great-great-grandfather installed it as a promise of what was to come. And it ran every day the inn was open." She let out a heavy breath and picked up a chunk of concrete. "It's just a fountain, but…"

"I'm so sorry, Millie."

She stayed like that for a while, shifting through the chunks on the ground. Finally, she stood up. "So much for holding on to past sentiments." She closed her hand around the chunk of fountain in her hand and gazed at the boarded house she'd put so much time and energy renovating and redoing since she'd arrived. "I guess it's new beginnings all around."

Man, he loved her determination. Life threw up roadblocks, but she didn't let them stop her. Instead, she plowed right through them, armed with a smile and a YouTube video. Time after time, she'd come toe to toe with disappointment and stared it down until it turned into opportunity. She was brave and strong and beautiful, and he wanted her to be part of his life more than he'd wanted anything in a long time.

"From what I hear, there's a how-to video on making your own concrete fountain. It doesn't look that hard." Repeating her catchphrase back to her earned him a full-fledged grin.

"And since I've already mastered tiling, roofing, and painting, a new hobby is exactly what I was looking for."

Braxton's heart did one of those somersaults that were becoming familiar whenever he was around Millie. But letting himself fall in love was terrifying. There were so many ways it could go wrong, so many ways everyone could end up hurt that he had absolutely no control over. The wounds from his past and pains of his present had etched deep scars on his heart. Every sensible part of his brain told him it was safer to walk away than risk everything again. But there was something about her bravery and determination that made walking away impossible.

He slid his arm around her shoulders and pulled her close. "The new fountain can symbolize the promise of the new Seascape Inn."

"Exactly." She looked up to examine her house and let out a long, weary sigh. "Six days until the open house. It was going to be a tight finish before I added hurricane cleanup to the list."

"You can ask the HOA to push it to the next meeting. Given the circumstances, I don't think any of the board members would have a problem with it."

"And put off the vote for another two months? I can't wait that long. My bank account will need paying customers long before then." She snagged her lip with her teeth and straightened her posture. "No, it will be done in six days. It might not look exactly the way I imagined, but we will have that open house and the board's going to love it."

Her pep talk sent a wave of confidence swirling through him. "I have no doubt. Where do we start?"

She pulled away from him enough to give him a look that she thought his comment was ludicrous. "We? No. You have your own mess to clean up over there." She pointed to his house. "You have a little girl you have to bring home in a few days. Which reminds me, have you checked in with them?"

"Video-chatted with her this morning. She's doing great and is as perky at six a.m. as ever." He missed his little girl fiercely, but knowing she was safe and happy brought him comfort.

"And she deserves a house in perfect working order when

she comes home."

Millie was right. Making sure his house was safe for Alice was a priority, but Millie's struggles were a priority, too.

As if reading his mind, she answered him. "What? After all I've done, you think a little hurricane cleanup scares me?"

He imagined all the dangerous positions she'd put herself in so far. "Your lack of fear is exactly what I'm worried about."

She grinned. "How about this. You go take care of your stuff, and I promise I'll save all the really scary tasks that involve power tools and tall ladders until I'm fully using the buddy system."

"The buddy system is good. I'm a fan of the buddy system."

"So I hear."

Maybe falling in love with her was a risk, but it was one he was willing to take.

"Don't worry, buddy. I'll be back."

Chapter Twenty

After putting on and taking off all thirty-two full-length wooden shutters that covered the doors and windows of her house, Millie decided she should be excused from doing any type of exercise for the rest of the month. Maybe even the rest of the year. Every muscle in her body ached as she hauled the ladder to the front of the house.

Luckily, the windows on this side all used shutters attached to the house that either swung open on either side of the window or propped open over the window. All she had to do was open them and secure them into place.

She leaned the ladder against the first wall, tightened the old tool belt she'd been using, and climbed up to get started. She'd just unlatched the first hook when the sound of tires crunching down her driveway caught her off guard. The only person she was expecting was Braxton and there was no way he'd finished his own house.

She swung the first side of the shutters open before she turned to check out the approaching car.

Sophia waved and pulled around to a stop in front of

where Millie had propped the ladder. "Hello! I was driving past and thought I'd check on you." She climbed out of her car and walked over to hold the ladder steady. "I can't stay long because there's a stingray in my pool. An honest-to-goodness two-foot-wide stingray swimming around in circles."

Millie latched the other half of the shutter in place and climbed down the ladder to her friend. "Really? A stingray?"

Sophia nodded. "I guess it came in with the storm surge and settled there along with half the sand from the canal. I had to go by Tessa's to borrow one of her big fishing nets to get it out." She pointed to the big net sitting on the passenger seat of her car. "But I thought I'd drop by and see how you fared during the storm before I rescue the poor agitated soul."

Millie leaned against the ladder, sitting on one of its rungs. "No physical damage besides the fountain, the boardwalk, and a pool full of debris."

Sophia's concerned expression melted into confusion. "That doesn't sound too bad."

"I kissed Braxton."

Sophia's eyebrows darted up in surprise. "Oh. That's an interesting turn of events." She paused for a second as if considering this new information.

Millie chewed on her lip, replaying the scene in her mind. So the kiss itself wasn't the problem. It was actually nice. Very nice, in fact. The troublesome part was what came after it.

"I also told him I liked him. I actually used those words. Like some seventh grader at a dance in the school gym."

Sophia chuckled and leaned back against the hood of her car. "Wow. You really pulled out the big guns."

Millie shrugged. "Apparently I don't do anything halfway."

A scandalous grin curled the corners of Sophia's mouth. "So what happened after you brought up the big L-word?"

"I didn't say the big L-word. I said the little L-word. Big

difference."

Sophia held up her hands in surrender. "My mistake. Still, what did he say?"

Millie glanced over at his house before answering. "He said, and I quote, 'Me too.'"

Sophia rolled her eyes. "Boys say the dumbest things."

It was enough to lighten the situation and Millie let out a snort of laughter. "Right?"

"So let me get this straight. You kissed the man you're *falling* for—"

Millie held up a hand to stop her. "Like."

Sophia nodded her apology. "Sorry, like. And he happens to be into you too. This sounds like a good thing but I'm getting the feeling that you think it's..." Sophia paused and stared expectantly at Millie.

"A giant mistake? Yeah."

"Right." Sophia nodded as if considering the story again. After a second her head tilted to the side. "Why exactly is this a giant mistake again?"

"Because he's Braxton Channing. He's like famous and stuff."

"He's not really that famous now. He hardly ever gets stopped for a selfie anymore."

"Fine, I'll take that one off the list. But it's not all him. I've got all this going on." She motioned to the house behind her. "My life is complicated. I have a new business about to open and I'll need to focus all my energy into Seascape if I hope to make it a destination spot once again. This whole thing is—"

Sophia cut her off. "Complicated?"

Millie let out a long breath and rested her head against the ladder rung behind her. "Basically. Yeah."

Sophia flashed her a sympathetic smile. "You'll be hard-pressed to find one love story that isn't complicated. Love isn't easy. But it is worth fighting for."

Millie let that resonate in her mind. Part of her wished she could walk away right now, but it was too late. Despite promising herself that this chapter in her life was a solo act, she'd fallen for the boy next door, which left her in quite the predicament. From here on out, there was only one scenario where this story ended happily and a whole lot of scenarios where it ended in heartbreak. How had she let this happen?

"I have too many other things going on in my life right now," she said. "What if I don't have time to fight for it?"

"Before this hurricane decided to careen into our beach, I was working on a huge order that was supposed to ship tomorrow. Now, instead of trying to get my shop back up and running so I can get that order out in the vicinity of on time, I'm on my way to scoop up an angry stingray with a net that only has a four-foot pole." Sophia jabbed her thumb in the direction of the net in her passenger seat. "We don't always see the next thing coming before it gets here, but that doesn't mean we can't embrace it."

Millie stared up at the clear blue sky as she considered her words. "This could end badly."

"It could," Sophia said. "Or it could be great."

But why did it have to be so scary? She'd moved to a new state all by herself and taken on renovating a huge house without any experience in home repairs. Both of those situations had just as much risk of ending badly, if not more so, but she hadn't let that stop her.

"Your thing could end badly, too." Millie pictured Sophia trying to chase a stingray around her pool with that net, and some of the tension that had been weighing on her broke. She looked down at the net inside the car. "That's the longest pole Tessa had?"

Sophia's serious expression changed into something more joking. "Dios mío. Right? That's what I said to her. She just laughed and said I'd be fine. But you don't see her over here chasing Mr. Ray, do you?"

Millie giggled. "Do you want help? Because I'll totally cheer you on from a safe distance."

Sophia waved her off. "Nah, I've got this. And you, my friend, have got your thing."

She looked over at Braxton's house. "We'll see."

"I'd love to stay and hear all the juicy details, but this whole stingray situation is time sensitive. I need to return him to the ocean before my saltwater pool becomes toxic for him. We can finish this conversation tonight. You'll be at Joyce's, right?"

Millie stepped away from the ladder and walked over to give her friend a hug before she left. "Joyce's?"

"Yeah, she sent a text inviting the book club and a few others over for a post-hurricane Lowcountry boil. She has a defrosting deep freezer full of shrimp and sausage she needs to cook before they go bad. You were on the text." She pulled up the message on her phone and flipped it around so Millie could read it.

"I must have missed the invitation. My phone's dead."

Sophia pocketed her phone and held out her hand to Millie. "I have a small generator at my house. I'll charge it for you and give it to you tonight. Joyce said to come over around six or whenever you get to a stopping point."

Millie jogged over to the porch to retrieve her dead phone, glancing around at all the cleanup that still needed to be done. "I think my break is over, but dinner tonight sounds great. Let Joyce know I'll be there."

"Will do." She got in her car and started the engine. "But fair warning, he's invited too." She jerked her head in the direction of Braxton's house.

"Like I said. Complicated."

For the next several hours, Millie worked without stopping.

Her muscles were sore and she was dripping with sweat, but it felt like she'd barely put a dent in the cleanup efforts. Yes, all the storm shutters were off and stacked on her back porch and she'd cleared all the debris off her long driveway, but she hadn't touched any of the fallen trees or the forest residing in her pool. And she hadn't even thought about repairing the things that were broken like the boardwalk and the fountain.

Visible progress or not, Millie was more than ready for a break when Tessa pulled up at six o'clock to take her to Joyce's.

"Sorry about the fountain." She pulled a face to show her sympathy as Millie slid into the passenger seat.

Millie tried to avoid looking at the pile of rubble and focused instead on buckling her seat belt. "Thanks. But if that's all I lost, I should consider myself lucky. How about you? How's the boat?"

Tessa headed around the newly cleared drive toward the street. "We were able to trailer the smaller boat and my brother took the other one north to get it out of the storm's path. Both made it through without a scratch, but the marina is a mess. It's going to take a while to get everything cleaned up there. But no one was hurt, so I think that's worth celebrating."

They turned onto the road and headed the short distance to Joyce's house.

The big gate was open and the long driveway was already lined with cars. "It looks like we aren't the only ones ready to celebrate tonight," Millie said. "Hurricanes are awful, destructive things, but it's inspiring to see a community come together."

Tessa parked behind the last car. "For sure. Every time we have one of these kinds of parties, I think what a shame it is we don't do this more often. Why wait until our freezers are defrosting to share our provisions with people?" She reached into the backseat and grabbed a platter full of sliced fruit. "Case in point. The fruit I bought at the beginning of the week thinking I'd have you and Sophia over for lunch is now overripe."

Millie pulled back the plastic wrap and snuck a piece of mango. "Well, I'm appreciating it now." She smiled at her friend and popped the fruit in her mouth as they both climbed out of the car. "For the record, it's not too ripe. It tastes great."

"Glad to hear it."

They walked up the wide stairs that led to Joyce's front porch.

"Oh, by the way, I think we figured out who wrote the love letters."

Tessa paused mid-step and stared, shocked. "What? How did you not lead with that news?"

"What news?" Joyce appeared in the doorway just a few steps above them. Tessa regained her momentum and continued up the stairs to join her.

"Millie found out who wrote those love letters to her aunt."

Joyce clasped her hands together. "We get to have book club after all! Who was it? A guest? Some heroic soldier who left for war?" But before she had the chance to answer, Joyce held her hands up. "Wait, don't tell me until we get all the girls together. Everyone should hear this news at the same time."

Joyce ushered them inside, and Tessa glanced around. "Is everyone here?"

"No. Not Betty. She evacuated with her granddaughter.

But I'll round everyone else up and we'll meet you on the patio. Help yourself to a drink from the cooler. Since ice is limited, they're only a touch cold."

Normally, going indoors was a relief from the warm, humid South Carolina weather but not today. As with all the houses along the coast, the interiors were a mixture of muggy, stagnant air along with the whirring sound of electric fans. Until the electricity was restored, outside was the more comfortable place to be.

Joyce's patio looked a little different than last time. All of the patio furniture and decorations were missing. Millie assumed they were still stored since redecorating seemed low on the hurricane recovery priority list. What was probably higher on the list was cleaning out the murky green pool that still had its fair share of storm debris in it. But what warmed Millie's heart the most was that coming together with friends and neighbors was top of the list. There was no doubt this was the kind of community she wanted to be a part of, the kind of place she wanted to be her home.

"I can't believe you didn't tell me about the letters when I saw you earlier!" Sophia said, joining them.

Millie grabbed a bottle of water from the cooler by the door. "I was a little distracted by other things. Like your stingray. How was the rescue mission?"

Sophia gave her two thumbs up. "Mr. Ray was successfully returned to the canal and no one was harmed in the process."

Camilla swept over, dressed more casually than Millie had ever seen her. "Tell me the end was beautifully tragic. Star-crossed lover? Lost at sea? Something that she never got over and spent the rest of her life standing on the widow's walk watching the sea?"

Millie laughed. "Last time I checked there isn't a widow's walk at Seascape, and sadly, I still don't know how it ended. The last letter was as optimistic as the first. The final sentence was 'until tomorrow.'"

Bonnie laid her hand over her heart. "How poetic. I wonder what tomorrow brought that ended such a beautiful love story."

"We'll worry about how it ended later." Joyce waved her hand as if brushing away the discussion. "First, how did you figure out who wrote them? Did he sign the last letter? Did you find something else in the office that identified him?"

"Nope." Millie shook her head, a slight grin pulling at the corners of her mouth. This revelation was going to surprise them as much as it had her. "Actually, I met him."

The news was met with widened eyes all around.

Millie nodded. "Turns out our mysterious Mr. C has been right here the whole time. The author of the love letters and the one who was in love with my aunt was none other than Braxton's friend Henry Donovan."

This time varying levels of shock registered on her friends' faces.

"No," Camilla gasped, her eyes staring off as if she was trying to connect the dots.

"Henry? But Braxton didn't buy that house until fairly recently, and I don't think Henry moved here until after Jade died," Tessa said, her eyebrows knitted together in confusion.

"Actually, according to Braxton, Henry grew up here. He was the reason Braxton decided to buy a house on Summer Island."

Bonnie nodded. "You know, I think I remember someone saying that. He left to be a golfer, right? When Braxton first bought the house, someone said now Summer Island will be home to two professional golfers."

"Wait, start at the beginning." Joyce rested her chin on her hand, her full attention focused on Millie. "I want to know everything."

Millie smiled and launched into the story of meeting

Henry at the memory care home. She told them everything from Henry thinking she was her aunt to what Braxton had told her about his first name being Christopher and referring to whatever happened as The Big Regret.

"Henry," Camilla repeated, when Millie was finished with the story. "I wonder why they never reconciled when he moved back. You'd think living next door to Mildred would have inspired them to talk again."

Sophia shook her head. "Mildred was already in the nursing home by then. And, actually, if you want someone who stood on a widow's walk and waited, it was Henry. Several times when I'd come over to help with Alice in those early days, I'd see him standing out on Braxton's deck, looking toward Seascape. I always assumed it was because he liked looking at the trees in the nature preserve next to it."

Tessa had a wistful expression. "This love story keeps getting better."

"And you still don't know why it ended?" Bonnie asked.

"He got confused before he said any details. And all Braxton knows is that Henry said he'd do it over if he had the chance." Millie replayed the scene in her mind. At the time, she'd been confused herself. But now that she knew Henry was talking about the affair with her aunt, had he said anything else she'd missed?

"But according to Braxton, Henry's memories can fade in and out, so there's still a chance he can remember what happened. Braxton said he'd keep asking from time to time, as long as it didn't upset Henry too much, to see if he can get more details."

"I guess we'll have to wait on the rest of the details. So, how about we switch to an equally enthralling and more recent story." Joyce flashed an accusatory grin of someone looking for some juicy gossip. "The one where you and Braxton keep spending an awful lot of time together."

Heat rose in Millie's cheeks, but she worked to keep her face as nonchalant as possible.

"We're neighbors so we help each other out from time to time. Nothing fancy." She shrugged for extra effect.

From the corner of her eye, she could see Sophia raise a questioning eyebrow, but she ignored it. Sure, there was more to the story, but since even Millie hadn't had a chance to talk about it with Braxton, she didn't feel like sharing it with these ladies yet.

Luckily, before her friends could ask her any more questions, Joyce's husband, Stan, announced that the food was ready as he stirred the contents in the giant pot cooking over a propane burner.

"Time to eat!" Joyce said in her loud, singsong voice. "Let me run in and get the paper towels." Joyce disappeared into the kitchen with Bonnie tagging along to help her while Camilla went over to talk with the group of men standing around as Stan dumped the contents from the giant pot onto the butcher paper-lined table.

"Don't think you've been saved by the dinner bell. This topic of discussion is far from over," Tessa said, stepping up next to Millie.

"Yes, especially since there are new details you haven't told Tessa yet." Sophia held her hand up to guard her mouth and leaned closer to Tessa as if sharing a secret. "She kissed him."

Tessa's eyes got large. "What? And I'm only hearing about this now?"

"It just happened and, at the moment, there aren't a whole lot of details to report. One kiss, then the thing with Henry and the hurricane. I've barely even talked to him since."

At that same moment, Braxton stepped out onto the patio. Almost instantly, he met her gaze across the crowded space, which sent warmth billowing through her, and suddenly she *knew.*

She still had a laundry list of complications and fears that plagued her. There were a thousand reasons she should walk away right now, but all of them paled in comparison to the way she felt when she was with him—safe, cherished, seen. She found herself wanting to be around him and share everything with him, from big wins like weathering a hurricane to the most simple daily tasks like checking out ghost crabs on the beach with Alice and Bear or playing chess with Henry. The time she'd spent with him had made her heart so full it made the risk worth it.

She could no longer imagine life without him in it.

Tessa gave her shoulders an encouraging squeeze. "One thing the hurricane and love letters remind me is that you never know what tomorrow might bring. Don't let opportunities pass you by."

• • •

Since Braxton lived right next door to Millie, his offer to give her a ride home at the end of the night so Tessa didn't have to seemed logical. And, to his relief, Tessa didn't argue.

But the truth was he wanted the chance to be alone with Millie. Since their kiss in the rain and the declarations that followed, neither one of them had addressed it. And now the subject was becoming awkward, like a sleeping giant both of them were carefully tiptoeing around for fear of waking up the crying beast.

Sure, one could argue that avoidance was justified. They'd both been busy and a lot of other very time-sensitive distractions had been vying for their attention, but that was never going to change. With Alice and Henry and Seascape, distractions popping up was probably the only thing in their lives that was a guarantee. But, if there was any chance of this thing between them moving forward, they were going to have to figure out a way to deal with the distractions.

Which brought him back to his original question. What was this thing between them?

There was the kiss, which he was a big fan of. He was definitely into doing that again. There was the insinuation that they would start spending more time together as a couple instead of just friends. But it had been so long since he'd done this dating thing that he wasn't even sure what to call it. Hanging out? Dating? Being boyfriend/girlfriend? Did they even have to put a label on it?

And then there was the confession.

She liked him. Those words had shot a lightning bolt through him, igniting every part of his heart, because he liked her, too. Maybe more than liked her. It was good to know he wasn't alone, that they were in this together.

But love? That was like cannonballing into the deep end. He wasn't saying he wouldn't get there. He might. In fact, after this week he was more interested in the deep end than he ever thought he would be again. But he liked to wade in slowly, test the waters, make sure he remembered how to swim. Was she okay with that? Or was she wanting something he didn't have to give her?

His goal was to keep all invested parties from getting hurt. Was he overthinking it? Perhaps. But he couldn't help it. It's who he was.

When the party was winding down, they said their goodbyes and walked out to where his sports car was parked at the end of the long driveway. It was his chance to have an uninterrupted conversation with her.

"Oh, the fancy car. I haven't ridden in this one yet," Millie said as she opened the door. The light from the interior lit her face. She was beautiful in every way, and a familiar excitement danced through him.

He grinned. "It's not the same kind of luxury ride as the minivan, but it gets you where you need to go."

She slid into the leather seat and ran her hand over the upholstery. "Nice. But I might miss the princess songs."

"Don't worry, I can still stream those." Braxton pressed a button on his phone and the bouncy theme song from Alice's favorite cartoon filled the sophisticated space. He bobbed his head as he sang along, which elicited a round of Millie's infectious giggles.

"I'm sure this is the exact track the designers imagined when they installed the high-end sound system."

"What? You think they had something more like this in mind?" He switched the playlist to something a little more romantic; the sounds of soft jazz filled the car.

Millie fastened her seat belt and settled in, looking comfortable. "If it was, they don't know what they're missing."

With power yet to be restored, the road was cloaked in a thick darkness as they pulled out onto the street.

"You don't realize how much electricity we use every day until you lose it," Millie said, leaning closer to the windshield to peer into the night.

Braxton switched his headlights to bright to make sure he could see any hazards that might still be left on the road. "The neighborhood did a good job getting the major debris off the road today. It looks totally different than when we drove by this morning."

Millie nodded. "I think everyone worked to get the trees cleared off the road before they focused on their own properties. When this neighborhood comes together, they can accomplish some pretty great things."

Pride swept through him. Being part of this community had saved him when his life had taken an unexpected turn. The people who lived in this place, a place that had become his home, were some of the greatest he'd ever met in his life.

"There's no place quite like it. When they're not sending you bogus violation letters, that is."

Millie giggled. "I wonder how many Braxton Channing violation letters I can expect from doing hurricane cleanup wrong."

He liked that she could laugh at hard situations. And he liked that she had the determination to change them.

The bottom line was that he liked her.

"I have to admit, I'm hoping for at least one. Sooner or later, whoever is sending them is going to slip up and give us a clue." He pulled into her drive, his headlights sweeping over the pile of yard debris stacked by the street in the process. "But it looks like you put a pretty good dent in the cleanup effort today."

Millie's mouth twisted to the side in a sort of skeptical look. "Some, I guess. But there's still a lot of work to be done."

There was a strain in her voice that he didn't like and wanted to find a way to soothe. She had so much riding on this proposal, and no one was as deserving as she was. She'd worked tirelessly over the past couple months and had accomplished great things. The neighborhood would be lucky to have her and her inn hosting guests in their town. And he had complete confidence the rest of the board would see it the same way he did.

"I wish I could be here to help you, but I'm leaving in the morning to pick up the munchkin."

Even in the dim light of the car's interior, he could see the excitement on her face. "Oh good! So you were able to reschedule your flight?"

"No. The airport will be reopened tomorrow, but flights were a mess. I'm going to drive, which will be easier all the way around." He paused, not really wanting to give her this next news. "I'm going to stay a couple days before we come back. I'll be gone for four days."

"A couple extra days in Atlanta will be good for both of you. Plus, it gives some extra days for the electric companies to get the power restored."

Braxton nodded. "That's the plan." He scratched his head, still wondering if he was doing the right thing. "But it also means I won't get to help you this week."

She reached across the car and wrapped her hand around his. "Please. You've helped me more than enough already."

"I really enjoyed it." To be honest, enjoy didn't even begin to cover how he felt about this week. He set out to help a woman on a ladder paint a wall and ended up falling for her instead. That was one hazard of home improvement he never considered. Which brought him back to the topic that he wanted to discuss with her tonight. Where exactly did this week leave them?

He cleared his throat. "So about last night…"

"Yeah, about that." She pressed her lips together and looked away as if considering something. The look didn't exactly inspire confidence. Was she rethinking what she'd said?

Her slight hesitation had him wanting to pull back to measure his words, but he pushed that feeling off. One of them was going to have to take the first firm step if they ever wanted to get out of this awkward tiptoe dance.

"I meant what I said." The words came out a little more matter-of-fact than he intended. He adjusted his tone and tried again. "I mean, I like…" He paused, trying to put into words exactly how he felt. Kissing her had been much easier.

"Us," he said eventually. "I'd like there to be a whole lot more of us in the future."

As soon as he'd said the words, any hesitation he thought he'd seen melted away and her mouth pulled up in a wide, playful grin. "So you're saying you're kind of into me?"

He held up his thumb and forefinger, his own grin taking

over his face. "A little bit."

"That's good to hear. Because I meant everything I said, too. I'm also kind of into you."

He raised his eyebrows in a playful question. "Kind of?"

She shrugged. "Fine. A lot. I'm a lot into you."

Excitement danced through him, but there was still one hesitation holding him back. It wasn't enough for her to be into him. There were two other very important people in his life. "I come as a package deal. I—"

It was Millie's turn to interrupt him. She reached up and laid her hand on his cheek. Her gentle caring flowed through him, reminding him how she managed to break through his barriers to capture his heart.

"I happen to like the whole package."

"Even this?" He hit the button on his phone and the princess song returned.

Millie chuckled, leaning into him. "Especially this."

"That's good to hear," he whispered just before his lips met hers. "So maybe we see where this thing goes?"

Her eyes sparkled. "I'd like that."

"What do you say we pick up right about here when I get back in town."

"Promise?" She leaned over and gave him one playful kiss.

Passion ignited in him. "Promise."

She opened the door and stepped out of the car. "Safe travels, Braxton."

"Thanks. I'll see you in four days."

Chapter Twenty-One

Four days later, Braxton pulled into his garage after the eight-hour drive from Atlanta with a wide-awake Alice—where did she get the energy?—and a clear plan for how the rest of his night would go.

He'd give his daughter a bath, put her to bed, and then spend the rest of the night getting caught up on the work he'd avoided since before the hurricane. That way his schedule would be free and Alice would be well rested and in a good mood for Millie's open house in the morning.

"Who wants a bath with lots of bubbles?" he asked as he unbuckled the toddler from the car seat and set her on the floor.

"Bubbles!" Alice screeched in delight and bounced toward the stairs. He grabbed their bags from the trunk and hurried to follow her up, staying close enough behind her to make sure he could catch her if she stumbled. The steep garage stairs always made him nervous, which was one of the reasons he didn't answer the phone when it rang in his pocket. He'd have to call whoever it was back later.

He opened the door to the house and Alice bolted for the interior stairs that led up to her bedroom. "Lots and lots of bubbles," she sang as she climbed.

"Yes, ma'am. Lots of bubbles and then we can read a night-night book."

The phone in his pocket buzzed again to alert him to a new text message. Whoever was so intent on reaching him must have no idea how much effort bath time took. He reached the top of the stairs, left the luggage on the landing, and pulled his phone out of his pocket, ready to text whoever it was that he'd call back after bedtime. But the message on the screen was from Jose, one of the HOA board members.

Call me as soon as you can. I have important info about HOA meeting.

They had a pretty full docket of things to discuss at the board meeting tomorrow night. There was actually so much more material than normal that Braxton wasn't sure how they'd get through all the items in the hour and a half they'd scheduled. But for some reason the only item he could think about at the moment was Millie's proposal.

Out of all thirty-two items on the list to discuss, the odds were that the phone call was about something else. In fact, there'd been a lot of discussion in the past few days about some new items that needed to be added because of the hurricane. It was far more likely that the call was about one of those issues instead of Millie's thing. But logic didn't keep the knot from forming in the pit of his stomach as he pulled up Jose's number to call him back.

He picked up on the first ring.

"Hey, buddy, what's so important it can't wait until tomorrow's meeting?"

A giggling Alice lay on the floor and held her tiny feet in the air so Braxton could take her shoes off. Tucking the phone between his ear and his shoulder, he unlaced her sneakers.

"This is more of an unofficial call, but I thought you deserved a heads-up."

Alice popped back up and grabbed the bottle of bath bubbles from the side of the tub and danced around the bathroom with it. The sight of her pure joy over something so simple made Braxton smile. He leaned over to start the bath water.

"I always appreciate a heads-up," Braxton said. He took the bottle from Alice and squeezed it into the running water.

"Lots and lots of bubbles!" she sang as she stood next to the tub watching the liquid bubble up into a thick foam.

"The board is going to vote no."

The knot in his stomach tightened as he shifted to hold the phone back up to his ear. "No? On what?"

There was a pause, then Braxton could hear the strain in Jose's voice. "On Millie Leclair's proposal. The overwhelming majority is going to vote no. I wanted you to hear it from me before you were blindsided tomorrow night."

Braxton sank down on top of the toilet seat and tried to wrap his mind around what he was hearing. "How can they all vote no? We haven't formally reviewed the documents yet, and they clearly show that Seascape has always been operational."

"Stan has made the point, and Gary is backing him, that a change in ownership would nullify that."

"But they haven't even been to the open house yet to see her plan. That was the deal. Review the documents and see how she fixed the place. Then make a decision."

Jose let out a sigh. "They say it doesn't matter. Voting yes is the start of a slippery slope. If we allow this hotel, we'll allow more until our coast is full of high-rises like all the rest of the commercialized resort towns."

"Big, big bubbles, Daddy," Alice sang as the bath water rose higher. Braxton turned off the tap, his mind racing through the different scenarios that might change the outcome of this vote. They only needed four out of the eight board members to vote yes and then he, as the president, would cast the swing vote.

"What about Jenna or Lori?"

"Same. And I hate to say it, but Jenna was swayed by the amount of violation letters in her file. She's not convinced it won't become a pattern."

"Those complaints aren't even valid. They weren't sent through the proper channels."

"A couple of them were. And knowing there were others, even if they're not official, is enough to make some people leery."

Frustration flanked by fear twisted inside him. This couldn't be happening. Millie had done everything they'd asked and she was going to get blocked by a technicality and a fear?

"What about Curt?"

"He and Jarod wrote the new ordinance in the first place. They both say they have no intention of overturning it."

Braxton might've understood why these people would vote no before. Even he agreed that rule made sense on paper. It was created to protect and preserve their neighborhood from big business and the kind of mass tourism that could destroy the natural beauty they worked to preserve.

But now? After meeting her? After seeing her passion and getting a feel for what kind of bed and breakfast she was going to run? How could these people who had embraced her into their lives still vote against her livelihood? She was in their book club for crying out loud.

Jose didn't wait for Braxton to rattle through the whole list. He went straight to the point. "Sophia is going to be the only yes, but she's not aware of how the rest of the votes will go." He paused, giving Braxton a chance to comprehend that even he was going to vote no.

Disappointment gripped him. "Even you?"

"It's nothing personal, Braxton. It's policy. Besides, my one vote wouldn't make a difference."

"Bubbles, Daddy, bubbles." Alice's cheerful voice interrupted his thoughts. With unbridled delight, she was trying to climb over the side of the tub into the bubble bath.

Braxton stood up and stripped the rest of the clothes off his bath-bound girl and lifted her into the tub. He then knelt next to it, watching her splash in the pink-tinted foam.

There was such joy in front of him. Joy that had no idea of the kind of life-changing disappointment was looming in the future. He pictured Millie celebrating the beautiful renovations with her two friends at this very moment. Millie whose welcome home text included a smiley face and a celebration emoji. A cheerful, unassuming Millie whose future was about to be crushed.

Acid roiled in his stomach. "Well, thanks for letting me know." A tinge of hostility slipped into his voice that he didn't bother taking out.

"Since you have a personal interest in this one, I thought you should know before tomorrow," Jose said. "I'm sorry it didn't work out the way you wanted it."

"I appreciate that." What he didn't appreciate was the fact that not one of the board members believed in something the rest of Summer Island seemed to see so clearly—that Millie and her inn would be a benefit to their community. But at least the heads-up gave him the chance to figure out what to do before the vote.

He was taking a page from Millie's playbook—just because they were down didn't mean they were out.

He hung up the phone and focused on finishing Alice's bath, thinking of how he could fix this.

"Well, kiddo," he said as he massaged shampoo into her hair. "Looks like Daddy's going to have to do more work than he anticipated tonight."

Chapter Twenty-Two

Millie stepped into the grand entryway dressed in her new brightly colored summer dress with a freshly groomed Bear by her side at exactly ten o'clock.

She'd done it.

Plenty of people had told her it was an impossible task, which at times she almost believed. Time and money had sat firmly in her way and even mother nature had tried to stop her, but she hadn't been deterred. She'd done it anyway. She, Millie Leclair, had restored the beloved Seascape Inn and now it was time to let the world see it.

Okay, maybe not the world. Just the people of Summer Island, but at the moment that was exciting enough.

The recently polished and resealed tile floors gleamed. The new furniture in the great room had a rustic charm that made the space look fresh while seeming as if it had always belonged there. The long dining room table had been refinished and was covered in snacks and treats that had long been a staple of Aunt Mildred's inn.

Everything was, in a word, perfect.

"Hello!" Bonnie peeked her head inside the door. "Has the open house opened?"

Excitement buzzed through Millie. "Yes, and you are my very first guest. Welcome."

Bonnie stepped into the entryway, her gaze sweeping around the space. "Oh, honey," she breathed out with a sort of wonder. "It's amazing."

Pride lit up inside her to the point that she wondered if she was actually glowing. She wasn't normally one to toot her own horn, but this time she had to agree. It was pretty great.

"Thanks." She hugged her friend. "It wouldn't have been possible without your encouragement."

"I knew you could do it all along. And now look at this place. It's even prettier than I remember it."

"You haven't even seen the whole thing. Check out the rooms upstairs and the new pool deck. And when you're through, grab a snack in the dining room."

"I can't wait." Bonnie grabbed one of the maps and information pages Millie had fanned out on the large round table in the center of the grand foyer. "Mildred would have loved this." She headed off in the direction of the stairs as the next group walked in.

Over the next hour, more people came through her front doors than she could count. Most of the faces she recognized, but some she met for the first time. She'd just finished greeting a new couple she didn't recognize from Summer Island when Sophia joined her in the entryway.

"It's a total success. Everyone loves it. Congratulations!"

Millie took in the view of guests hanging out in the living room and through the windows she could see more gathered around the pool. This was the exact scene she had worked for. This was what she moved to Summer Island to do. Seeing this house filled with the happy hum of conversation and people relaxing and enjoying themselves made all the grueling hours over the past two months worth it.

Millie motioned to the guests. "I'm pretty sure they're all discussing the beauty of the tile work in the guest bathrooms. Those are clearly the crowning jewels of the house."

"They're rather stunning, if I do say so myself." Sophia grinned. "I hate to eat and run, but I have to get back to the shop. I'll talk to you tonight after the HOA meeting?"

Millie hugged her. "Thanks for everything."

When Sophia opened the door to leave, Braxton, dressed in a pressed dress shirt and slacks, was walking up the steps. She held the door open and waited for him to come in.

"Welcome home, Braxton. Just wait until you see all the work Millie's done while you were gone. The house looks amazing."

Braxton's gaze met Millie's first, and warmth sparkled through her. "I can't wait to see it." Then he turned to Sophia. "Are you leaving? I have a couple of HOA items I wanted to talk to you about."

"Work calls at the moment, but I should have some free time later this afternoon. You can call me if you need to, or we can talk before the meeting." She looked over at Millie. "And I'll see you afterward to celebrate."

For a second, Millie could've sworn a pained expression passed over Braxton's face. His jaw tensed and something flashed in his eyes that she couldn't quite identify. But as soon as it appeared it was gone, replaced by his charming smile.

As Sophia disappeared outside, Braxton walked over to her. His hand settled on the small of her back and he brushed a kiss across her cheek. "Hello."

"Hello yourself. Welcome home. Where's the little miss?"

Braxton slid his hand in his pocket. "She's with Lena this morning. I have to get caught up on some work and then I'm headed over to see Henry. But I wanted to see your big reveal."

There was something about him that seemed a little stiffer than normal, almost formal. But she tried to shake off the feeling. Surely she was imagining it, right? The stress of the open house and the vote later today was probably making her overanalyze everything.

"It looks great, Millie." He walked past her and stood at the top of the two steps that led down to the great room. "Really, everything turned out spectacular."

Millie joined him. "I have to admit, it all came together better than I hoped. Even the couches that got held up by the hurricane were delivered on time. And I'm a little bit in love with them." Sometimes it was hard to believe this was her house. Those beautiful couches and all the other accessories that made the room stunning were her things. She had to keep pinching herself to make sure this wasn't some elaborate dream.

Braxton nodded. "You did an amazing job." He turned his focus to her, his blue eyes gazing into hers. "Whatever else happens, you should be very, very proud of yourself."

The words caught her off guard. She took a step back, apprehension nudging out the joy that had been sparkling through her all day. "What do you mean 'whatever else happens'?"

Once again, that same tense look passed over his face. But with a slight shake of his head, the worrisome expression was replaced by his charming grin. "Nothing. This is your moment. You should enjoy it."

She studied him. It wasn't nothing. Something was off. "Is everything okay?"

He took a beat too long to answer. "Nothing to worry about." He pressed his lips against her forehead in what should have been a reassuring kiss. "But after the open house, can we talk?"

Nothing good ever came out of those three little words.

A chill ran through her. Before he could answer her, Joyce and Betty walked through the front door.

"Isn't this place just lovely!" Joyce gushed, walking straight over to them. "I can't even believe it's the same house."

Millie tried to squash the gnawing apprehension and plastered on a smile. "Thanks. I'm pleased with how it turned out."

"Pleased? You should be over the moon." Betty patted her hand. "It looks even better than I remember it looking when we were young."

Betty's gaze darted around the space as she moved her head slowly to take it all in. "Doesn't this bring back memories?" There was a certain wistful quality about her voice that filled Millie with pride.

"Well, this isn't all of it. You should see all the work that was done upstairs. The guest rooms turned out great. And the sweet flower arrangement you sent this morning, Joyce, is in one of them. Thank you so much for that." She gave Joyce a quick hug.

"You are welcome, dear. We're all so proud of you."

"Yes, we are," Braxton said, his eyes meeting Millie's.

"Enough jabber-jawing. I want to see the rest. Braxton, care to escort a feeble old lady up that staircase?"

Braxton offered his arm. "It would be my pleasure."

Betty slid her hand through the crook of his elbow.

"Enjoy. And when you come back down, don't forget to stop by the dining room for some classic Seascape treats along with some new favorites."

The trio started toward the stairs, Joyce and Betty discussing Mildred's famous brownies.

Braxton glanced back over his shoulder at Millie. "I'll find you later. It's all good."

Millie nodded and watched them walk up the steps. It

didn't feel all good. Something was off and she didn't want to have to wait thirty more minutes until the open house was over to find out whatever it was. Her mind spun with possibilities, none of them good.

Had he changed his mind? Did something happen in Atlanta that made him rethink his relationship with her? A knot formed in the pit of her stomach.

Before she could think too much about it, she was interrupted by Jose, one of the HOA board members, and his wife who were leaving.

"The house is beautiful. Congratulations on the remodel."

The compliment calmed some of her fears. "Thanks. I'm thrilled with how it turned out. And with your help tonight, lots more people can experience the charms of Summer Island while staying at this charming bed and breakfast."

Jose glanced around the space. "That is the vision, isn't it?"

Millie, feeling encouraged, leaned in as if sharing a secret. "And I personally promise to make sure every one of my guests follows all of the HOA rules. That's my guarantee to the community."

Jose shifted, looking slightly uncomfortable. "That's good to hear."

So maybe she'd taken her sales pitch too far, but she wanted every HOA board member to know she was a team player. Seascape Inn would be a benefit to their community, just like it used to be when Aunt Mildred ran it.

"It certainly is lovely," his wife said. "Thank you for showing it to us."

Millie waved goodbye to them and stepped up to greet a new group who walked in the door.

The next twenty minutes was a constant stream of people coming and going. Whatever apprehension had set with Braxton's can-we-talk request had been buried under the delight of hearing person after person sing the praises of Seascape. People loved the renovations and property.

She was floating on the success of the event when the Callahans, a couple she'd just met, came up to her again.

"The property really is gorgeous, dear. It's beyond anything I could've imagined," Mrs. Callahan said.

"Thanks." Millie smiled at her. "I'm so glad you came by to see it."

"Braxton told us about this place a while back but wasn't sure it would still be available. We were thrilled to get the call last night that it was. And after seeing it, Braxton was right." She clapped her hands together, looking delighted. "This is exactly what we've been looking for."

Millie held her hands up as if putting Seascape on display. "Well, now you've found us."

"Yes, we have. I know I balked at the price tag last night, but after seeing it, we think it's right on par," Mr. Callahan said.

"Price tag?" While she and Braxton had talked about what she could charge for a room once it opened, their discussion had always been theoretical. She'd never decided on anything. Was he already advertising her room rate without her approval? No, that didn't sound like him.

"I know we aren't supposed to sound too eager, but I don't care. Now that I've seen it, I have to have it. We already talked about it and we're willing to go two percent above the asking price if we can sign now." Mrs. Callahan turned and looked out the back window. "I can already visualize what the new house will look like."

Confusion circled in her mind like a dark storm. "New house?"

Where to even start piecing together what they were talking about? Exactly what were they looking for? Asking price. New house. Braxton.

And then it hit her like a lightning bolt through storm clouds.

How could she have been such a fool?

A successful real estate agent who was well aware of her aunt's passing showed up on her doorstep the moment she arrived, asking about her plans for the place and going over every reason why it would be impossible for her to keep it. And then she'd believed him when he said he was on her side. Had she not learned anything in the course of her life?

Her old boss had only wanted her ideas to get himself a promotion. Her ex had only wanted her by his side when it looked good to be committed but was not actually committed enough to stay around after he got the new job he wanted. Even her mom had left because chasing a career was more important than raising her daughter. Why would Braxton be different? Of course it had been his plan to broker this deal and walk away with the big fat commission.

Can we talk? Yeah, she had some words for him, all right.

"I'm sorry for the confusion, but Seascape is not for sale," she said, as levelly as she could, considering a hurricane raged inside of her.

"What?" The shock in Mrs. Callahan's voice was expected. They'd been just as blindsided by the same man.

"Fine. We'll go five percent over asking," Mr. Callahan said.

Millie tried to keep her expression as polite as possible. "It's not a money thing. The reason for the open house was to announce the grand reopening of the historic Seascape Inn, which will now be a luxury bed and breakfast." Satisfaction sparkled through her as she delivered the last line. She couldn't wait to say the same thing to Braxton when they *talked.*

"Well, I…" Mrs. Callahan didn't bother to finish her sentence. She simply huffed and marched out of the front door.

"If you change your mind, give us a call. Our offer still stands." Mr. Callahan handed her a business card and followed his wife out.

Millie was still holding the card when Braxton, Betty, and Joyce appeared in the grand foyer. Braxton's brow furrowed as he stared out the open front door.

"It's simply divine, dear," Betty said.

"Very lovely. Everything turned out beautifully," Joyce added. "I love that paint color you used in the guest rooms."

"Thanks." Millie tried to focus on her friends, but her mind was consumed by Braxton.

"Was that the—" Braxton started but Millie cut him off.

"The Callahans? Uh-huh. Friends of yours?"

His questioning look was worth the snark, but she ignored it for now. She wasn't going to do this here. Not in front of her friends.

She focused her attention on Joyce and Betty. "Thank you both so much for coming and for all your support. I really appreciate it." They said their goodbyes and she hugged both ladies, the whole time trying not to get distracted by the elephant in the room.

Once they left, she turned to Braxton. Propping her hands on her hips, she glared at him. She wasn't sure if hurt, disappointment, or frustration burned in her gaze, but all three were circling through her. How could he?

"Were you going to tell me you invited them, or were you planning on making the entire deal without getting me involved?"

Braxton's brow was still furrowed in confusion. "What are you talking about?"

Millie nodded her head at the now empty doorway. "The Callahans showed up to look at the property you're showing them, and they're ready to offer five percent above the price you set. One problem. This is *my* property."

The creases in his brow deepened. "I admit, the Callahans are my clients, but I didn't invite them today."

Millie cocked an eyebrow. "They said you told them this property would be perfect for them and then called last night to tell them it was available."

Braxton shook his head. "I mentioned this property to them months ago, but I haven't said anything to them since. And I certainly didn't call them last night."

Millie dropped her hands to her sides. They still tingled with the rush of anger, but confusion was clouding everything. "Then who did?"

"That's what I'd like to know." He ran his hand through his hair and let out a sigh. "Look, I swear to you I have nothing to do with the Callahans being here today. But the fact that they're here isn't awful. The truth is you might be looking to sell."

Millie crossed her arms in front of her chest, anger sparking inside once more. "I assure you, I'm not looking to sell."

Braxton pressed his lips together and gave her one of those I-feel-sorry-for-what-I-have-to-say puppy-dog looks. "I have some bad news."

"What kind of bad news?" Millie couldn't help but be skeptical. She wanted to fully trust this man she was falling for, but the current situation combined with her not so stellar track record kept stepping in her way.

"The board is going to vote no."

It took a second for the words to register because that scenario wasn't even on her radar. "No? H-how do you know? The vote isn't until tonight."

"Jose called to give me a heads-up. Everyone has already made up their mind. The vote will be seven to one." Braxton shook his head. "I'm so sorry, Millie."

Millie stood there, stunned. "Jose's voting no? But I just spoke with him. He said the place was beautiful."

"And it is. This has nothing to do with the renovations or with you. They're afraid of the precedent allowing a hotel will set. They don't want a bunch of hotels and vacation rentals taking over our neighborhood."

A sagging disappointment joined the party of intense emotions pulling her down as she tried to process this information. "So it was all for nothing. I jumped through all of their hoops and there was never any intention of them saying yes." Tears stung her eyes.

Braxton reached out and pulled her into a hug. "It wasn't for nothing. Look at what you did. This place is amazing."

She relaxed into his chest, allowing the tears to escape. This wasn't how she saw today going. At all.

"And on the bright side," Braxton continued. "The house being in prime condition will get us a much more generous offer."

Millie pulled away from him and stared at him with a horrified expression. "What do you mean a better offer? I'm not selling."

"But…" He took a step back, giving her space, which she appreciated. "You might have to. You said yourself that you can't afford to keep it without paying customers." Braxton's words were kind but matter-of-fact, like he'd already made the decision for her.

"So that's it? You think I should just give up?"

"Absolutely not. Millie Leclair doesn't have the quitting spirit."

At least they agreed on that. If he believed in her, then they could surely find a way to convince the board.

"That's why, after I got off the phone with all the board members last night, I looked up every property in Summer Island you might like. There are several options that would make perfect bed and breakfasts."

Millie let out a sad chuckle and shook her head. "Let me get this straight. You knew about the vote last night, but instead of calling me, you spent the rest of the night looking up properties to sell me?" She couldn't decide what offended her more: that he didn't tell her or that he'd already decided her next move for her.

"Not sell you. Show you. And there are some good options. In fact, there's this one on the beach over on the south side of the island that you'll love. I have an appointment for us to go look at it tomorrow."

Millie threw her hands up in the air. Was he not listening to her at all? How could he tell her not to give up and then suggest the same thing? "I don't want to look at another house, Braxton. I want *this* house. I want to run my family's inn."

"At this point, that's not an option." Braxton's words were firm as if this whole situation was already set in stone.

"Then we make it an option," Millie countered. She hadn't come this far and done this much to give up that quickly. She retiled the freaking roof for goodness sake.

"How? I've already personally spoken to every board member and no one is swaying. And once the vote is cast, the decision is final."

Millie shrugged. "I don't know, but I'll figure out a way. I'm not giving up because a bunch of neighborhood know-it-alls are scared about setting a precedent."

Braxton sighed, looking frustrated. "You're going to go bankrupt chasing after a dream that can't be."

"But it's *my* dream to chase after."

"I get that, but you can't go about it recklessly. You have to be reasonable."

His words cut through her like a knife, going straight to her heart. This was the kind of guy she was falling for?

Someone who was going to talk her out of her dreams? Someone who didn't believe in her?

She'd walked down that road before. She knew how that story ended. It might've been a new town with a fresh look, but apparently it was the same cast of players. Only this time, Millie wasn't falling for the same mistake.

"Right. Reasonable like you. Who has wanted to sell this property, my property, from day one?"

Braxton took another step back, looking offended. "Is that what you think of me?"

Her heart ached as the cold truth trickled in. Everything she'd been so sure of just yesterday was crumbling around her. The board was voting no. Her already exhausted bank account was about to be stretched to the point of breaking. But worst of all, the man she was falling for wasn't the man she thought he was.

But she'd been down before, and she'd learned enough to know that just because she was down didn't mean she was out.

"Thanks for the heads-up on the board's decision, but you can delete your property search. And you can tell the board Millie Leclair is not giving up the Leclair property."

• • •

This conversation was not going at all like Braxton had planned.

Had he dreamed about selling the property for a long time? Sure. And did he make a few phone calls the day he found out it had been left to a distant heir that lived up north? Yes. What real estate agent wouldn't? But he let that business opportunity go the second she told him she wasn't selling. This conversation had nothing to do with him as a realtor and everything to do with her situation.

"First of all, I don't want to sell your property. But our hands are tied. I can't sit here and watch you self-destruct because you're stuck on a goal that can't be accomplished."

Hurt flashed in her eyes. "You think I'm being reckless and am going to self-destruct?"

So maybe that hadn't come out exactly like he meant for it to. "Perhaps that was a bad choice of words, but I worry about you. I don't want you to get hurt."

"But you don't believe in me. You don't think I can do this."

He sighed. "I believe in you. You can do amazing things. But this..." He motioned to the room around them. "Some dreams are impossible."

Millie pressed her lips together and stared out at the gathered guests. "Right."

"We'll find you another property you love. And with the differences in the prices, you'll have plenty of money left over. We'll fix it up however you want."

"We?"

Braxton could tell she was upset, so he treaded carefully. "Yeah. It won't be this property, but you'll still be living out your dream of opening a B&B. I think it's your best option."

Millie looked up at him with a storm brewing in her eyes. "Really? Because I think my best option is not being with someone who doesn't back my dreams."

Braxton huffed out a breath. Why wouldn't she listen to reason? "I am backing your dreams, but sometimes dreams need to be modified. I can't just stand here doing nothing and watch you get hurt just because you wouldn't consider better options."

Millie met his gaze. "Then maybe you shouldn't be standing here at all." She walked across the foyer to the already opened door and leaned against it. "I started this on my own, and I'm going to finish it on my own."

Pain seared his heart. He knew this kind of hurt. It was different from the physical ache of a torn muscle or a broken bone. This kind of pain cut deeper, and no amount of physical therapy could make it better. Hadn't he promised himself he'd never be in a place to hurt like that again?

Their relationship, if he could even call it that, was at an impasse, which he probably should've expected. Really, there never should have been anything there to begin with. Even in his most optimistic moments he'd known deep down it was a long shot. She didn't know how to play it safe and he didn't have it in him to watch her get destroyed. Wasn't this conversation the very reason he had decided he was out of the relationship game for good? He should've listened to his own good advice the first time.

He walked over to the open door and stepped out on the porch to leave. But the problem with the heart was that it didn't always listen to reason. "For what it's worth, I sincerely wish you all the luck in the world."

Millie's gaze was unflinching as it met his. "Goodbye, Braxton."

He gave her one last lingering look, then jogged down the steps to his car.

Just like that, it was over.

Whoever said it was better to have loved and lost had obviously never been in love to begin with. There was no pain in the world that compared to the pain of a heart breaking. And if the only way to avoid ever feeling like this again was to not fall in love, Braxton swore that from this moment on, he'd never do it again.

Chapter Twenty-Three

By the time Braxton got to Summer Island Memory Care Home, he was in a foul mood. If there'd been any way he could have skipped his daily chess game, he would have. But since he'd been out of town, he at least needed to check on his friend. It was his responsibility after all.

After being buzzed into the facility, he plodded across the grand room to their normal table, careful to avoid conversation with anyone else.

"You're late," Henry grumped. It was his standard welcome. No matter what time Braxton arrived Henry always said he was late. Normally, he played along, but not today. He wasn't in the mood.

"No, I'm not. I'm actually early. But the timing doesn't matter. I'm here. Let's play." Even though he was sitting in front of the black pieces, he picked up his pawn and made the first move.

Henry studied him. "What's wrong with you?"

Braxton massaged his temples, trying to rid himself of the memories of everything that had transpired since he woke up this morning. Really, if he could've rewound to the beginning of the summer, he would have. "I'm having a bad day."

Henry reached across the board and returned Braxton's piece to its original position and made his own first move. "You think you're the only person in the history of time to have a bad day? We all have bad days. I might be having a bad day too."

Braxton moved a different pawn in a counterplay to Henry's move. "Are you?"

Henry shrugged. "I don't know. Maybe. Some bozo just stormed in and tried to steal my turn, which is crappy. And what's-her-name over there keeps telling me I can't have any cookies." He motioned to Veronica who was talking with another resident near them.

"You already had your cookies, Mr. Donovan. Two of them. You can't have any more because you're watching your blood sugar."

Henry snorted. "I'm a grown man and I still have to ask permission to eat a cookie." He moved his knight. "See. Bad day. But you don't see me storming around, do you?"

Leave it to Henry to remind him not to take his life too seriously. "Don't give Veronica a hard time. She's just doing her job."

"That's what people keep telling me. But she'd be doing a better job if she wasn't so stingy with the cookies."

Braxton could feel his tight grimace give way to the beginning of a grin, taking the edge off his dark mood. Maybe taking a step back and focusing on someone else was a good thing. "Besides the cookie thing, how are you?"

"Fine, I guess."

"Have you been taking your medicine?"

Henry shrugged, focusing on the board. "I do what they tell me."

"And you've been sleeping all right?"

Henry raised an eyebrow. "Are you going to keep asking me questions so we can avoid your thing?"

Yep. That was pretty much the plan. "I'm checking on you. It's my job."

"Apparently I'm good. Let's check on you for a while." Henry folded his hand on the board and leaned in, waiting.

This was one of the times when Braxton hated this disease the most. He could've used Henry's advice right about now. It seemed unfair to sit across from the one person whose wisdom he valued more than anyone else's and not have access to it.

Braxton picked up his pawn and moved it forward one space, plunking it down with more force than he'd intended. "I might have messed things up with this woman."

Henry nodded. "It's always about a lady, isn't it?"

Memories of the fight with Millie replayed through Braxton's mind, and he fiddled with the chess piece in front of him. "Not anymore. I'm done."

Henry shook his head, looking defiant. "Done? No. You're not done. I didn't coach you to run away when things got tough. I taught you how to fight for things you wanted."

"What if I don't want this?"

Henry motioned to the chess table. "Then we'd be playing chess instead of sitting around talking like a bunch of old, old…" His face screwed up as he searched for the right word.

"A bunch of old hens?" Braxton suggested.

"Right. That."

Braxton sat back against his chair and crossed his arms in front of his chest, glaring at the man across from him. "Fine. Let's play chess. It's your move, old man." He was acting like a sullen teenager, but he didn't care.

Today hadn't gone as expected. Heck, his life hadn't gone as expected.

Henry studied Braxton for a second. "Don't walk away

because it's hard. Walk away when it's over."

The truth of his words stung and Braxton squeezed his eyes shut, trying to block out his feelings for Millie. "How do you know when it's over?"

Henry snorted. "If you haven't left everything on the course, it's not over. Quitting early only leads to regret. Fight for what's worth fighting for."

The words hit Braxton with more volume than if he'd used a bullhorn. So maybe he wasn't getting Henry's advice the way he'd hoped to get it, or the way Henry had given advice in the past. But he was still passing on his wisdom in the only way he could. Maybe Braxton had messed up the chance to find out all the details of Henry's Big Regret, but he wasn't going to miss this chance to ask him about it again.

"Was Mildred The Big Regret? Mildred Leclair?" The question had a high likelihood of upsetting Henry, something Braxton tried to avoid. And if Henry showed signs of frustration, he'd back off. But for some reason this part of the story felt important, especially considering his current circumstance.

"Mildred," Henry whispered. A parade of emotions flickered across his face so quickly Braxton couldn't quite interpret them all, but they finally landed on a look Braxton knew well—confusion. Henry stared out into the distance as if searching for his lost memories.

After a few seconds, Henry looked up, the all too familiar blank look settled on his face. "Mildred Leclair owns Seascape Inn."

It was probably as close to confirmation as Braxton was going to get. He would've loved to hear the story of young Henry and Mildred. He wanted to know what happened that ended their love story and why Henry walked away. But for now it was enough to know that if he had to do it over again, he would've fought harder. If Braxton was looking for advice, this was as close to it as he was going to get.

"That's what they tell me," Braxton said.

"I could tell you some stories."

Braxton chuckled. "I bet you could."

The last of the anger he'd held on to from his argument with Millie faded away, leaving only the relentless ache of the heartbreak.

He made his next move on the chessboard and considered his situation.

So life hadn't worked out the way he thought it would. There'd been quite a few heartbreaks he wasn't counting on and plot twists he never saw coming, but it was his life. These were his people and, for better or for worse, they were worth fighting for. Especially Millie.

In his attempt to protect everyone, he'd really messed some things up. He saw that now. He'd been so busy trying to protect everyone from getting hurt that he'd never considered how that protection was hurting them.

Life was full of ups and downs. Getting hurt was inevitable. What mattered were the people you had in your corner to help get you back on your feet.

Braxton had some pretty great people in his corner. People worth fighting for. And he had an idea of how he could fight for Millie. He just hoped he wasn't too late.

Chapter Twenty-Four

As soon as Millie finished cleaning up what was left of the snacks laid out on the dining room table, she headed straight to her closet to change into her pajamas.

Yes, it was only four o'clock in the afternoon, but she didn't care. She didn't have anywhere else she needed to be tonight. Besides, she was done with today. Today was stupid.

"I mean, if they were so intent on saying no, they could've at least mentioned it before today, don't you think? If I'd known this open house was going to be pointless, I wouldn't have worked sixteen hours every day for the past eight weeks to get it ready," she said to Bear as she yanked on her favorite flannel pajama pants. They were way too warm for this hot summer day, but at the moment it didn't matter. She needed something warm and cozy after the day she'd had. So what if she had to lower her AC another ten degrees so she didn't sweat to death?

The only thing that made her feel slightly less like an idiot in this whole situation was that Sophia had been as blindsided by the HOA news as she had. At least Millie wasn't the only one fooled by the community. Unfortunately, though, after making several phone calls, Sophia confirmed Braxton was right. The board had made up their mind.

"Because, what? They're threatened our tiny operation will be so successful that investors from all over will be snapping up their properties and turning them into hotels?" She huffed and stormed out of her closet with Bear following behind. "Well, I'll tell you one thing, Bear. I'm not giving up. We didn't come this far and do this much to walk away now."

Although, if she was being completely honest, Braxton wasn't totally wrong. From where she stood, her options were limited. She was out of money, and after the vote went through tonight, she'd be out of a job.

"But like Aunt Mildred always said, when you get to the bottom of your barrel, it's time to find another barrel." She just had no idea where she was going to find it.

She let out a weary sigh. "No one ever said starting over would be easy," she whispered to herself. But she'd hoped it wouldn't be impossible.

For the time being, though, she needed a task to keep her busy, something that would help take her mind off all the ways today had been a disaster. And she had just the job in mind.

Opening the door to the office, she stepped into the room and surveyed the stacks and piles of papers. Sorting through all the documents stored in here would take forever, but if ever there was a time when she needed to be buried by a project, this was it.

The only problem was figuring out a place to start.

Since she couldn't find a logical beginning point, she plopped herself on the floor next to the desk. All along the wall between the desk and the six-foot-tall rusted metal filing cabinet in the corner were rows of document boxes with file folders stacked on top like mini Leaning Tower of

Pisas. Millie gently picked up the first one, fully aware that if she made one wrong move the entire structure might come tumbling down.

She went through folder after folder, sorting the contents into piles to keep, shred, or recycle. The minutes slipped away as she sifted through the history of Seascape. Most of the papers weren't worth keeping. There were invoices for food deliveries and books containing the carbon copies of old phone messages. Some of the folders at the bottom of the first pile were details of weddings and other private events they'd hosted. There were even a few yellowing photographs of people with big shoulder pads and even bigger hair who attended these events in the eighties.

After a little over an hour, when she finally cleared the precarious stacks of file folders, she kneeled in front of the first box.

She shot Bear a sidelong glance. "What are the chances, Bear, that one of these boxes holds a pile of cash?" The dog's tail thumped against the ground in response.

It was worth hoping for, right?

"Here's to finding stacks of Benjamins." She pulled off the top and stared inside.

Even though her hope of finding money hidden away in one of these boxes was wildly unrealistic, she couldn't help the pang of disappointment. "Nope, just more papers," she reported. Well, if she was being technical about it, the box contained an assortment of notebooks. She picked up the first one and thumbed through it.

The pages were filled with line after line of Aunt Mildred's scripty cursive handwriting. She paused on one page to read a few sentences. After she did, she flipped a few pages and read some more just to make sure this was what she thought it was. Her excitement growing, she pulled out the other notebooks, thumbing through them. They all appeared to be the same thing.

A genuine smile crept across her face for the first time since the blowup with Braxton. She might not have found a box of money, but she'd definitely discovered a treasure.

She held up one of the notebooks for Bear to see. "Guess what we just found? Aunt Mildred's journals."

On a day when it felt like the world was against her and she was fighting an impossible battle all on her own, she needed this.

Drawing in a deep, calming breath, she opened the first journal and read. Aunt Mildred's wisdom dripped off the pages. Her notes and reflections to herself about the things happening in her life resonated with Millie. She could've spent hours going through them. In fact, she would spend hours going through them when she had more time. But for now, she'd just read one more entry, then carry the box of journals to her bedroom.

She flipped the page and started reading.

Life has a funny way of changing the way one sees things. Things I felt so sure of in my youth I now find myself rethinking while things that had me stumped before now seem so clear. I suppose that's the beauty of wisdom.

I've often said that I don't have regrets. I've had lessons, some harder than others, that have gotten me to where I am today. Although some nights, when the rooms are not full and I am alone in this big empty house, I wonder.

I loved once. I don't write about it often and talk about it even more seldom, but I think about him frequently. It was a breathtaking romance. The kind that changes lives. The kind that changed my life.

And then it ended.

The relationship, that is. Not the love. I dare say, I'm just as in love with him today as I was back then. Perhaps that's why I have never been interested in anyone else. My heart still belongs to the one who stole it many years ago. His words, some from my memory and some from notes that I have kept, remind me even today of the person I want to be, of the person I could be. They remind me that the people we love and the people who love us make us better. They remind me that life was never meant to be conquered alone but among those we cherish. And while I cherish the rich friendships that have surrounded me throughout my life, there will always be a hole where one was supposed to be.

I still maintain my position of no regrets, although there are times when I wonder what could have been. What could have been if I'd been quicker to listen and slower to anger on that fateful night? What could have been if I had been slower to judge and quicker to find common ground? What could have been if I had taken time to sort through a minor misunderstanding and offer forgiveness instead of letting my own pride halt all conversations?

Perhaps then things would have turned out differently. Perhaps that hole which reminds me of what I once lost would have remained filled as a testament to what my life had gained. And if that were so, I would've liked to know how that story played out. I think I would've liked that very much.

Tears rolled down Millie's cheeks. The wounds from

everything that had happened were still fresh. The sting of betrayal had clouded her mind earlier, but she was justified, wasn't she? She needed to stop things before she allowed herself to get hurt any more. If she'd been smart and stuck to her original plan of this chapter being a solo act, she never would've put herself in a position to get hurt in the first place. She squeezed her eyes shut, trying to block out the memories from earlier today.

But after thirty years of clarity, would today be the one day Millie wished she could do over? Should she have been quicker to listen and slower to anger? One thing was for sure: even after everything that had happened, she still loved Braxton. He'd touched her in a way no one else ever had. He gave her confidence, made her laugh, and reminded her she was worthy. She had an odd suspicion that was the kind of love that would leave an unfillable hole in her heart if he wasn't there anymore.

Millie dropped the book to her lap and stared up at a picture of her great-aunt that was propped on top of the file cabinet. Aunt Mildred was in her later years here, looking stoic and confident in front of Seascape. It was the picture Millie always thought showed off her aunt's strength. Look at the amazing things she achieved on her own!

But today she saw a different side of that picture. She saw a woman whose one regret was that she'd let love slip through her fingers because of what she said started as a minor misunderstanding.

"If it's any consolation," she said to the picture, "after all this time, he never stopped loving you either."

Her eyes drifted down as she considered this insight to the love story that had captivated her all summer. She was barely even paying attention to what she was staring at when something on the bottom drawer of the file cabinet made her pause.

She'd never taken a lot of time to study the labels on either of the two old rusting file cabinets in the office. Honestly, there didn't seem to be much need. The office as a whole didn't seem to have much organization to it. But now she could make out the first three faded letters written on the paper label. *HOA.*

Intrigued, she wiped her eyes and crawled over to the drawer to get a better look. She moved the stack of file folders and stacks of papers out of the way and read the full label: *HOA Board Documents and Deed Restrictions*

On demo day, someone mentioned Aunt Mildred had been president of the very first HOA. It hadn't surprised her. She loved this town and this neighborhood and would have done anything to see it prosper. Protecting the coast and the sea life had been a passion of hers. Millie remembered her working hard to make sure they preserved the beach for generations to come. What sort of items had been important to her when she was helping to make the deed restrictions?

She opened the drawer and scanned the files inside. The first folder was labeled "Deed Restrictions." She opened the file and pulled out the first document inside. An old sticky note that had long lost the stick fluttered to the floor. Millie pushed the drawer in to retrieve it. She picked it up and read it.

Mildred,

Thanks for your dedication to the community. It's our turn to look after your welfare. We're calling it the Mildred clause. Viva la Seascape.

Article 12 Section E

Intrigued, Millie flipped through the document that was very similar to the one she'd received from George two months ago. She swept her finger down the page, searching for the correct section. She had to flip the page to find it, but there it was. Article 12 Section E. Someone had even circled it. Millie read the legal words. When she finished, she read them again, just to make sure she'd understood it correctly the first time.

A fresh fire surged through Millie. If it was saying what she thought it was saying, this was huge. The Mildred Clause could be the magic bullet she needed to save Seascape and her dreams.

Since the legal wording always threw her off, and since this was an old version of the deed restrictions, she wasn't sure if it was still valid. But lucky for her she knew someone who could answer both of those questions.

If she was reading this right, she had less than an hour to get his opinion and get to the clubhouse to stop that vote.

Chapter Twenty-Five

Braxton glanced at his watch as he paced in front of the entrance to the clubhouse. It was seven o'clock, time to start the meeting. Where was she?

The thought of seeing her filled him with a mixed bag of emotions.

On the one hand, excitement swelled inside him. He had news to share and he wanted to be the one to deliver it to her. He'd taken a page out of Millie's playbook and gone after the impossible. And it worked! Perhaps he should've tried harder earlier and they wouldn't be in this mess. But, to be fair, he hadn't put it all together until he was with Henry. The important part was that he got here, and while it might not be enough to save everything, it was enough to give her time to figure out her next move.

On the other hand, guilt, disappointment, and icy apprehension pricked him at the thought of seeing her. To put it simply, he wasn't sure where they stood. Okay, fine, that wasn't quite accurate. He knew exactly where they stood. He'd played a part in that decision the moment he walked out—see guilt—

ready to give up on them. But that had been a weak moment, before he realized...well, before he realized a lot of things. He wasn't sure where they could stand after this, but he had pretty strong feelings about where he wanted that to be.

He glanced at his watch again. It was now two minutes after seven. He was officially late to the meeting. His stomach plunged as he took one more look at the parking lot. She wasn't coming.

Heaving a sigh, he turned to head into the clubhouse. Millie not being there wouldn't affect the outcome, but he would've loved to have seen the look on her face during the process.

He was halfway down the hall when he heard her voice.

"Wait! Braxton!"

Excitement. When he was in her presence, the emotion that won out was excitement. It gushed through him as he stopped in his tracks and turned.

Millie, dressed in blue flannel pajama pants and an oversize sweatshirt, was racing through the door with George Rodriguez on her heels.

"Stop the meeting!" She pumped her fist in the air, still jogging to catch up with him. Then she grinned. "I've always wanted to say that."

She stopped in front of him, a little out of breath but looking awfully cheerful for a woman whose future was actively in the process of getting crushed.

"I have news," she said, sucking in a lungful of oxygen.

"Me, too." Braxton started to launch into what he'd found, but she held up a hand to stop him.

"No, me first." She motioned to George. "We have proof that they can't vote against the inn."

Braxton raised an eyebrow. "Well, by all means, let's stop that vote."

They rushed the rest of the way down the hall, and he

held the door open for her and George. The entire board was already assembled, sitting around the long conference table.

"Finally," Stan breathed out. "We can get this thing started."

Braxton took his seat at the head of the table while Millie and George made their way back to the extra chairs. "I apologize for my tardiness. I was taking care of some last-minute things."

Sophia pushed the computer toward him with a questioning look. He gave her a discreet half smile and hoped she got the message. "We have a lot to discuss today, so without further delays, let's get tonight's meeting started."

Braxton banged his gavel on the table.

"First up on the agenda is the grievance and subsequent proposal by Millie Leclair of 121 East Shore Drive that was presented at the last meeting."

Anticipation grew inside him as he shifted his gaze to Millie. "But before we move to the vote, I think there has been some new information to be presented in that area. Ms. Leclair."

"I'm sorry, Millie, but you've already had your chance to state your grievance." Stan's face wrinkled with disapproval as he turned to Braxton. "This is highly unprofessional. We have procedures." Stan gave her a stern look.

"Indeed you do, Mr. Huffington." George offered a curt smile to the table and opened his briefcase. "What you have failed to do is follow those procedures, which is why we are here."

Millie stepped up next to him, her wide, joyful grin lighting up her face. "I found something today when I was going through my aunt's office that changes my grievance."

"In light of our new discovery, the old grievance filed at the previous meeting is no longer valid. The new grievance has to do with improper addition and deletion of rules and restrictions to the legal document." George pulled out two packets. Even Braxton could tell from his end of the table that they had the same cover page as the Oceanside Estates Deed Restrictions he was familiar with.

George held up the two documents. "I have a copy of the two previous adoptions of the deed restrictions. This version, voted into adoption in February of 1994, was amended to include a new clause. If I may…" He lowered his glasses to his eyes and started reading from the document. The room was completely silent as he read a clause that basically said it was not allowed to create new rules and restrictions that would adversely affect the current operations of properties already established in the neighborhood. "And if such a restriction is created to protect the future of the neighborhood, the adversely affected property can continue to operate in the same manner it has been."

George looked over his glasses at the board members seated at the table. "Basically, according to this, you can't stop Seascape from operating as an inn as long as it is doing so in the same manner it was when the new restriction was written. As long as Millie is planning on offering six guest rooms in the original structure, she is well within her rights of operating as it always has."

Millie stood next to George looking as though she might break into a happy dance.

Braxton wanted to celebrate right along with her. She'd done it. Somehow, even with the odds stacked against her, she'd figured out a way.

Although everyone at the table didn't seem as excited as he was. There were murmurings as several people whispered with the person next to them.

Finally, Jarrod Cross spoke up. "I appreciate your findings, however, that is an old adoption. I feel fairly confident that clause is not in our current deed restrictions."

George nodded, looking thoughtful. "You're right. It's not, which is very curious. This clause was added in the 1994 adoption to article twelve, which, as you all well know, is the article titled 'Basic Rights and Protections for Residents.' According to this article, items added to this section are for the purpose of protecting the rights of the residents and cannot be taken away." He paused and removed his glasses, focusing on Jarrod.

Braxton had never seen George in action before, but he now understood why he was considered the best lawyer on Summer Island.

"This new clause shows up again in the adoption of 2004, as it should. However, it is curiously missing from the adoption of 2014, which just so happens to be the same adoption with the new clause that forbade hotels. I'm sure it was an oversight and not an intentional act to take away the rights of one of your residents." He passed the two copies of the deed restrictions to Jarrod.

Braxton hadn't been living on Summer Island in 2014. It would be a few years later that he'd buy his house, and still a couple more before he joined the HOA board. He had no idea what had gone down then, but he was here now and he had the power to fix it.

"Thank you, Mr. Rodriguez, for pointing out this unfortunate oversight. That certainly is a valid grievance." He turned to Sophia. "Let's add this item to new business so we can discuss how to fix it in more detail."

Sophia, who was now grinning from ear to ear, snagged the laptop and pulled it back in front of her, typing furiously.

Braxton surveyed the table. "And actually, Millie is not the only one with additional information on this topic." He pulled out a stack of papers from his bag and lightly tossed them onto the middle of the table. "It seems someone has been sending Ms. Leclair forged violation letters in a bid to delay the renovation efforts on her property. Not only were many of these violations not valid, and most of them not registered, they were sent using an unauthorized signature."

Most of the faces at the table wore looks of shock and confusion. But one face, the face he'd expected, looked nervous. "I did a little digging today and found that one of our board members was using these scare tactics for his own benefit."

Stan shook his head. "This is ridiculous. Now we're on a witch hunt to prove who changed the bylaws?"

Braxton fixed his gaze on him. "Not exactly. But to prove unethical behavior on the board? Absolutely." He slid the final paper in his bag toward Stan. "And I happen to have proof that you have a deal with Tellinger Construction so that every lot you bring them in this neighborhood that they build out gives you a handsome little under-the-table payout."

He shifted his gaze to Millie, whose mouth was hanging open.

Stan glanced at the paper before tucking it inside his portfolio. "You don't have proof. What you have is a suspicion and a desire to pin your girlfriend's misfortune on someone."

Braxton settled back in his chair, clasping his hands on the table in front of him. "Perhaps. But the evidence is pretty condemning and our lawyers are in the process of looking into it."

Stan glared at him with a look that could've burned straight through a stone. "I don't need to sit here and listen to accusations being slung at me. If you have something to say to me, you can contact my lawyers."

He stood up with such force that his rolling chair shot backward and hit the wall. He stormed out of the room, slamming the door behind him.

As soon as the stunned silence started to turn to muffled murmurs, Sophia turned to him. "So now what?"

"Since I've never dealt with anything like this, I'm not entirely sure of the procedure here." Braxton shifted his focus to Jose. Since his parliamentarian had just stormed out of the room, he figured maybe the standards chairperson would be the best to ask. "Jose, help me out here. In light of this new information, it seems to me that if Millie Leclair is planning on offering six guest rooms in the original structure, then we have nothing to vote on. Is that correct?"

Jose reached for the stack of letters Braxton had thrown on the table and pulled them toward him. "I will need to study the bylaws some more, but it appears so." He flipped through the pages of violation letters. "And it would seem that we also need to issue Ms. Leclair a formal apology. Let's add that to the new business as well."

Braxton tried to keep his face as professional as possible, but there was a small part of him that wanted to give the entire table the finger.

Of course, he couldn't point any fingers without pointing back at himself. He, too, had fallen victim to fear of the future. Instead of fighting for what he believed in, he also had caved, hurting Millie in the process.

Braxton looked across the table at Millie. She met his gaze and love swept through him like a warm breeze. Falling for her was no longer a simple possibility of someday. He was all in, cannonballing into the deep end, fully in love with Millie Leclair.

"Congratulations on the reopening of Seascape Inn. Summer Island is lucky to have you."

There was a hint of sadness in her eyes, one he had put there, and she offered him a pained smile. "Thanks."

There was so much more he wanted to say, so much more he needed to say, but now wasn't the time. It would have to wait. He just hoped all the damage he'd done could be overturned.

Chapter Twenty-Six

Millie had done it! She fought the system and she won. It took all her self-control to not throw her arms in the air and cheer.

"Since we also have a vested interest in the discussion during new business, we'd like to stay for the remainder of the meeting." Despite the glorious news, George still looked as serious as he had when they first walked into the room.

Millie didn't want to stay for the whole meeting. She'd kind of hoped they could say what they needed to say then skip out of the room to celebrate their victory. But since she needed to see this thing through, she tried to contain her excitement.

"Of course. Please, have a seat." Braxton held out his arm to motion to the chairs at the back of the room.

That was another reason she wasn't thrilled about staying. She didn't want to sit at that end of the table, directly across from Braxton, trying to avoid eye contact for the next however long this meeting was going to take.

She sank into the chair against the wall to wait it out. For the next hour and a half she alternated between trying to contain her excitement about the big victory and curb the ache from what had happened with Braxton. It was an odd opposition of emotions, and by the time they'd come back around to discussing the process for fixing the deed restrictions and looking into Stan's ethical violations, Millie was more than ready to get out of her own head.

"Now that we have that all in place, I think that covers everything. If no one else has anything to add, our meeting is officially adjourned." Braxton banged his gavel on the table.

Millie sprang up from her chair. She needed to release some of this built-up energy before the anxiety ate her up.

But before she had the chance to move, Jose had rounded the table and was standing in front of her. "Congratulations, Millie. For the record, I'm sorry your first couple of months in Oceanside Estates hasn't been the most enjoyable. I hope there are no hard feelings." He extended his hand.

Millie shook it. "Of course not." After all, life was too short to hold grudges. She had gotten what she wanted and now it was time to move forward. In the end, they were all on the same side. Their goal was to make their neighborhood, the place they all called home, the very best it could possibly be. "And just like my great-aunt, I'm also dedicated to fighting for what's right to preserve our coastline and to make sure the town prospers. I'm proud to be part of Summer Island's legacy."

"Your passion is evident. Have you ever thought of being on the HOA board? We could use someone with your determination on our side."

Millie grinned. "Maybe someday, but right now, I think I'll have my hands full with the inn."

Jose nodded. "I certainly understand. But don't think I'm going to stop asking."

He had barely stepped out of the way when Sophia bounded up, throwing her arms around Millie and almost knocking her over. "You did it! How on earth did you find that clause?"

"Luck," Millie said. And maybe a little help from her aunt. "I'll tell you all about it later."

"You better." She stepped back and examined Millie's worn, oversize sweatshirt and pajama pants. "And what's with the outfit?"

Millie looked down at her flannel-clad legs. Everything had happened so fast after she found the old deed restriction that she hadn't had time to change. "You don't like my power suit?"

Sophia laughed. "It definitely makes a statement. What do you say we get out of here and celebrate the reopening of Seascape Inn?"

"That sounds like a plan." After the roller coaster of a day, Millie could use some relaxing time with friends.

Sophia nudged Millie's side playfully. "How about dinner and champagne on the patio of my favorite new bed and breakfast?"

It was official. For better or worse, Millie was the owner and operator of a seaside hotel. True, it'd been her goal since the reading of the will, but it was still a little surreal to know it was actually happening. Exhilarating, but surreal.

"That sounds like the perfect place to celebrate," Millie said.

Sophia beamed. "Great! I'll take care of everything. All you have to do is put on your party shoes." She took a step back and examined Millie's outfit, giving a shrug. "Or house shoes. You know, whatever."

Millie laughed. "Perfect."

"Tessa is going to be so excited! And stunned. I can't wait to tell her about Stan." She gave Millie a quick hug, then pulled a phone from her handbag. "We'll see you at your place in about an hour."

Millie's gaze flickered across the table to where Braxton was talking to George. A mixture of emotions ricocheted through her. Part of her wished she could avoid him. Going on with the exciting new parts of her life and pretending like there'd never been anything between her and Braxton seemed like the easier choice. She'd always planned on this gig being a solo act anyways.

But he had figured out who'd sent the violation letters in an effort to save Seascape—she needed to know how he'd done that, by the way—and there was a chance that his intentions during their argument earlier, even if misguided, had come from a place of care and worry about her.

There was also the whole matter of falling in love with him...

She didn't want to be played for a fool, but she also didn't want to walk away only to get thirty years down the road and wonder what if. Their next conversation would not be easy, yet she couldn't ignore it. So she drew in a deep breath, squared her shoulders, and started toward the other end of the table.

It wasn't a long table, but she kept getting stopped by board members offering their congratulations on reopening the inn or offering their apologies for the oversight. By the time she reached the head of the table, George was the only one standing there. She glanced around, but Braxton, along with all of his things, was nowhere to be seen. He'd left without even saying one word to her.

A wave of disappointment threatened to crash over her. It seemed she had his answer. Maybe it was a good thing. They'd already said everything that needed to be said. It was over.

George squeezed her shoulder. "Congratulations, Millie."

Millie forced a smile. "I couldn't have done it without

your help. Thanks for dropping everything and coming with me tonight."

"My pleasure. I love it when the good guy wins." He grabbed his briefcase from the table next to him and held his hand out to the door. "Since I gave you a ride here, can I give you a ride home?"

Millie considered the offer, then shook her head. "No, thanks. I think I'd like to walk tonight." She could use the fresh air to help clear her head. After all, tonight was a night for celebrating.

George nodded as if he understood her internal dilemma. "Have a lovely evening. We'll talk soon."

Millie headed outside and down to the road for the mile walk home. It was a gorgeous summer evening. Sometimes, especially on nights like tonight, it was hard to believe she really lived here. But it was official now. For better or worse, this town was her home. She was going to carry on the Leclair legacy of hospitality right here on the beautiful South Carolina coast. It had been a long trek to get here, much longer than anticipated, but here she was all the same.

She walked along the very same road she'd driven down on her first day on Summer Island. That day, she'd been wide-eyed and naively optimistic about the future. She had no idea how hard life was about to get, which was probably a good thing. There was a reason the future was a mystery. If Millie had known all the challenges waiting for her, there was a good chance fear and overthinking would've made her turn her car right around.

But she hadn't, and she was better because of it.

She looked up, admiring the palm trees that lined the street. They were quite a bit lighter in the frond department since the day she first arrived, and all slightly tilted because of the hurricane's relentless wind. But they were still just as beautiful as they'd always been, and she'd dare say quite a bit stronger because of what they'd been through.

"We did it, didn't we?" she said to the trees. "We withstood the storm. And look at us now." She'd fought every battle over the past two months and now the victory was hers. She should be proud. All her hard work had paid off. Once again, her future gleamed before her. But, regardless of all the excitement and celebration, there still seemed to be something missing. A sort of hole in her otherwise full life.

She tried not to look at Braxton's house as she walked past it.

A summer romance. That's all it was. And now that summer was over, it was time to move on. She could chalk it up to a mistake or getting swept away by the excitement of her new adventure. Maybe if she kept saying it to herself, her heart would get on board.

She turned onto her new faux cobblestone driveway and looked up at the house. Her house—no, her inn—and a thrill swept through her.

"Welcome to Seascape Inn." A smile spread across her face. It was good to be home.

She picked up the pace as she walked down the driveway. She wanted to make sure the twinkle lights were on before her friends got here for their celebration on the patio. But as she mounted the steps to her front door, something caught her attention, and she paused.

There, taped to the front door, was an envelope with her name written on the front.

She pulled the envelope off, looking around to see if there was any sign of who had left it. Since no one seemed to be around, she gently opened it and pulled out the page inside, unfolding the thick linen paper.

At the top was the bold *BC* in the design she recognized as Braxton's logo from his golfing days. Below it, the page was filled with Braxton's scratchy handwriting.

Tears instantly filled her eyes and she looked up. He'd written her a letter on monogrammed stationery. For months, she'd read and reread the beautiful letters written to her aunt and wondered what it would feel like to be the receiver of one of them. What was it like to know you were loved so completely and have the written evidence to back it up every time a doubt arose?

Only, she wasn't sure what it was going to say. To be honest, she wasn't sure what she wanted it to say. Yes, she was head over heels in love with Braxton Channing, but did he love her the same way? And if he did love her, was love enough to get them through this? Or was it better to walk away now before she got even more hurt?

But ignoring it wasn't going to make any of this any easier. Her aunt had ignored a letter once and look where it got her. Good or bad, she had to know what was on that page. So she blinked back her tears and started reading.

My sweet, fearless, unstoppable Millie,

I'm not too proud to admit when I am wrong. And today, my love, I was wrong. I tried to control the situation in a vain attempt to keep you from getting hurt. I didn't ask your advice. I didn't listen to what you needed. Letting fear and pride overtake my better judgment, I trudged full steam ahead, confident I could fix it. And in the process, I managed to make a huge mess that caused you additional pain and grief. For that, I am truly sorry.

The truth is, I don't need to protect you. You are the strongest, bravest, most determined person I have ever met. You are more than capable of moving mountains on your own, and it has been a privilege to walk beside you the past few months. Your confidence is inspiring and your joy changes lives.

It has changed my life. My world is a better place because of you. For so long I had been trapped under a cloud, but then you showed up and shined your light into my darkness. You reminded me how to hope, something that I thought I had lost forever. Your cheerful smile and warm, positive spirit are like a breath of fresh air, and because of the time I've spent with you, I feel like I can finally breathe again. You accepted me for who I am, and that makes me want to be a better person.

I would list all the things I love about you, but there are so many reasons, they would fill an entire book. One day, I hope to get to tell you each and every one of them. You deserve to know how special you are and how richly you have blessed all the lives you've come into contact with. But what I want you to know now is what I should have said before.

I am completely, one hundred percent in love with you.

I want there to be an us. More than anything, I want to navigate through life with you. But even if that can't be, it doesn't change the way I feel about you. Now and for always, my heart belongs to you.

Forever,
Braxton

Tears slid down Millie's cheeks as she read the beautiful words written on the page. Braxton Channing loved her, and he'd written it down in her very own love letter for her to hold on to for the rest of eternity.

Yet, unlike the love letters in her aunt's office, she didn't just want to hold on to this piece of paper. She wanted to hold on to the relationship behind it.

"I hear there's cause for a celebration." Tessa's bouncy voice caught Millie off guard. She'd been so consumed with the letter she hadn't even heard her pull up.

Millie turned to face Tessa, fully aware she looked like a hot mess. Not only was she still wearing pajamas that should've never seen the light of day, there was a high likelihood she now had black mascara streaks running down both cheeks and her nose was probably the same color as Rudolph's.

The sight certainly caught Tessa off guard. Instantly, her cheerful smile morphed into a look of concern. "Oh, honey, what's wrong?" She jogged up the last few steps to join Millie on the porch.

Millie swiped at her eyes. A few of them were sad tears left over from the pain and heartache that had gotten her to this point. But for the most part, right now, she was happy. Really, really happy. A smile spread across her face to prove it. "Braxton loves me."

Tessa grinned. "Yeah, he does."

Millie sniffed and used the sleeve of her sweatshirt to wipe whatever was remaining of her mascara off her cheeks. In her heart of hearts, Millie had known all along, too, yet her own fear of being hurt again caused her to doubt it. But in her new life, the one where she called the shots, nothing controlled her. Not even fear.

Excitement fueled by an overwhelming love bubbled up inside her until she couldn't contain it anymore.

"I gotta go!" She threw her arms around her friend and squeezed before she shot down the steps. She needed to get to Braxton and she needed to do that now.

Tessa adjusted the straps on the canvas grocery bag hanging from her shoulder. "Okay. I'll just be here.

Celebrating by myself.""

Millie held up her hand in a sort of apologetic wave as she headed for the side of the house.

She broke into a run when she reached the backyard. It was times like these when she wished her property wasn't so large. All she was trying to do was get next door, but by the time she got to the washed-out boardwalk, she was huffing and puffing harder than the big bad wolf. Maybe it was time to add some cardio to her daily workout routine. Or, you know, adopt a workout routine.

She paused at the top of the sand dune, resting her hands on her knees, to catch her breath. The sun was setting and the sky was full of breathtaking pinks and purples.

Still breathing hard, she walked down the other side, admiring the daily phenomenon. And that's when she saw him. Braxton was at the edge of the water between their two houses, watching the sunset.

The light from the setting sun cast a golden glow that highlighted his profile, making him look like a vision out of a dream. He really was attractive. But he was also so much more than that. Kind, generous, funny, a devoted father. She couldn't wait to get to spend forever with him.

Slowing her pace, she walked out across the sand to meet him.

"You know, they say there's a green flash the instant the sun dips below the horizon."

By the way he jumped, she'd caught him off guard. But it only took a fraction of a second for the surprise to melt into the charming grin she knew so well.

"That's what they tell me." He left his spot at the water's edge and strolled over to meet her. He left slightly more distance between them than usual, but it didn't stop the magnetic pull drawing her to him.

"Where's the little one?"

He held up the monitor. "Already in bed. Lena's there, so I thought I'd take a walk." He took a tiny step closer to her. "But I got distracted by the view."

His gaze locked with hers and the air around them electrified.

She wanted to kiss him, but there were things that needed to be said first. "I got your letter." She held the paper up between them.

"I meant what I said, Millie. I'm so sorry. Of course I believe in your dreams. I just might need some help on the fear-management side so I don't jump into problem-solving mode and run over everyone else."

Millie grinned at him. "I'm pretty sure that's why they invented the buddy system. Everything is better with a buddy."

"True statement." There was a flirtatious twinkle in his eyes that pulsed through her.

"And while I'm never going let you talk me out of my dreams, you do have some pretty good advice when it comes to staying safe. I promise to do a better job of listening next time."

Braxton cocked an eyebrow. "Next time?"

"I mean I'm assuming there will be a next time. Forever seems like a long time to go without an argument."

A look of pure joy that started in his eyes took over his whole face. "Forever, huh?"

She took another small step toward him and put her hand on his cheek, gazing up at his ocean-blue eyes. "I mean, forever is a pretty good start. We'll see where it goes from there."

"I love you, Millie Leclair."

"I love you too."

Millie stood on her toes and pressed her lips against his. He kissed her back, long and deep and gentle. It washed over her like a soft, rolling wave, filling every part of her with a fiery warmth. His arms wrapped around her, pulling her close, and she melted into him. The world faded away, and she allowed herself to get lost in the moment. Lost in him.

Although her eyes were closed, she could imagine the beautiful green flash tonight when the sun slipped below the horizon. A brilliant, soul-changing one.

Music drifted into the night from the direction of Millie's house, and the faint sounds of laughter filled the air.

Braxton, still holding Millie in his arms, pulled back and smiled. It was an expression that mirrored how relaxed and free Millie felt. Then he quirked one brow and looked over her shoulder toward her backyard. "Are you having a party?"

Millie turned to look. From where they were standing, the trees blocked her view of the patio, but she recognized the voices. Those were *her* friends, hanging out on *her* patio, waiting to help celebrate *her* success. Yep, her new life was turning out to be pretty okay.

"Oh, yeah. Want to come? We're celebrating a bit of good news I got today. I'm not sure if you heard, but the HOA cleared the way for Seascape's grand reopening." She shrugged, trying to make it look like no big deal.

Braxton chuckled. "I don't know how you did it. You will never cease to impress me."

"Speaking of being impressed, how did you finally figure out that Stan was behind the letters? And that he was doing it all for a kickback from a construction company?"

Braxton shrugged. "I didn't put it together until I called the Callahans to see who had told them about the open house. I couldn't figure out why Stan would even care, but then I remembered that he has been trying to get the HOA to buy the older houses that go on the market for years. His reason was that many of the houses were being extensively redone, and the HOA could smooth out the process. It didn't all connect until the Callahans told me who they were planning on using as a builder. It happened to be the same one Stan wanted to use for the HOA and whose owner is one of Stan's poker buddies."

"I can't believe you had time to pull all the evidence together."

Braxton grinned. "The evidence I had was circumstantial at best, but I handed everything over to our lawyer and their private investigator will figure out the rest. Plus, his reaction was incriminating enough, don't you think?"

Millie giggled, remembering Stan's response to the paper Braxton had given him. Then she jerked her head in the direction of her house. "Well, now that we've solved that mystery, shall we celebrate?"

"I'd love to. But we have to keep this party contained. You have a big day tomorrow."

Millie stared at him, her eyes narrowing a bit. "Oh, do I? What exactly is on my agenda?"

"*Coastal Life* magazine is doing a feature article on a new up-and-coming luxury boutique inn and its dynamic owner. The reporter and photographer will be here around ten."

Millie's jaw dropped open. "*Coastal Life* magazine? Is coming here? To do an article about Seascape?"

Braxton nodded. "And a full photoshoot. I hope you're not mad. I know I said I wouldn't make any more decisions without you, but I was already working on this. I can call them tomorrow and cancel it if you'd rather not—"

"Are you kidding? Do you know what kind of exposure being in something like *Coastal Life* will bring Seascape?" Images of Seascape on the glossy magazine pages flipped through her mind. Tons of people would be admiring beauty shots of her beloved property. It was almost too much to take in. "This is amazing. How did you get them to agree to come?"

Braxton took a step back from her and shoved his hands in his pockets. "I offered their sister magazine, *Links and Parkland*, an exclusive interview about rejoining the PGA tour."

If the news of getting a feature article in one of the most popular beach magazines shocked her, this news left her flabbergasted. "What? You're playing golf again? When? Where? How?"

Braxton chuckled. "Let's start with the when. I started talking with my agent about it earlier this week and we'll make the official announcement just before the magazine comes out. My first tournament won't be until February, so I have some time to dust off the old clubs."

Millie had never seen Braxton play golf, not in person at least, but she could tell just from the way he lit up when he was talking about it how much he loved it. "What made you change your mind?"

"You, actually." He tucked a strand of her hair that had broken free from her ponytail behind her ear. "You reminded me how to be brave. And how to not let any obstacle—even if that obstacle is me—stand in the way of something I love."

Millie's heart was so full she thought it might burst. What had started out as one of the worst days of her life was rapidly becoming one of her favorites. "How about tall ladders? Have I inspired you to conquer that?"

Braxton chuckled. "I'm still working on that one."

Millie breathed in, trying to memorize every detail about this moment. Being here on the beach, talking about the future with the man she loved.

A noise came from the baby monitor in Braxton's hand and she leaned closer to him to see the image of Alice stirring in her crib. Her heart swelled even more.

"Looks like someone is a little restless tonight. She's having a harder time getting to sleep than normal," Braxton said.

"I don't blame her. Today's been full of excitement." She watched the little girl she'd come to adore. "Why don't we check on her before we head to the party? Together."

Braxton's grin widened. "I'd like that." He gently kissed her forehead before he took her hand and they headed in the direction of his house. "I guess everything worked out in the end, after all."

"End?" She stared into his loving eyes. "This is only the beginning. And I can't wait to see how great our story is going to be."

Acknowledgments

As always, there are a ton of people who helped make this book possible, and I owe each of you a huge debt of gratitude.

First of all, a huge thanks to my fabulous husband and amazing kids. Your love, encouragement, and willingness to eat more than your fair share of frozen pizza when I'm on deadline is a gift. I'm lucky to call you mine. None of this would be possible without you.

To Liz, Amy, and the entire team at Entangled, thank you for your wisdom and expertise. I'm so grateful to get to work alongside you!

And last but certainly not least, a huge thank you to my readers. I'm honored you'd choose to escape in one of my books. I hope you enjoyed Millie and Braxton's story and walk away feeling hopeful and encouraged. And, if you're inspired to grab a hammer and tackle a home DIY project—all the better!

Xoxo,
Rachel

About the Author

Award winning author Rachel Magee writes sweet contemporary romance with fun characters, witty dialogue, and plenty of happily-ever-afters. Her stories are usually set in sunny locations where she doesn't mind spending lots of time 'researching'. When she's not out scouting the setting of her next book, you can find her at home in The Woodlands, Texas with her wonderful husband, their two adventurous kids, and a couple of spirited pets. Find out more about what Rachel's up to at RachelMageeBooks.com.

Discover more Amara titles...

WRITTEN FOR YOU
a novel by Robin Bielman

Free-spirited Reese has always been the complete opposite of steadfast Cameron. While Reese nurses a broken heart, and Cam searches for inspiration for his new screenplay, supporting each other is what best friends do. But something's changed between them, and as sexy sparks fly, they hope the phase will pass. Not only does her new dream job threaten his career, but their friendship and family ties can't possibly survive the romantic mess they would create.

A LOT LIKE LOVE
a Blue Moon Bay novel by Jennifer Snow

When Sarah Lewis inherits a run-down B&B from her late grandmother in coastal Blue Moon Bay, the logical thing to do is sell it. But when she learns that interested buyers will only tear it down, she feels a sense of obligation to her family legacy to restore it to the landmark tourist destination it once was...and that means hiring the best contractor for the job, who happens to be her old high school crush.

THE MATCHMAKER BRIDE
a Blue Hill Brides novel by Ginny Baird

Successful matchmaker Meredith Galanes is great at finding love...for other people. When she's broadsided by questions about her love life on national TV, she panics and blurts out the first guy that comes to mind. Never mind that he hates her—the feeling is mutual. She'll just have to convince him to play along until she secures her syndication deal. In return, she'll help him win back his ex. It's a simple plan, but to pull it off, they'll have to survive each other first...

ACCIDENTALLY FAMILY
a Pecan Valley novel by Sasha Summers

Life for Felicity, and her teen children, is finally back on track. After her divorce, she wasn't sure if her sweet family would ever be the same. But things are good—right up until her ex's spirited toddler lands on Felicity's doorstep. If life's going to throw lemons at her, thank God she has her best friend, Graham, to help her make lemonade out of them. How did she never notice how helpful and kind he was?

Made in the USA
Coppell, TX
23 August 2021